What readers are saying about
the Hunter Rayne highway mysteries:

"A great take to bed read for anyone who loves crime fiction in a traditional fashion."

"Those were the best mysteries I've read in a long time! As soon as I finished the first one I bought the second and felt empty when I finished it! The characters were awesome and so there that I somehow think they are in my life ..."

"This is a great read for anyone who likes mystery, intrigue and those that are looking for good reads from up and coming Canadian authors."

"Great trucking detail, hardboiled characters, no-nonsense dialogue ...."

"... this book caught my attention from the very first pages and it only got better. I recommend this book to anyone who has a love for a good mystery."

" ... Hunter Rayne would make a great TV detective, driving around the country in his rig visiting different states and helping to solve crimes. He is that interesting of a character."

Also by R.E. Donald

ICE ON THE GRAPEVINE

SLOW CURVE
ON THE
COQUIHALLA

a Hunter Rayne highway mystery

— — — — — —

R.E. Donald

PROUD HORSE
PUBLISHING

First print edition 2012 by
Proud Horse Publishing,
British Columbia, Canada
ProudHorsePublishing@gmail.com

First digital edition published September 2011

PUBLISHER'S NOTE:
This is a work of fiction. Names, characters, places and incidents either are the product of the author's imagination or used fictitiously and any resemblance to actual persons, business establishments, events or locales is entirely coincidental. The story is set in 1995.

PRINTED IN THE UNITED STATES OF AMERICA

*To Jim, who started me on this road in 1994,
and to my father, who kept the wheels turning.*

"I have never found a companion that was so companionable as solitude."

Henry David Thoreau

CHAPTER — — — —
ONE

Funny how the last hundred miles always seem like the longest part of a trip home. The nose of Hunter Rayne's big Freightliner pointed west, into the sunset. He had just come out of the mountains southwest of Hope and was travelling the straight, flat stretch of Highway 1 that runs through Sumas Prairie in the lower Fraser Valley. Somewhere between him and the horizon, beneath the scalloped rows of gilt edged clouds, the port city of Vancouver mushroomed along the shores of Burrard Inlet, her sharp edged buildings sprouted against the looming shadows of the Coast mountains.

Hunter was on the last lap of a four thousand mile trip. He'd hauled a load of baby cribs from Vancouver to L.A., a refrigerated load of cucumbers and tomatoes from L.A. to Edmonton, and now he was returning home with a refrigerated load of Alberta beef. He was impatient to close his own front door behind him so he could exchange the road weary jeans and wrinkled blue shirt, the cleanest he had left after two weeks on the road, for some loose soft sweats. All he wanted to do tonight was to take a long soapy shower, then put up his feet and suck on a beer, maybe do a little channel surfing before he fell asleep at the helm of his remote control.

As he slowed his rig behind a dusty motor home with California plates, boxed in by a Trailways bus and half a dozen cars tailgating each other in the passing lane, Hunter flipped open his cellular phone and punched the '1' to call his dispatcher. Hunter was an owner operator under contract to Watson Transportation, a load broker and freight forwarder in the Lower Mainland of B.C., run by a former driver named Elspeth Watson.

"Watson!" El answered impatiently, as she usually did.

"Yo, El!" He raised his voice towards a small microphone mounted above the windshield. "The Blue Knight's just your side of Aldergrove. Where do you want me to drop the beef?"

"The yard, Hunter," El said. There was a brittle edge to her voice, and she hung up before he could acknowledge. Must have caught her at a bad time.

Less than an hour later, Hunter wheeled into an industrial park on Annacis Island, braked the big Freightliner to an easy stop behind a gray cinderblock building, and left his truck idling to cool the engine down. He hadn't expected El to still be there, but the dispatcher's Chevy pickup was parked beside the door to Watson Transportation's office. The building was dark.

With a crooked frown, he climbed the few steps to the office and tried the door. It was unlocked, and he could hear nothing save a brief spit and crackle from the CB radio inside. His chronic suspicion, occupational disease of police officers and former police officers everywhere, told him that something was wrong. He eased open the door and entered the office, planting his steel toed sneakers with care until he could see around the front counter into the alcove where the dispatcher's desk was located.

Elspeth Watson was slumped forward in her big captain's chair, her elbows resting on heavy thighs, forehead cradled in her hands. Her broad, rounded back ballooned and deflated with big, slow breaths.

Hunter backed quietly to the other side of the counter and cleared his throat. El raised her head and looked at him blankly, her skin blotched with red, the bangs of her brown hair flopping limply over her forehead like the comb of a rooster.

He offered her a tentative smile, which she didn't return. Instead, she dropped her gaze to the frayed armrest of her chair, and began to pick at the dirty foam rubber that bulged out of a tear in the black

2

vinyl. Her fingers looked swollen, and were smudged with ink and carbon. Hunter could hear the soft whirr of El's computer and muted traffic noises from the street.

Without looking up, she said, "Randy Danyluk's dead," and closed her eyes.

Suzanne's bladder was painfully full, and it confused her. How long had she been sitting here? She pulled on a corner of yellow cloth that protruded from under her thigh and realized that she was crushing the clean laundry, putting creases in tiny teeshirts and shorts, the girls' nighties, underwear of Gary's and her own. She'd been folding the laundry and stacking it in piles on the bed, it seemed like a lifetime ago, but she could still hear the news music from the T.V. in the family room, so it was only a while. Twenty minutes, or maybe half an hour. Such a short time that she was sure she could still wind things back to where they were, the way her life was at the start of the evening news.

She felt another stab of pain in her bladder and rushed to the bathroom. After, washing her hands at the sink, she caught sight of her face in the mirror. It took her by surprise. The girl in the mirror was older, she was not the same Suzanne who'd washed her hands at this sink less than an hour earlier. Oh, it looked like the same face, but she knew it wasn't the same person looking out of the mirror anymore. She watched her reflection with a curious detachment, and felt no affection for it, only a mixture of pity and disgust. She shook her head slowly and turned away.

The girl in the mirror, she thought, is a person whose father is dead.

She stood at the entrance to the family room, thinking that there must be something she should do. She should talk to someone who would know what to do, but the only person she could think of who would know was her father. Or maybe El. But she'd just spoken to El. El had told her about the accident, and then what had she said? Take a stiff drink, El said, and call a friend to come stay with you until Gary gets home.

Gary. If only Gary were here.

Suzanne sat down on the couch and picked up the remote control. She pressed the mute button, and stared at the frivolous images on the screen, not knowing or caring who they were or what they were doing or why.

It wasn't until little Veri padded into the room and tugged on her shirttail that Suzanne stirred. She pulled the toddler onto her lap and wrapped her arms tightly around the sleep-warm body, burying her face in the little girl's hair.

Veri squirmed. "Mommy. Mommy! Ow!"

Suzanne loosened her hold, kissed the top of the child's head, and began to rock her gently. "I'm sorry, sweetie. I'm so sorry. Oh, God! I'm so sorry."

CHAPTER
TWO

At eight thirty Friday morning, Hunter was sitting on the lawn behind his basement suite with Gord Young, his landlord, when the phone rang. The grass beneath their feet was cool and still slightly damp, its fresh scent mingled with the smell of the tall cedars that stood guard at the bottom of the retired doctor's sloping North Shore lot. Hunter had supplied fresh coffee, and the landlord had brought down a small carton of Half & Half, a replacement for the cream that had gone sour after three weeks in Hunter's fridge. Gord's Siamese cat, who was stalking robins between the apple tree and the laurel hedges in the back yard, stopped in mid-stride and glared at Hunter when he abandoned his lawn chair to answer the phone inside his suite.

It was El. "Listen, Hunter, can you get out to the airport by one o'clock? I need you to pick up Gary's truck in Winnipeg and drive it back out here."

"Uh, well, I ..."

"I know you were looking forward to a couple of days in town, but Suzy needs him. He's already caught a flight home to Kamloops. You'll get paid for your time, goddammit!"

"It's not that, El. You just took me by surprise, and I ... "

"Damn!" A telephone rang loudly in the background. "Hold on," El said, and Tanya Tucker started singing in Hunter's ear.

While he waited, Hunter rubbed the whiskers on his cheek, then ran his hand through his hair. He was staring thoughtfully at a

5

photograph on his desk when El came back on the line. The two teenaged girls in the picture were standing on Ambleside Beach in West Vancouver with the Lions Gate Bridge behind them, and strands of their long hair, a few shades lighter than his own, had blown across their faces as they squinted into the afternoon sun.

"Well?" said El. "Can you be there by one?"

"Almost everything I own is in the washing machine right now, but ... " - he wondered if Randy's daughter looked anything like his own - "I should be able to finish the laundry, get a haircut and pay my bills before noon, I guess," he said.

"I knew I could count on you. You're a prince!" Another phone started ringing. "Shit! It's flight 182 Air Canada your ticket will be at the counter call me from Winnipeg." And she hung up.

"No golf for me this afternoon," Hunter said to his landlord as he plunked himself back down into the lawn chair. He took a sip of his coffee, then rested the mug on his thigh while he gazed out past the cedars. The waters of Burrard Inlet stretched like sheet steel between the bare, straight trunks.

Gord's eyebrows raised above the dark frame of his bifocals. "Back to work already?" he asked. His face was tanned and lined, and although he was in his seventies he had a full head of hair that was still more brown than grey. He was barefoot, and wearing baggy shorts and a tee-shirt with BICYCLE STANLEY PARK stenciled across the chest.

"That driver I was telling you about? He owned four or five trucks besides the one he was driving. I've got to go pick up his son-in-law's truck in Winnipeg, so he can get home to his wife."

Gord nodded, his face grave. "I see. That's too bad." He paused, staring into his coffee cup. "So the driver was a close friend?"

Hunter smiled wanly. "He was a friend. Not that close, but a good friend." He'd lost friends before, colleagues on the force. People die in the line of duty, but you carry on. Most times, you carry on. Sometimes, you don't.

A robin exploded into the air, landing in the apple tree where it began a loud and frenzied clamour. The Siamese trotted over to

6

Gord's chair and settled primly on its haunches, ignoring the commotion.

"He and his wife were good friends of El Watson, the woman I work for. She hired his trucks, or he hired hers when they couldn't handle loads with their own drivers. It's his daughter El's worried about. Two little kids to look after - she's not much more than a kid herself - and suddenly her father's trucking company lands in her lap."

Before Hunter left for the airport, wearing a clean and only slightly wrinkled cotton work shirt and carrying a duffle bag with a couple of others, he looked again at the photograph on his desk.

He'd give anything to keep those girls safe and happy. He wondered if the last thing that went through Randy's mind was that his death would cause his daughter pain, and knew he would have struggled mightily to stay alive for that reason alone.

"Soon, kids," he said aloud, nodding. He tried to remember when he'd last spent time with his girls. Weeks ago, months maybe. "Yes. Soon."

Suzanne could hear Jolene scolding little Veronica for spilling the Cheerios and hoped the two of them would settle down quietly with the Muppets. The phone was bound to start ringing again soon, and she still had to retrieve the messages from earlier calls. Drivers would be reporting in. Shippers would be calling to schedule pick ups. She looked down at the coffee mug on her desk. Her fingers were curled around the handle, but she couldn't remember if she'd already taken a sip or not.

She'd hardly slept at all last night, and whenever she had dozed off during the early hours of morning, she would awake with a suffocating sense of dread before remembering the news about her father. Perhaps it was all a mistake, she thought. Everything around me looks so normal. He'll walk in the door in a minute or two, and he'll tell me it was all a big misunderstanding.

She had been showered and dressed before either of the kids woke up.

When she'd first arrived at the office, which was in her father's house less than two blocks away from the house he'd helped her and Gary buy, she went upstairs with Veri in the crook of her arm and Jo trailing behind her. Her father had left a few dishes in the sink, a bottle of multiple vitamins beside a used glass on the counter. A scratch pad beside the phone read coffee filters and popsicles (orange & grape!!). He always kept little treats on hand for the girls. Her father's bed was unmade but looked cold, and several pairs of pants were draped over a chair beside it. It wasn't unusual for her father to be gone for days at a stretch, even though he no longer drove his truck full time. He'd be on the road for a couple of days, then home for a night or two. Why should this time be any different?

When Veri started to squirm and Jo began to whine, Suzanne had shushed them firmly and they all had stayed still, listening to the silence, feeling the emptiness of the house, waiting almost expectantly, until a shiver of something like fear ran up her spine and she had hurried downstairs. She deposited the girls in the T.V. room adjoining the office, and turned on their morning cartoons.

The phone buzzed and Suzanne jumped. She felt an unpleasant tingling in her limbs that she supposed came from lack of sleep. The phone buzzed twice more before she could steel herself to pick it up.

"Ranverdan Transport," she said. "Good morning," she added hastily, but whoever was on the line had already started to talk.

"... not deliver yet. Where Randy? Where my Seattle freight? Why he not deliver to Edmonton yet?"

"Please ... who is this, please?" Suzanne's stomach dropped. She knew who it was. The traffic manager at Ranverdan's largest account, a man she had hardly ever talked to because her father always looked after him personally.

"This Victor Sung at Waicom in Vancouver. Why Randy not call? My Edmonton warehouse call this morning, say no deliver Seattle freight yet. Was suppose to be deliver yesterday. Where Randy? Randy not answer cell phone. Let me speak wif Randy."

Suzanne caught her breath. Could she say, "He's dead. Randy's dead." Or could she say, "Your freight is at the bottom of a cliff and we can't deliver it until ... ." Until when?

8

Could she talk to this man at all?

"Hello? Hello? You talk to me? Hello, miss?"

"Yes ... yes ... I'm sorry." She clamped her left hand over her mouth to keep from sobbing, took a deep breath. "I'll check and call you right back."

"I need to know right now. I hold on."

"No ... I ... I can't do that. I'll call you right back, Mr. Sung." Cutting off his objections, she jabbed at the next line button with her finger and speed dialed Elspeth Watson.

"Gary, where are you?" she whispered as she waited for El to answer. "I need you with me, Gary. Where are you?"

Elspeth Watson gritted her teeth. "Yes, Mr. Sung, it was a very serious accident. I'm afraid that Mr. Danyluk - Randy - was killed in the accident." She covered the mouthpiece and added under her breath, So who gives a fuck about your freight, asshole!

"Oooooh. Randy? Killed?" His voice was suddenly subdued. "How it happen? Randy a very good driver, I know him for a long long time."

"How'd it happen? We don't know for sure. Wednesday afternoon, when Randy hadn't called in for almost twenty four hours, we asked the R.C.M.P. to scout the route for his rig. They found it yesterday at the bottom of a ravine on the Coq just south of Merritt."

"Coke? What you mean, Coke? Coca-Cola?"

"Not that Coke. Coq for Coquihalla. Co-ka-ha-la," she enunciated slowly. "The highway. How do you think we get your freight across the mountains between Hope and Kamloops? Pack animals?"

"Oh, oh, oh. Coquihalla. Yes, I know Coquihalla." There were a few seconds of silence. "Very sad. Very, very sad. I know Randy a long time. He a very good man. A good driver. How it happen? No brakes?"

The man's grief was clearly genuine, maybe he wasn't such an asshole. El softened. "It doesn't look like brakes, 'cause he was on an uphill curve. We don't know how it happened yet. The R.C.M.P. will investigate." Sung's right. Randy was a good driver. There had to be a good reason. "Maybe he swerved to avoid an oncoming car, lost control of his rig. Maybe it was some kind of mechanical failure. Heart attack, even." Randy was in his early fifties, she thought, and kept himself in pretty good shape, but you could never tell. She remembered the initial reason for Sung's call. "The R.C.M.P. may not release the tractor trailer and its freight for a few days. I'm sorry."

"R.C.M.P.? Oh, oh, oh. I see." There was a long pause. "Freight not a big problem, compared to Randy. We ship again, no problem. I call you when ready in Seattle?"

"Yes. Okay, Mr. Sung. You call me here." El figured Suzanne didn't need the hassle.

Victor Sung sighed. "I very sorry about this thing. Randy was a good man."

Suzanne had just finished feeding the girls their lunch back at home and was wiping tomato sauce soaked alphabet noodles off Veri's high chair when she heard the front door open, and Jolene's excited "Daddy! Daddy!" Next thing she knew, Gary's arms held her close as she sobbed into his chest.

"Shhhhh, honey. It'll be okay, Suzy. We've still got each other," he said, and for reasons she didn't understand, it irritated her. She looked up at his face, then, and saw pain and sympathy in his eyes, and immediately felt guilty for her irritation. She guessed it was hard to know what to say at a time like this, especially for a man.

"Daddy? What's wrong?" Jo and Veri both stood looking up at them with worried little faces. "Mommy? Why are you crying?"

Later, when she'd put the girls down for their nap, she and Gary sat thigh to thigh beside each other on the couch, his arm circling her shoulders, his long hair still damp from the shower, his white cotton shirt smelling freshly of soap and deodorant. He'd gotten them each a beer, and Suzanne could feel the alcohol melting its way through her body after only a few sips.

"I can't believe it. It just doesn't seem real, you know what I mean? I keep expecting to wake up and find out it's just a nightmare," she said.

"I know exactly what you mean. I pulled out of the yard in Seattle before your dad's trailer was finished loading on Tuesday - and he waved at me from the loading dock. I thought he wanted to talk to me, so I go to stop the truck ... but then he waved me on." Gary stuck his beer can between his knees to free up his hand to demonstrate the wave. "Like he was saying, no big deal, I'll tell you later. You know? You always think you can talk about it later." His voice dropped to a whisper. "Now I'll never know what he wanted to say. That was the last time I saw him."

Suzanne pressed her face into his chest.

"Poor Suzy." Gary hugged her tighter and kissed her hair, before sitting back and taking a long pull on his beer. He sighed, then said, "This ain't gonna be easy, babe."

What was he trying to say?

"You're gonna have to make some tough decisions. About the business, you know?"

She knew it was true, but she didn't want to hear it. "Not today, Gary."

"It can't run itself, Suzy." He tipped his head back to drain his beer can.

"I know that." That feeling of irritation was rising again. "But I've forwarded the phones to El Watson in Vancouver, and she said she'd look after the calls whenever I needed to get out of the office until after ... ." She hated to say the word. "After the ... funeral. I'll make up my mind then."

"Your dad had a lot of years of experience. It's not easy to run a trucking company and make money at it."

"Please. Not today, Gary." The comfort she'd drawn from his closeness had evaporated. "Not yet." She stiffened.

"Okay, babe. I'm sorry." He hugged her again, hugged her with both arms and nuzzled her hair until she relaxed.

In a low and gentle voice, he said, "Your dad was one special guy, Suzanne. I feel privileged to have known him."

Suzanne smiled, the corners of her mouth trembling, and the tears started again.

There were over twelve hundred miles of highway between Winnipeg and Kamloops, where Randy Danyluk had lived, and over two thirds of it was flat. After spending the last three weeks on the road, Hunter started the two day drive without enthusiasm. The green and silver rig Gary had been driving was a late model Western Star like the rest of the Ranverdan tractors. As Hunter got used to the gears and controls, threading his way through the streets of East Kildonan towards the Trans Canada Highway, he marvelled at how Randy had managed to put six such tractors on the road while most drivers he knew struggled to make the payments on one. Like his own tractor, a 1991 tandem axle Freightliner with a 350 horsepower Cummins engine, a navy blue workhorse that El had nicknamed "The Blue Knight". By the time Hunter finished making the payments on what would then be a six-year-old truck eight months from now, El would be prodding him to trade it in. Randy had to have been one smart businessman, and he must have worked like the devil for years.

The highway dragged itself across the prairie landscape. After a late dinner stop in Virden, near the Manitoba-Saskatchewan border, Hunter dug through a case of tapes he found beside the seat, thinking music might break the monotony of night driving. It was mostly country, or country rock. Clint Black, Ricky Scaggs, Jerry Jeff Walker, Prairie Oyster. He stuck in a John Anderson tape and turned it on as he pulled back onto the highway. The third time it started to repeat, he pushed the eject button and let the drone of road sounds fill the cab.

With nothing much to distract him, Hunter's thoughts began to follow the oppressive shadowed pathways in his mind that only seemed to take shape, like recurring nightmares, after dark. Most long haul drivers prefer to drive through the night, when the traffic is lighter, but for Hunter, the price exacted by the darkness was too

12

high. As if his usual black musings weren't enough, tonight he was passing Regina.

Regina, over twenty - no - twenty four years ago next month. The R.C.M.P. training depot. Six months they'd sweated and strained and ached together, he and Ken and the others, polished boots and buttons and shined the buckles on their belts, cleaned rifles and guns and the floor beneath their bunks, drilled and studied and pushed themselves till they thought they would hit the wall.

"What's your first choice?" Ken had asked. They were lying on their backs, staring at the ceiling, tired limbs draped along narrow, spartan beds. Around them, fellow recruits prepared for lights out, shining boots, writing letters, or exchanging banter. A few were already asleep. "Vancouver?"

Hunter looked at Ken in disbelief. "Of course not. I've spent my whole life there, why would I want Vancouver?"

"Where then?" Ken took his arm out from behind his head and scratched his groin through the grey woollen blanket. "Ottawa? Pomp and circumstance?"

Hunter snorted. "Is that where you want to go?"

"Hell, no!" He tucked his arm back in behind his head. "Hell, no!" he repeated with a grin.

"Ever been up north?" Hunter asked.

"You're not talking about Flin Flon, are you?" He grinned again.

Hunter shook his head.

"That's what I thought."

A few weeks later, the graduating recruits gathered to receive their postings. They were high on the drug of imminent success, charged with an almost uncontrollable energy and enthusiasm and a sense of comradeship unlike anything they had ever felt before, as if they'd endured a bloody battle together and knew, at last, that they would survive, triumphant.

"Constable J. Hunter Rayne." The corporal's voice barked into the hushed group. "G Division, Whitehorse Detachment, Whitehorse, Yukon."

A cautious cheer went up, and Hunter raised both arms in the air in a giddy victory salute.

A few minutes later it was Ken's turn. "Constable Kenneth A. Marsh."

Ken's nostrils flared and he held his breath.

"G Division, Whitehorse Detachment, Whitehorse, Yukon."

"Yeeee-HA!" Ken punched the air with his fist, his body lifting off the chair with the force of it, and leaned forward to give the recruit seated in front of him a resounding kiss on the top of his head. Hunter bit his lip to keep from laughing.

Boots clattering down the wooden stairway of the meeting hall, Ken caught up to Hunter on the way out. He knocked off Hunter's hat, then wrapped his arms around Hunter's chest in a ferocious bear hug. "Watch out, Mad Trapper! Stand by, Lost Patrol! Here come Constable Rayne and Constable Marsh, blood brothers and spiritual descendants of Samuel Steele, set to tame the lawless Yukon!"

Hunter pushed him away, growling. "Lawless, like hell! Dammit, Ken! There's probably been more Mounties per capita in the Yukon than anywhere else in the goddamn country!" He surreptitiously wiped his eyes with his sleeve as he reached down to retrieve his hat. Damned if he didn't love the silly fool like a real brother.

Now Ken was dead. And Randy was dead. Thinking of Randy, the doting father, set Hunter on that other inexorable train of thought that led to his own daughters, who lived with Christine, his ex-wife. It seemed to Hunter that he had been waiting all his life for the time when he could finally hunker down and talk to his girls, when they'd be old enough to really talk, to articulate their deep down hopes and dreams. He'd always believed that as they got older, he would get closer to them. Instead they were growing farther and farther apart. Like he and Ken had.

Hunter clenched and unclenched his jaws, grinding his back teeth. Regrets. They lay like a heavy black tarpaulin, stretched across his heart. If only he and Ken had ... If only he and Chris ... Damn! He caught himself edging up over sixty five miles an hour, eased up on the accelerator, and set the cruise control.

He spent what was left of Friday night in a pullout between Regina and Moose Jaw in the sleeper of the truck, tossing and turning between memories of the Depot and thoughts of his daughters, and finally falling asleep surrounded by the stale, tobacco stained odor of the last occupant's sweat.

CHAPTER — — —
THREE

Elspeth Watson couldn't get the office door unlocked fast enough, teased to distraction as she was by the smell of the hash browns and Egg McMuffin in the warm bag that rustled against her belly. El loved her work. She loved her unadorned and utilitarian office, its smudged walls and scarred grey tile floor, the cold concrete and chain pulley doors of her warehouse. She loved the smell of propane forklifts and big diesels and wet cardboard and sweating men that went along with it. But she took particular pleasure in Saturday mornings, with their slower pace and the hot breakfast she was permitted the leisure to indulge herself in.

At the end of May, the sun was well above the neighboring buildings by seven o'clock when she lowered her ample rump into the captain's chair. She watched the dust motes swirl above the customer service counter as she settled in to eat her breakfast and drink an enormous mugful of coffee. The phone rang before she'd had a chance to cancel the call forwarding, which meant she had to pick it up before the fourth ring. Her mouth was still full.

"Watson!"

"El? It's Suzanne."

Poor kid. "Mornin', Suzy." El swallowed. "How're you doing?" She grabbed the coffee to wash the lump of muffin and sausage down her throat, but it was too hot to take more than a small sip.

"I just wanted to let you know that I'm in the office today. I've switched the phones back."

"Uh ... well ... okay, then. I've got a few things in the works, Suzy... uh ... I'm expecting some calls on your line about ... " Oh, damn! The kid won't know what's going on! "Are you sure you want the calls coming to you? There's some stuff ... "

"That's okay, El. If I have any problems, I'll give you a call."

The kid sounded pretty together, but the drivers were used to dealing with Randy, a veteran, like herself, who knew every side of the business - more than just an office clerk. "Sure." El could feel the first faint smoldering of heartburn.

"Feel free to take some more time off, Suzy. It must be awfully hard for you, especially with those little tykes to look after."

"Thanks, El. The kids are used to coming here, and being here makes me feel closer to Dad. It's better than sitting at home and stewing about it, you know? Dad and I learned that after Mom died, remember?"

El remembered. Randy had barely taken any time off work when his wife died. Suzanne had already moved back to Kamloops and taken over her mother's work in the office by then. Cancer. The last couple of months Ronnie had hardly gotten out of bed. Ranverdan was a real family company. Ranverdan - after Randy and Veronica Danyluk.

"It isn't fair that you've lost your mom and your dad, both, in such a short period of time," El said gently. Hell! Randy's death just wasn't fair to anybody, herself included! "He was a very special man, your father. A lot of us are going to miss him."

"How could it have happened?" El could tell that Suzanne had started crying, her voice turned wet and nasal. "Dad of all people! He was such a good driver, everybody said so."

"I know, Suzy, he was. He was the best."

"Then how, El? What could have happened? Why him?"

"I'm sure they'll find out. I'm sure it was something beyond your dad's control. These things happen."

"Like what? What things happen? I always worry about Dad and Gary in the winter, when the drivers talk about the ice and snow on the Coquihalla, but why now?"

El fidgeted with the phone cord. "An oncoming car, maybe. Your dad was a good driver, but there were other people on the road that night, and there's always some jerk driving too fast, or driving drunk, or falling asleep at the wheel. Fate doesn't play favorites," El continued. "Then there's always the chance he might've had a heart attack. It doesn't seem right, but I've seen it happen to younger men than him."

Suzanne said nothing, but El could hear her breathing through her nose with a soft snuffle.

"Are you sure you're ready to take the phones back? I've got things under control."

"Yes. Yes, I need to." And more softly, "Dad would want me to."

After she hung up, El took another bite of breakfast, but the spell was broken. She swallowed it in a hurry and grabbed the receiver again. Why wait for the drivers to phone her?

At about ten o'clock, her phone rang for the umpteenth time and El bustled in from the warehouse to grab it somewhere around the seventh ring. It was Hunter Rayne, calling collect from a payphone in a restaurant near Swift Current.

"Hey, Hunter." She was only slightly out of breath as she settled into her chair. "How's it going?"

"Just tickety boo," he said. "I'm right on schedule, should be arriving in Kamloops sometime Sunday afternoon. Got a flight home booked for me?"

The guy almost always sounded this cheerful. Sometimes it was downright irritating. "I'll have Gary meet you at the Ranverdan yard. You can drop the rig there. Listen, about your trip back to Vancouver, I had a great idea ... "

"Hold on, El. Let me just remind you that I'm due for a couple of days of R and R."

"That's precisely what I've got in mind, sweet cheeks. I figured you could take a couple of days off, rest up a little, do some golfing, maybe a little fishing ... uh ... you still there, Hunter?"

"Yes, El," he said, slow and clipped. Ouch! He was already suspicious. It was scary, the way he could read her like a book, even over the telephone.

"Well, it's like this. Ranverdan's one of my biggest operators and I can't afford to see them screwed up. Things could be a little shaky for a while, until Suzanne either sells the business or gets a partner to help her run things properly. Uh ... since it's in your best interests as one of my drivers to see my operation prosper ... maybe ... I just figured ... "

"Yes?" He obviously wasn't going to make it easy for her.

"It's this way, Hunter. Suzanne's really shook up about her dad's death ... as she should be, of course ... and she's torturing herself about how it happened ... and I thought perhaps with your connections ..." Surely he still had friends in the Kamloops R.C.M.P. "Maybe you could make a few phone calls, you know, pull a few strings ... get a little inside information about the accident before the inquest. The sooner she comes to terms with it, the better, don't you think?"

Silence.

El pressed her lips shut and raised her eyebrows, watched two crows sparring with each other on the rail of the chain link fence across the yard. She cleared her throat.

"Hunter?"

"Sure. I'll make the calls as soon as I get home." El rolled her eyes. The fox!

"It would do her a lot of good - a lot of good, Hunter - to talk to you in person about it. You're so good at that kind of stuff, you know, fatherly advice. And I'll be driving up on Wednesday morning for the funeral, you and me can ride back together, okay?"

"I'm not staying for the funeral. El ... "

Shit! Sounded like he was losing patience. Before he could finish his sentence, she added, "Suzanne says you can use Randy's truck, his

19

boat, his golf clubs. You can stay at his place in Kamloops, and haven't you been talking about visiting friends on the Shuswap? That's only an hour or so drive away, isn't it? Please don't say no, Hunter, not until you've thought it over. Call me from Kamloops, okay? Call me after you've met Suzanne. If you still want to come home, I'll buy you a ticket on the first flight out, I promise."

She could hear him let out his breath in a big rush of air. He sighed again, then said, his voice like granite, "Remember what you just said, El. I'll call you from Kamloops."

She wiped her forehead in mock relief as she put down the phone. Sheesh! Good natured as he was, seems Hunter was only prepared to be Mr. Nice Guy on his own terms. She hoped that his meeting Suzanne would tip the scales.

El grabbed a sugar doughnut from the Tim Horton's box, a weekly bribe from one of the drivers, and finished it off in three bites before she headed back out the warehouse door.

Hunter hung up the receiver feeling cheated. Some days on the road felt lonelier than others, and this was one of them. He'd been looking forward to a few minutes of friendly banter with El, but the turn the conversation had taken precluded that. He frowned at the phone, debating whether to call his daughters' number, but a kid in a black baseball cap elbowed in beside him and asked if he was finished yet. Hunter nodded and, pushing open the restaurant's outer door, headed back out to the green and silver truck.

Daylight driving was a pleasure, especially in fine weather. The green prairie wheat rippled and flowed across the fields like water, splashing up waves of reflected sunlight. The warm wind tightened the skin on Hunter's left cheek, and the smell of grass and earth eddied through the truck's open window. Occasionally a single sweet note of birdsong pierced the solid hum of his eighteen wheels. The prairie sky was as big as he'd ever seen it, blue and wide, with far away clouds scudding across the surface of the distant fields where they dipped away towards the other side of the globe. He sensed that, somehow, its vastness was good for his soul.

20

Late Saturday afternoon Hunter checked into a motel just outside of Calgary. It cost thirty five dollars and smelled like an ashtray, but it had a bed, a bathroom, and a place to park the truck. He showered and shaved and treated himself to a steak in a nearby restaurant. Then he wandered around a drugstore, picking up a day old Vancouver newspaper and a Tom Clancy novel. Back in his motel room, he sat on the bed to read. He couldn't get comfortable. He plumped the foam pillow behind his back against the headboard and stretched his legs out on top of the thin bedspread. The bed frame squeaked with every movement. He couldn't sit still and finally gave up trying.

He walked back up the street, past the restaurant and drugstore, past rows of closed shops and offices and empty lots, and found a licensed lounge in a small hotel. The room was dark, and loud country music blared from speakers on the ceiling. He sat down at a table near the entrance and ordered a beer. The carpet in the entranceway smelled of vomit. Every time he looked up, a blonde woman sitting at the next table was staring at him. She wore tight jeans, a sleeveless red blouse, and red high heels, and there was a tiny gold chain around her ankle. Hunter finished his beer quickly and walked the six blocks back to the hotel. He tried again to read the novel, but nodded off before he finished the first chapter.

After complimentary coffee and doughnuts, which he ate standing up in the motel's musty smelling lobby, Hunter was on the road again by seven Sunday morning. On the stretch of road past the foothills and through the Rocky Mountains, every second that navigating the hills and curves didn't require his full attention, his eyes were drawn like magnets to the peaks of the Rockies. He took a hamburger break in Revelstoke, and about four o'clock on Sunday afternoon he pulled into Ranverdan's fenced yard in northeast Kamloops.

A tall, well built man in his thirties, his thinning blond hair drawn back into a tight little pony tail, was leaning against the side of a small house trailer, smoking a cigarette. He was dressed in blue jeans, black cowboy boots, and a white cotton shirt with sleeves rolled up to display muscular forearms. His eyes were hidden behind Oakley shades. After signaling to Hunter where to park his rig, Gary Rodgers locked up the trailer and the gate, and steered Hunter to a black 4x4 Ford pickup parked on the street.

"Suzanne is waiting for us back at the office," he said. "And Big Mother Trucker wants you to call her."

Gary drove a few blocks towards the river and pulled in beside a wine colored mini-van parked in the driveway of a boxy two-story house with chocolate brown wood siding. He led Hunter through the front door and down a small hallway to the office, a converted rec room on the ground floor, and motioned to a small sofa. Sticking his head back out the door, he hollered up the stairs. "Suzanne! We're here!"

The low-ceilinged room was paneled in dark wood and had a rusty brown carpet, but was made bright by a large, spotless window revealing the South Thompson river, its lushly treed flood plain, and the sandy sage covered hills beyond. The office was tidy and spacious and comfortable. There was a big yellow teddy bear perched on the arm of the sofa and a coloring book with crayons spread out on the carpet. As he sat down, Hunter picked up a polka dot baseball cap from the sofa and placed it at a rakish angle over one of the teddy bear's button eyes.

A slight young woman with long brunette hair entered the room and smiled at him as she made her way over to the desk. She wore faded jeans, canvas shoes, and an oversized sweatshirt of robin's egg blue that made her look tiny and fragile. Her eyes looked tired, inflamed against the pallid skin of her face.

"Okay," she said as she shuffled through some papers, "El told me how much to make the check out for, but you should look at the numbers first. We decided that Ranverdan should just pay you direct. Watson isn't going to take anything on it, so it's less hassle this way."

Hunter approached the desk. She met his eyes, then dropped her gaze to the sheet of paper she held extended to him. He accepted it without looking at it. "Suzanne," he said. He waited until she raised her eyes again. "My sincere condolences. Your father was an exceptional man. He'll truly be missed."

Suzanne blinked rapidly, nodded and tried to smile. Just then a racket of thumping and squealing descended the stairs in the hallway, and seconds later two blonde little girls giggled and jostled their way across the room towards their mother.

"Can Veri and me have a popsicle, Mom? Dad says it's okay. Can we?" The oldest was about five and she was the one doing the talking. The other, who looked about three, got suddenly quiet when she saw Hunter, and pulling on her lower lip, inched sideways and wrapped her other arm around her mother's legs.

"Will Daddy get it for you?" When the girls nodded vigorously, she said "Okay, then" and gave them a little shove towards the door. "But use a Kleenex," she called after them. "Watch the drips!"

Hunter smiled as he watched them scamper away. "Nice kids," he said. "I had two girls, very much like those two, but now they're young adults. Closer to your age." He shook his head. "Time goes by so fast." He remembered holding one small sticky hand in each of his, stooping a little to pilot his tiny family and their popsicles from the concession stand to where their mother waited on the beach near Dundarave pier. "You wish life could just stand still for a while."

They were both lost momentarily in their thoughts, then Suzanne reached for a pen and started to write out the check. "How do I make it out? El keeps calling you 'Hunter', but the paperwork says 'J.H. Rayne'. Is that a mistake?" She looked up at him, and he noticed again how tired her eyes were.

"Hunter's my given name. It's J. Hunter Rayne." He scanned the numbers on the paper she had given him. There was nothing listed to cover a flight back to Vancouver. Damn that Elspeth! She'd done it to him again.

"This looks ... uh ... fine." He nodded, conceding defeat. "Just fine."

CHAPTER
FOUR

The man on the Harley was well aware that he was exceeding the speed limit - hell! he'd doubled it! - and didn't need a cop to remind him of the fact. And he sure as hell didn't intend to pay a fuckin' fine for it either! He checked his left side mirror, watched the RCMP cruiser's brake lights brighten and fade as the cop realized he couldn't make a U-turn on the narrow road. Good ... no! ... oh, shit! The cop's flashers went on, and his brakes lit up again. He must've decided to stop traffic and make the turn, maneuvering his cruiser across both lanes between the big ditches. The biker saw that the road in front of him was clear, and opened up the throttle. If he could just get off this fuckin' country road, away from the open fields and into an area with trees and houses to hide his bike from view before the cop closed the gap.

The Harley responded - ah, what a sweet little mother she was! - and the flashing red and blue receded momentarily behind him, until he was forced to slow on the approach to an intersection. Right or left? He didn't know this street. What was he heading for? A dead end or a clean escape route? Ri-i-i-i ... no ... hard LEFT! He swerved with a split second to spare in front of an oncoming pickup, which fishtailed wildly, horn blaring. The biker grinned and sneaked another look in the mirror. The driver of the pickup had stopped right in the intersection and was standing on his running board, shaking his fist above the roof of the cab. The cop had to come to a full stop until the pickup was out of the way. The biker laughed into the wind and sped on.

Another intersection, both sides now concealed by alder and cottonwood, heavy with the brilliant greens of spring. This time he chose the right. He rode like stink, looking for a chance to turn left before the cop reached the corner. Aha! Here it was. He careened to the left, his rear wheel skidding and catching the unpaved shoulder, sending a spray of gravel into the ditch. Past one driveway, two, three. Shit! A dead end! Nothing but heavy bush. What now? Did he have time to backtrack, get back onto the last road and disappear down another side street before the cop could spot him? He didn't think so, but he had nowhere else to go so he turned around, the sole of his left boot connecting soundly with the asphalt.

The second house he'd passed was set well back from the street. Its dirt driveway ran between the ramshackle house and some outbuildings adjacent to a small corral. He swerved into the driveway, hoping that no one was home. Rounding one of the outbuildings, almost too fast, the biker saw a small enclosure fenced with solid weathered planks about six feet high. He rode right up to it, undid the latch, and swung the gate wide. As soon as the Harley lurched through the opening he killed the motor and leaped off the bike to close the gate. The falling bike caught him behind the left knee and brought him down. What the ... !? The kick stand had sunk into fuckin' deep mud! The chrome of his poor sweet chopper was half submerged in fuckin' black mud! The biker struggled to his feet, swung the gate closed, and scrambled up to drape himself over the top of the fence. With much struggling and kicking, he managed to reach down the far side and close the outside latch, then launched himself back to the ground just as he heard the cruiser's siren reach its peak. Slipping in the mud, he lay where he fell, listening, straining to hear the movements of the police cruiser over his own panting breaths.

He wouldn't have been here if it hadn't been for that fuckin' boss of his last night. Fuckin' EX boss, he corrected himself. Saturday night in Surrey, always a few assholes looking for trouble and he, Dan Sorenson, had been ready for them, as befitted a bouncer at the King George Inn. He'd turfed at least six guys by midnight, and was feeling pretty pumped. It was a great job! He'd flash the Harley tattoo on his left biceps and the black cobra on his right forearm, backed up by his six foot three, two hundred and forty pound physique, and most dickheads got suitably respectful and left quietly. There were usually one or two a night he had to push around, and that was okay, too. In fact, that was even more fun.

But maybe last night he'd been a little too pumped. It seemed like a righteous thing to do at the time, but he shouldn't've thrown that drunken asshole through the stained glass partition. The venerable image of old King George (it wasn't really King George, it looked more like the King of Clubs) had shattered into a thousand orange and red and yellow pieces. So his fuckin' asshole boss had paid him out and told him not to come back. And then of course he'd gotten drunk (the first time he'd fallen off the wagon in three years), and then Simone had cried about it this morning like he knew she would, and that had made him feel fuckin' awful, and that had made him want to ride the thunder, and that was why he had been speeding through the Surrey countryside on 176th Street this fine Sunday afternoon.

The siren travelled west to east, then east to west, and now was receding into the distance. If he could lay low for an hour or so, he'd be home free.

So, thanks to his fuckin' ex boss, here he was ... belly down in some kind of stinking mud ... he heard a snuffling sound and felt warm breath, then a vigorous nuzzling at his neck.

Pigs! Fuckin' PIGS!

"I won't expect to hear back from my friend at the Kamloops detachment until tomorrow afternoon," said Hunter. "At that time, I should be able to get the results of the preliminary investigation for you, at least."

26

They sat around a table on the back patio at Suzanne and Gary's house. Gary had barbecued a couple of sirloins, and Suzanne had brought baked potatoes, green beans and a tossed salad from the kitchen. The little girls had been fed earlier, and now played boisterously on a lawn strewn with colorful plastic toys. Conversation during dinner had been sparse, the sense of bereavement hanging in the air between them like smoke.

"What are you planning to do tomorrow morning?" asked Suzanne. When Hunter shrugged, she turned to Gary. "Why don't you take Hunter riding? You've been trying to get me to go with you for months." She turned back to Hunter. "If you used to be a Mountie, you must be able to ride, right? Gary's got connections at a dude ranch up in the hills above Kamloops Lake."

The youngest child, little Veri, began to scream. Hunter winced involuntarily. Gary and Suzanne both leaped to their feet, but Gary motioned his wife to sit down. "I'll take them upstairs," he said. "You keep Hunter company." He picked up the little girl and tossed her in the air. "Bath time!" he said. "You, too, Jolie!" Both girls were giggling as he carried them, one squirming under each arm, into the house.

Hunter volunteered to help Suzanne with the dishes, and to his surprise she asked him to wash. Their automatic dishwasher needed repairs, she said. Hunter approached the unfamiliar task with care and concentration.

"How're things with the business?" Wrist deep in suds, Hunter turned his head to watch Suzanne wipe the countertop. She looked so young, her small-boned hands so fragile.

"El's been a lifesaver," said Suzanne. "She's covering us with her own guys to make up the runs we can't handle. Suddenly we're short a truck and two drivers, what with Gary being pulled off the road, and Dad..." She wiped hard at something Hunter couldn't see. Her hair swung forward to hide her face. "She's doing it at cost, too. I don't know how to thank her."

"El was very fond of your Dad. She wants to help." Hunter paused as he ran water to rinse the soap suds off a glass. "Anything I can do?"

"Aren't you going riding with Gary tomorrow?"

"We don't have to go. I'd feel guilty about taking Gary's time. He's staying home because of you, after all. You know what I mean?"

Suzanne dried a glass, polishing it slowly with the towel. "I guess the truth of it is, things might go smoother for me if Gary spends some time with you tomorrow. He doesn't know much about running the office, and for now, it seems more work to teach him things than to do them myself." She still held the glass, but stared out the window into the twilight. "The kids and I have our set little routine.

"I guess I get comfort from sticking to the routine, you know? It makes me feel like I'm carrying on ... for Dad. It makes me feel he's still close, you know? And I need that right now." She put down the glass and started fingering the hem of the towel, waiting for Hunter to put more dishes in the drainer. "I wasn't always real close to Mom and Dad. For a long time, I thought I was smarter than they were." She snorted softly. "I have regrets, I guess. Some kind of guilt I have to deal with, maybe. Although I feel I cheated myself as much as them, those years I was away and figured I didn't have time for them ... it must've hurt. Being a parent now myself, I can imagine how it must feel." She grabbed a handful of cutlery and started massaging it with the towel. "Kids are stupid. At least, I was." She looked up at him.

"I don't know why I'm telling you this. You must be one of those good listeners that people talk about," she said with a sheepish smile.

"Well, I have been called that." He smiled. "You learn more from listening than from talking. Besides, I can never think of much to say." He wondered if his daughters would ever feel like they didn't have time for him, or maybe they felt that way already. Suzanne seemed like such a nice girl. She seemed so much like his own nice girls.

28

Gary came back from putting the kids to bed. "They need kisses, Mommy," he said, and nuzzled Suzanne's neck making playful smacking noises. She ducked out of his reach and left the room. "So you and me are on for a ride tomorrow morning, Hunter? I'll pick you up at eight."

"Do you think Suzanne's coping alright?" Hunter asked. Gary had made a right turn off of Highway 97 past Savona and was driving the pickup along a narrow two-lane road that snaked up into the sandy hills. Hunter knew that the brave face Suzanne allowed him to see might be very different from the one she showed to Gary when they were alone.

Gary grimaced. "She's taking it pretty hard, I think. I wish I could comfort her somehow, but she kind of shuts me out. Maybe I just don't know what to say." Hunter wasn't sure, but he thought there was a trace of bitterness in Gary's voice.

"That happens. Grief is a very private thing for some people." He fixed his eyes on a small plane that was following the course of the unseen river to the south. "It's like a private conversation with ... well, with her father. You or I feel like we're butting in on it. And not welcome."

"That's exactly what it feels like! But - dammit! - I just hate to see her hurting like that!"

The road dipped and twisted, and the truck whined as Gary geared it down to second. Grass and scrub trees were giving way to low clumps of plantain and white clover. The sand colored slopes that rose on either side of the roadbed were dotted with sagebrush.

Hunter nodded. "Unfortunately, grief is something you have to meet head on, take the lumps." Easier said than done, he admitted to himself. "Otherwise it can ambush you later on." The truck rattled over a cattle guard built into the road, which was now unpaved, as they began to climb another hill. The side mirror showed billows of pale dust rising in their wake.

"Life's a bitch and then you die," recited Gary, staring grimly at the road ahead.

Hunter studied the younger man's face, those parts not hidden behind the dark glasses. It was a strong, symmetrical face, with taut, healthy looking skin. The mouth was sensual and expressive, although the lips were less than full. Hunter suspected that the dark glasses were a conscious vanity, because he'd noticed last night how Gary's face lost much of its strength when his eyes were exposed. They were a washed out blue with short pale lashes, and just a little too close together.

As they crested the hill, a long blue expanse of water came into view. Kamloops Lake. A short distance ahead was a log archway, into the topmost pole of which were burned the words Lazy K Ranch, and below that, Welcome. Soon they were looking down on the untidy cluster of log buildings and network of fences that comprised the Lazy K.

Once they'd parked the truck, Gary introduced Hunter to his friend, Jack Turpin, who was busy saddling up a group of bored looking horses. Jack looked the part of a lanky, laconic cowboy, dressed in faded blue denim and tall dusty boots.

"Kingston's tied up, so I'm taking half a dozen dudes out this morning," he said. "You guys will be on your own. You mind?"

Hunter shrugged agreeably.

Gary shook his head. "Not a problem. I know my way around," he said. "That realtor's truck," he motioned towards a Jeep Cherokee with a logo on the door, "belong to a dude?"

Jack shook his head and raised one eyebrow meaningfully.

Gary nodded and pursed his lips. "Already?" He sighed deeply before bending to pick up a saddle. "Shit."

It felt good to be in the saddle again. With the empty brown hills unrolling in front of him and the sky weightless overhead, Hunter sensed the same promise of freedom that he felt behind the wheel on a good day, maybe even more so. A couple of hours out, they reined up at a viewpoint and dismounted, settling themselves on a couple of large rocks as their horses pulled half-heartedly at spiky clumps of grass, snorting drily, bridles clinking.

30

Gary pulled a couple of cans of beer out of an insulated bag and handed one to Hunter. The tab popped inside with a crack that startled the horses, and Hunter held the can at arms length as the beer foamed out of the hole and formed small frothy beads in the dust between his outstretched legs. It wasn't ice cold, but it was still cool and wet. They both took several long swallows, then turned to grin at each other.

"Bliss, eh?" said Gary. He sucked his breath in audibly through closed teeth. "I love this cowboy stuff!"

"The ranch is up for sale?" asked Hunter.

Gary nodded. He took a few thoughtful sips, then looked sideways at Hunter. "Just between you and me," he said, "I'd love to buy the place."

Hunter nodded. He wondered if Gary was just dreaming, or if he actually had a way to finance a purchase of that size.

"Suzanne doesn't know, and I trust you won't say anything. Unfortunately, this doesn't seem like the right time to bring it up." He sighed heavily. "There's no way we could afford it, of course, unless she sold the company, and even then ... I haven't a clue what Ranverdan would sell for. Have you?"

"No idea. Are the trucks all paid for?"

Gary shrugged. "I wouldn't even want to ask right now. Suzanne ... well ... it's like Ranverdan is part of her dad, or maybe her dad is a part of it, or whatever. No, I wouldn't even want to ask."

"Even then," said Hunter, "running a ranch isn't something you can learn overnight. Why's he selling? Maybe he can't turn a profit on it. Could be he's just trying to unload a big money pit, pretty as it might be."

Gary turned over his empty beer can and shook it, watched a few flecks of foam drop to the dirt. "Kingston's only fifty five, but ever since I've known him, he's talked about retiring and moving to southern California. I didn't think he'd be ready to sell for another five or ten years, I thought he was having too much fun, but maybe he figures the market's hot. The annual Kamloops cattle drive is getting to be a big thing, starting to attract people from all over the

States. You know, the City Slickers scene? The Baby Boomers and their increasing leisure time, that sort of shit.

"Oh, well. I'm not going to push it. When Suzanne's ready ... " Gary pulled out another beer, offered it to Hunter. Hunter accepted, and Gary opened one for himself. "When Suzanne's ready, she'll remember."

"Remember?"

"Yeah. She and I met at university, back when we were both studying Recreation, which was a popular field for people who didn't like math or English, right?" Gary flashed a small self-deprecating smile. "We were big on plans but short on practicality - like, we never worried about how we were going to pay for it, but our dream back then was to one day have our own guest ranch. She was working part time in a restaurant then, and talked about how she'd be able to run the lodge, decide on the menus and stuff. She got excited about baking her own pies. Rhubarb. She loved the idea of rhubarb." He laughed softly, shaking his head. "And I would look after the stables, mend the fences, tend bar - I was working part time as a bartender - and do all the handyman stuff. We had it all worked out.

"The trucking business never came up. Becoming truckers is not something either of us would ever have predicted ... or wished for. Driving truck." He sighed, then looked over at Hunter with a quizzical frown. "How about you? You were with the R.C.M.P. How in hell did you ever end up in this business?"

A ghost of a smile on his lips, Hunter stared off at the horizon. "Just luck," he said quietly. "Sheer good luck."

CHAPTER
FIVE

Suzanne was on the phone when Murphy walked in. For a bear of a man - a thick neck atop rounded shoulders, a barrel chest that segued into a big belly - he stepped with surprising delicacy around the toys littering the office floor and smiled a sweet apology as he perched his big body on the edge of the sofa. He wore slightly mismatched olive colored work pants and shirt, and carried a well worn peaked cap in his hands. Suzanne jotted down the details of the call - a pickup in Vernon to be scheduled for Friday afternoon - thanked the caller, put down the receiver, and looked up at the big man.

"Hello, Murph," she said, and burst into tears.

Before she knew it, her arms were around him and he cradled her head against his sturdy chest, rocking her gently from side to side.

"Poor little Suzy," he crooned. "Poor little Suzy."

Murphy had known her father ever since the big Newfoundlander's first trip out west from eastern Canada some twenty years ago. They both loved to tell the story of how Randy had been fueling up his truck when Murphy'd pulled up beside him at a service station in the town of Golden, just west of the Rockies. The big Newfie had tumbled out of his cab, fallen to his knees, and kissed the filthy asphalt. "Sweet Jesus! Holy Mother of God!" he'd cried. "T'anks to you both for getting me t'rough 'dem bleedin' big mountains!" Her father had laughed so hard he'd cried, and Murphy had gone red in the face and threatened to punch him to Kingdom Come. They became fast friends and a year later, when Suzanne's father started Ranverdan Transport, Murphy had moved out west to Kamloops to drive for him.

Murphy's work shirt smelled of dust and diesel and old sweat. Suzanne pulled away and looked up at the ruddy, round face. "I'm okay, Murph," she said.

"I come as soon as I got back in town once't I heard. I'm so sorry, darlin'. So sorry. Your dad and me ... well, you know about your dad and me ... I loved him like a brother, I truly did."

She nodded, trying to smile through her tears. "I know, Murph."

"If there's anything I can do, you just whistle, hear? You just whistle and I'll be there, whatever you need, eh?"

The phone rang and Suzanne broke away to answer. "Ranverdan Transport," she said.

"I'm trying to reach Hunter Rayne. Is he there?" The male caller had a pleasant, confident voice.

"No. Is there a message?"

"Ah, good. I have the right number. Could I reach him on his cell phone, do you think?"

"I don't know, he might be out of range, but I can take a message for him here. He should be back by about two or two thirty."

"Fine. Tell him that Sergeant Bill Earl of the Kamloops R.C. ..., oh, just tell him that Bill Earl called. He'll know what it's about."

"About my father?" Suzanne's heart began to race. "This is Suzanne Rodgers. Randy Danyluk is my father. Is it about my father?"

"My condolences, Ms. Rodgers. Please have Hunter give me a call when he gets back."

"Have you found something out about the accident? Do you know why ... what happened? Was it ... did my dad ..." She wasn't aware until after she'd spoken that her words would sound so desperate. She tried to compose herself, adopt a more businesslike tone. "Is there any evidence of how the accident happened?"

"I'm sorry, ma'am. I'm afraid I can't tell you anything. Please, you'd best just have Hunter give me a call."

Murphy's face when she looked up was grave, almost angry. "Who was that?" he demanded.

Suzanne looked up at him, surprised at his vehemence. "The R.C.M.P."

"They hung up on you?" His face had begun to redden. "Those bastards ... haven't they got any feelin' for ... "

"No, no, Murphy. It's not like that at all. You know Hunter? He's one of El's drivers. He used to be in the R.C.M.P., and that was a friend of his."

"Hunter? No, I can't say's I know him. Maybe seen him down at Watson a time or two, but the name doesn't ring any bells." He was still scowling.

"He's about Dad's height, five ten or so, I guess. Not a big guy, average build, short light brown hair, but not military short. Plain dresser, but kind of tidy looking. Reminds me a little of Bryan Adams, except older, but not as old as Dad." She frowned, trying to think of how to describe him. "You'd remember his eyes. He's got those intense kind of eyes - stares right into you - I'm not sure what color, maybe blue."

Murphy smiled and shook his head. "I don't go lookin' at fellows' eyes, darlin'. And I don't know this Adams fellow, either. Can't place him, sorry. No, wait. You say he used to be in the R.C.M.P.?"

She nodded.

"Sure," he said. "Tidy, shortish hair, has that policeman kind of look about him. I've seen the guy."

"Well, he's checking with his friends, trying to get some information for me, just as a favor. El asked him to."

"He is, is he? Good for him, then." The scowl metamorphosed back into Murphy's familiar good natured grin. "Meanwhile, don't you forget what I said." He tipped an imaginary hat. "If there's anything I can ever do for you, Suzy darlin', just you whistle."

When Hunter and Gary pulled into the driveway of Randy's house, Suzanne had opened the front door to greet them by the time they stepped out of the truck. Hunter could feel himself stiffening up already, and was stretching his legs and back with a certain painful satisfaction as Suzanne approached, the two little girls dancing along behind her.

"Your friend phoned, Hunter. Bill Earl? He says to call him back." Hunter gathered from her eager tone that she was anxious to hear what Bill had to report, and he couldn't bear to disappoint her. Leaving her and Gary outside with the kids, he went into the Ranverdan office to make the call.

When he got off the phone they were still outside chatting as they watched Jolie pretend to drive Gary's truck while Veri bounced up and down noisily on the passenger seat. Suzanne turned at his approach, rubbing her palms on her denim covered thighs, her eyes wide in anticipation.

"Not much to report yet," Hunter told her. "No obvious evidence of any kind of collision, so on the surface it looks like a single vehicle accident. Bill suggested I speak directly with the officer in Merritt who's handling the investigation, but says he probably won't be able to tell me much more until the master mechanics have gone over the vehicle."

"A single vehicle accident? Are you trying to say that Dad just drove off the road?"

"Any driver can find himself nodding off at the wheel at one time or another," said Gary.

Suzanne turned on him. "Dad wasn't just any driver!"

Hunter noticed Gary's jaw stiffen, and hastened to intervene. "Nobody's saying that the accident was your dad's fault. There could be any number of reasons besides an actual collision. Blowout, mechanical failure ..."

"El said maybe ... The autopsy!" she blurted out. "Wasn't that this morning?"

"Yes, but that just confirmed the cause of death. It didn't reveal the cause of the accident."

"And?"

"Bill said he died of multiple injuries."

36

"I thought ... El said that maybe it was a heart attack. She said maybe that was why he drove off the road. I'd hoped that ... at least that way I'd know he didn't suffer much." She paused, her hand combing the hair back off her forehead as she stared at the ground. "At least did they say when he died? How long he'd lain there before ... ?" Her eyes were pleading, desperate.

Hunter shook his head. "I doubt that they can pinpoint it that accurately."

"Oh, God! I just need to know that he didn't lie there ... Surely they could tell something. How long before he ..."

"I'm sorry. Bill didn't have the actual report in front of him, so he didn't have too many details, and he probably couldn't answer that question if he did."

"Almost two days he was down there. Almost two days before they found him. If he didn't die instantly ... Oh, God!" She covered her mouth with her hand, took several deep breaths through her nose. "Don't tell me he was still alive! If only we'd called the R.C.M.P. in sooner. If only I'd gone myself ..."

Gary moved to his wife and gently put his hands on her shoulders. "Suzy, don't torture yourself. It's over, and there's nothing anybody can do." He stroked her hair as she looked at him blankly, then began to draw her close. "You don't have to know these things. Your dad wouldn't want you to worry. Shhhh, now."

"Don't shhhh me! I'm not a little girl, goddamn it!" Suzanne pulled herself away. "He was my father, and I have to know. I have to know!"

She turned and ran into the house. Gary's mouth twisted and he kicked the tire of the 4x4. "Shit!" He looked in the direction his wife had disappeared. "Shit!" he said again, then seemed to realize that the bewildered faces of his two little daughters were pressed against the windows of the pickup. He sighed and turned to Hunter with a pained look on his face. "See what I mean?" he said. "I hate to see her hurting like that, but she won't let me ..." His voice trailed off.

Her distress made Hunter uncomfortable, too. "I'll take a run down to Merritt and see what else I can find out," he said, and hoped like hell that he could find out something that would set her mind at rest. Bill Earl had told him to contact Garth Pullen, the General Duty member of the Merritt R.C.M.P. detachment who was working on the case.

Gary's jaw muscles were tensing again, his hand was balled at his side. "Thanks," he said through clenched teeth, then slowly and deliberately relaxed his hand, rubbing it against his jeans. "I'll get you the keys to Randy's Suburban."

Randy wouldn't like the fact, Hunter knew, that his daughter was suffering so much on his account. Randy wouldn't like it at all.

It was a fine spring day, still not too hot to let his elbow lean out the window and the wind roar past his left ear. Randy's deep green Suburban was clean and comfortable. It felt solid and benevolent. Hunter couldn't believe how much he found himself looking forward to the afternoon. He was feeling that same old stirring of the senses he used to experience in the force. He loved investigative work, always had.

It had been over three years since he'd resigned from the R.C.M.P. That was a year after he'd made the pension, a year after he'd passed the twentieth anniversary milestone. He'd endured the usual ribbing from his younger colleagues, and accepted the welcomes and congratulations from fellow "lifers". Then Ken died. Accidentally shot himself while cleaning his gun, was the official version. Ken, his friend from those first crazy months at the Depot in Regina. Ken, whose career had paralleled Hunter's own.

Ken's death hit Hunter hard. He carried on though, because he knew he'd get over it. He told himself that other members had died, retired, disappeared from his life. Pay your respects and get on with it, he told himself, trying to drown out the voice that kept repeating, Why, Ken? Why did you do it? Try as he might to pretend it was business as usual, it was like his heart had gone numb. Like it just wasn't pumping enough blood to move his muscles, or to send oxygen to his brain. Just reporting for duty was exhausting, and he

38

could never seem to clear his head. What else could he do? It was over.

The night he decided to resign from the force, Hunter had gone for a long drive and ended up having coffee at the Husky truck stop in Chilliwack well after midnight, where he met a driver with an '86 Freightliner to sell. A few months and a driving course later, Hunter had his commercial driver's license and was on the road. At first he drove for an outfit that sent him all over the continent for less than ninety cents a mile and was so late cutting his checks that he missed the first payment on the bank loan he had needed to pay for the truck, and then he had the good fortune to meet a driver who referred him to El. She made him buy a later model truck, but promised to keep him west of the Mississippi and pay him promptly. So far, she'd kept her word.

The Coquihalla climbed out of the Thompson valley and the temperature dropped. Kamloops' sandy brown hills, lightly furred with spring green, gave way to mountain slopes covered with endless ranks of dark evergreens, white spruce, fir and lodgepole pine. Here and there brown and white Hereford cattle grazed in ragged clearings, and high on the left side bank, where the hill had been sliced away to build the road, he saw a young moose, standing behind the wire fence and gazing at the greener pastures on the other side of the highway. The Suburban sprinted up the long hills and coasted down the short slopes until it reached the long smooth decline into the Nicola Valley. The view, one of Hunter's favorites, unfolded below like a giant map. Beyond his left elbow, the Nicola River twisted north and east between brilliant green borders, past Quilchena and back towards Kamloops, and southward, over the steering wheel, the town of Merritt sprawled in a trough between dark swollen mountains.

Constable Garth Pullen was in the detachment canteen drinking coffee and doing paperwork. He was in his late twenties, a big blond with a full, tanned face. A luminous, earnest face. He had brought the thin file on Randy Danyluk, and pulled out some of the photographs for Hunter to see. "There were no skid marks, no broken glass on the road, nothing to indicate that another vehicle was involved. That's why we didn't know the vehicle was there until it was reported missing. Here. The cab was badly crunched, but hung together. The trailer busted wide open - look at this! - and there were wet crushed cartons strewn all over the hill. Mostly computer parts, looks like." He sorted through the photographs for a couple of close ups. "It wasn't raining the night he went over, but it had rained hard in the mountains a few hours before we found him. Poor bugger!"

Hunter pored over the photographs while the constable concentrated on his paperwork. The cab was lying on its right side in a small rocky creek bed, its roof and sides dented, but intact. The familiar colors sent a small shock between Hunter's shoulder blades. "Ranverdan Transport" was printed in deep green letters framed with silver on a wide seafoam stripe that ran from the grill to the back of the sleeper and up to the roof. The stripe was outlined in silver and surrounded by an elegant metallic green background and glinting chrome trim. The strong logo bespoke of quality. Safety. The plain aluminum ribbed trailer was twisted and bent, its king pin had torn away from the fifth wheel coupling and the trailer was lying almost on its roof on the steep slope above the cab. Both the rear doors were open, one hanging by a single hinge from the misshapen side wall.

Two photographs had obviously been taken through the driver's door from above. They showed Randy Danyluk's body, the right side of his face pressed against the shattered glass of the passenger side window, arms tight to his sides, bent at the elbow with forearms hidden between his chest and the passenger seat. His legs were bent slightly at the knees from the weight of his work boots, one draped along the seat, the other straddled the gear box. His back was twisted. His visible eye was closed. Traces of dried blood blackened the corner of his mouth and his left ear. His dark brown hair, mixed with strands of grey near his temple, looked recently trimmed. His pale green shirt was still clean and unwrinkled.

Garth Pullen collected up the file with the rest of his paperwork, then suggested Hunter meet him in the parking lot. "I'm patrolling the Coquihalla south of Merritt this afternoon anyway, so if you want, you can follow me up there and I'll show you the site. Not much left to see, but you can get the lay of the land," he suggested. "The vehicle's here in Merritt. We've got a mechanic coming up from Vancouver to check it out. He should have a report for us by the end of the week."

The R.C.M.P. cruiser and Suburban pulled out of the Coquihalla's outside southbound lane onto the graveled shoulder just south of an inconspicuous overpass, and Hunter followed Constable Pullen on foot across the four lane highway to the site. There was a space about twenty five feet wide between the end of the cutaway hillside and the rounded concrete barrier that bordered the highway where it passed over the ravine. The ground in that space had been well disturbed since the discovery of the truck, so there was no information to be gathered from tracks there anymore. Until you got right to the edge of the highway and looked down, the ravine and its banks weren't visible from the road. It was a steep pitch to the creek bed below, dotted with small shrubs and trees, and blanketed by long grass. The grass and trees in a fifteen yard swath were crushed and broken, no doubt disturbed more by police and salvage workers than by the original accident. The constable pointed out the location of the cab and the trailer, speculated on the truck's initial path down the abrupt incline, and wished Hunter a good day.

Hunter slid and slipped his way down the slope to the creek. There were still odd bits of debris: crushed plastic and glass from the headlights, cigarette butts and bits of paper, a few metallic scraps from the shattered grill. A patch of grass was stained by spilled diesel fuel, and its oppressive smell fought with a light fresh breeze off the creek. He stood, balanced on two rocks embedded in the creek bottom, and looked up at the highway overpass a hundred and fifty feet above. He could hear the faint whooshing past of traffic but could see nothing. A raven croaked and set off in a glide and a swoop from a nearby tree. Hands on his hips, Hunter looked around once more and then began to climb back up the steep hill, ratcheting himself upwards by grabbing small branches and handfuls of grass.

When he reached the highway, he sat down on the white concrete barrier and looked back down into the ravine. He wasn't sure why he'd gone down. A man died there. Perhaps he'd been conscious before the end, heard the mountain runoff rushing pizzicato towards the river, heard the trucks rumble by, heard the world carry on in ignorance of his pain, indifferent to his solitary passage from their world. The raven was circling overhead as Hunter passed the site again on his way back to Merritt, the Suburban coping easily with the long, slow, uphill curve.

CHAPTER
SIX

Gary had taken the kids to the playground after their nap, and there weren't usually many phone calls to the Ranverdan office on Monday afternoon. Suzanne decided to take advantage of the block of uninterrupted quiet to bring the computer records up to date. She sat in front of the monitor, a glass of Coke fizzing gently on the desk beside her, and entered information from the small stack of waybills the Ranverdan drivers had faxed or dropped off at the office over the past several days. The waybill from her father's last trip was missing, of course, but she had the basic information from the faxed pickup order. She paused to consider what to do about it. Enter it into the computer and bill Waicom Electronics for the freight charges, as usual?

She took a few sips of her drink, wiped the condensation from the bottom of the glass on her jeans before setting it back on the desk. Could she ever charge them enough to compensate for the death of her father? Her fingers began to pat the keys again in the rhythm so familiar to her from entering waybills thousands of times before. Or should she maybe pretend that the shipment had never existed? If it hadn't, her father would be alive right now. Tears filled her eyes until she couldn't read the computer screen, and they rolled down her cheeks leaving small itchy trails on her skin.

But the stupid reality was that the shipper would want to make a claim for delayed and damaged freight. Ranverdan Transport would owe Waicom money for the accident that had killed her father. She fought a sudden surge of irrational hatred for Waicom Electronics. It was their bad luck as much as ours, she told herself. They can't be responsible. But she wanted to lash out at someone, blame someone for her father's death, and for her pain. Why did it have to happen? She slammed her fist again and again against her thigh. "Why?" she cried with each hit. "Oh, Dad, why?"

The ringing of the phone jarred her, and she cursed it. She wished she'd forwarded the phones to El again, but it was too late.

"Ranverdan Transport," she said, pronouncing the words precisely, trying to sound as normal as possible as she wiped the tears away from her eyes with her free hand.

"Hello, there, Ranverdan Transport," a male voice as smooth as chrome came over the line. "Who am I speaking to?"

"This is Suzanne Rodgers," she said, reluctantly.

"Hello, there, Suzanne Rodgers. This is Steve Mah. How are you this afternoon?"

The voice was presumptuously over-familiar, and she felt her lips twist in irritation. She was not in the mood for friendly. "Can I help you?" was all she said.

"I certainly hope so. I'm the shipper down at the Waicom distribution warehouse in Seattle. I just wanted a little information about that accident you folks had."

Suzanne clenched her jaw and said nothing, flooded with horrified wonder. Why right now? Why would Waicom have to call now?

"Like, how did it happen? Have you heard?"

"I don't know." She barely managed not to choke on the words. She wanted to tell him, The driver was killed, and the driver was my father, but she couldn't speak.

"Surely the police have talked to you about it. Don't they know how it happened?"

"Why do you want to know?" she asked, her eyes on the cursor that blinked hypnotically on the computer screen.

44

"Oh, just curious," he replied easily. "We had almost a hundred thousand dollars worth of electronics on that trailer, so it's a matter of some interest to us, as you might expect. Haven't the police given you any theories?"

Suzanne stared at the cursor. You're not finished, it seemed to say. "If you're that interested," she managed, her voice thin and cold, "I suggest you contact them directly."

"Ooooo," the caller said, "a little sensitive about it, aren't we?"

Suzanne didn't trust herself to say anything, and debated hanging up the phone. She was squeezing the telephone receiver so hard, her hand hurt. She wanted to get back to the keyboard. Her work was incomplete, the cursor said.

"I'm sorry," the caller continued. "I shouldn't be so glib. I know that the driver was killed. He was the boss at Ranverdan, wasn't he? He was a good guy. I'm sorry."

"I'll ... we'll ... let you know if we hear anything further," Suzanne was able to say, and exhaled with relief when the caller thanked her and hung up. Immediately she punched in the code to forward incoming calls to Watson Transportation.

El sounded only too happy to take over.

The owner of Nicola Towing and Wrecking in Merritt was busy on a tow job, but his nephew, who was working in the murky garage, saw no reason why Hunter shouldn't have a look at the wreck, as long as he didn't take anything. "The cops have to see if there was anything wrong with it, you know? See what caused the accident, if anybody can get sued. The guy died, eh?" The kid scratched his nose with a grease stained sleeve and pointed a blackened thumb towards the back of the compound. "Just had some guy phone up about the trailer, right? Said the stuff in it was his, and I told him he better talk to the cops. Couldn't hardly understand him. Chinese, eh? Couldn't hardly speak English."

He pointed at a German shepherd lying flat on its side on the cool concrete floor in the corner of the garage. His name was painted in black on the galvanized water bucket beside him. "Wrecks there won't let nobody into the yard when he's on duty," said the kid. "Will ya, Wrecks? Good boy!" The dog thumped his tail lazily and raised his head, clinking a chain on the concrete.

The twisted trailer was strapped to a big flatbed parked next to the green Ranverdan Transport tractor beside the chainlink fence. Straps held the rear doors of the trailer shut, but holes around the door and along the upper corner gaped wide enough to allow Hunter to see cardboard cartons in chaotic heaps inside. The dented and scraped door of the cab was unlocked, so Hunter hoisted himself up to look inside. The windows were shattered in places and streaked with mud and bits of grass. A bent sheet of acrylic was wedged under the seat, and Hunter wiggled it back and forth to work it free. It was a standup picture frame containing a color snapshot of Suzanne and the two little girls, everybody smiling. He placed it gently on the seat, then backed out the door and jumped to the ground. He circled the ruined cab but could see no sign of damage that pointed to a collision with an animal or other vehicle. Best to wait for the results from the experts. Just as he was heading out of the yard, a huge tow truck drove in and a big, beefy man with a black goatee stepped out.

Hunter introduced himself as a friend of the family, and explained that Suzanne was naturally upset and wanted to find out all she could about how it had happened.

The big wrecker shifted a wad of gum from one cheek to the other and looked over at the cab. He shrugged. "Nothing I can tell ya. Sorry." He chewed loudly and rapidly for fifteen seconds, eyes looking upwards, left and right, left and right. "Wasn't speed, though. I had to take the rig outa gear for the tow, right? It's a mild grade there, eh? Maybe three, four degrees, eh? Most guys with that many horses can do fifty miles an hour up that hill - forty five, minimum." He chewed again. "The rig was in second gear, like he'd just started up, right? Had to be goin' less than ten miles an hour, don't ya think?"

Hunter found himself in the Suburban heading south on the Coquihalla again with unanswerable questions running through his mind. Why wasn't Randy Danyluk wearing a seat-belt? A few hundred yards in either direction, and the truck would have run into the soft slope of the hill. Damaging, for sure, but much less likely to be fatal. Why had the accident occurred precisely at that deep, hidden ravine? Why was the truck in second gear? Could the driver have intentionally steered off the road, travelling slowly enough to ensure that the truck left the road at that particular spot? Could Randy have had reasons, known only to himself, for engineering the accident and his own death?

Hunter shook his head. He kept telling himself that he wasn't a cop anymore. His cop's instincts had to be rusty and chances were, this was just his imagination running wild. Whatever Suzanne wanted him to find out, chances were her father just fell asleep at the wheel.

He drove past the site of the accident and turned around a few miles south at the next exit. Then he tried to recreate the last few miles of Randy Danyluk's final trip as he approached the accident site. It was easy to see the approach during daylight, but Randy was driving up here at night. He would have had to keep the speed down in order to find the ravine and leave the highway without hitting either the side of the hill or the concrete barrier. That took planning.

Hunter pulled over and parked on the shoulder a dozen yards from the overpass, then walked over and looked down into the ravine. Wind blew across the highway, but deep in the ravine the air was still. There was no movement except for the flicker of sunlight reflecting off the water as it trickled across the rocky creek bed. A glint of light caught his eye. Twenty feet down the slope a raven was pulling at something shiny in the long grass. On impulse, Hunter started leaping down the hill, hollering and waving his arms. The raven squawked and took to the air. The shiny object it had been pulling at, tangled in the matted grass, was a thin metal strip, the kind used by Canadian customs to seal a trailer loaded with freight that was being bonded on to an inland customs warehouse. The seal had been broken.

Broken or cut.

Hunter slipped it into his shirt pocket and, for the second time that day, scrambled up the steep hill.

The sun hovered just above the western ridges as Hunter sat with Suzanne on the vast wooden deck off the kitchen of Randy's house. They sat in matching Adirondack chairs made of red cedar and looked out at the cutaway sand hills along the river, coated with gold by the horizontal shafts of sunlight that clung to whatever still rose above the creeping shadows.

"Sometimes he'd forget," said Suzanne in response to Hunter's question about whether her father always wore a seat belt. "Sometimes I'd have to remind him, even in the car."

Hunter had hated to give her this "if only". He had enough of his own to know how cruel and persistent "if only's" could be. He could see it boring its way like a tick through her troubled young forehead to lodge itself permanently in her consciousness, where it would secrete its poison every time she thought of her father's death.

As if she could feel what he was imagining, Suzanne shook her head and ran her hand over her forehead and through her hair, pulling it back off her face as she stared off at the horizon. "I don't understand. He was such a good driver, a defensive driver. He never even had any close calls. Never. Most of the time, I'm nervous when somebody else drives, you know? When I'm a passenger?" She turned to him, as if searching his eyes for understanding, and he nodded. "I have to watch the road as if I was driving myself. But with Dad, I could close my eyes and go to sleep. He was the best driver ..." Her voice trailed off and she sighed.

Hunter nodded again, and they both watched the sun slide behind the graying uneven hills, leaving molten strips of cloud in its wake. The sound of voices and laughter drifted from a neighboring yard, along with the faint smell of a barbecue.

"Maybe it's because I used to ride with him when I was little. I would fall asleep on the back seat of the car. I remember the sound of the windshield wipers, and the rain on the roof, and Mom and Dad

48

talking in quiet voices about wherever we'd just been, or who we'd just been to visit. You know, my grandparents or whoever. I always felt so safe. So safe."

Hunter hesitated. All the questions he was rehearsing in his head sounded so official. After twenty odd years of being a police officer, he didn't know how to sound like a truck driver just trying to help out. "Your father - did you notice anything unusual about him in the past few weeks? Did he seem upset, preoccupied? Anything different about him somehow?"

"Why? What are you trying to say?" She jerked around to face him, her eyes suddenly sharper and darker.

"Suzanne, I ... ." He took a deep breath. "I didn't know your father as well as you did. If there's anything ... uh ... out of the ordinary, about his death, the only way I can find out is by asking questions. I'm not implying anything. It's too early yet. I just don't know. You do still want me to try to find out why it happened? Or do you want me to butt out?" Hunter tried to look her in the eye, but she had turned away and was watching her fingers stroke the rounded edge of the arm of her chair.

"Dad made these chairs himself," she said with a dreamy smile.

Hunter waited, admiring the evolving sunset, which had turned the farthest mountains purple, and painted pink and gold and violet streaks in the clouds. He cleared his throat.

"Sorry, Hunter. I guess it just shocked me a bit. The possibilities, I mean." She met his eyes. "Was he acting different? Yeah. Maybe. He did seem a little worried about business. The week before, he spent a lot of time in the office, going over old paperwork and comparing numbers. He asked me for a computer print-out of all the business we'd done with Waicom since last September. Waicom Electronics is one of our regular accounts. We haul imported computers and computer parts from the port of Seattle to their distributors in western Canada, usually eight or ten loads a month. In fact, that's what Dad was ... ." Her voice trailed off as she rubbed her forehead, then her cheeks, with both hands. Hunter noticed how slender and pale her fingers were; her wedding band slid up and down above her knuckle.

"The shipper called me today. Waicom, I mean," Suzanne said. She closed her eyes and sighed. "He wanted to know more about the accident. I guess they've got a right to ask, but I found it hard to be polite."

"What was your dad looking for in those printouts, do you know?"

"I guess - well - no, I don't know for sure. I just assumed the contract was coming up for renewal, and he wanted to be sure the rates we were charging were all right. I assume he was worried that we were going to lose the account to a competitor." She frowned. "I don't know how I'm going to handle that. I've never had to negotiate any contracts with the customers before. If they were already complaining about their rates, and now with a damage claim to settle. Did you see the load? How bad did it look?"

"The trailer must've rolled over a couple of times and shook the cartons up like peas in a rattle. The whole load looks pretty well trashed."

She seemed almost to welcome the distraction of thinking about business. "I guess we'll have to get the freight to their Edmonton warehouse somehow so they can assess the damage."

"More likely they'll just want the goods held at customs and examine them there. No point clearing them through Canadian customs if they're worthless."

"Customs? They've already cleared."

He frowned at her, confused.

"At the border," she explained. "Waicom stuff always clears at the border. You look like you don't believe me. What's wrong?"

Hunter shrugged. Maybe the customs seal he had in his shirt pocket had more significance than he'd expected, but there was no point involving Suzanne. "I don't think you should be worrying about all those "possibilities" you mentioned, not yet. You've got enough to deal with. Why don't you give me the details on the load. I'll find out when it'll be released by the R.C.M.P. and pass the

50

information on to El. She'll keep Waicom from bugging you until you're ready."

She stared at him for a moment, making him wonder if he had inadvertently set disturbing new "possibilities" coursing through her mind, then she pushed herself out of the chair, pausing a few seconds to run her hand along the smooth surface of the armrest, and disappeared into the house.

Hunter sat, his eyes on the fading hills, his mind on something distant. Driving in the dark, the wipers making a rubbery scrape against the windshield of a second hand '69 Oldsmobile. The steady hiss of tires on wet pavement, the cool kiss of rain through the slightly open window. He and Christine exchanging amusing comments, voices warm and low. Braking slow and easy, signals clicking, making careful turns. Powerfully aware every second of the precious cargo tucked into the car seats behind him. Listening for their soft breathing, melting inside at the sound of their little sleepy sighs.

He closed his eyes and took a deep breath, then rose and followed Suzanne into the house and downstairs to the office, checking his watch on the way. He had a few phone calls to make.

CHAPTER
SEVEN

Tuesday morning, Hunter awoke while the sky was still a pale blue wash underlined by the golden ridges of the eastern hills. He threw a fishing rod and tackle box into the back of the Suburban, lowered an aluminum boat onto the roof rack, and scratched a quick note to Suzanne. "Gone fishing. Borrowed your Dad's boat and some of his gear. Back before ten o'clock."

He drove east on the Trans-Canada highway for the better part of an hour until he reached the town of Chase, where he found a park with beach access to Little Shuswap Lake. He didn't want to catch a fish but he was looking forward to spending a few quiet hours on the water. The light trolling motor putted him out to an unpopulated bay, where he turned it off and sat sipping on a styrofoam cup of gas station coffee and absorbing the cool peace of morning.

The early sun tinted the tangled sprays of salmon berry and wild roses above the shoreline with a rich, deep yellow and threw long, damp shadows along the mottled rocks and mounds of last year's leaves. The lacy green brilliance of the shore and the deepening blue of the sky repeated themselves in the mirror that stretched shivering in every direction from under his drifting boat. He could hear the grinding of a distant diesel truck as it wound along the western shore of the lake, and the haunting ululations of a loon too far away to see.

Water plashed gently against the aluminum hull, close and clear, in time with the tremulous rhythm of the boat beneath him.

The faint odor of gasoline was superseded by a slightly fishy scent as Hunter opened the tackle box. A fishing license was taped to the lid. The date beside the firmly written signature was March 15, just over two months ago. How often had Randy Danyluk sat in the boat since then? When was the last time? Hunter felt a comfortable sadness settle around him like the melancholy echoes of a distant hymn. He took his time selecting a lure and fastening the leader to his line, then, knowing he wouldn't catch a thing, chose to sit and jig rather than eclipse the fragile music of the morning behind the noise of the motor. He heard a splash and turned his head to see an osprey struggle into the air with a trout thrashing in its talons. Life and death, forces so irrevocably entwined, one can't exist without the other. A simple philosophical concept, but on a personal level, the necessity of anyone's death was so very, very hard to accept.

A breeze came up, cool and fresh, and the surface of the water shuddered and cracked into a thousand tiny flames, flickering silver against the dark water, and sending the vibrant green reflections of the spring leaves scurrying back to the shore. The rhythm of the waves slapping the aluminum hull picked up, and the loon called again.

"Hope it's just like this where you are now, Randy," he whispered.

"And I won't be staying for the funeral, El."

That's what she thought he'd said. Did the guy have a thing about funerals or what? This time she didn't argue. "About the clearance, you were right, as usual," she said. "I talked to a buddy of mine at Border Brokers. They usually clear Waicom's freight at the border all right, but the load Randy was hauling had paperwork presented to customs that showed the freight was bonded on to the customs warehouse in Edmonton. He faxed me a copy of the A8A." As she spoke, she held the curling fax paper up in front of her, shook it once to straighten it out.

Hunter said something else, but some jabbering from her CB drowned it out. El could hear a steady whooshing sound behind his voice, and guessed he had his window down as he drove.

"Close your damn window! I can't hear you!" She adjusted the volume knob on her CB as she spoke.

The whooshing sound almost disappeared. "Did your buddy say why the A8A had been prepared?"

"Looks like nobody except the guy who wrote out the A8A knows why it was done. And I recognize the handwriting, Hunter," El said. "It's Randy's."

"Any idea why he would've done that, El?"

"Nope."

"What do you know about Waicom?"

El paused before answering. She'd known that Waicom was a big account for Ranverdan, but just how big and how profitable, she hadn't known until now that she'd started helping Suzanne out. A steady account like that would buy a lot of bread and butter. "Like what?" she asked. "They import computer electronics from the Orient, distribution to western Canada, mostly Vancouver, Edmonton and Winnipeg, controlled out of Vancouver. What else do you need to know?"

"What about the people? You talked to any of them?"

"Yeah. The traffic manager in Vancouver and the shipper in Seattle. Why?"

"Anything strike you about them? Anything not quite right?"

El's jaw dropped. Hunter was being a cop! This wasn't a trucking conversation, this was a goddamn police investigation! The idea that Hunter thought there could be more to Randy's death than a tragic accident sent a shiver up her spine.

"El? Can you hear me?"

"Yeah." She could hear him alright. "Are you saying ... ?" Her other line started ringing. "Just a sec." She put Hunter on hold, then punched his line again. "Don't go away! I'll be right back." She put the new caller on hold, then did the same with the rest of her lines to keep them from ringing, and went back to Hunter. "Are you saying that there could be ... foul play involved?"

54

"Whoa! I'm not saying anything. I'm just looking at the possibilities here."

El rubbed her jaw, noticed too late that there was carbon on her fingers, and rerubbed it with the back of her hand. "Maybe a couple of things. The traffic manager sure backed off in a hurry as soon as I mentioned the R.C.M.P., and the shipper has been real curious about the cause of Randy's accident. Nothing obvious, though. But guess what?"

"What?"

"There's a Waicom pick up scheduled for tonight that I still don't have a truck for."

"Book me on the first available flight out of Kamloops. I can be at the airport by noon."

"You got it." El put the receiver down gently, leaned back in her captain's chair, fingers linked behind her head, and directed her gaze towards a smudge on the ceiling. In her experience, Hunter Rayne was generally an easy going guy, good natured, friendly, easy to work with. After a while, you could forget that he'd spent most of his life being a cop. But she'd always sensed something beneath the surface, seen him watching people, his eyes narrowed like those of a circling wolf, wary and glacier cold, like blue ice. She'd often thought how she'd hate to ever make him mad. El suddenly became aware that her blood was racing. Whatever Hunter was on to, if Randy's accident was no accident, she wanted him to let her be a part of it.

"Holy shit!" she said as she remembered the flashing hold buttons and lunged for the phone.

Bill Earl, a good natured R.C.M.P. corporal and former colleague of Hunter's, was a member of the Kamloops band of the Shuswap Indians. He had been one of the first recruits in the R.C.M.P.'s Indian Special Constable Program, and had been posted back to his home town immediately after training in Regina. He eventually became a regular member of the force. He suggested to Hunter that they grab some lunch while they talked, then he would drop Hunter off at the airport in time for his flight. At Hunter's request, Bill brought a copy of the autopsy report, issued by the coroner's office in Kamloops, which hadn't been in Constable Pullen's file. Hunter told Bill he hoped it would tell him whether the injuries were entirely consistent with the accident, or whether one or more of them could have been inflicted before the truck went off the highway. They scanned the report together, and Bill was the first to sit up straight and take a bite of his sandwich.

"You're gonna have to talk to the doc, Hunter. The injuries are described well enough in the report, but there are no speculations about blows from heavy objects or blunt instruments. You know how it is, they weren't looking for anything like that." He gestured with his sandwich, and a shaving of roast beef fell onto the table top. "I know, I know. You're gonna quote that Massachusetts study that said as many as one out of every ten highway deaths may be murder. Be realistic, will you?" Bill shrugged as he picked up the errant piece of meat and popped it in his mouth. "Single vehicle accident, nothing to indicate foul play. The guy was in a smashed truck at the bottom of a ravine for two days. A fifteen story drop, for God's sake. No seat-belt. It would've been a miracle if he'd survived. The coroner's not gonna be looking too closely at what might've hit him. Gear shift. Steering wheel. Thermos bottle. Who knows?"

"C'mon, Bill. I can't talk to the coroner's office. I'm a truck driver now, remember?" He raised his eyebrows. "Well?"

"Okay, okay! I guess I can make the time to call. But on something that looks this clear cut, I don't know how much more I can do for you."

"I'm not asking for anything else," Hunter said and bit into his own sandwich.

Bill grinned. "Just in case you do, then."

"Maybe just a little information is all. Here, have my donut." Hunter pushed it over and Bill's hand hovered over it.

"This a bribe?"

"There's been some indication that there were irregularities with the load. Do you know if Constable Pullen has been in communication with Canada Customs on it at all?" He noticed he'd

56

fallen into the cop talk without even thinking. Who was it that said, Policemen never go anywhere, they always proceed?

"Not to my knowledge, Hunter. You've been there. It's like a guy almost has to fight to be allowed to spend time investigating leads on something like this. We're up to our ears in missing persons, assaults, B&E's, DUI patrols, you name it!" Bill waved the donut around as he talked. "The kind of time we'd like to give to a case and the kind we can afford to are miles apart. Outside of paid time, forget it! Most of us got families, too. We got lives outside the force."

Hunter felt a tug of guilt and tried to ignore it. In a flash, he saw Christine's tear-streaked face as she told him why she wanted a divorce. He saw the stunned betrayal in the eyes of his two daughters when he told them, yes, it was true - he wouldn't be coming home again. *We got lives outside the force.* Like he had a thousand times before, he slammed the door on his useless regrets, wrenched his wandering thoughts back to Randy's accident.

"There's only so many hours in a day, man," Bill continued. He stopped waving the donut and took a bite, then said, "So, in case I should be talking to Pullen again soon, what irregularities does your information point to?"

"I don't know. Maybe some kind of contraband. I've got nothing solid, but the deceased had been looking into past shipments he'd handled for the customer, and had taken it upon himself this particular time to avoid clearing it through customs at the border. I've got friends asking around. The customer is pretty uptight about the load being impounded in Merritt, has been hounding the trucking company and the wrecker, but it seems he's not prepared to talk to you guys about it. Just suspicious behavior, nothing definite."

Bill nodded and looked at his watch. "I may not be able to connect with Garth or the doctor today. I'll see what I can find out, but I can't promise you anything."

Hunter nodded his thanks. "So, how's the family? You've got two boys and a girl, right?"

"Yep! The boys are great. Jason wants me to take him fishing every chance I get. I love it! The girl's the oldest - just turned fourteen. I guess you know what that means." He stood up and picked up the file from the table, and his hat from the chair beside him. "Trouble comin' up! Big trouble! How're your two girls?"

"Good." Hunter nodded, with a half smile. "Yeah, they're good."

He hoped this was true.

At about five thirty on Tuesday evening, Hunter pulled an air-ride trailer into the graveled yard at Waicom Electronics' Seattle warehouse to pick up a load of computer electronics destined for Edmonton. A Ranverdan rig was already backed up to one of the loading dock doors. A man signaled to Hunter from inside the adjacent door, and he backed his own trailer up against it, set his brakes, and shut The Blue Knight's engine down. Before he stepped out of the truck, he reminded himself to play it cool, not move too fast. If there was something going on here, it wouldn't do to reveal his interest in it.

At the warehouse counter, Hunter was greeted by a wiry Oriental, probably in his mid-thirties, with unnaturally curly hair and a neat goatee. He stood with his hip against the warehouse side of the counter, and seemed to be checking over the information on some paperwork line by line with a pen. He wore a diamond stud earring in his left ear and a heavy silver buckle on the belt of his jeans. When Hunter introduced himself, the shipper clapped him on the shoulder. "All right! You're the other Ranverdan man!"

Hunter gave him a tight little smile and involuntarily narrowed his eyes. The man's familiarity was grating, and he didn't like being touched.

"Old Pete there," the shipper indicated a long faced man in an olive green shirt standing near the rear doors of the Ranverdan rig, "is hauling the Winnipeg. Once we finish loading him up, it's your turn."

Hunter nodded, and they both watched a warehouseman run a skid past the standing man, the forklift's engine roaring through the

Ranverdan trailer's open doors, then muted as it slowed to maneuver the skid into place. The air stank of propane.

"Oh, yeah. I'm Steve Mah." The shipper dropped his pen on the stack of paperwork and stuck out his hand. Hunter kept the handshake brief. "I notice you're not driving one of the company trucks. That your own?" Hunter nodded. "Too bad about the old man. He seemed like a nice enough guy. You know, you see trucks in and out of here every day, you tend to forget how dangerous it can be, driving in those mountains. Poor dumb fuck. You ever fall asleep at the wheel?"

Hunter didn't like his words, his tone, nor the little smirk that accompanied the question. He stared at the man, grim faced, without answering, then realized that hostile behavior wouldn't help if he hoped to get any information from the man, and tried to smile. Maybe he'd been a civilian so long he'd lost the patience he cultivated while he was on the force, the patience that allowed him to put up with all sorts of low-lifes, jibes and name-calling without letting his personal feelings show.

"Not yet, I haven't," he said, and reached behind Mah to tap the counter with his knuckles. "That's wood, isn't it? Particleboard, at least?"

The shipper laughed. "Glad to hear it. You know when to pop those little white pills, huh?" A conspiratorial smile and wink. Hunter again fought back his irritation and returned the smile.

"So, they know yet how it happened?" continued the shipper. "You figure he really did fall asleep?"

Hunter shrugged. "Haven't heard," he said. "You got any theories yourself?"

The shipper's smile faded briefly. "You're the driver. I'm just a landlubber. You'd be in a better position to guess."

"Yes, but you must've seen him a few hours before it happened. I didn't."

"You got a point, there ... Hunter, wasn't it? One of those last name first names, huh? Pretty good. You're really in for a guy your age." Another smirk. "I just figured, what with the grapevine you guys have, that somebody would've heard something. No, huh?" He turned back to the paperwork and Hunter walked a few steps away to where he could watch both Mah and the loading without turning his head.

"Is Pete one of the regulars?" Hunter asked.

"He's been in a time or two." Mah didn't look up from his paperwork.

"The stuff goes in bond?" He ventured after another minute of silence.

"Who told you that?" Mah stopped writing something and looked up.

Hunter shrugged innocently.

"No, it doesn't go in bond. The paperwork's already been faxed to our broker at the border by the time you clear the yard here. We'll make sure you've got everything in here," Mah slapped a big manila envelope lying on the counter, "before you put your little ass back in your big Peterbilt, there."

"Freightliner," said Hunter, grinning, with effort.

"Whatever," said Mah.

"Got my paperwork ready?" The long faced man named Pete walked up to the shipper with his hand out. He passed Hunter as if he weren't even there.

"Hold your horny little horses, Petie," said Mah, as he cocked his head to listen to a woman's voice over the paging system.

Hunter exchanged introductions with the other driver. Pete Whitehead looked to be in his fifties, a humorless, nervous man with dark hair combed straight back from a receding hairline. As they spoke, he looked repeatedly from his watch to Mah, who had been called to the phone behind the counter.

"Since day one," Pete said in response to Hunter's question of how long he'd been with Ranverdan. "I drove the first truck Randy bought, aside from his own." The man's eyes made contact with Hunter's for a split second, then were snatched away as if they'd been scalded.

"The funeral's tomorrow."

60

"Yeah. I'm stopping over for it, but only because I can still make Winnipeg for Friday delivery," the man said, his eyes darting from Mah to his watch to the floor of the warehouse. "Randy wouldn't want the trucks to stop running, not for his own funeral, not for anything else either."

"You think his daughter can keep them running?"

The man shrugged. "It's the drivers who'll make it work."

"You hauled the Waicom stuff much before?" Hunter could see that Mah was just about to hang up the phone.

"Sure." Pete's eyes flicked to Hunter's chest, then back to Mah. He cleared his throat, and Hunter thought he was about to say more, but the shipper was approaching, a fat manila envelope in his outstretched hand.

"Here you go, Petie," Mah said. "Have a good trip. Don't go driving our freight off any cliffs now, got that?"

Pete Whitehead scowled at the floor for a moment, then walked stiffly away. Mah returned to his desk and again picked up the phone.

For the next fifteen minutes, Hunter supervised the uneventful loading of his own trailer. The warehouseman wore a heavy duty set of ear protectors, and Hunter had to yell over the roar of the forklift to even get his attention. After his trailer doors were closed and padlocked, he went back to the counter to pick up the paperwork. Mah was watching him, the familiar smirk taking shape on his face as Hunter approached.

"Time to saddle up, cowboy," he said. "Got enough little white pills to see you through the mountains?"

Drugs wasn't a subject Hunter felt comfortable smiling about. This time he didn't even try. He ignored the comment. "Anything I should know?" he asked. "Anything to watch out for at customs?"

"Like what? Customs make you nervous, cowboy?" Mah snorted. "Surely a clean cut looking dude like yourself won't have any trouble with the geeks at customs."

Hunter smiled crookedly. For whatever reason, he seemed to have lost any shred of rapport he'd managed to establish with Mah. He wondered if it was something he'd said, or simply because he hadn't been successful in hiding his dislike for the man. Or was it something else? "Should I be nervous?"

"You tell me, cowboy," said Mah, still with that irritating smirk. "You tell me."

CHAPTER
EIGHT

"I'm going to bed now, Sorry. Don't forget to take the dog out before you fall asleep, okay?"

Dan Sorenson lay on his side on the couch watching a Kung Fu rerun on T.V. He turned his head and pushed his lips out for his wife to kiss as she leaned over the back of the couch. Simone's short bobbed hair, shiny brown and springy, tickled his ear. Her hair was soft and sophisticated, just like her voice. She had a voice like a caress, it often made him shiver inside, and she spoke with the charming hint of an accent that betrayed her French Canadian heritage. He reached up to pull her to him, but she had already slipped away.

"Don't forget to walk the dog now, Sorry," she said as she left the room.

"Okay, okay, Mo. I said okay, already." Sorry rubbed his nostrils with his index finger, then smoothed his moustache. It had only been a few days since he'd lost the bouncer gig at the King George, and she was already trying to make it sound like he wasn't shouldering his share of household responsibility. Okay, so maybe his jobs were always part time and seemed to have undependable hours and no steady pay check. Christ! She knew when she met him that he wasn't a nine-to-five kind of guy. In fact, being a wild one was what had attracted her to him in the first place, wasn't it? If she'd wanted financial security, she could've married a fuckin' doctor, or a lawyer for Chris'sake.

The doberman shared the couch with him, curled up in a black and tan circle beside his ankles. He poked the dog with his bare foot. It opened one pleading eye, then curled itself up a little tighter. "Fuck it," said Sorry, and turned his attention back to the T.V. He was in the mood to root for the bad guys. If only the bad guys didn't have to fight in slow motion, that decrepit suck, Carradine, wouldn't stand a fuckin' chance. He'd love to see that saggy faced wimp screaming in pain and pleading for his life for a change. *Take that, Grasshopper!*

When the show was over, Sorry kicked the Doberman awake and pushed it off the couch. It followed him out to the kitchen. He opened the back door and the dog scooted outside. "Okay, Doobie, go take a dump," Sorry said, leaving the door wide open so he could keep an eye on it while he grabbed a snack. He opened the fridge and peered inside. Damn! He'd forgotten that the inside light was out. He'd promised Mo that he'd pick a new bulb up at the Home Depot. Okay, okay. Tomorrow.

The three little brown paper bags in the fridge were the lunches Mo had made for her and Sasha and little Bruno. Off limits. He hauled out a packaged loaf of bread and tossed it on the counter beside a half empty jar of no name cheese spread. He picked up the milk jug, but there wasn't much left. If he just took a couple of swigs, maybe Mo wouldn't notice. As long as there was enough left for the kids' cereal in the morning, he reasoned, it would be okay.

The fridge door swung shut, and suddenly he found himself face to face with the Mother's Day cards he had helped Sasha and Bruno make for Mo a couple of weeks ago while she was at work. Sasha's was made of purple construction paper and had flowers and a sun with a smiley face on it. Bruno's was brown. As always, Bruno had insisted on drawing a Harley. Beneath the cards was still a picture from Christmas, when Sorry had rented a Santa suit, and there he was behind a fake white beard that wouldn't stick to his moustache so the mouth was just a black hole, and sitting on each knee was a blond haired little mugwump with a big, silly grin that almost broke his

64

heart. He aborted his drink of milk in mid swig and ran the tap for a cold glass of water instead.

"Fuckin' bread and water," he muttered to the dog as it trotted back into the kitchen, its nails clicking softly on the linoleum. "You eat better than I do, Doobie."

He'd promised the kids a new wading pool. He'd promised Simone a new summer dress for work. He missed the days of tailor-made cigarettes and a fridge full of decent food. Not only that, his Harley needed work again, which meant that he needed money for parts. As he settled himself back on the couch, glass of water in one hand, four floppy pieces of bread spread with no name cheese in the other, he resolved for the thousandth time that tomorrow would be different.

"Tomorrow," he told Doobie, "I'm going to find myself a fuckin' job."

Hunter called Bill Earl on Wednesday at about noon. He'd stopped at a roadside restaurant in Blue River, just west of the Rocky Mountains. He was at a pay phone, near the doors to the restrooms. The hallway smelled of Pine Sol.

"Bill! It's Hunter," he said when the corporal came on the line. "What've you got?"

"In a word, it's possible. Hang on a sec." Hunter could hear Bill flipping pages. "According to the doctor who performed the autopsy, there were three clear points of impact on the skull, two of which were severe enough by themselves to have likely caused immediate unconsciousness and concussion. One of the head injuries would be quite consistent with a severe blow to the back of the head administered prior to the accident. He definitely wasn't dead at the time of the accident, but he could have been unconscious. The amount of blood in his lung and body cavities proves that his heart was still beating at the time of the crash. He had enough critical injuries to kill three men, she said. The combined head injuries were potentially fatal, as were the internal injuries caused by his splintered ribs, including a punctured lung. The pattern of damage to the ribcage is consistent with his chest hitting the steering wheel. His spine was broken in two places, as we saw in the autopsy report, which can be attributed to the body tumbling around in the falling cab." Bill's breath whooshed into the phone. "The poor guy didn't stand a chance of surviving that crash."

"Where do we go from here?" Hunter asked, pressing closer to the phone as two obese women with tight perms emerged from the ladies' room. A cloud of powdery perfume surrounded them and he tried not to inhale. "Where are we going to start? My guess ... ."

"Whoa! Hold on there!" Bill interrupted. "In the immortal words of Tonto, what do you mean 'we', White Man? The doctor said, and I quote, It is possible - and I underlined the word possible - that one of the blows was administered prior to the accident, but there is no way of confirming that. It is also quite possible, and most probable - this is still a quote - that all the injuries were sustained during the crash itself." He paused, and Hunter was silent. "Nothing's changed, Hunter. Still doesn't warrant a murder investigation. We just can't afford the time to chase down every wild goose."

"But don't you think it's possible that someone - someone who knew how to drive a truck - could have propped Randy, unconscious from a blow to the head, in the driver's seat, wedged his foot under the clutch pedal with his heel on the accelerator, and managed to steer the rig off the highway, and then jumped clear of the cab before it went over the edge?"

"You're the trucker," said Bill. "You tell me."

Hunter sighed. "Obviously, I do think it's possible." His fingers played absently with the twisted phone cord. "Did Constable Pullen talk to Customs and Immigration? What about the customs seal? Did the lab take a look at it?"

"I haven't heard back from Garth yet, but the lab guy confirms that the seal was broken by something, not cut. The way he described it was a semi-sharp metal object, something like the back of a knife or a screwdriver or something, put extreme pressure on the band in one place until it snapped. There was uneven stretching of the seal at the point of pressure, possibly indicating prying or levering. Same story, I'm afraid. They said it could've been intentionally broken with an instrument, or it could've been the pressure from the latch as the doors burst open. So we've nothing to rule out foul play, but nothing pointing to it either. By the way," his voice got tentative, "exactly what is your stake in this anyway?"

"What about the padlock?"

"What padlock?"

"Was the trailer door still padlocked?"

"Hell if I know. You haven't answered my question. How'd you get involved in this? You never struck me as the caped crusader type."

There was a short silence. Hunter pursed his lips and exhaled slowly. "I'm doing a favor for a friend." He paused. How did he get involved? El had asked him to help out Suzanne, help to set her mind at rest. "It's the guy's daughter, Bill. She said she needed to know how the accident happened, she needed to know it wasn't her father's fault."

"And you think she'll feel better if you tell her that you think her father was murdered? Boy! Are you opening a can of worms!"

But Hunter knew it was something else now, something that went beyond helping out Suzanne. Randy Danyluk had been a friend, a savvy old trucker who liked to drive and who liked to fish. He was somebody's father, doing the best he could. A father who would never have another chance to hunker down and really talk to his daughter. A daughter who reminded Hunter of his own. "Something else, Bill. The old gut feeling. Now I need to know, too."

Before Bill had a chance to comment, Hunter continued. "Sounds to me like a closer look at the trailer could be in order. Can you pass that on to Garth? Or the traffic analyst?"

"Roger. I hear he's got the master mechanics working on it in Merritt today. You going to be back this way again soon?"

"I should be passing through again in a couple of days on my way back from Edmonton, and I'll be in touch. Think you might find the time to go fishing sometime when I'm in town?"

"Could do. As long as you wouldn't mind if my youngest came along. He'd never let me hear the end of it if I ever went without him."

"I'll look forward to it. And thanks, Bill."

"No problem, guy. Glad to hear your gut's still workin'. Guess you can take the man out of the Mounties, but you can't ever get the Mountie out of the man."

Hunter heard Bill chuckling before the line clicked dead.

There wasn't a big crowd, but it wasn't a bad turnout, El thought, for a Wednesday afternoon. She didn't mind funerals, not that she made a hobby of attending them, but she could admit to drawing a certain amount of comfort from saying an official goodbye. It showed respect, she thought, not only to the dead person, but to the relatives of the dead person. Obviously, Hunter didn't agree. He'd said from day one that he had no intention of being here. She looked around the small chapel, nodded to two or three drivers that she knew. Recorded organ music played softly in the background, not loud enough to mask the coughs and whispers, the shuffling of feet and the occasional creaking of the wooden pews. It was a tasteful little chapel for a funeral home.

Stan Murphy slid in beside her, surrounded by a cloud of Old Spice. He looked stiff necked and uncomfortable. It was no wonder, she thought, since the collar of his white shirt sliced into his heavy red neck, and the fabric of his navy sports jacket strained between his shoulder blades like an overstretched tarp. He looked as if he'd been shrink wrapped. Must've been a few years since he'd last taken his Sunday best out of mothballs.

"Nice to see you all dolled up for a change, Elspeth darlin'," he whispered.

El made a face at him and whispered back. "You're a pretty sight yourself, Murph." She looked down at her own black slacks, grey blouse and black blazer and realized that she must look shrinkwrapped, too. Her blouse gaped between buttons and her thighs stretched the polyester of her slacks to its limit. Side by side

68

they must look like an economy size version of the Bobsey twins. "For a Newfie," she added, jabbing him in the ribs with her elbow. She knew that Murph's big heart must ache as much as hers did, saying goodbye to his best friend, and figured that a little distraction wasn't uncalled for.

"Ow!" he cried, then clapped his hand over his mouth. El followed his gaze.

Suzanne and Gary, along with Randy's two little granddaughters, were being ushered into the chapel from a side door by a mournful looking older gentleman with silver hair and a black suit that fit his thin frame perfectly. His serene demeanour marked him as the funeral director, or whatever. The sad little family filed into the front pew. Even the little girls were silent with downcast eyes. El wondered how long that would last. The organ music stopped.

The serene gentleman stood behind a polished wooden podium, cleared his throat, and began to speak in appropriately reverent tones into the hushed chapel. "We are here today, as the friends and family of ... ."

There was a crescendoing clack clack clack of high heels on the hardwood outside and a rush of white noise as the chapel door swung open. The man at the podium carried on, obviously above this sort of interruption, but all heads in the chapel turned to follow the progress of a hard-faced blonde woman, probably in her late forties, wearing a tight-fitting, shiny black dress and four inch heels. She teetered up the carpeted aisle and grabbed hold of Murph's arm. "Shove over, Murphy," she whispered in a harsh smoke-and-whiskey voice. "Let me in." The woman's perfume overpowered Murphy's cologne. It was something cloying. A knock off Poison, maybe.

Murph shoved over, and El shoved over, and the man beside her shoved over, until they were crammed like cabbage rolls into the pew. El gave up trying to hold herself in, her thigh jostling Murphy's for space on the bench. She glared at the woman around Murphy's barrel chest, but the woman seemed oblivious, staring straight ahead behind a pair of oversized dark glasses. El reined her attention back to the service.

"... not as an ending, but as the opening of a new chapter ... "

"Murph!" That smoky loud whisper again. "Where is he, Murph? I want to see him." Murphy shrugged, put his finger to his lips. "Where's the casket, Murph? I want to see him."

Murphy whispered something in the woman's ear, and she covered her face with reddened hands and began to sob, silently at first, then louder, disturbingly so. Murphy looked at El with a pained expression, then stood up. El caught sight of Suzanne's ashen face, her eyes wide with shock and pain. Gary quickly rearranged the little girls and sat down next to his wife, putting his arm around her shoulders as she leaned her head against his chest. Murph had taken the woman by the elbow and led her to a seat at the back of the chapel, where El could still hear her whining and snuffling.

" ... who taught us to pray," the man's velvety voice carried on with, "Our Father, who art in heaven, hallow-ed be thy name ... " and El shut her eyes, tight, very tight, trying very, very hard to picture Randy's face, and she joined in.

"... for thine is the kingdom, and the power, and the glory, forever and ever ... "

Amen.

The house was silent, although occasionally the whine of a motorcycle or the fading rumble of an unmuffled car on the highway a few blocks away wafted through the open window along with the soft night air. Gary had just turned out his light, arranging his body inside the sheets with a few small grunts. Suzanne lay on her back, her eyes open wide and staring unfocused into the darkness above her. Gradually the light fixture on the ceiling took shape, making a huge elliptical shadow in the grey light from the window. She felt exhausted and empty, but she knew she wouldn't sleep, not for a long time.

"Gary?"

He answered with a short muffled hum.

"How could Dad have even touched that woman, after Mom?"

70

There was a big sigh, like he knew Suzanne would never understand what he was about to say. "Like I said before, it's just a physical thing, Sue. Men sometimes ... ." He sighed again. "Don't make it into a big deal. It doesn't mean your dad loved your mother any less. We both know how much he loved her."

She heard his arm rustling in the sheets, then his fingers stroked her cheek, his touch soft and warm, like a baby's breath. "Any relationship he might've had with that woman was probably all in her head. She's a head case. Don't let her spoil your dad's memory. She's not worth it."

A tear trickled wetly into Suzanne's ear. "I wish I could stop thinking about her."

Gary moved closer, put his arm across her stomach and nuzzled her neck. "Remember how your dad used to take Jo and Veri out for ice cream in his tractor? And how he let them play hide and seek in the sleeper? And remember how they giggled that time he put Jo's teddy to bed in his bunk, wearing his Caterpillar hat?" He ran the tip of his nose along her jaw, then kissed her gently on the chin. "Remember? Huh?"

She nodded, laughing and crying at the same time. He stroked the hair at the crown of her head, straightened loose strands at the top of her pillow. She was glad he didn't try to make love. She hated to ever turn him down, but tonight, well, thinking of her dad and that woman, Suzanne couldn't stand the thought of sex.

"Gary?"

"Hmmm?"

"El said today after the service that if Ranverdan gets to be too much for us, we should tell her, that we could work something out. It sounded like she didn't think we'd be able to handle it."

Gary propped himself up on his elbow and looked into her eyes. "She wants to buy the company?"

Suzanne shrugged. She supposed that was what El meant.

"Did she say how much?"

"You know I couldn't sell Dad's company. I couldn't even think about it."

"But if we can't make it work ... "

"Who says we can't make it work? Why shouldn't I be able to make it work?" Suzanne's voice rose, and she could feel her anger rising. Why had she even mentioned El's offer? How could she have thought that Gary would take her side? Every time she discussed the business with Gary lately she ended up feeling she had to defend herself. And now with El it was the same way. Suzanne knew that El was convinced she couldn't make it work, either.

Gary sighed and lay back down, leaving only his hand nestled against the crown of her head. "Settle down, Sue. Let's not talk about this now." His fingers resumed their gentle stroking. "Look, you've had a very emotional day. Don't even think about it. Take it easy, be good to yourself for a few days, okay, honey?"

Take it easy. That's almost what El had said, too. Make it easy on yourself, she'd said. Give me a call if you need any help, she said. But what she really meant was, you haven't a hope in hell of making this work and you'd better bail out before you run the business into the ground. And Suzanne guessed that what really made her mad, what upset her most of all, was that she suspected in her heart that El and Gary were right. She was just a glorified office clerk who'd done a little dispatching and bookkeeping for her dad, and what did she know about running a trucking company? How could she dare to think that she could keep her father's company alive?

"Okay, Gary. You're right," she said. "It's been a rough day - a rough week - and I need some time before I make any kind of decisions." She leaned over and kissed his cheek. "Good night, love," she said, and patted his fingers, which were still stroking her hair.

"Good night, babe. I love you," he whispered. He took the fingers away and turned himself over, burying his face in the pillow.

"I love you, too," she whispered back, but she felt empty, like she had no love to give him. She knew she did love him, and Jolene and Veronica, with all her heart, but she felt as though all the love that had been in her today, love that had poured out of her like blood out of a gaping wound and left her feeling numb and lifeless, like a drained battery, that love had all belonged to her dad. Now she had nothing left to give anybody, not even herself.

She hoped she'd have some more tomorrow.

Hunter arrived in Edmonton without incident on Thursday morning. John Semeniuk, the receiver at Waicom's Edmonton warehouse was middle aged, near sighted and obese, and smelled of garlic sausage. While the warehousemen went to work unloading the trailer with their forklifts, he put down a half eaten sandwich to sign for the load. His big open-mouthed smile disappeared as he read the paperwork. "Too bad about Randy, eh? I knew him for years, from back at my old job, even. Great guy." He shook his head, his jaw denting the huge cushion of fat beneath his chin. "Real straight shooter Randy was. Had a lot of friends around here." He reached for his sandwich.

Hunter felt respect for the man's obvious sorrow. "I hadn't known him that long, but I've never heard anyone say a bad word about him. This has been real tough on his daughter." He paused, watching the man tuck a stray round of sausage between slices of heavy bread. "Any reason you can think of why the load he was carrying last week didn't clear at the border?"

The sandwich stopped in mid air, and Semeniuk's eyes became guarded. "Why are you asking?"

Hunter shrugged. "I'm trying to help his daughter out. Evidently someone at your Vancouver office is giving her a hard time because the R.C.M.P. haven't released the freight yet, but it's still in bond anyway, so we wondered if there was some problem with the clearance. Randy did up an A8A bonding the freight on to Edmonton, but never had a chance to mention it to his daughter, or anybody else as far as we know."

The big man stared at his sandwich. "Can't say. Can't help you."

Their conversation was interrupted by a languid male voice. Hunter glanced over his shoulder and saw one of the warehousemen who'd been unloading Hunter's trailer standing behind him, a tall athletic looking man with a tight pony tail and a two-day beard. He gave Semeniuk the skid count and asked if there was anything to load on Hunter's trailer.

"No, that's it, Frank," Semeniuk said curtly. "Finish picking the Red Deer order." The warehouseman gave Hunter an appraising look, rubbing the black stubble on his jaw with the back of his hand as he turned away.

Hunter was pulling The Blue Knight away from the loading dock when Semeniuk signalled to him from the warehouse steps. Hunter stopped the truck and climbed down as the fat man jogged over to him. Semeniuk was breathing heavily and oily sweat glistened on his forehead. "I'd like to help Randy's daughter, but all I can tell you is, talk to Mel Collins at City Customs Brokers. He was a good friend of Randy's."

"What else?" Hunter leaned close to hear him over the sound of the engine.

"Sorry. That's all I can tell you." He waved Hunter away as he turned and walked quickly back towards the warehouse. As he drove out of the yard, Hunter saw the warehouseman, Frank, standing at the small window in the warehouse door, stroking his chin with his hand.

CHAPTER
NINE

Hunter had a pickup to make in Edmonton in the afternoon, half a trailer load for Vancouver. Ranverdan had some freight from up north that would fill the rest of his trailer. Hunter would have lots of time to pick it up in Kamloops over the weekend and still have the load delivered to Watson's yard in Vancouver by Sunday night. Mel Collins couldn't take time off to see him during the day, but agreed to meet Hunter at a hotel not far from the Yellowhead Trail after five o'clock. The location was Collins' choice, Hunter having asked him to suggest a place that would have space nearby to park a tractor-trailer.

Collins, a short, wiry man of about fifty wearing glasses and sporting a pale yellow golf shirt and light brown slacks, was standing beside his station wagon at the empty end of the parking lot and began walking towards The Blue Knight as soon as Hunter pulled in. Together, the two men walked in awkward silence to the hotel lounge, where they made their way to a table as far away from the big screen T.V. as they could get. Hunter ordered a glass of draft beer and Collins ordered a bottle of Coors Light.

"Do you know Suzanne, Randy's daughter?" Hunter began.

"I've spoken to her a number of times, but we've never met. I have to call the Ranverdan office sometimes about arranging weekend customs clearances, locating lost paperwork, that sort of thing. Why do you ask?" Collins was soft spoken and came across as precise and polite.

Hunter had planned an approach that he hoped would justify his inquiries. He couldn't just flash his badge anymore and say he was conducting a police investigation, and why else would someone like Mel Collins agree to answer his questions? "Suzanne ... is ... concerned about the load that Randy was hauling at the time of his death. She's been getting some pressure from the company who owns the freight, Waicom Electronics. It appears that the freight was supposed to clear customs at the border, but Randy decided not to let that happen. He cut an A8A bonding it on to Edmonton." He debated whether to mention that it was John Semeniuk, the receiver at Waicom, who had referred him to Collins, and decided against it. Semeniuk had seemed fearful of someone or something, although the source of his fear wasn't likely to be Collins. In his mind's eye, Hunter again saw the warehouseman's face at the window, the aggressive set of his jaw as he'd stroked his two-day beard. "Seeing as you're a friend of Randy's, I wondered if you might know anything about it." The beer arrived and both men silently watched the waiter deal out coasters and set the glasses on them.

"Who are you?" Collins took a sip of beer and placed the glass back precisely in the middle of the coaster.

Hunter ran his finger through the condensation on the side of his glass. "A friend of Suzanne's." He sat back. "To be honest, I didn't know Suzanne before Randy died, but my dispatcher, Elspeth Watson, has known them both for a long time. She asked me to help out, both as a driver, and to poke around a little, you know, set Suzanne's mind at ease." Collins was staring into his beer, either thinking it over or being stubbornly silent, Hunter couldn't decide which. Seconds passed. Hunter sighed. He'd hoped he wouldn't have to say it. "I used to be with the R.C.M.P., that's why they think I can get information that they can't get on their own."

When Collins looked up there was a slight smile on his thin lips. "I've had a couple of run-ins with Elspeth Watson. Guess you couldn't say no." They both laughed.

The customs broker's face grew serious, and he dropped his voice so that Hunter had to lean forward to hear. "Randy didn't tell me everything, but he suspected there was something illegal going on. It had something to do with the Waicom Electronics shipments from Seattle, but he didn't know what it was. He said there were some weight or piece count discrepancies, a few other things that made him suspicious, but he didn't volunteer any specifics. He called me on Tuesday morning from Vancouver, said he was picking up a load in Seattle, and wanted a chance to examine the load before anybody else did. He said it would be set to clear at the border as usual, but he didn't want the regular people involved, so he was going to bond it on to Edmonton. We do the customs work for Waicom here, so I was going to get a buddy of mine at customs to unseal the trailer on the pretext that the paperwork was lost and I had to remove invoices from the cartons. It'd be at our bond warehouse, so it wouldn't have been any problem. Then Randy and I were going to go over the freight to see if it was all in order." He drank some more beer, set down the glass, and turned it in little circles on the coaster.

"Did you know what you were supposed to be looking for?"

Collins shook his head. "I don't know if Randy knew either, except that it was probably illegal. He wouldn't let anybody or anything tarnish Ranverdan's good name. That company was his pride and joy, and Randy himself was straight as an arrow. He'd have dropped Waicom like a hot potato if he found out there was smuggling involved." He smiled wanly. "Randy was so happy when his daughter got involved in the business after Ronnie died. He figured he had a few good years of driving left in him, then he was going to go fishing and leave the day-to-day operations to Suzanne. Life isn't fair, eh? He never got a chance to reap the rewards of all his years of hard work, he and Ronnie both." He looked mournfully at Hunter, then drained his glass. "I doubt that I can tell you anything else that'd help."

"You said Randy would've dropped Waicom like a hot potato if he'd found something illegal going on. Do you think Randy would have contacted the authorities as well?"

"Damn right. He wouldn't let something like that go. Not a chance."

"Straight as an arrow, huh?" said Hunter.

Collins nodded. "Straight as an arrow."

The June heat was enervating, the air still and parched, when Hunter arrived in Kamloops on Saturday afternoon. He called ahead, and was met at the yard by Suzanne. She and the two kids were sitting on lawn chairs in the scant shade of the old house trailer finishing up soft ice cream cones. Dressed in a checked white and pink sundress with bows at the shoulders, Suzanne looked not much more than a girl herself. Her hair was held in a loose ponytail by a bright pink terry cloth band, and her nose was pink from the sun. She asked him to unhitch the trailer and park his rig, saying that Gary would look after the freight transfer later, assuming Hunter didn't mind staying the night. The full trailer would be back in the yard, ready for him to hook up to again by ten on Sunday morning.

"I haven't had a chance to talk to you since last time you were here, Hunter, so I wanted to pick you up myself and ask if you would come to dinner. Anyway, Gary's out with his friends." She shrugged and dropped her eyes. "You are still looking into things, aren't you? I mean, I know it's not your job or anything."

"El won't let me forget," he replied, smiling. He decided not to say anything yet about his meeting with Mel Collins. He was afraid of telling her too much too soon. All he had for now was speculation and suspicion. "Here, I'll give you a hand."

They folded up the lawn chairs and stowed them in the trailer, then she buckled the little girls into the back seat of the minivan and drove it out the chain link gate. Hunter padlocked the gate, threw his duffel bag in the back of the van and jumped into the passenger seat for the short drive to Randy's house. Suzanne dropped him off, and said there'd be a cold beer waiting for him at her and Gary's house whenever he was ready.

Hunter showered, changed into clean jeans and a clean shirt. He went downstairs to the empty Ranverdan office and seated himself

78

behind Suzanne's desk. His plan was to contact Bill Earl first to see if there was any news, then call his daughters, hoping he'd find at least one of them home on a Saturday afternoon. Was it really almost a month since he'd last talked to them? That thought gave him a sudden sense of urgency that he knew was ridiculous, but he decided to call them first. Punching in their number, then his calling card number, he drummed the fingers of his left hand on the desk as he waited for the connection. The line was busy.

He was lucky enough to find Bill Earl at the detachment, just closing out his shift. Bill had reviewed the mechanics' report on Friday as soon as it arrived. The Western Star tractor had been in top condition, no indication that the brakes, transmission or steering could have failed. Careful examination of the tractor's paint had revealed no traces of a collision prior to leaving the road. Any damage was entirely consistent with the bouncing and rolling a fall down the steep bank would have generated, and all paint scratches could be attributed to rocks along the rough slope and at the bottom.

"What do you get from that, Bill?" Hunter asked.

"Just what it says, Hunter. It was a single vehicle accident, probably caused by driver error. He fell asleep, maybe, or he wasn't watching the road, or he made the mistake of swerving to avoid hitting a deer or a moose. Why?" His voice was wary. "What do you get from it?"

Hunter raked his damp hair back from his forehead. "Veteran driver like Randy Danyluk -- who knew better than to swerve to avoid a moose, who knew better than to drive if he was drowsy -- no mechanical problems with the vehicle, no sign of a heart attack or stroke, it looks more and more like it wasn't an accident. That's what I get from it." There was silence at the other end of the line. "Well?"

"Not enough, Hunter. If you can dig up something else, something more substantial than your gut feeling - like a motive, maybe - I might be able to recommend to Staff Sergeant Walker that we put some manpower on this. But right now, I don't need to make waves. Walker's reprimanded me a couple of times for poor judgment, which of course wasn't poor judgment at all. It was just a different way of looking at things, which Walker, being a WASP, would never understand, but that's beside the point. The upshot is, I can't afford any more black marks from him. I've got to keep working with him because I have to stay here in Kamloops. I want my kids to grow up here on Shuswap land, listen to Shuswap stories, talk to Shuswap people. I can't go out on a limb for somebody else's hunch. Can you understand that, Hunter?"

Hunter took a breath to respond, but Bill carried on without giving him a chance.

"Now, if it was my gut feeling, I'd probably already be dangling from that limb. But it's your gut feeling. I got every respect for your gut, Hunter, but it's your gut, you take the risks. Know what I mean?"

"Thanks, chief. You're making it tough on me, but I know where you're coming from. I may already have something on the motive." He gave Bill a quick rundown on his conversation with Mel Collins. He asked Bill to pass it on to Garth Pullen so he would take a closer look at the trailer before it was released from the compound, and to let him know if anything new turned up. "Did you find out if there was a padlock?"

"No sign of one. If it flew off into that long grass, no telling how long it might take to turn up."

Hunter winced. Bill was right. It was sheer luck that he'd found the customs seal. "I'll get you what you need to jump start an official investigation," Hunter promised, "and then we'll go fishing."

By the time he arrived at the Rodgers home, Suzanne had set the kids up in a little wading pool in the back yard. They were happily, if noisily, chasing naked plastic dolls through the grass clippings in the water with a monster truck when he arrived. Suzanne handed him a chilled can of beer and joined him at the shaded patio table. He ran the beer can across his forehead before he popped the top. The short walk from Randy's had made him feel like he needed another shower.

"According to the pathologist, your father died quickly and didn't suffer. He was probably unconscious by the time the truck hit bottom. Unfortunately, the mechanics didn't turn up anything in their examination of your father's truck, so there are no new clues about the cause of the accident." He shrugged apologetically, feeling a need to give her some kind of new information to ease her disappointment. "The R.C.M.P. haven't closed the file yet, so something could still turn up. By the way, it's beginning to look like your father suspected some kind of hanky panky with the Waicom loads from Seattle. I've got nothing definite yet, but it explains why he didn't have that load cleared at the border. You're sure he never mentioned anything to you?"

"Nothing. Like I said, he'd asked for records on past Waicom shipments, but he never told me why. I assumed ...." A puzzled frown creased the skin above her nose. "You think that might have something to do with his ... accident?"

Hunter cocked an eyebrow and tried to smile. "Possibilities, remember? Just looking at all the possibilities."

Some kind of tragedy in the wading pool brought three year old Veri running to her mother in tears. She pressed her sorrowful little face into her mother's lap, her dripping swimsuit leaving big wet patches on Suzanne's cotton dress. The older girl, Jolene, shouted defensively from the pool. "I didn't do anything, Mom!" Hunter excused himself and went inside to use the phone in the hallway. Third time lucky, he thought. Maybe this time he'd get through to his daughters.

He was half way through punching in his calling card number when Gary swung the front door open.

"Hey, pal! How's it going?" Gary asked, flashing a big smile. "Staying for dinner? Sue picked up a nice spring salmon this morning."

Hunter's finger hovered over the phone pad. He'd lost his place.

"How's your beer?" Gary continued. "I'll get you another."

Hunter depressed the connection button with his fingers, then decided to put the receiver down. He'd try again later.

Hunter stood at the edge of the patio and looked out at the sandy, sage dotted slopes on the other side of the river. As much as he'd like to keep quiet about his suspicions, he was going to have to tell Suzanne and Gary what he was doing, and why. He didn't want word of his unofficial investigation getting back to them through the grapevine. That would be worse. By telling them tonight, he could also make them promise not to discuss his suspicions with anyone else. He didn't want the murderer, if there was one, given a reason to cover his tracks any more than he already had. At the same time, he had to make it clear to them both that this was still only speculation. Bill could be right. However good a driver he'd been, Randy's death could still have been caused, inadvertently, by himself.

Hunter got the subject out of the way before dinner, trying to downplay its importance. Suzanne took the news calmly, nodding and chewing on her upper lip. She was obviously getting used to the concept of possibilities.

"Gary? You were at Waicom that night," said Suzanne, turning to face her husband. "What happened there? Did Dad say or do anything unusual?"

Gary shrugged. "I ... I never thought about it. I don't remember anything ... unusual."

"Walk yourself through it," suggested Hunter, leaning back in his chair.

Gary frowned, running his thumb idly across his chin. "Let me see," he said. "I got there first. In fact, Randy was late, so my trailer was almost fully loaded before he pulled in."

"The Winnipeg load," said Hunter.

"Right," said Gary, nodding, meeting Hunter's eyes. "So, really, I was on the road before his trailer was even finished loading. I don't see how I can help. I wasn't even there when he left."

"But remember what you told me the night you got home?" asked Suzanne, leaning forward, her hand stretching out towards him along the table. "Remember? You said Dad was trying to tell you something? You said that now you'd never know what it was. What did you think he was trying to say?"

Gary's frown deepened and he pursed his lips. "Shit! I don't know."

"Do you remember saying that to me?"

He shrugged helplessly. "What I told you, Suzanne, was that when I pulled out your dad waved at me as if he wanted me to stop, as if he wanted to tell me something. But then he changed his mind and waved me on. He never said anything. I assumed that whatever it was could wait, that he'd decided to tell me later."

"Had you and Randy ever discussed Waicom in the past?" asked Hunter.

Gary looked annoyed. "Yeah, we discussed Waicom. Waicom was a big customer. Why wouldn't we discuss it?"

"Did Randy ever say he was suspicious about Waicom's loads?"

"Suspicious? Like what?"

"Did anything about Waicom seem to make him uncomfortable?"

"No. He liked Waicom. Waicom was a big customer, like I said. A good customer. Anything Randy said to me had to do with keeping Waicom happy, as a customer. There wasn't even a hint of anything ... suspicious, as you put it ... in what he said."

"Did you see Randy talking to the shipper that night?"

"Yeah. They talked. Why wouldn't they?"

"Any disagreement? Any arguing?"

Gary shook his head. "It was just like any other night." He sighed and took a sip of beer. "Sorry. Nothing unusual happened. Unless you want me to make something up, I just can't make it any more exciting than it really was."

When Suzanne had gone into the house, Gary put his beer down and leaned forward in his chair to look up into Hunter's face.

"You really think it's possible that Randy was murdered? Randy was just normal people, for God's sake. Not Mafia. Not into drugs or ... or ... crime. Christ! Get real! Have you thought about what you're doing?" he asked, then gestured with his head toward the door Suzanne had just disappeared through. "To her. I know you were roped into this by her and El, but don't you think it would be better for Suzy to just accept her father's death and get on with life? Christ!" Gary sat back in his chair and snatched his beer can from the table. He threw his head back and drank, then leaned forward again.

"You say there was no sign of a collision with another vehicle. So how else could a loaded eighteen wheeler be forced off the road?

What the hell do you think happened? Some fuckin' Sasquatch pushed the truck off the road with his bare hands?" He shook his head and snorted. "Or some hijacker drove the truck off the road, then climbed out without a scratch, left the load smashed to rat shit, and disappeared into the mountains? Get real."

Hunter shrugged, brushing his can of beer back and forth against his knee. In a way, Gary was right. If his investigation turned up nothing, he would have made Suzanne suffer this continued uncertainty for no good reason. But for Hunter, the alternative was worse. Could he rest knowing someone got off scot free after taking the life of a good man like Randy Danyluk? God knows, he had enough regrets haunting him already. "You've got a point there, chief. I expect the inquest may finally conclude the accident was a result of driver error. There's a good chance Suzanne will end up having to accept the fact that her dad drove off the road and nobody will ever know why. Maybe in a couple of weeks she'll be ready for that. In the meantime, I'll try not to stir things up too much, but maybe it helps her to know that somebody cares enough to look at all the angles. Okay with you?"

Gary made a face, but said, "Go ahead. I don't care how you want to waste your time. Just don't upset my wife."

Suzanne walked out carrying the salmon on a platter lined with aluminum foil. She showed Gary and Hunter the lemon, onion and bacon slices spread across the rich pink-brown flesh inside the fish, allowing the two of them to admire it thoroughly. Then she dotted its silver skin with more lemon and onions, and sealed the fish in the foil.

"Here you go, men," she said, washing her hands of it. "The rest is up to you."

Monday the sun rose on the sky side of a heavy grey cloud blanket, and by eight o'clock it had started to rain in North Vancouver. The landlord's cat came to Hunter's back door, a sliding glass door that opened onto a concrete patio overhung by the sundeck of the landlord's suite upstairs, where it stood mewling pitifully until Hunter let it in. It rubbed against the leg of his jeans as it passed. Hunter left the door half open and stood there for a moment, deeply inhaling the scent of rain-soaked grass and cedar mixed with a subtle taste of ocean air. It was a nice change from the dry heat he'd left behind in Kamloops the day before.

He carried his coffee to the small desk in his den and started going through his mail for bills, writing checks, and bringing his ledgers and journal up to date. The cat jumped lightly to his desk and walked across the piles of paper, nudging his pen with its brown muzzle and purring sensuously. Finally it curled up in the warm glow of his desk lamp with its head tucked beneath its paw.

The last two checks he wrote were made out to Lesley Rayne and Janice Rayne. He and his ex-wife, Christine, had agreed that when the girls reached sixteen they themselves would be responsible for banking and disbursing their father's contribution to their living expenses, a contribution Hunter planned to continue making until they were finished their formal education. The strategy had seemed to accomplish what it was intended to: they were both well aware of the value of a dollar, and had both begun building a savings account towards buying their first apartment. He was proud of them, but a little sad. His sadness confused him. He'd been highly responsible at their age, too. He hadn't been unhappy, but he didn't look back on his adolescence and youth as being fun. Somehow he'd gone from being a serious and introspective child to being a mature and sober adult, skipping what were supposed to be the carefree years in between. Or ever. These days, in his mid forties, he was as close to carefree as he'd ever been. He made a glum mouth as he entered the final balance in his checkbook. He'd have to drive out to El's office today so he could deposit his paycheck tomorrow morning before his next trip out.

A little whistle floated in through the open back door, followed by a hoarse, "Cat! Food, Cat!" Hunter poked the sleeping Siamese with his pen. It looked out from beneath its paw with one blue eye, then curled its head deeper. When he tried to pick it up, the cat suddenly burst awake, squirmed out of his grasp, and sunk its small fangs into his hand before shooting out of the den and out of the door. Hunter followed, inspecting his hand to see if the skin was broken. It was. His landlord was leaning on the sundeck railing and grinning down on Hunter and the cat. Gord wore knee length khaki shorts and a Hawaiian shirt. One bare foot rested on the lower railing.

"Morning, Gord! She bit me again." Hunter held up his injured hand.

"Oh dear! Badly?"

"I'll live."

The Siamese darted off the patio, clambered halfway up the trunk of the apple tree, and without the tiniest pause, leaped back down to the ground, scooted across the wet grass and thundered up the wooden steps that led to the sundeck where Gord stood. Expressionless except for an almost imperceptible lift of his eyebrows, the old doctor watched the cat until she disappeared into the house, then turned back to Hunter.

"Feel like a coffee?" Gord asked. "Anne dropped off some peanut butter cookies yesterday."

"Aha! You just said the magic word. You know I can never turn down a peanut butter cookie." Gord's daughter, Anne, made them just the way he liked them, crunchy on the outside and chewy on the inside.

Hunter polished off two peanut butter cookies before his first mouthful of coffee. Gord's coffee was a little weak, but strong enough for this time of day. They sat at the kitchen table, looking out at the grey sky and the tall cedars at the foot of the garden, the deep green of their swooping branches softened by a fine curtain of rain. Beyond and between the cedars Hunter could make out a flat grey stretch of Burrard Inlet, its waters only a shade darker than the clouded sky. "So how's Anne these days?"

"Oh, fine, I guess. Loves her job, but she's always complaining about the pay. How does that saying go? She's trying to indulge champagne tastes on a beer budget." Gord nodded sagely. "Takes after her mother. Myself, I'd take a Moosehead over a Dom Perignon any day."

"Heard from the other girls lately?" asked Hunter. Gord had three daughters and a son.

"I talk to them all pretty much every day. Some days I'm tempted to let the answering machine they gave me take all my calls, but then I'd have to put up with them banging on my door. They've all got to keep tabs on me. I guess they're afraid I'll drop dead or at the very least break my leg any day now."

"Pretty close family, yours. I'm lucky if I talk to Jan or Lesley more than a couple of times a month." He smiled at the retired doctor. "Or is lucky the right word?"

"Lucky? I'd say it's just normal. I never used to get all this attention. When their mother was alive, it was usually 'Hi, Dad. Can I speak to Mom?' Unless they needed money or medical advice, of course. I guess they figured I was indestructible in those days, or else they knew their mother was looking after me properly. God knows, now that I'm old and feeble, they obviously don't think I can look after myself. And I guess they don't think John can look after me, either." Gord's brother John, a retired geologist, was slightly older, just as active, and Gord's roommate. Hunter considered his upstairs neighbours something of an Odd Couple, and got a kick out of their frequent bickering.

"Where is John?" Hunter asked as he accepted Gord's offer to refill his coffee. They were drinking out of pottery mugs, their pot bellied contours shaded from dark brown to cream.

"He's pretty well moved up to the Shuswap for the summer again this year. I plan to go up next week with Holly and her gang." Holly was Gord's oldest daughter, who was married and had three children.

"What are you going to do with the cat?" Hunter asked, looking around with some trepidation.

"Don't worry, you're safe. She had muddy feet, so she probably went to sleep on the clean laundry." Deadpan, Gord pushed his bifocals up on his nose. "The cat comes with me. She hates riding in the car, but once we get to the lake, she's really in her glory. Hunts all night, sleeps during the day. Besides, with your schedule, I wouldn't expect you to volunteer to look after her." He reached for another cookie.

"Although I know how well you two get along."

CHAPTER
TEN

Whenever he had to spend the night in Vancouver, Randy Danyluk used to stay at a hotel in Surrey that catered to truckers, and he often hoisted a beer or two with Elspeth Watson in the hotel's pub, known as The Goal Post. When Hunter went in to pick up his check at Watson Transportation on Monday, El invited him to join her and Randy's friend Stan Murphy at The Post that evening for a drink or two in Randy's honor, an unofficial wake. Until then, his day was free, and Hunter intended to devote it to a couple of neglected priorities: his daughters, and a little personal recreation.

Jan and Lesley lived with Hunter's ex-wife Christine in a three-bedroom townhouse in a park-like complex in North Burnaby. For the past few years, since Jan had learned to drive, Hunter seldom had occasion to go to the townhouse. It was usually more expedient to meet the girls at a restaurant or somewhere. He figured that by now their classes would be over for the summer, and thought that during the day he might have a good chance of finding them at home. He had their monthly checks with him, and if nobody was there, he'd have to slip the checks in an envelope under the door mat and leave a message on their answering machine.

He parked on the street. The complex was across the street from the Burnaby Mountain Golf Course, and Hunter peered through the trees beside the boulevard to see if the course was busy. A threesome was putting on the closest green, and the foursome behind them ranged across the fairway, waiting, about two hundred yards away. The members of the foursome looked Japanese. Hunter walked across the street to the townhouses.

The clouds were thinning and the rain had stopped, leaving the air damp and fresh, the pavement mottled with patches of wet and dry. A robin hopped along the lawn beside the sidewalk leading to the stairs, and a group of tiny black-capped chickadees chased each other through the crooked branches of a spreading pine tree. The complex was made up of three-story buildings arranged in staggered rows, and each townhouse had its own outside entrance. The outer walls were a combination of white stucco and chocolate brown wood siding, and the buildings looked as clean and well maintained as the gardens that surrounded them. Hunter climbed the stairs to a second floor suite and knocked on the door. He could hear music faintly from behind the heavy door. He knocked louder, and fifteen seconds later the door jerked open. He smiled broadly.

"Dad! Hi! What are you doing here?" It was Lesley, his youngest, who at nineteen looked like a nineties version of the girl Hunter had fallen in love with in 1968. She had long, sandy blond hair, shot with brass and gold strands, that framed her face in a careless cascade of waves. Her skin was clear and her eyes a gentle blue. She wore a short pale green skirt and a short sleeved blouse with gold and green patterns of tropical foliage.

"Just came by to drop off your checks." He thought he sounded almost apologetic. He cleared his throat and raised his voice. "Got time to go for a walk? Get some ice cream, maybe?"

"Sorry, Dad. I'd love to, really, but if I don't hurry I'll be late for work. I've got a job at Ricki's in Metrotown, just started last week. It doesn't pay much, but it'll give me spending money and I can probably work there part time all year. And I get a discount on clothes, see?" She twirled on her bare feet in the doorway. Hunter thought he had never seen anyone look so vibrant, so very beautiful. His throat constricted with pride. He took a deep breath, rubbing the back of his neck and looking out towards the street, struggling to hide his emotion.

90

"Oh, well, next time ... I guess." He shrugged. "How about Jan, is she home?"

"Nope. Jeez, Dad, you're really out of touch!" Lesley shook her head and laughed. "Jan's started this great job with a high tech company. They phoned her Marketing teacher at B.C.I.T., and he sent her to see them, and they hired her right away! She's doing some kind of a marketing research project for them over the summer that fits right in with what she was taking last year, and it might turn into a permanent thing." She banged her forehead with the heel of her hand. "What was that name again? Oh, yeah! Digi-Lab Systems. In Discovery Park, off Gilmore Street. Have you heard of them? They were in the paper a couple of times."

Hunter shook his head sheepishly and pulled the checks out of his shirt pocket. "Here you go. I don't get to read the papers much."

"No, I guess not. You're always out of town."

"How's your mom?"

"She's fine. You should come by for dinner sometime, Dad. It'd be really nice for us all to be together for once. Listen, sorry, I gotta run! My ride will be here any minute."

Hunter raised his hand in an understanding wave. "Okay, Les. See you again soon, I hope." She smiled and swung the door shut.

He started to walk away, heard the door open, stopped and looked back. His daughter's head poked sideways out the doorway, her hair swinging lightly across her lower shoulder. "Dad! Thanks!" She waved the checks as if to fan her cheek. "And next time ... phone first, okay!?" The grinning young face disappeared and the door banged shut.

Hunter walked slowly back towards his car. He leaned his arms on the Pontiac's roof and rested his forehead against them for a moment before jerking open the door and getting inside. Why was it that he so often ended up feeling angry with himself after talking to his daughters? He felt like he was out of the loop, and that he could do something to get closer to them, but he didn't know what, he didn't know how. He felt suddenly frustrated and restless and vaguely dissatisfied with life. He was sure it was all tied in with his daughters, but he didn't know what to do about it.

He drove the short distance to the golf course, grabbed his golf bag out of the trunk, and was lucky enough to get onto the course almost immediately with a threesome of seniors. He clobbered the ball so hard on the first tee, his drive hooked badly and ended up on the far side of the second fairway.

His second drive must've been a good two hundred and eighty yards.

The sun was shining in Surrey as Hunter drove up to The Goal Post, an establishment euphemistically billed as a "sports bar". In fact, it wasn't much more than an old fashioned beer parlor attached to a third rate hotel called The Riverside Inn which abutted a rundown industrial area in Surrey. But the rooms were clean and cheap and the place catered to truckers, so there was always a tractor trailer or two parked in the back lot and a driver or two parked in the beer parlour.

Hunter's eyes took a while to adjust to the dim light inside the double sets of doors. It seemed almost criminal to be walking into a dark smoky room before the sun went down. There was the usual hubbub of voices and sporadic cracking of billiard balls, overlaid with an old Bruce Springsteen song. A television screen flickered at each end of the bar. Before he could see them, El's voice boomed across the room from a booth on his left.

"Yo, Hunter! Get your cute butt over here!" Several heads turned in his direction, appraising eyes moving up and down his torso. He frowned when he caught sight of her, and her laugh rattled like a tommy-gun in his direction. He slid in beside a beefy man with a round, florid face, who was seated on the red vinyl bench across from El. The man wore army green, and had a black baseball cap pushed back on his head. He grinned at Hunter and extended his hand.

"Murphy. Stan Murphy," he said, "but most of the boys calls me Murph." The big man had a none too subtle east coast accent, making his pronunciation close to 'byes' and 'Marph'. "I hear you're drivin' for us these days, fillin' in part of the big hole that Randy left behind."

Hunter shook the man's hand. "I just go where El tells me," he said with grin. "Nobody can take Randy's place." He poured himself a glass of beer from the nearly empty jug in the center of the table.

"You got that right," said Murph. "Me and Randy knew each other for years, eh? We worked together ever since I come out here from down home. I'm gonna miss the old bugger, that's for damn sure." He raised his beer glass and drank.

"Speaking of going where I tell you," El said to Hunter, pushing the sleeves of her faded purple sweatshirt up above her elbows, "you're confirmed for the Waicom pickup in Seattle tomorrow. Gary's going back on the road, so I've got him doing the Edmonton run. That way he won't be away from home very long. It means you'll be hauling the Winnipeg load. You okay with that?" She scratched the pale underside of her fleshy forearm without looking at it.

Hunter nodded, then caught the waiter's eye and signalled for another jug of whatever draft brew they were drinking. "Yes, Miss Watson," he said, trying to think of a way to repay her for the 'cute butt' remark, but determined not to make any reference to her ample size, even in jest.

The 'Miss Watson' drew a chuckle from Murph who, like most of the drivers, probably had trouble thinking of El as anything but one of the boys.

El made a face at Hunter, then turned on Murph. "You shut up, Newfie! You're treading on pretty thin ice there 'bye'! How long's it been since you kissed a cod, anyway?" Her machine gun laugh barked again.

"Elspeth, my girl, you've never been kissed till you've been kissed by lips that've kissed the cod." Murphy puckered up and leaned towards El, who drew back in mock disgust.

"You look like a friggin' cod yourself when you do that," she said. "Say, Murph, they say that Newfoundlanders always go home. Isn't it about time you went back to the Rock yourself?"

"I'll go when you least expect it, darlin'. Line me up t' haul a load of cigarettes or liquor, and I might suddenly get an irresistible urge ta go back and visit all my buddies down home."

"Don't hold your breath, 'me bye'. I'll never trust you any farther than I can throw you, and I don't think I could get my arms around your belly to even lift you off the floor."

"That's cause your poor arms have too much of your lovely self to go 'round first, precious," Murphy said with a wink, and poured El another glass of beer. Unlike Hunter, Murphy obviously had no compunction about taking a shot at El's size, but Hunter decided Murphy had the right, being of similarly generous proportions himself.

The first time Murphy excused himself and disappeared to the men's room, Hunter said, "I've got to ask you something, El, about Randy." El's expression sobered immediately. "Now that the experts have ruled out medical and mechanical causes for Randy's accident, what do you figure the chances are that Randy really did fall asleep at the wheel?"

"They have? No medical or mechanical causes?"

"That's right."

El frowned, "Well then, how the hell ... ? To answer your question, not a chance. There's no way Randy would've fallen asleep at the wheel. He was too cautious to ever let that happen. Besides, he'd just had a layover in Vancouver. It's not like he was pushin' himself."

"You figure he would have swerved to avoid a deer, a moose maybe?"

"No way. With all the experience he'd had? He knew better. He must've hit half a dozen over the years." She scratched her chin. "What's left?"

"There's always the chance that he swerved to avoid another vehicle, maybe even a pedestrian."

"A pedestrian. Way out there?"

Hunter shrugged. "It's possible. Not probable, but possible."

"And?"

"The other possibility is that it wasn't an accident."

94

"What do you think, Hunter?"

"I'd be willing to bet it wasn't suicide."

El nodded. "The medical and mechanical experts could be wrong." It was more of a question than an assertion.

"There's always that chance."

"Hard to believe it could've been Randy's fault in any way. He practically wrote the book on driving the Coq, helped a lot of young drivers make it through the mountains their first time." El sighed and peered into her beer glass, then hoisted it towards Hunter's.

"Here's to the best goddamn driver either of us have ever worked with," said El, her voice ragged.

Hunter acknowledged El's toast. A silent minute passed.

"Hunter," El said, "if Randy's death was no accident, if it was ..." she lowered her voice to a whisper, but her eyes were intense, "... murder .... If it was murder, I want you to find the bastard who's responsible for it, and I want a piece of him. You understand? I'm not normally a violent woman, but I'd gladly rip his fuckin' head off." She glanced towards the washrooms. Murphy was threading his way between tables on his way back to the booth. "Later," she said.

The both watched Murphy, who had changed direction and was hailing someone who'd obviously just come in the door. "It's that aging bimbo from the funeral," whispered El as Murph escorted a rough edged blonde woman towards their table. Hunter threw her a quizzical look, but there wasn't time for an answer.

"Carla, meet Elspeth Watson, our illustrious dispatcher." Murph gestured grandly. "And Hunter Rayne, truck driver extraordinaire, not unlike my good self. Pardon me, I should say, Miss Elspeth Watson," he said with a bow. El gave him a raspberry. "Friends, this is Miss Carla Hurley. I've invited her to join us."

The blonde slid in beside El. The woman's age showed in her skin, which was slack and lusterless, although the style of her hair and dress was youthful, in an almost trashy sort of way. Hunter guessed she was about his own age, but had lived hard.

"You're lookin' good, darlin'," said Murphy. "Nice to see you without them dark glasses. Not a trace of that shiner any more." He gently tipped her chin up with a thick finger to get a better look, then turned to El. "Carla's ex is a mean bugger. Last time Randy and I was here - come to think of it, it was the night before his accident - this fellow ... Bilodeau, right, Carla? Anyway, this Bilodeau come in here all tanked up and started hollerin' at poor Carla, tryin' to drag her outa here. Randy gave him right what for and he backed off. The man's a coward at heart, like all bullies. Later, when we wasn't watchin', he socked the poor darlin' over by the ladies' powder room there," he pointed at the washroom, "By Jesus, Randy scared him off right proper after that." He turned to Carla. "I still say you should've let them call the police and had him put in jail."

Carla looked around nervously. "Let's not talk about that bastard. Rick, I mean." The waiter placed a glass of rum and coke in front of her and she lifted it up high. "To Randy," she said in a smoke roughened voice. "The best damn driver I ever met! And I miss him like hell!" Her glass was half empty when she set it down to light a cigarette.

Hunter couldn't help wondering how many drivers Carla had met, and how she went about determining which one was the best. Her manner seemed artificially gay, and Hunter saw her hands shake as she held a transparent pink lighter to the end of her cigarette. She smiled with an obvious effort, and the creases of her smile emphasized the heavy texture of makeup on her skin. She had one gold incisor, and her hair looked heavily sprayed.

"So," began El, smiling in Carla's direction, "how long did you know Randy?"

Carla took a long drag on her cigarette and screwed up her face as if thinking were a painful process. "Since about February, maybe early March, wouldn't you say, Murph? I split up with Rick just after New Years, and Randy and me started seeing each other a couple months later." El's face looked blank, almost uncomprehending, leading Carla to elaborate. "Whenever he was in town, that is. We saw each other here, mostly," she said, gesturing around the room with her cigarette. She giggled at Murphy. "At least until closing time, hey, Murph?"

Hunter didn't know what kind of a relationship Randy might have had with this woman, but watching her simpering, he was pretty sure he didn't want to hear any of the details she might be prepared to divulge about it right now. He cleared his throat and nodded towards Murphy. "Say, Murph? I guess you weren't born in Canada, then, were you?"

Murphy seemed to welcome the change of subject. "Right you are. Newfoundland was still a free country in them days, I'd hate to say just how long ago."

"Sheesh," said El, "it sure ain't free any more. It's costing B.C. taxpayers a bundle."

"Don't get started on Newfoundland, now, El." Murphy looked hurt. "Why don't you pick on Quebec, instead?"

"Or the Yukon," added Hunter, again hoping to change the direction the conversation was taking. "Ever been to the north, Murphy?" He smiled at Carla. "Did you know that, in Dawson City, they have a big baseball game every year on the longest day, on a hill overlooking the town?"

"Yeah? So?" she said, with a puzzled smile.

"The game is played in broad daylight, but it starts at midnight."

They ordered food soon after Carla's arrival, and Hunter switched from beer to Coke. By ten o'clock he was ready to leave. He was about to say his goodbyes when a tall, skinny man with unkempt brown hair, an out-of-control moustache and broken front tooth came striding up to the table and grabbed Carla's arm. He wore torn blue jeans that sagged low on his bony hips and a black muscle shirt that revealed two indistinct, blue tattoos on his stringy upper arms.

"Where the fuck have you been?" he demanded, ignoring the others at the table. "You said you was coming to Pat's place tonight!" He looked around the table and added with a sneer, "Excuse me. I need to have a little ... uh ... discussion with my wife."

"I am not your wife, you asshole! Take your hands off me!" Carla jerked her arm away and knocked over El's full glass of beer.

El shot Hunter a look of alarm. Murphy stared down into his beer, concentrating as though he were counting to ten. Hunter's eyes narrowed as he watched the newcomer closely, then his jaw stiffened.

"Stop fucking around and get off your butt, girl!" Bilodeau grabbed for her arm again.

"NO! Get out of here! Fuck off, Rick!"

Without taking his eyes off Bilodeau, Hunter nudged Murphy, and the big Newfie slid along and stood up so Hunter could get out. Murphy sat back down, and Hunter stood face to face with Carla's ex. The skinny man, already inches taller than Hunter, stretched himself upward and looked contemptuously down his nose into Hunter's face. A ghost of a smile played over Hunter's mouth, and he kept staring straight into Bilodeau's eyes. The skinny man's sneer gradually gave way to an angry frown, his chin thrust stubbornly forward.

"Might be a good idea if you left," Hunter said in a low and even voice. "Carla's spending some time with friends."

The skinny man's moustache twitched as he spat out, "Who the fuck are you?"

"I'm a friend of Randy Danyluk's," said Hunter.

Bilodeau snorted. "That asshole." He looked accusingly at Carla. "You still snivelling about that prick? He's history, got that!? Dead meat."

Hunter took a step forward and lowered his head slightly, his eyes boring straight into Bilodeau's face. He jerked his thumb towards the door. "Might be a good idea if you left," he repeated levelly.

Bilodeau raised his right hand to shove his palm into Hunter's chest. In a split second, Hunter had the man's skinny wrist immobilized in the grip of his left hand. Hunter took another step forward, pushing Bilodeau's raised hand back behind his ear. Bilodeau, looking surprised and confused, tried unsuccessfully to free his arm, his head rotating from side to side to avoid Hunter's eyes. He finally took a step backwards.

"I can't leave if you're fuckin' holding my arm, can I?" His sullen frown returned. "Let me go, asshole."

Hunter released the skinny wrist, and Bilodeau started angrily towards the door, throwing chairs out of his way as he went. Halfway across the room, he turned and shouted, "Next time you won't be with that dead fucker's friends, you bitch!"

By this time a burly waiter had arrived at the table. He wiped the sopping table with a smelly cloth, and asked if they wanted another round. Hunter debated with himself, decided that he should stick around for a bit longer. He ordered another Coke.

El and Murphy made a half hearted attempt at resuming their banter, but the picnic had been rained out. Carla soon relaxed, thanks as much to a double rum and Coke as to Bilodeau's departure. Murphy made a gallant effort to cheer her up.

"He's bad news, that one," said Murphy, looking at Hunter, heightened respect evident in his expression. "Too much of a shaggin' coward to meet you head on, so you'd better watch your back leavin' here, buddy."

Hunter shrugged and turned to Carla. "Are you going to be alright on your own tonight" he asked her. He didn't like the woman, but he felt sorry for her. Many of the victims of domestic violence he'd seen during his career seemed to be fighting a fatal instinct beyond their control, being drawn to abusive partners like moths to a flame. Randy must have been like a prince to her. Her relationship with him, however casual it had been for Randy -- and he couldn't imagine Randy intending her to become part of his family -- must have been a valiant attempt on her part to break out of the vicious cycle of her relationship with Bilodeau, and perhaps others like him. "You think he might come back looking for you?"

"Nah. Rick's an asshole, but his bark is worse than his bite. I'll be okay." She took a deep drag on her cigarette, then emptied her glass and pulled a full one over in front of her and sucked on her cigarette again. Her hands were shaking.

"Look. I've got a friend who lives near here with his wife," said Hunter. "He's an ugly son-of-a-bitch, but he and his wife are good people. They'll probably put you up for the night if they've got room. Give Rick time to cool off. What do you say?" Hunter smiled to encourage her.

Carla shrugged and flicked the ash off her cigarette into the black plastic ashtray. "I'll be okay," she repeated. "I don't want to be no trouble, you know? I'll be okay."

By the time Murphy and El escorted the other two out to Hunter's car it was almost eleven o'clock. The parking lot was dark and quiet, except for another party saying their goodnights a few cars away. Hunter held the door open for her as Carla threw her cigarette on the ground and slid into the passenger seat. Hunter started up the Pontiac's engine and let it run while he watched El get into her pickup, and Murph enter the hotel where he had a room booked for the night.

"So Randy showed your ex ..." Hunter fumbled for a word before deciding he didn't need one, "... the door last time he was here, did he?"

"Hah! Rick's my ex, alright - an ex-mistake on my part. Yeah, Rick got really choked at Randy. Randy was a pretty skookum guy for his age." Carla looked over at Hunter with a grin and added, "Take it from me, he was in good shape for a guy his age."

Rummaging noisily in her big purse, she continued talking. "He backed Rick up against the wall, grabbed him by the front of the shirt, and threw him on his butt. Told him to leave me alone. Shit! Was he mad!"

"Who was mad? Randy or Rick?"

"They both were, but I'm talking about Rick. Before he left, he yelled across the room, like he did at me tonight, only worse." She sneered and tried to imitate Bilodeau's voice. "You're such a big man with your friends around, but wait'll I get you alone." She went back to her own voice, but the sneer remained. "Hah! Randy still would've wiped the floor with him. Asshole."

Carla pulled a lighter and her cigarettes out of her purse. "Mind if I smoke?" she asked. Hunter wrinkled his nose, and she said, "Nah. I can wait. And thanks, eh?"

He looked at her questioningly.

"For helping me out with Rick. He can be such a creep when he's drinking. I can handle him pretty good usually, but I've been feelin' kind of low lately, eh? Because of Randy, you know?" Her face looked almost comically mournful, sagging like an old hound's.

"Are you and Rick still married?" asked Hunter.

'Hell, no! Never were. We lived together for about a year, then I threw the bastard out, but he still hasn't got it through his thick skull that it's over." She snorted loudly.

"Is Rick a driver, too?"

"Hah! Since I met him, Rick's never done an honest day's work!"

"By the way," said Hunter, "what happened afterwards? I mean, after Randy had that little dust up with Rick? Did you see Randy again before his accident?"

Carla seemed to be staring at something just beyond the tip of her nose. "Well, yeah. I stayed with Randy that night. In the hotel." She nodded back over her shoulder, then cocked her head to one side, a sad smile on her face. "In the morning we had breakfast at the White Spot, and walked from there over to the mall at Surrey Place. Randy bought me a nice pair of shoes, white sling-backs, for the summer, and I helped him pick out a couple of little sun hats for his granddaughters. He always liked to bring them little presents, he said." Her lips trembled. "I haven't worn those sling backs outa my apartment yet. I don't want them scuffed up, you know? I want them to be always brand new, like he just gave them to me." She started sniffling.

"There are some unanswered questions about his plans for that night, his daughter's trying to piece them together to solve a problem for one of their customers. Did Randy say anything to you, or did he talk to anybody that you know of, about what he was going to do?"

Carla frowned. "You sound like a cop," she said.

Hunter chuckled. "Nope. I'm just trying to get his daughter out of a jam."

"I can't help. Talk to Murph. He's the one Randy discussed business with. In fact, Murph was a little pissed at Randy that night, something to do with work. After we left the Post, Randy stopped to have a talk with him, sent me on up to the room. Don't ask me. Talk to Murph."

They fell silent as Hunter turned the Pontiac into the driveway of a small bungalow in Whalley. The headlights revealed a lawn in need of mowing, but the house looked tidy, with a fairly recent paint job. A battered and rusting mustard colored Volvo sat in the driveway. Through the house's front window they could see the flickering purple lights of a television.

The front door was open before they reached it, and a tall burly man stood bare chested and barefoot on the concrete stoop under the light of a naked bulb. He had very blond hair, parted in the center and hanging to his well-muscled shoulders, and a long drooping moustache.

"Hey, Hunter, my man!" he boomed. "How the fuck are you!? Long time no see!" He pumped Hunter's arm enthusiastically, animating a tattoo of a black cobra, its hooded head dancing over the muscles of his right forearm, its tail wrapped several times around the thick wrist. "Come in, come in!" He motioned them both into the T.V.-lit living room.

"Carla, this is Dan Sorenson," said Hunter, "and this is his lovely wife, Simone."

A slender brunette wearing short shorts and an oversized black tee shirt rose like a dancer from a fat, afghan covered sofa and extended her hand with an elegant smile. She turned on an old-fashioned floor lamp and turned off the T.V.

"Hunter, it's nice to see you again!" Simone had a soft voice with a light and delicious French accent. "Sorry and I were just talking about you the other day, wondering what you have been doing these days. Sorry, get Hunter a beer or something."

"No beer left, Mo. I think we've got some of that unbeer crap, though." Sorry turned to Hunter and said, "Hey, man, want some dealcoholized shit? Some dork brought it to a Christmas party and it's been in the back 'a the fridge ever since." He grinned broadly.

"How about coffee?" Hunter replied. "You got any?"

"Sure, Mo can make some. Carla, was it? That okay with you?" Sorry winked at Simone, and she padded off to the kitchen.

"Sure. Can't stand that dealcoholized shit, myself." Carla laughed hoarsely. "Mind if I smoke?" she asked, with a cigarette already halfway to her lips.

Sorry reached out his hand. "Sure, but it'll cost ya." His braying laugh bounced off the walls as she offered him the pack.

Carla and Simone settled into the sofa on either side of a sleeping doberman while Sorry and Hunter sank into two massive, mismatched armchairs. A pasteboard coffee table sat on a brown rag rug in the center of the small living room. A large grey cat prowled around the outskirts of the room, then disappeared into a dark hallway. The walls were decorated with Harley Davidson posters and the window was flanked by limp curtains of some shiny, lime green fabric. The coffee was instant, but it was hot and strong. Hunter took a sip, then balanced it on the arm of his chair.

"Carla's ex was giving her a hard time at The Post tonight, so I was wondering if you might have room for her to stay here, just for the night till he cools off." He looked first at Simone, then at Sorry.

"No problem, so long as she don't mind the animals," Sorry indicated the sleeping Doberman with his chin, "she can crash here on the couch. Will that do for ya?"

Carla shrugged and smiled. "Sure. Just great. So long as the dog don't mind."

"We have three bedroom, but the kids are in two already," apologized Simone. "But you are very welcome, Carla. We often have a guest on our couch!" Simone's laugh rang like a tiny silver bell.

"What are you doing these days, Sorry?" Hunter asked. "Last time I saw you, you were driving for a vegetable farm near Cloverdale, right?"

"Christ! That was last summer, man. They wouldn't let me take a week off to go camping, so I quit in August. I was working as a bouncer at the King George, but I just got fired." He laughed and slapped his knee. "I liked my work too much! I sometimes get a few hours swamping for a guy who does local moving, has a couple five tons."

Simone made a face, her lips pushed out in an attractive pout. "That man hasn't called you since two weeks already." She turned to Hunter. "And when he does call, that's only a few days work."

Sorry shrugged. "No wonder we can't afford beer and smokes, eh?" He laughed, then mirrored Simone's petulant expression. "Is it my fault that people only move on the first and the fifteenth?" He turned back toward Hunter with a grin. "The big problem is, I can't afford to fix my bike either."

"You've still got your Class 1, don't you?" asked Hunter. "Is your license still clean? Want to do a trip to Winnipeg tomorrow, as a team?"

"Do you know what you're saying? You and me, cooped up together for three thousand miles? Think you can stand it?" Sorry's laugh bounced off the walls again. "You're on, Hunter! I could sure use the dough. What's it worth?"

It was well after midnight before Hunter managed to get away. He'd settled the details for the trip, admired Sorry's Harley, parts of which were spread out on an old pink blanket in the garage, and bid the two women goodnight. As he headed back to North Vancouver on the 401, he tried not to dread travelling to Winnipeg with the jolly biker. He didn't much like team driving at any time, but he could think of worse partners than Sorry. In spite of his devil-may-care lifestyle, Sorry was a good driver and a hard worker when he wanted to be. Besides, most of the time Hunter was driving, Sorry would be in the sleeper and vice versa. This way he could be back from Winnipeg in less than half the time, and be able to devote more time to investigating Randy's accident.

No, he corrected himself as he drove across the newly renamed Ironworker's Memorial Bridge to the North Shore. He could no longer think of Randy's accident as an accident.

He thought of it as murder.

CHAPTER
ELEVEN

Sorry watched Hunter's no-name car back out of the driveway and saluted its dark windows as it cruised away. He took a last deep drag of his cigarette and flicked it into the driveway before he closed the door, then killed the front porch light with an easy blow from his fist.

Simone and the blonde sat side by side on the couch, making female small talk. Sorry leaned an elbow up against the archway and rubbed his nostrils with the back of his hand. Damn but Mo was still a fine looking woman! Some of his friends' old ladies looked almost as wasted as the blonde. Deep lines on her face, grey pouches under her eyes, that Carla looked like she had been driven hard, a lot of miles over some bad roads. But his Mo was still one fresh and sexy mademoiselle.

As if she sensed his thoughts, Mo looked up at him and smiled. "It was nice to see Hunter again after all that time," she said.

Sorry shrugged. Yeah, he had been glad to see Hunter again, it's just that Mo was always trying to steer him towards so-called good influences and he didn't like to encourage her. He just wasn't as enthusiastic about good influences as she was.

"So it looks like you'll be getting some work?" she asked.

"Yeah. For sure, I will." Sorry nodded. "Yeah. It's good that he came by."

Mo braced her hands on her bare thighs and stood up. Looking down at the blonde, she said, "It's been very nice meeting you, Carla. I'm working early tomorrow, so I must go to bed now. Perhaps I will see you in the morning. Please, make yourself right at home."

She padded over to Sorry and raised up on her toes to kiss him on the mouth. He caught her in a quick hug, then slipped one hand down to grab a handful of her soft butt. Her butt tightened in his hand, and she pushed herself away. "Behave yourself! We have a guest!" she whispered.

Sorry thought he detected a saucy glint in her eye. He grabbed for her again as she walked away, but she slapped his hand down with a little giggle. "Good night, Carla," she said as she left the room.

The blonde settled herself in the corner of the sofa and tucked her legs up under her, then began rummaging in her gigantic purse. The clicking and clunking noises made Sorry think that she must carry around lots of makeup. He studied her face again, and couldn't see where it had helped.

"Whatcha lookin' for?" he asked, grinning and stroking the moustache that crept down both sides of his mouth. "Got somethin' else to smoke, by any chance?"

The blonde looked at him and grinned, flashing a gold tooth. "Maybe. Now that the coast is clear. Your friend reminds me of a cop."

Sorry laughed heartily. "That makes two of us. In fact ... sa-a-a-y, what's that you got there?"

She was holding up a big fat joint, waving it in front of his face as if she were trying to hypnotize him. He decided to be a willing subject.

"You light it," she said, tossing it into his lap. "Yeah, a lot of truckers are straight that way. Randy was."

Sorry looked up at her from under his bushy brows as he sucked the flame of his Bic into the other end of the joint.

"Randy was straight like that," she repeated. "He was a friend of mine that just died. Sometimes I figured he was just too straight for his own good." She reached out to grab the joint from his

106

outstretched hand. Her fingers were skinny and knobby. "He didn't like me to do weed."

Sorry nodded, holding his breath.

"Yeah, your friend's a hard guy to figure," the blonde continued. "Right off he struck me as standoffish, not real friendly like, then suddenly he's playing some kind of white knight and fixin' me up with you guys."

"Yeah," Sorry said, trying not to let too much smoke out of his lungs. "I always figured he must've OD'd on Roy Rogers when he was a kid." Sorry waved wildly towards the joint, exhaling in a rush. "Aren't you gonna smoke the fucker!? Don't let it burn itself up for Chris'sake!"

She took a big toke and passed it back, then dove down into her bag and came up with a roach clip made out of silver and turquoise. She waved it at him with another flash of her gold tooth. "Be prepared, that's my motto," she said with a raw laugh. "Me and the Boy Scouts."

By the time Sorry's lips couldn't get around what was left of the roach, the blonde was giggling and primping like Sorry's six year old daughter, Sasha, except she wasn't nearly as cute.

"It's just so-o-o-o-o funny," she managed to get out between giggles. "Brain washed by Roy Rogers." Giggle. Giggle. "I'll bet he calls his truck Trigger." Giggle.

"Tee hee hee," Sorry responded, frowning. Nothing worse than an ugly broad trying to act cute. He sat watching her for another couple of minutes. Looked like Mo had already brought her a pillow and a blanket. With any luck, she'd be gone in the morning by the time he got out of bed. He yawned loudly, stretched himself to his feet, and said, "Nitey nite. Don't worry about bedbugs, but watch them fleas."

She giggled again, reached over and tousled the doberman's ears. The dog, still curled up on the couch, looked up at Sorry beseechingly. "Hang in there, Doobie," Sorry said, and slapped the poor mutt's rump on his way out of the room.

He tiptoed down the hall to the bedroom, peeled off his jeans, and tucked himself under the sheet beside Mo. He ran his hand along her hip, but she whimpered softly in her sleep and pulled away, so he turned over and settled himself on his stomach.

Just before he fell asleep, he heard the blonde giggling again in the living room. "Brain washed by Roy Rogers," he muttered, then chuckled into the pillow. "Too fuckin' funny ... ."

Hunter slept until half past eight. The skies were clear again and his bedroom was flooded with yellow light. He could hear the whine of the landlord's vacuum upstairs, and the squawking of a crow from the direction of the tall cedars at the foot of the yard. He started the coffee maker before heading into the shower, and emerged to the final gurgles of a fresh pot. He picked up yesterday's clothes from the floor where he'd dropped them. The unhealthy reek of stale smoke wafted up from them until he'd buried them under a load full of laundry and closed the lid of the washing machine over them. After two mugs of coffee and a quick breakfast of cold cereal, he headed out to deposit his check and pay some bills.

His credit union was in a small strip mall on Marine Drive. As he drove through the parking lot, he noticed signs plastered across the drug store windows reminding shoppers of Father's Day on June 19th. Last year he'd made a point of being in town on Father's Day. He'd sat around all day, catching up on his reading, doing laundry, he even borrowed Gord's vacuum and cleaned the four rooms of his downstairs suite. Finally, at seven o'clock when he still hadn't heard from either of his daughters, he drove to West Vancouver and went for a walk beside the Capilano River and along Ambleside beach, then treated himself to a hamburger, fries and a chocolate milkshake at the Park Royal White Spot. He sat at the lunch counter along with several other solitary men. At home afterwards, he found a message on his answering machine. The girls had called him from Penticton where they'd gone camping with friends, and wished him Happy

Father's Day in a giggling chorus. He wondered what they had planned for him this year.

When he got back to his suite from the credit union, the answering machine was flashing. He pushed the play button, half expecting to hear the ghost of Happy Father's Day. Instead, he heard El's voice. "Hunter! Goddammit! Why don't you have your cell phone on! It's Gary. He just called from an emergency call box near the Coq summit. Looks like somebody fooled with his brakes and he just about ended up like Randy. Call me!"

Since Gary's frantic phone call, every time the phones went quiet for a minute or two and gave her time to think, El started fretting. She had wanted him to report his suspicions to the police, but Gary'd refused. "What the fuck can they do?" he'd asked. She didn't know if they could help, but she thought they should be told. Hunter would know what to do. Who the hell would want to hurt Gary? Or Ranverdan? Was whatever happened to Randy, and now to Gary, the product of some stupid vendetta against the company itself? Or was somebody trying to force the sale of the company? What the hell was going on? Where the hell was Hunter?

The phone buzzed again and she grabbed for the receiver, resenting and welcoming the distraction at the same time. "Watson," she barked.

It was Hunter.

"Jesus, Hunter! Get in here, would ya! Some psycho is trying to murder the whole goddamn Ranverdan fleet! We gotta do something!"

"Whoa, El. Slow down there," said Hunter, his voice smooth and slow.

El took his irritating calm as a rebuke. She had to bite her tongue to keep from screaming back at him.

"Okay," Hunter's level voice continued, "tell me what happened."

"I told you, Goddammit! Somebody tried to murder Gary!"

"El. I said slow down." There was a warning in his voice. El bristled, but held her tongue. "Start from the beginning."

Another phone started to ring and El cut the caller off, whoever it was, then put all of her lines on hold so her conversation with Hunter wouldn't be disturbed..

"Okay," she said. "From the beginning. I told you last night that Gary was back on the road today, right?"

"Yes. You said he'd be hauling the Waicom load from Seattle to Edmonton."

"Right. Well, first he had a load out of Prince George that he was hauling from Ranverdan's Kamloops yard to here. Newsprint."

"A full load?" Hunter asked.

"Yep. Forty five thousand pounds." El paused for effect. Both she and Hunter knew that a load that heavy demanded full braking power on the killer hills of the Coquihalla. "He left at about eight this morning, and did the usual brake check prior to descending the first summit. Everything was in order. No sweat on the first descent, he said. Everything worked. He took it easy and had no problems." She took a breath. There are two summits on the Coquihalla highway between Kamloops and the town of Hope. For a southbound driver, the first summit lies between Kamloops and Merritt, the second summit, a good forty two hundred feet above sea level, lies between Merritt and Hope. "He says he did the brake check again, like he's supposed to, before starting the second descent this side of the toll booth.

"So, he's starting on that first downhill grade, low gear, the load's pushing pretty hard. So he pulls his spike, eh?" The hand valve should have activated his trailer brakes. "And nothing happens! Zip! Nada! No trailer brakes. His drives couldn't hold the load all on their lonesome, so pretty soon they're smokin'." She paused again. Although the curves on the descent from the Coquihalla summit were relatively gentle, the grade, averaging six percent, extended for over ten miles. Relying on nothing but drive axle brakes on a hill that long was almost suicidal. Smoking brakes on the drive axles meant that they were already overheating.

110

"So he's barrelling down the hill, drive brakes smoking, pulling on a dead spike, and he has to take the turn up one of the runaway lanes. After he stops shakin', he says, he checks his trailer brakes and sure enough, the slack adjusters had been backed off. He figures somebody did the dirty work while he was taking a shit in the restrooms at the brake check." She paused, waiting for a comment from Hunter.

"Where is Gary now?"

"I gave him the number for the local towing outfit, 'cause he was going to need help getting back to the highway, and he said he didn't want to risk pulling that load the rest of the way until after he's had the tractor checked out. He said the ride up the runaway lane was pretty rough, and there might've been some damage to his tractor, besides the glazed brakes. Meantime, I pulled Murph off of another job and sent him up to get the newsprint, so Gary's got to wait for him to get there before he heads to Hope. Murph'll have to do the Seattle, too, looks like." El drummed her fingers on the desk, waiting for Hunter's response. "Well?" she said.

"How long has Gary been driving?"

"What are you getting at?"

"I've heard of guys turning their own slack adjusters the wrong way, just by mistake."

"What?! You think he's bullshitting?"

"If you were a macho guy, overeducated for the job and married to the boss, would you admit screwing up like that? He'd become the butt of other drivers' jokes for the rest of his life."

"We're not talking about a simple screw up here." El sat forward in her chair and banged a fist on the counter in front of her. "The guy could've fuckin' died!"

"I'm not saying it didn't happen like he told you, but I'm not prepared to just assume it did, either. What else did he say? Did he see anybody hanging around his truck?"

"How the hell should I know? Look. The guy calls me from a call box in the middle of nowhere just after having the shit scared out of him. I'm supposed to interrogate him?" This was getting real tiresome. She just wanted to hand the thing off to Hunter and let him run with it, and here he was throwing the damn thing back in her face. "Something screwy is going on at Ranverdan, Hunter. If I had the answers, I wouldn't have called you, would I?" It occurred to her that all her lines were still on hold. Customers would put up with a busy signal for only so long.

"Does Suzanne know?"

"No. He said not to tell her, at least not yet. He doesn't want to worry her." El herself was of two minds about that. Sure, it would be a shame to upset the poor kid any more than she was already by her father's death. But, hey, welcome to the real world, kid. The sooner you face it the better. Trucking is a tough business, and if you can't stand the heat, get outa the kitchen. It wouldn't be hard for Suzanne to unload the business, either. In fact, Ranverdan's assets, including plummy accounts like Waicom, would fit in real well with Watson Transportation's current operation. "Look, are you coming in or not?"

"What can I do right now, El? I'll have to talk to Gary before I do anything. Call me when you hear from him, okay? I'll see you this afternoon when I pick up my truck."

El grunted. Hunter was right, damn him.

Suzanne ran the last envelope through the postage machine. With a grind and ka-ching, the machine spat it out into the wire basket where it slipped off the pile of other invoices. That was it. The last bit of paperwork for now. The kids were napping. The phones were quiet. Suzanne frowned. It didn't feel right. What was happening? Had business fallen off so much since her dad's death? Had the company suddenly started to wither and die? What should she do about it? What could she do to even find out?

Although it wouldn't help business any, she decided to use the time to search for those computer records on Waicom she'd pulled for her dad. Perhaps she could find something Hunter could use. Maybe something there could provide some clue as to why her father had decided not to clear that Waicom load through customs. She

112

went to the five drawer steel filing cabinet, its key perpetually in the lock, pulled out the Waicom file folders, and brought them back to her desk.

One folder was for correspondence. There were some letters relating to damage claims, a few e-mail messages requesting photo copies of delivery receipts, and a small stack of annual contracts, the most recent one dated January of the current year. She scanned the letters and notes, but saw nothing out of the ordinary. The remaining folders held the Waicom bills of lading. Suzanne started with the most recent, and glanced at the key information on each bill of lading before turning it over and going on to the next. Here was a calendar of the past months measured in shipments instead of days. For each waybill, she took note of the date, the pieces and weight, the destination and the driver. After the first half a dozen bills, she flipped them faster and faster, just looking for notes or scribbles or anything else that might red-flag a shipment, might create some kind of suspicion. Nothing.

Where were those printouts she'd pulled for her father? She went to the desk he used to use when he needed a space to work in the office. He'd given the best and biggest desk to his wife, and then to Suzanne. His own small desk was facing the side wall, out of the way. She remembered him sitting there with the computer printouts and the file folders of waybills. He'd been making notes on something. If it wasn't the waybills, it must have been the printouts. She tried the large side drawers of the desk, but they seemed to contain nothing except blank waybills and claims forms, various manuals and tariff pages, job application forms and empty legal pads. She rifled through all the file folders without finding anything that had notes or writing of any kind. Then she tried the upper side drawer. It was locked. The center drawer contained nothing but an assortment of pencils and pens, rulers and staples, paperclips and blank post-it notes. She rummaged around in it for a key. No luck.

She pulled on the locked drawer again. Where would her dad keep the key? Surely he wouldn't have carried it with him. She went to her own desk and had begun to search the top drawer for a key when she was interrupted by the phone.

"Hi, babe."

"Gary!" His sexy voice on the phone always gave her a shiver of pleasure.

"Just thought I'd let you know about the change in plans. I had a little brake trouble on the Coq today so ..."

Her stomach dropped. "What happened? Are you alright?" She couldn't keep the sudden panic out of her voice.

"Nothing to worry about, Sue. They just overheated a little."

"Overheated a little? My God, Gary, are you ... ?"

"I'm fine, Sue. I said it was nothing." He sounded irritated, implying that she was acting like some silly worried woman, someone who didn't know how serious a brake problem on the Coquihalla could be.

Suzanne clenched her jaw, said nothing. She could feel the heat rising in her face.

"I just wanted to let you know that the scheduling has been juggled around a little, mostly because I'll be delayed getting into Vancouver." He told her that he'd be hauling a load from Vancouver to Kelowna, then making a pickup in Kelowna bound for Calgary.

"What about the Waicom?"

"Murph's on it."

"Murph?" Suzanne was confused. Why the hell hadn't anyone consulted her? What was going on? Drivers weren't supposed to make decisions like that without talking to their dispatcher.

"El said she'll have me home Thursday, no problem."

El! No wonder it had seemed so quiet. Even though Suzanne was back in the office full time, ready and eager to work, the drivers were still calling El! Things they should be discussing with her, Suzanne - granted, in the past she would often have consulted with her father before making any decisions - they were now addressing to El. Were the customers calling El, too?

"She will, will she," Suzanne said grimly. "What the hell has she got to do with dispatching Ranverdan trucks to Ranverdan accounts?"

114

"Suzy."

"Just what the hell business has El got fooling with our schedules?!"

"Suzy, settle down. She's just trying to help, you know that."

"If she's got a load for us, she can goddamn well call me and I'll let her know if I can send a driver. She's got no business dispatching ... our trucks." Suzanne came very close to saying "my trucks", but it didn't feel right. In her mind - and in her heart - they were still her dad's trucks.

"She's just trying to help, take a load off you, you know?"

Yes, thought Suzanne. And what was Gary doing? Why had he called El about the brake trouble instead of calling her? "Why didn't you call me first?"

A hiss came over the phone as Gary exhaled loudly between his teeth. "This is exactly why I didn't call you first. Listen to yourself. You're in a panic about it."

Suzanne knew she couldn't respond without keeping the hurt and anger out of her voice, which would just give him more ammunition. She took a deep breath.

"Maybe if you didn't react so emotionally to everything ... ," Gary went on.

"Are you saying I shouldn't have reacted emotionally to my father's death?"

"Of course not. This is getting ridiculous. Look, everything's okay. No harm done. El's just helping out until you're ready to take over yourself."

"I'm ready now, and I'll damn well tell her that."

"Give your head a shake, girl. Right now, without El's help, you could end up in big trouble. Let's talk about this when I get home," he said. "How're the girls? Are they sleeping?"

They changed the subject, but it didn't get the subject off her mind. Suzanne was still shaking when she hung up.

CHAPTER
TWELVE

Hunter always enjoyed the two and a half hour drive between Vancouver and Seattle. The road was good and the scenery, varied. Rural fields and light industry alternated with small towns and shopping malls catering to shoppers from both sides of the border. There was an easy stretch of curved mountain highway and always plenty of trees, plenty of green. He liked the Indian names he read on the green and white highway signs. Lummi. Snohomish. Snoqualmie. Tulalip. The name Sedro Woolley had intrigued him so much he'd looked it up in the auto association guide. The name came about when the logging town of Sedro, from the Spanish word for cedar, merged with the railroad town of Woolley. While he was at it, he learned that Issaquah means "snake" and Enumclaw, "place of the evil spirits".

He hadn't yet spoken to Gary. Hunter had arrived at Watson Transportation's yard to pick up The Blue Knight just after El had redispatched Gary to Kelowna, and their schedules wouldn't permit a face-to-face discussion, which is what Hunter wanted, for several days. The realities of making a living made a proper investigation impossible. Gary rejected El's suggestion to take a few more days off, just as he'd rejected her suggestion to contact the police. But he intended to keep a close eye on his vehicle from now on, he said.

Hunter had broken the news to El about his co-driver to Winnipeg, asking her to find a return load out of Winnipeg for him by Thursday. He planned on picking Dan Sorenson up after he'd crossed the border back into Canada.

"What!?" El practically choked. "That *sorry* excuse for a human being!? How could you stand being cooped up with him all the way to Winnipeg and back?"

Hunter, with a half grin, shrugged.

"Remember when Ron Taber hired him on for a run to Montreal?" El continued. "When Ron got back here, all he'd say is that the only way he'd ever travel with him again is if Sorry rode in the trailer - preferably a reefer." El's machine gun laugh. "A reefer with something non-edible, he said. Otherwise the goddamn trailer would probably be empty by the time he opened the doors."

The phone rang, and Hunter paced the floor in front of the counter while El took the call. He noticed some strings of scrap paper on the floor, white with small holes spaced half an inch apart, the torn and discarded edges from computer printed waybills. He picked them up and threw them in the waste bucket, along with the cobwebby dust that clung to them, then wiped his hands on his jeans.

"Listen, El," he said when she was off the phone, looking around to make sure no one else was within earshot. "If anybody asks, you're the one who hired Sorry, okay? He might come in useful when it comes to getting information, and I don't want anybody connecting him with me. Too many people still think police when they see me coming. Nobody has to know, not even Gary and Suzanne. They might let something slip to the wrong people. Okay?"

"Are you kidding? Sorry's a funny guy, but he's about as straight as a corkscrew air line." El shook her head. "He's been wearing a black hat all his life, for God's sake! You really believe you can put him in a white one?"

Hunter had rubbed his jaw. "Yeah," he said. "I do."

There was a ten minute delay at the border, but traffic moved smoothly along the I-5 and Hunter reached the warehouse in Seattle slightly ahead of schedule. When he pulled up at Waicom's loading dock in the Free Trade Zone, Murphy's green and silver Ranverdan rig was already backed up to one of the doors. As Hunter walked up to the shipping counter, the warehouseman approached him and volunteered that the shipper was taking a smoke break. "I'll go get him. Just wait here." Hunter noticed that they had already started loading Murphy's trailer. He walked inside the trailer, his footsteps on the wooden floor echoing inside the aluminum cave, but it was too dark in the nose to read the address labels on the cartons. The loaded cartons all looked the same. Computer monitors. He assumed they were for Edmonton. When he walked out, Steve Mah was waiting for him, scowling and twisting the diamond stud in his ear.

"What're you looking for, man? That's not your load."

"I'm looking for Murphy. You seen him?" Hunter was now convinced he wouldn't be able to get much information from Mah. Mah seemed wary of him, almost suspicious, and Hunter thought about what he'd recently said to El. *Too many people still think police when they see me coming.* Whether it was the way he walked, or talked, or how he dressed, or something indefinable, it seemed that twenty years of being a cop were impossible to erase. Lowlifes like Mah seemed to have some kind of a radar. Or could it be that somebody had warned him?

Mah jerked his head toward the coffee room door just as Murphy came strolling through. The big Newfie had a friendly grin on his round, ruddy face.

"Hey!" Mah shouted to the warehouseman. "Load this guy's trailer first." He pointed a rude finger at Hunter, that familiar smirk returning to his face. "The man's got farther to go."

Murphy and Hunter sat side by side on a stack of pallets as they watched the warehouseman load Hunter's trailer. Murphy twirled a keyring round and round one plump index finger.

"How 'bout that Bilodeau?" said Murphy, referring to the incident at The Goal Post. "One ugly bugger, eh?"

"Sure is. No love lost between him and Randy, was there?"

"That's for damn sure. I sure wouldn't want to turn my back on that weasel, if I was Randy." Murph clucked his tongue against his teeth and shook his head. "A real scumbucket, if ever there was one."

"You know him from before?"

"Just seen him around the Post. Deals drugs, I think."

"I thought Carla had a thing for drivers. He's not a driver?" Hunter watched the forklift run a skid of computer parts into the dark interior of his trailer. He wondered how open he could be with Murphy.

"Not as far as I know. Doesn't look like the bugger's done an honest day's work in his life, if you ask me." Murphy glanced sideways at him. "You think he might've had something to do with Randy's accident?"

Hunter half smiled, said nothing.

"Randy was my buddy, my best buddy," said Murphy. "If you're lookin' for a guy who might've had it in for him, I can help."

Hunter nodded. The forklift backed out of his trailer and roared off towards the back of the warehouse.

"You might want to look up a fella by the name of Chuck Wahl. He was an old friend of Randy's. They used to drive together, company drivers with Transcan Express, some years before Randy started up Ranverdan. And before Chuck went to prison. He did time. Chuck." Murph glanced up at Hunter from beneath his heavy black brows. "Light fingers. From what I heard, his loads were often short a few cartons, T.V.'s, car stereos, that sort of thing."

"Did Randy have something to do with him going to prison?"

"No, no, nothin' like that. I don't know how he got busted, but after he got out of the clink, Chuck started running as an owner operator, " Murphy dropped his voice, "and managed to snare a great account. A new company called Waicom Electronics." He raised one eyebrow, pausing for effect. "That was when Waicom brought their stuff into Vancouver and distributed it to Edmonton and Winnipeg. Their stuff, the computers and that, comes from China, eh? One split load a week. A good contract for a single operator, steady work. Then Waicom expanded, and started bringing their stuff in through the port of Seattle." Murphy gestured towards the warehouse. "And the guy in Vancouver wanted Wahl to keep handling their freight, but guess what?

"Our boy-o's an ex-con, so he can't cross the border, right? So he calls up his old buddy Randy and says, can you do me a favor and run this stuff up to Vancouver? No problem, says Randy. Ranverdan hauls the freight to Vancouver, Chuck keeps the Edmonton and Winnipeg consolidation run. Everybody's happy." Murphy dropped his keys. They chunked on the concrete floor and he left them there, leaning closer to Hunter's ear as the forklift roared past again. "Except Waicom keeps growing, and now they want their loads from Seattle to go direct to Edmonton and Winnipeg. And the new traffic manager, the boss's nephew straight from Hong Kong, likes Randy. He throws old Chuck out on his ear."

"And Chuck blamed Randy?"

"Wasn't Randy's fault. Chuck just couldn't do the job. So now Chuck's got a truck to pay for, but no more good customer, and not bein' the most charmin' fella, he's not havin' much luck finding any new ones. So he asked Randy to hire him on with Ranverdan." Murphy bent to pick up his keys. Hunter saw him exchange glances with Mah, who was back behind the shipping counter some forty feet away, out of ear shot.

"And Randy refused?"

"You got it. Randy might've felt sorry for Chuck, but there was no way he wanted a proven thief hauling his customers' freight. Besides, he needed drivers who could cross the border. Old Chuck was pretty bitter about it. Figured Randy owed him."

"What's he doing now? Do you know?"

"Haulin' shit loads for shit rates in some shit bucket of a truck, from what I hear." Murphy shook his head. "Poor old bugger."

They both watched the forklift nose another skid into the trailer, back out and roar away. Murphy went back to spinning his keys. Mah's head was no longer visible behind the shipping counter. He was probably sitting at his desk against the wall.

"You haul the Waicom loads very often?" Hunter asked Murphy.

Murphy shrugged. "I take my turn, like the rest of the boys."

120

"How about Randy? Did he?"

"Mostly just the Vancouver loads. He gave himself a lot of the short runs, day runs, overnighters, so he could spend a little time in the office every couple of days, be in town for little Suzy, especially when Gary wasn't." Murphy's face went sour. "Him too, eh? Randy gave the kid more than his share of the plummy jobs, too. Gary's never had to pay his dues. The rest of us had to fight for our days home - and nights. The life is startin' to get to a few of us, eh?" He shrugged. "Ah, what the hell. You let diesel get into your blood, you gotta pay the price."

"Us? Who do you mean, Murph?" Hunter watched the big Newfie's face closely. This was the first sign he himself had shown of ill will towards Randy. Although it wasn't surprising in itself, because long-haul drivers are often discontented with their lot -- even the ones who wouldn't trade life on the road for a nine-to-five job and a million bucks -- and their bosses are the first target of resentment. Irregular schedules and up to weeks at a time without a night home take their toll. Broken dates, missed birthdays and anniversaries, lonely wives, all adding up to failed relationships and unhappy truckers.

"We're gettin' on, you know, some of us. Pete for instance. And old Mike." Murph threw his keys from one hand to the other, stuffed them into his pants pocket. "It's nothin', really. Dog in a manger stuff, eh? If I've gotta be on the road and miss my sweetie's birthday, why shouldn't they?" The forklift maneuvered the last skid into position at the back of Hunter's trailer. Murphy laughed, slapping his thighs with both hands and preparing to stand. "All in all, though, Randy was the best. We got nothin' to complain about, but you know how drivers are. Nothin' makes us happier than findin' something to bitch about, eh?"

Hunter nodded, smiling. "Why do you think Randy would have been hauling the Waicom on that particular night then, Murph?"

Murph's big shoulders heaved in a sigh. "Goddamn it, I don't know."

Mah whistled shrilly and motioned for Hunter to come over to the shipper's counter. Hunter and Murphy both stood. Hunter started over towards Mah.

"Should've been me," Murphy said grimly, turning away. At least that's what Hunter thought he heard.

"What?" Hunter stopped abruptly and swung around. "What was that, Murph?" he called at Murphy's broad back, trying to raise his voice above the roar of the returning forklift.

The big man kept walking, and disappeared behind the forklift into the back of his trailer.

When The Blue Knight rolled off the scale at the Pac-Highway weigh station, right on time, Sorry was nowhere in sight. It was just after nine. Hunter parked to one side and dialled Sorry's number on his cell phone, and Simone answered, "'Allo." She said that Sorry's friend, the one who was giving him a ride, had been late coming to pick him up, but they were on their way. "He'll be there. He's very excited, Hunter, to be driving with you again. He wouldn't miss it, don't you worry."

Hunter stepped down from the rig and stretched his arms and back. The asphalt of the pullout was stained with skid marks and oil. Traffic whooshed by on the adjacent highway, and a light breeze played in the leaves of the birches beside the road. A driver Hunter knew passed his tractor-trailer over the scale and pulled over. "Hey! Hunter! How's it going?" he called through the passenger side window.

"No complaints, Bob. El's got me doing some runs for Ranverdan. I'm just waiting here for a guy who's supposed to team with me to Winnipeg. How 'bout you?" Hunter had to shout over the drone of the engine.

"Fine, fine. Just back from a trip east. I'm taking the wife and her two kids camping the rest of the week. I'll have to ask El to find me a good long run after that! I'll need a break!" He laughed. "Maybe Florida. Say, too bad about Randy. Now, there was a good operator. Knew his stuff. Y'know, I saw him here at the weigh scale,

122

and I figure it musta been the night it happened. It was a Tuesday night then, too, just about this time."

Hunter held up a finger to say just a minute, and jogged around the front of Bob's rig to the driver's side. He looked up at Bob and said, "Makes sense you'd've seen him here. Stan Murphy and I are doing the exact same runs tonight. Did Randy seem okay to you that night?"

"Randy? Sure, he was fine, same old Randy. He was stopped right here, where I am, and right there, where your rig is, was Chuck Wahl's old Ford tractor. They'd done a check on his equipment here that night, and pulled him off the road 'cause his tires weren't up to snuff. From what I hear, the money that should go into maintaining his equipment goes down his gullet instead. It's guys like him give us a bad name. The man's in the wrong business!"

"So you saw Randy talking to this Chuck Wahl?" Hunter prompted Bob before he could digress further.

"Sure did. In fact, I stopped to say hello and joined in their conversation for a bit. Randy offered Chuck a lift, since his rig was grounded. Randy and Chuck went way back, I hear. Somebody told me that Chuck taught Randy how to drive."

"So did he give Chuck a lift?" A pickup with a hole in its muffler passed on the highway, forcing them to shout.

"Far as I know. As I was leaving, I looked in my right hand mirror and Chuck was climbing into the cab with Randy. I guess Chuck's damn glad he didn't ride along with Randy any further than he did." Bob nodded emphatically.

"Where did Randy drop him off?"

"Beats me. Some place close by, I'd guess." Bob shrugged, peered into his side mirrors, one after the other.

"Say, Bob," said Hunter. "Where would I find this Chuck Wahl? Do you know?"

Bob snorted loudly. "Where would you find him? Nearest bar! The question is why would you want to find him?"

Hunter shrugged. "Business stuff." Anything he said to Bob would spread like wildfire. He hoped that he could make it sound too dull to gossip about. "We'd like to find out if Randy said anything to him about a problem with customs paperwork that night. If he did, there's some questions he might be able to clear up for Randy's daughter."

"Try the Goal Post here in Surrey, or the Canyon Hotel in Hope. He's been seen parked at both places on more than one occasion. I'm not sure whether he lives here or in Hope, but I think he gets most of his loads from a freight broker in Coquitlam. Wayne McCormick. That's the broker's name, I think. You heard of him?"

Hunter nodded, and glanced behind the trailer. Another rig was just finishing up at the scale. "Say, good to see you again, Bob, but we're holding up the parade here! I better let you go." Hunter gave the door of Bob's Kenworth a resounding slap. Bob grinned and tipped his hat. Hunter heard him turning up the volume on his CB as he drove away. It was guys like him who made the trucker's grapevine as fast and effective as it was.

Moments later, the loud but smooth roar of a Harley Davidson rose above the other highway sounds and came to a purring halt beside The Blue Knight. Sorry dismounted from behind a hefty biker whose beard, sunglasses, helmet and hair obscured his entire face. The faceless man nodded to Hunter, ignored Sorry, who had removed his own helmet, and revved the big bike's engine. It leapt away and swerved easily into the space between two semis that were just pulling away from the weigh station.

"Lookin' good!" Sorry walked around the big Freightliner, rubbing his chest and nodding in approval. He was wearing blue jeans and a plain black tee shirt, and had a grease stained army backpack hanging on the bulky curve of one shoulder. "First class, Hunter! First class! Hey! How come you don't have the name on it? You need to paint The Blue Knight in flashy gold letters right across the door."

Hunter shook his head. "Climb in, Sorry. I'll drive to Kamloops, then you can take over to Calgary. Sound fair?"

"Fair enough. Except I have an important question."

They both pulled their doors shut and clicked their seat belts into place. Hunter looked over at his passenger and lifted his eyebrows.

Sorry grinned and rubbed his hands together. His laugh filled the cab and spilled out the open windows.

"When do we eat?"

CHAPTER
THIRTEEN

"Okay, chief." Hunter had thought it over, and decided Sorry's appetite would give him a good opportunity to look for Chuck Wahl, the man seen getting into Randy's truck the evening before his death. "We stop in Hope. The Canyon Hotel. Ever been there?"

"Yep. Buddy of mine works there, slingin' suds. His old lady wanted to move outa the city, go back to the land. So they buy a little house up there, then she gets a job in Aldergrove and spends half her day commuting and the other half complainin' about it! Broads! Right?" He laughed. "So, the Canyon's one of your regular stops?"

"Never been there." Hunter pulled the rig out into the left lane to pass a camper pulling a boat with a massive outboard motor. A great ski boat, no doubt. He wondered if the girls had learned to water-ski. He had intended to take them, when the time was right.

"Ahem," said Sorry. He was looking sideways at Hunter with a sly grin. "What's up? Sounds to me like you've got one of them there ulterior motives."

Hunter shrugged, trying to decide how much he should tell Sorry about the situation. If he expected to enlist the biker's help, he was going to have to fill him in on it sooner or later.

"Don't bullshit me, man! The Canyon isn't exactly on the auto club's recommended list. What's the attraction?"

126

Hunter told Sorry about Randy's accident. "There's nothing concrete enough to warrant the police getting involved. I'm just poking around, for now, seeing what I can turn up. There's a guy might've had it in for Randy who spends a lot of time in the bar at The Canyon Hotel. Not only that, but it sounds like he was with Randy leaving the Pac-Highway scales that night. It could mean absolutely nothing, or it could be important. Like I said, I just want to nose around a little."

"Yeah. Shake the tree, see what falls out, eh?" Sorry slapped Hunter on the shoulder. "You may look like a trucker, but deep down you'll always be a cop! Like a wolf in cheap clothing." He laughed lustily.

Hunter scowled at him, but couldn't suppress an amused smile.

"So you need information on this guy, I can help. I'll have a word with Crab. That's my bud." Sorry got serious. "I owe you, man. I still owe you."

Hunter and Sorry had a stormy history that went back some fifteen years. The first time they met, Hunter busted the big biker for drugs and it stuck. It cost Sorry twelve months in Oakalla. The next time their paths crossed, Sorry was drunk and stupid and tried to pull Hunter's head off. He sobered up and smartened up in a hurry when he found out, the hard way, that Hunter had been a student of ju-jitsu since the age of twelve. A very good student. He was also bewildered to learn that the taciturn Mountie had a sense of fair play that even extended to bikers. Sorry got out of that encounter with a few bruises and a new respect for Hunter, and the incident led to Sorry becoming a covert source of information and eventually a good friend. Five years after their first encounter, Hunter had put a lot of his own time into an unsanctioned investigation to get Sorry off the hook when he was railroaded into taking the fall for a gang murder. Since then, Hunter had known he could trust the jolly biker with his life. And now Sorry was prepared to help him, as he'd expected.

Hunter nodded. "Dinner's on me."

Hunter was true to his word. He picked up the tab for Sorry's steak, which came with a golden mountain of french fries and some overcooked vegetables, and a piece of bumbleberry pie with ice cream in the hotel restaurant. Hunter only had pie, and stayed behind in the restaurant nursing a coffee while Sorry, feeling well fed, entered the bar. It was a beer parlor, nothing fancy, and about half full. Hank Williams Jr. bellowed a drinking song from the jukebox. Sorry greeted his buddy, Crab, and climbed aboard one of the battered revolving stools at the bar.

Crab held up an empty beer glass, but Sorry shook his head. "Can't do that stuff anymore. Messes up my head. Gimme a Coke." He laughed. "Hi! My name's an alcoholic, and I'm Sorry." He laughed again, and noticed a few heads swivel in his direction. He looked over at Crab and said, "Yeah, I know. My wife always tells me to turn down the volume, I'm way too loud," and laughed some more.

Crab squirted bar cola into a glass. It sloshed over a little when he slid it across the counter to Sorry. They made a little conversation, about their bikes, their old ladies, mutual friends. "So what brings you here?" Crab finally asked.

"I'm lookin' for a guy named Chuck Wahl. You know him?"

Crab nodded. "What do you want him for?" he said, with the emphasis on him.

"It's about work. The guy has a truck, right?" Sorry left it purposely vague, and hoped Crab wouldn't be interested enough to ask more questions.

"Yeah. He hangs out in here sometimes." Crab got around to wiping the spilled cola off the counter. "Don't expect to see him tonight, though." He gestured with his head to a table beside the blaring jukebox, and Sorry turned to look. Two mean looking women in halter tops and shorts sat with an even meaner looking man in a muscle shirt and jeans.

"See the broad with the big tits?" asked Crab, leaning forward and speaking softly.

"Hu-mun-ga ma-ma!" cried Sorry, then clamped his hand over his mouth and swung back to the bar.

128

"Old Chuckie likes to diddle her when her old man's on the road. See the cowboy sittin' beside her, the guy with the big biceps?"

Sorry nodded, grinning guiltily. The guy in question had been scowling in his direction ever since his little faux pas.

"He's her old man." Crab gave the counter a last swipe with his towel and added, "And I don't think he likes you."

Sorry swirled his drink around, making the cola slosh over the sides again, then continued skating the glass around in tight circles on the wet counter. "I heard that old Chuck was here the night that rig went off the Coq, 'bout two weeks ago. You hear about it?"

"Heard something about a wreck. Don't know what night it was."

"Did you know the dead guy?"

Crab shook his head, then rubbed the back of his neck, his eyes darting back and forth across the room. "Nope." Someone yelled at him, obviously signalling for more beer, because Crab filled two glasses, put them on a wet, cork lined tray, and waded into the room.

Sorry gulped his drink, debated whether it was worthwhile pumping Crab for anything else, decided not to risk it. He put down the glass, which had held more ice than cola, and slid off the stool. He had to take a piss.

He was at the urinal when the door opened and closed. Nobody showed up beside him. He looked behind him and saw Big Tits' boyfriend, the dude with the muscle shirt, standing, arms crossed, in front of the door. It wasn't a very big room. One cubicle, two urinals, and a rust stained sink. Sorry shook Uncle Albert gently and tucked him back in his jeans.

"Hey! Don't be shy," he said, gesturing towards the next urinal with his left arm. "I promise not to laugh." Then he swung around and blocked the attack with his left, let go a piston shot to the guy's gut with his right.

Boyfriend said, "Ooooof!" and doubled over. Sorry kneed him in the throat, grabbed him by the muscle shirt, intending to push him back against the door. Boyfriend slid right out of his shirt to a sitting position on the floor, and tweezered Sorry's ankles with his legs.

129

Sorry started going down to his left, but managed to grab the sink, which creaked dangerously but held. He yanked his right foot out from between the guy's legs and pivoted around, slamming his boot sole into the side of the guy's face.

Boyfriend said, "MMmmph!" and started to bleed from the nose. Sorry stood panting at the sink, watching the guy roll his head back and forth against the door. In pain, Sorry hoped. He ran some water, soaked a wad of paper towels in it, and threw it in the guy's face.

"See? I ain't laughin'," said Sorry, and pulled the guy to his feet. "What's your problem, asshole?"

The guy pulled his muscle shirt back into place and spat on the floor, then scrambled to his feet. "Cocksuckin' motherfucker," he muttered through the wad of wet paper.

Sorry lowered his head and sucked in his breath, preparing to take another run at the guy, but Boyfriend held his arms up and said, "Okay. Okay. Enough."

"I asked you a question, slime dog. What's your problem?"

"Nothin'. No problem."

"Then why'd you come in here after me? You got a funny way of bein' sociable."

Boyfriend scowled. "I don't appreciate assholes makin' wise ass comments about my old lady." He took an unexpected run at Sorry and his right fist managed to connect with Sorry's ducking skull, just above the left ear. The skull won. Boyfriend's fist glanced off and his momentum carried him around far enough around for Sorry to grab the guy's left arm and twist it up behind his back as he slammed Boyfriend's face into the mildewed crack between the wall and the cubicle door. Sorry jammed his free elbow into Boyfriend's kidney.

"While you're here," he panted, "how's about tellin' me where you were two weeks ago tonight."

"Why?" Boyfriend said to the crack his nose was in.

"Never fuckin' mind, why." Sorry's elbow dug into Boyfriend's kidney. "Where were you two weeks ago tonight?"

"Aaaagh!" said Boyfriend.

Sorry's elbow dug again.

"Sumas. I was in fuckin' Sumas on fuckin' business."

"You heard anything about that accident on the Coq that night?"

"I don't know anything about any fuckin' accident."

"How about Chuck Wahl. You know where Chuck Wahl was that night?"

Boyfriend managed a fresh burst of energy, meaning that Boyfriend suspected Chuck Wahl of doing just what Crab said he did, meaning diddling Boyfriend's girlfriend with the big tits. Sorry pushed all his weight against Boyfriend's back, mashing his face further into the crack.

"You obviously know who I'm talkin' about. You know where I can find the motherfucker?" Sorry growled into Boyfriend's ear, giving Boyfriend's kidney another affectionate little poke.

"Nnnmmph," said Boyfriend.

"You useless piece of shit," said Sorry. "If you promise to be good, I'll let you go home to mama."

As Sorry left the bar, he grinned and waved at Crab, and blew a noisy kiss at the woman with big tits.

"Your boyfriend'll be out in a minute, sugar," he said. "He's just fixin' his face."

Hunter waited patiently until he had guided The Blue Knight out of the town of Hope and got up to speed on the first gentle incline of the Coquihalla Highway before he turned to Sorry and said, "Well?"

Sorry chuckled and twirled the end of his moustache. "Can't wait for the juicy bits, can ya?"

Hunter frowned in mock exasperation.

"Seems old Chuckie likes a certain piece of tail in town, and all things point to him keeping a date with her the night of the accident. Could very well be our boy Chuck rode with your friend all the way to Hope that night." He wiggled his bushy blond eyebrows. "The lady's old man seems to think so, anyway. He didn't say it in so many words, but he did get his nose out of joint over it."

Hunter waited for the echoes of Sorry's laugh to fade, then asked, "Did you find out anything else?"

"Yep. Chuckie likes big knockers."

As the Coquihalla wound and climbed and dipped in the headlights of The Blue Knight, Sorry fell asleep against the window, making damp snuffling noises in a regular rhythm. Hunter pulled over just beyond the toll booth and nudged Sorry's shoulder with the heel of his hand.

"Huh?" The biker jerked awake.

"You want to crawl in the sleeper until we get to Kamloops?"

"Hell, no! I'll be fine, boss," he said, rubbing his eyes. "I'm wide awake now."

Five miles and seven minutes later, the snuffling started again.

Gary had arrived home late on Thursday night. Although Suzanne had rehearsed what she wanted to say to him, she'd kept her mouth shut when she saw how tired he was. We'll talk in the morning, she'd decided. Now the kids were fed and dressed and it was time for her to take them over to her father's house to open the office, and for the dozenth time she stood at the door to the bedroom. Gary slept on his stomach, his head half buried beneath the pillow, shielding his eyes from the daylight that flooded the room. The top sheet, pale blue with navy piping, was bunched at his waist, exposing his naked upper body. The sight of his sculpted back and shoulders, rising and falling almost imperceptibly with the rhythm of his silent breath, distracted her thoughts and gave her an involuntary thrill of pride. This powerful human male belonged to her, he loved her, he had chosen her to bear his children. As it often did, the child in her felt a sense of wonderment at the woman she had become.

She approached the bed. Should she wake him? Yes, she decided. He'd slept long enough. She sat beside him, lifted the pillow, uncovering his head, and suppressed an urge to nibble his ear. Playfulness didn't suit the seriousness of what she had to say. Instead, she stroked his cheek, her knuckles sliding gently over the rough stubble of his beard. His exposed eye opened, rolled sideways

132

to look at her, then closed again. Several seconds passed. Then with a throaty roar, Gary came to life. Suzanne found herself lying on her back, pinned between his legs and his chest. His arms encircled her, his hands groped her body playfully, and he nuzzled her head and neck, growling like a Rottweiler.

"Gary," she said, trying not to giggle. "Stop it!" He drew back, displayed a mischievous smile, and then resumed his ferocious nuzzling. She giggled in spite of herself, and the pace of his groping slowed. He scooped her up, holding her tightly against his chest and drew her across his body. As he lowered her back to the bed beside him, his mouth covered hers and she found her senses swimming in the warm depths of a kiss, dimly aware of his stubbled chin scraping hers. His skin was hot, his body scent stale from sleep, stale but strongly arousing. She fought to keep her senses from overwhelming her will. It would have been so easy to surrender.

"Gary," she said into his ear. "We have to talk."

"Shhhh," he said, covering her mouth again with his.

"Gary! The kids!" she said, as she pushed against his shoulders.

"They're too busy with Sesame Street to worry about what we're doing." He kept up his nuzzling.

"No, Gary. They're ready to go to Dad's. They'll come looking for me." Suzanne pulled herself up on her elbows, pulled herself away.

Gary groaned. "Oh, baby," he whined. "Look at me."

Suzanne looked guiltily and somewhat wistfully at his erection. They hadn't made love since before her father's accident. She hated to shut it down, on her own account as well as his. But there'd be lots of time to make it up to him, later. "I'm sorry," she said, making a sorry face. "Tonight, okay?" This had turned into a bad time to talk, but she couldn't put it off again. She couldn't let him leave. She climbed out the other side of the bed, then perched herself at the foot, out of his reach.

"Tonight, I'll be gone again, remember?" He leaned back against the headboard, pulling the pillow up behind his shoulders.

"No, Gary. You won't."

"Yeah. I will. That overnighter to Seattle, remember?"

Suzanne looked down at her lap, pressed her lips into a thin line. She had to sound firm, she told herself. It didn't suit her, telling her husband what to do, but this was too important to let that stop her. "I'm taking you off the road," she said.

"What?" He scrambled out from under the sheet and sat on the edge of the bed. "You're what?!"

"I'm taking you off the road." She lifted her chin, lips still pressed together, and stared him down.

"Suzy. What are you saying?" He looked incredulous. "Huh! Just like that. Good morning, honey. You're fired." He shook his head. "Huh! Just like that."

"I didn't say that."

"Well, what the fuck do you think it means, taking me off the road? That's my job, Suzy. I'm a truck driver, remember?"

"C'mon, Gary. You never really wanted to be a truck driver. You can get another job."

"Doing what? This is Kamloops, remember? This ain't the big city. What the hell other kind of job do you expect me to get, just like that, huh? You gonna give me your job in the office?" He slapped his bare thighs. "Fuckin' fired by my own wife!" He leaned toward her, peering into her eyes. "Now comes the big question. Why?"

"I don't want you ... getting hurt." She dropped her eyes.

"Go on," he said. "Explain this to me, please."

"Somebody tampered with your brakes on Tuesday. You could have been killed. I ... I don't want to lose you, too." She couldn't look at him. "Why, Gary? Tell me. Why is somebody trying to kill you?"

"What? You think ...?" He slid over to sit beside her. "Suzy." He took her hands, one in each of his, and made her look into his eyes. "Suzy, honey. You're serious, aren't you? You're really scared that somebody's trying to hurt me. Oh, Suzy, baby. It's okay. I'm okay. You don't have to worry. Hey, c'mon. What makes you think I'm in any danger?" His voice was gentle, his eyes dark with concern.

"You know," she said. "The problem with your brakes. El told me more about it than you did."

"Goddamn that El! Why can't she keep her fat mouth shut?!" Gary frowned and drew Suzanne closer, put one arm around her shoulder. "That's silly. Why would anybody want to kill a nice guy like me?" He grinned, prodding her to lighten up.

"Whoever killed Dad. It might have something to do with Waicom, like Hunter said. You were there, too, at Waicom. Maybe you saw something that you shouldn't have. Maybe it was you they were after in the first place. Maybe they think you know something?"

Gary sighed. "I don't know anything. I didn't see anything. There's nothing going on at Waicom, as far as I know. This whole thing is just somebody's overactive imagination." He put a finger under her chin, smiled and winked. "Hey, c'mon, Suzy. We're just regular folks. This isn't a T.V. show or a Shwarzenegger movie. Nobody's trying to terminate me. Look. Let's just put all this scary stuff behind us and get on with our lives, okay?" He gave her a hug. "It's been a tough couple of weeks. Losing your dad like that, it seemed like our whole lives suddenly fell apart. But we've got to pick ourselves up and get on with it, you know?"

"We can't just pretend nothing happened, Gary. If Dad was murdered, we can't just forget it and go on about our business."

"Who says your dad was murdered? Do the police think he was murdered? No. The police say it was an accident. The only person who thinks ... thinks," he repeated, "that your dad might have been murdered is a retired RCMP detective who's getting bored with being a truck driver and wants to create a little excitement in his life. Why don't you fire *him*? Tell him to butt out of our lives and leave us alone, huh?"

"You're wrong, Gary. Hunter isn't inventing anything. There's more to it than that. Dad figured that something screwy was going on at Waicom. That's why he didn't get the load cleared at the border that night, remember? If there's a chance - any chance at all - that his suspicions about Waicom got him killed, I don't want you going anywhere near them. I don't want you to have anything at all to do with them, you understand?"

"So, fire Waicom then, not me." Gary stroked her hands with his warm, dry fingers. "Look. Put yourself in my place, babe. I'm a man. I want to look after my family. I don't want to live off my wife's money, which is what I'd be doing if you took me off the road. Let me work, hon. Sure, keep me away from Waicom if it makes you feel better, but at least let me work until something else turns up. Sure, driving truck wasn't my first choice as a career. In fact, I'd rather we sold the company and went into another business all together, danger or no danger. That's no secret. But I don't want to push you to sell your father's business. Take your time, babe. Do what you need to do, it's okay."

Suzanne leaned her head against his shoulder. She'd meant to be strong and businesslike, stay in control, but she knew she was relinquishing control to Gary, and doing it gladly, without putting up any kind of a fight. She nodded, grateful for his strength and for his tenderness and for his love. He was what she needed, and maybe he was right.

He tipped her face up towards his own and kissed her, once, twice, three times softly. His lips lingered on hers, and his strong tongue parted them, gently and deliciously working its way into her mouth. She felt the rest of her tension melting away, felt her senses start to reel.

"Mommy! Veri lost my yellow crayon!"

Gary stopped kissing but didn't pull away, speaking out of the side of his mouth. "You already got somebody else lined up for the Seattle run tonight?"

"Uh huh," she answered, with the beginning of a smile.

"You can fire me until Monday, then. Looks like I've got something way more important to do tonight."

"Uh huh."

El had managed to line up a load out of Winnipeg, so Hunter and Sorry were turned around and on their way back to Kamloops by

Thursday afternoon. El told Hunter that Suzanne and Gary would expect to see them late Friday night, and that Randy's house was again at Hunter's disposal. They had a meal in Revelstoke Friday evening, and Hunter drove the last shift into Kamloops. Sorry stayed up in the cab, feeling much revived after a meal of spaghetti and meatballs with garlic toast and salad, followed by a large piece of lemon meringue pie. It stayed light until they reached Salmon Arm, a town of about twelve thousand at the southwest tip of Shuswap Lake.

"This is where Helen moved to, isn't it?" Sorry's voice was solemn for a change. Sorry had met Ken, and he'd also met Helen, Ken's widow. He knew that, for twenty one years, Ken had been Hunter's closest friend. He knew that they had started their careers together at the R.C.M.P. training depot in Regina, and that they had ended their careers in neighboring detachments in the Vancouver area. He also knew that Ken had ended his career with a bullet.

"Yes." Hunter took a deep breath, let it out again. "Helen thought she'd have an easier time with their son in a small town." He hadn't thought about Helen for a long time. She wasn't easy to think about. Thinking about her and Ken churned him up inside.

"Smart lady." Sorry couldn't stay solemn for long. "I grew up in a small town, and look how good I turned out." He interrupted another laugh with, "Hey! Will ya look at that? Pierre's Point." He pointed to a sign beside the highway.

Hunter nodded, smiling. Back in the early eighties, when Pierre Trudeau was still Prime Minister of Canada, he had passed through Salmon Arm on the train. The good people of Salmon Arm met the train with an organized protest against some government policy, and the flamboyant Pierre responded to the citizenry with the infamous one-finger salute. A representation of the prime ministerial middle finger appeared on the sign advertising a campground on Shuswap Lake. The rest of Canada may have forgotten Pierre, but Salmon Arm never would.

Hunter kept his mouth shut tight, trying not to encourage his companion. He usually enjoyed talking to Sorry (listening was more like it), but they'd been on the road together since Tuesday, except for the hours each of them had spent in the sleeper. For some reason, the old saying about a tree falling in the forest came to mind. If Sorry were in the middle of a forest where there was no one to listen to him, would Sorry make a sound? Knowing Sorry, he'd end up talking the ear off a grizzly.

Gary came to pick them up at the Ranverdan yard in Kamloops. Hunter parked The Blue Knight, and he and Sorry carried their bags towards Gary where he stood smoking beside the chain link gate under the amber glow of the security lights. As they walked towards Gary's 4x4, Hunter introduced Sorry as Dan Sorenson.

"Dan." Gary nodded, sucking in a lungful of smoke.

"I'm Sorry," said Sorry with a straight face.

"Huh?"

"Look, I said, I'm Sorry."

Gary looked at him with a mixture of wariness and bewilderment.

Sorry clapped him on the shoulder and grabbed his hand, pumping it heartily up and down. "Sorenson? Sorry? Get it?" He let go a laugh. "Nice to meet you, pal."

Gary rolled his eyes and snorted. "So you're not saying that you're sorry to meet me?" He tossed his cigarette butt on the bare, dry ground, and it bounced away in a little spray of sparks. He smiled out of one corner of his mouth, unlocking the back door of the 4x4 and ushering Sorry into the back seat.

"Damn right, I'm Sorry!"

"Well, I'm not."

Sorry laughed again. "Say, you're a lot more fun than Mr. Clean, here." He jerked his thumb at Hunter.

Hunter rubbed his jaw as he climbed in beside Gary. He was looking forward to a long shower and a stationary night's sleep. "You're gonna be sorry you said that."

They reached Randy's house in minutes, and Gary informed them that the key was under the mat. Hunter told Sorry to go ahead and let himself into the house. Once Sorry had gone, Hunter asked Gary if he'd had any further problems on the road, and Gary said no.

"I'd like to talk to you about it," Hunter said. "Are you going to be around tomorrow morning?"

Gary shook his head.

"Well, we've got to talk," said Hunter, "so we'd better do it now."

Gary sighed. "Look, you know how I feel about this ... this ... investigation of yours."

"Even after what happened with your brakes?" Hunter glanced over at the house. The upstairs lights had gone on. Sorry had found the kitchen.

"Maybe I overreacted, gave El the wrong impression. It was probably some sick fucker's idea of a joke and I just happened to be in the wrong place at the wrong time, you know?"

"Some joke," said Hunter grimly. "Humor me, okay? Tell me what happened."

Gary shrugged, lighting another cigarette and slipping the lighter back into his shirt pocket.

"When had you last checked your brakes?"

"Right there at the brake check, man. I'm not about to run a full load over the Coq without brakes! You think I'm stupid?"

Hunter's smile said, I'm not stupid either. Gary's resentment was obvious, and reminded Hunter that he was no longer an officer of the law and, whatever his motives, he was meddling in someone else's life. But he couldn't back off now. He cared too much about what had happened to Randy. He couldn't back off unless Suzanne asked him to, and maybe not even then. "Just tell me what happened, Gary."

Gary had set his trailer brakes before leaving Kamloops. He'd tested his brakes at the first brake check outside of Kamloops at the entrance to the Coquihalla, and everything was working fine when he came down from the first summit into Merritt. As usual, he checked his brakes again at the brake check on the lower half of the Coquihalla. Everything was in order.

"It was business as usual. Then I took advantage of the john there. You know how it is. Sometimes you need to sit in there for a while?" He took a deep drag on his cigarette and blew the smoke out the window. "I could've been in the john for a good five minutes, maybe more. Who checks their watch, eh?"

"Did you see anybody else at the brake check while you were there?" Hunter leaned his back against the door, turning so he could watch Gary's face.

Gary rubbed his nose with the back of his hand and exhaled another lungful of smoke. "I wasn't paying a lot of attention, but I know there was a rig parked there already, and another came in right behind me. Let's see," he mused. "I think the one already there was a chip truck, one of those white ones. The one that came in behind me parked right beside me. A scummy looking independent, an old Ford, maybe. I don't remember a company logo, didn't read any names or anything. The cab was white, I think. Dirty. There were quite a few cars, too, parked on the other side of the lot. I couldn't say how many. It's a regular rest stop, too, eh? Not just a brake check."

While he was in the restroom, he had vaguely heard a few rigs check their brakes and carry on, he said, plus he heard several men use the washroom. "I can't remember exactly. Like I say, I wasn't paying much attention. Why would I? When I came out, the rig beside me was gone, and there was another rig parked there. A CF tractor pulling a set of joints, and the driver was just coming out of the john when I left."

Someone who knew what they were doing and who was working fast could've backed the trailer brakes off while Gary was in the restroom. It could be done in as little as two minutes. But how would they know he was going to be in the restroom long enough for them to crawl under the trailer and fiddle with the slack adjustors without being seen? It would make more sense if there were two of them, one to keep watch for Gary coming back, the other to do the work. But even supposing someone had it in for him, how would they know he was going to be stopping there in the first place, let alone that he'd be there long enough for them to sabotage his brakes? And wouldn't they figure he'd have the sense to use the runaway lanes when his brakes failed? Was it just a warning?

"You remember seeing any of those rigs before?"

Gary shook his head. "One CF rig looks pretty much like another, and the CF drivers usually hang out with drivers from the other majors. At least, I can't remember meeting any."

"What about the white Ford?"

He shook his head again. "I didn't recognize the rig, so I didn't pay any attention to the driver. I don't think I even saw his face."

"Was there a passenger?"

Gary shrugged. "Didn't notice."

"Can you think of any reason someone might want to hurt you?" Hunter stared intently at Gary. Gary and Randy had both been running a load from Waicom up the Coquihalla that night. If, in fact, someone was trying to kill Gary, did that mean that Randy had been killed by mistake, or did someone actually have it in for Ranverdan Transport?

Gary snorted. "And where were you the night of the murder?" he said in a sneering voice. "Jesus Christ! I told you before. It's not like any of us are members of the mafia, or those Asian street gangs, whatever you call them. Get it? Nobody here is dealing drugs or smuggling. This isn't L.A. or New York. This is fuckin' Kamloops. I'm just an average joe, just like Randy. Average Joe Trucker. No crime. No enemies. No fuckin' murder! Can't you understand? This scare about murder is ruining my family, what's left of Suzanne's family." Gary pounded his fists on the rim of his steering wheel.

"There was no fuckin' murder," he said. "Why don't you just leave us alone."

CHAPTER
FOURTEEN

Hunter was awakened by the sound of a door clicking shut somewhere in the house. He pulled his arm out from beneath the pillow to check his watch. Eight o'clock. Could it be Suzanne entering the office downstairs? As he swung his legs over the bed and began to pull on his jeans, he heard the jingle of bottles as someone opened the refrigerator door. Of course. Sorry's hungry again, he thought. Hunter strolled out to the kitchen shirtless, still zipping up his fly. It was Suzanne.

"Good morning," she said.

"Good morning. Excuse me." He turned away to finish fastening his jeans, then crossed his arms across his chest. "I thought you were my co-driver."

"Sorry to surprise you. I just thought I'd bring over some stuff for breakfast." Suzanne gestured at the fridge. She wore cut off jeans and a sleeveless cotton shirt of pale blue, its ends tied beneath her breasts, leaving her midriff bare. "Eggs. Bacon. There's milk and butter, and coffee." She indicated a tin beside the automatic coffee maker on the counter. "Oh, and some orange juice in the freezer. I could make it if you like."

"Thanks," he said. "Don't go to any trouble. I think I'll put on some coffee, then go have a shower. I'd like to talk to you, though. Are you going to be around for a while?"

She nodded. "You go ahead, shower. I'll make the coffee, then I'll be downstairs," she said. "I'm expecting a couple of calls this morning. Gary's looking after the kids."

By the time Hunter was showered and dressed, Sorry was pouring himself a cup of coffee in the kitchen. Soon Hunter joined him on the sundeck, looking out at the sandy walls of the river gorge rising on the other side of the green flood plain, and at the muted swirls on the surface of the river. The air sparkled with morning birdsong, underlaid with the rustling of treetops as a fresh breeze brushed past their faces. Sorry started nodding and scratching his stomach, a satisfied smile hiking the ends of his moustache. His bare toes wiggled ecstatically.

"Beauty, eh?" he said. "I can see why some guys decide to move outa the smog surrounding the big city. Waking up in Surrey ain't quite like this."

Hunter squinted up at the cloudless sky, took a swallow of fresh coffee, and agreed. The sun had already warmed the rough skin of the deck's cedar railing. It promised to be a hot day.

"Talk about your fresh air, eh?" Sorry inhaled loudly through his nose, then started to cough raucously. As the coughing wound down, he thumped his fist against his chest. "Where's my smokes?" he said, and padded back inside.

Sorry volunteered to make breakfast, so Hunter refilled his coffee mug and went downstairs to see Suzanne. She was working at the computer, reading something on the desk and typing without looking at the screen. She looked up and smiled as he straddled a chair across from her.

"Well?" she said. "How's it going?"

Hunter shrugged and returned her smile. After what Gary had said last night, he didn't want to be the one to initiate a discussion of the "investigation". He wanted to give Suzanne a chance to back away from it first. "How's it going for you?" he asked, smiling sympathetically.

She sighed. "Gary doesn't believe in you," she said. "He doesn't want me to pursue things any further. He says you're chasing a long shot, it's probably all in your imagination, and that it will only upset me, prevent the wound from starting to heal, he says."

Hunter kept his quiet smile, nodding slightly to indicate that the decision was hers.

"I can't do that," she said, tucking her hands between her knees and rocking gently. "I couldn't live with myself, knowing that Dad might have been murdered and I didn't do anything about it. Sometimes it's hard to believe that Dad's really gone, let alone that there was something ... criminal about his death." She leaned back and sighed again. "You will keep looking into it, won't you? I know it's asking a lot of you, but I don't know who else to turn to."

He nodded.

"And now I'm worried about Gary, since that business with his brakes," Suzanne continued. "I'm afraid he's in danger, too, but he insists there's nothing to worry about. Do you think that someone, whoever it is, might think Gary knows something incriminating when he really doesn't? Do you think he could be in danger without knowing it?"

"Why do you say that?" Hunter asked.

"Because he was at Waicom that night, too, remember?" she said. "If they saw Dad signal to him, even if he didn't stop to talk there at Waicom, maybe they think Dad told him something later, that they might've met somewhere along the road for dinner or something. I want to show you something." She went over to a desk against the wall, took a key out of her pocket, and opened the top left hand drawer. She pulled out a sheaf of mismatched papers, brought them over and laid one on the desk in front of Hunter. "Look at that," she said. "I can't make head nor tail out of Dad's notes, but look at that." She kept her slender index finger pressed against the page, her small well-trimmed nail pink from the pressure.

It was a note, undated, written on a blank Waicom bill of lading in an almost childish scrawl.

John (home) - 403 - 256 - 1213
Please don't say anything to
anybody and please don't

144

"Please don't" was underlined heavily, both times. Suzanne pulled her finger away, clasped her hands against her body, and looked briefly away. "It sounds so ... desperate, somehow. Don't you think this could mean something?" she asked. She still stood close to him. The skin of her bare midriff was clear and smooth, gently convex like a child's.

Hunter frowned. "What else did you find?" he asked, moving his chair back a little and holding his hand out for the other papers.

"These computer printouts. Dad made a few notes on them beside the list of shipments from Seattle to Edmonton, but I can't make out what they mean."

"Beside specific shipments?"

She shook her head. "No. I looked up the bills of lading, too. There's nothing."

"Who do you think wrote this?" he asked, picking up the unsigned note..

"My guess is John Semeniuk."

"The shipper in Edmonton. Shipper or receiver or whatever he is," said Hunter. "That'd be my guess, too. I think he knows more than he's telling." He's scared, Hunter thought, remembering the greasy sweat on the man's face when Semeniuk told Hunter about Mel Collins, and remembering the warehouseman's grim face at the window. He didn't want to voice his thoughts out loud. No need to frighten Suzanne any more than she was already.

"Can I see your dad's notes?" he asked.

"I'll make copies," she said, picking up the bill of lading. "This too."

"While I'm here, can you tell me anything about a driver named Chuck Wahl?"

Suzanne frowned. "The name rings a bell. I think Dad worked with him a long time ago, but I haven't heard anything about him lately. Sorry."

"Could you tell me a little about the drivers who work for Ranverdan now?" asked Hunter. "Other than Gary, of course."

"Sure," she said. "What do you want to know?"

"Oh," Hunter shrugged, "general information. Say, how long they've been with the company, how well your dad knew them, that sort of thing."

Suzanne ran through the list of Ranverdan drivers. In addition to Gary and Randy, there had been seven other drivers working for Ranverdan at the time of Randy's death. Four of them were full time, and the other three were called in to drive the Ranverdan rigs when the other drivers were off duty, or drove rented tractors when the need arose. The full timers were Stan Murphy the Newfoundlander, Tom Buckingham, Tom "Tiny" Kubik, and Pete Whitehead, all veteran drivers in their forties and fifties who'd been with Ranverdan for at least ten years. The part timers included Pete's son, Jason, who worked on his uncle's ranch when he wasn't driving, Mike Albert, a semi-retired older driver who ran a local antique shop in partnership with his wife, and Suzanne's cousin, Tyke Wilson, a young man who still lived at home with his parents.

She gave Hunter a brief run-down on each driver, and said she could supply phone numbers and road schedules if he needed them. "The drivers are a big part of why it's important for me to keep the company running. They've all been so loyal to Dad, for so many years. And most of them weren't just employees, they were good friends. I think it means as much to them as it does to me, keeping Dad's company alive." She smiled sadly. "I'm sure they'll tell you as much, when you talk to them."

"I think I'll do a little more digging before I talk to any of them. No sense starting rumors until we get a better fix on what might have been going on." No sense tipping the murderer off, he thought to himself. "Do you know if any of them seemed to have any special interest in Waicom? Did some drivers handle the Waicom loads more often than others?"

"They all would've handled Waicom loads at one time or another. Dad set up the schedules so all the drivers would swap runs a lot, including him, although he didn't like to be away from the office

146

for more than a couple of days at a time. That way he got to keep in touch with all the shippers, make sure they had no complaints. Almost like he was doing sales calls when he was on the road."

"Your dad was a smart guy."

Suzanne nodded and turned her head away, but not before Hunter saw her eyes fill with tears.

"Hits you sometimes when you're not looking," he said.

She nodded again, and turned away to face the big picture window at the back of the office. Beyond the pane and across the lawn was a big willow tree with branches that almost touched the grass. He left her there, alone.

After breakfast, Hunter went back down to the office. Suzanne had left a stack of photo copies in an envelope with his name on it, but she herself was gone. Besides John's note, there were copies of the computer printouts marked with scrawled notes, a couple of weeks worth of dispatch schedules, and a list of the drivers with their addresses and phone numbers. Hunter sat down at the desk to study the computer printouts, but the copies were faint and the print relatively small. The handwritten notes were almost illegible, and obviously abbreviations. He regretted leaving his reading glasses in the sleeper of his truck, and decided it would be less painful to go over the printouts later. Besides, Sorry was getting restless. He had paced around the room throwing the kids' pink stuffed dog in the air, until he finally sat down and stuffed its head between the sofa cushions.

"When are we leaving?" he asked.

"As soon as we can get a lift out to the yard," said Hunter.

"Where do we stop to eat?"

Suzanne came back a few minutes later with Jo and Veri in tow, and Sorry gave the two little girls horsy rides around the room while they waited for Gary to arrive with his 4x4. The kids giggled and squealed with delight, and Suzanne laughed like a kid herself at Sorry's antics as he whinnied and snorted and scrambled around the floor on his hands and knees. Hunter felt a warmth in his chest. It was good to see Suzanne enjoying herself. He wondered when his own daughters would become young mothers. It was hard to believe they were already almost the age he was when he met their mother.

As they passed the turnoff to Merritt, Sorry whined about not stopping for ice cream at the Dairy Queen, which was visible from the highway - "Shining like a beacon", said Sorry - so Hunter promised to stop for a meal at The Canyon Hotel again in Hope. Automobile traffic was still fairly light on the Coquihalla. The elementary school year still had another two weeks to go so the big summer migrations had not yet begun. The temperature dropped as they climbed back into the mountains, Sorry dozing and Hunter watching the road, and also scanning the sides of the highway for a glimpse of wildlife. He always enjoyed sighting the occasional moose where the Coquihalla wound through marshy sections of the high country. Once he'd seen a cinnamon colored bear loping across a field towards the road, thick coat shimmering across its powerful shoulders.

Sorry came to life again about fifteen minutes before they reached the toll booth mid way between Merritt and Hope. He launched into a running commentary on passing vehicles and road signs, punctuated by bellows, whoops and belly laughs.

"Look at that no-mind in the Porsche! He thinks he's Mario Andretti or something. Whoa! Look at that. If I had my Harley, he'd be eating my dust. ASSHOLE!"

"Whoo-whee! Look at them legs! Talk about your short shorts, eh, Hunter? See that? Did ya see that? Hi, baby! She's flashin' us, Hunter. She's flashin'." He reached for the horn, but Hunter fended him off.

"Juliet Creek? What kinda Indian name is that? Where's Romeo? Isn't there something here called Romeo? Oh, wherefore art thou Romeo? Where the hell do they get these names, anyway?"

In self-defense against Sorry's non-stop chatter, Hunter searched his memory for details about the Coquihalla region. "Andrew McCulloch," he said.

"Huh? What about him?"

"Andrew McCulloch was the guy who picked those names. He was a Shakespeare nut. Let's see, there's also Falstaff, Iago, Portia, Lear and Othello. I don't remember what order they come in, but they're mostly names of stations along the Coquihalla section of the old Kettle Valley Railway. It ran from Hope all the way to some town in the Kettle Valley, somewhere around the middle of the B.C.-Washington state border. Andrew McCulloch was the chief engineer."

"Like, the guy who drove the train?"

"No. The other kind of engineer. The guy that built the railroad. Did you see the movie First Blood with Sylvester Stallone?"

"Yeah?"

"Part of that movie was filmed from the cliffs near the Othello-Quintette tunnels McCulloch built, not far from Hope. At the time the railroad was being built, back in the early 1900's, McCulloch planned the route through there, but other engineers said it couldn't be done. They figured on building a mile long tunnel bypassing the gorge. McCulloch surveyed the gorge from a wicker basket hanging off the cliffs, and built five short tunnels which did the trick. Saved them tons of money. Smart guy. Lot of guts."

"So what happened to it?"

"What happened to what?"

"This railway," said Sorry. "I never heard of it."

"If I recall correctly, it was completed in 1916 and ran until the late forties."

"No wonder I never heard of it."

"You should take the kids hiking up there to see the tunnels one day."

"Did you?"

Hunter concentrated on his mirrors as he pulled the rig into the left lane to pass a slow moving R.V.

"Did you take your kids to see the tunnels, Hunter?"

"No." Hunter pursed his lips and shook his head. "No, I didn't."

A few miles past the toll booth, Hunter pulled off the highway into the mandatory brake check area. He tested his brakes, then pulled over just past the concrete building that housed the restrooms. "I'll just be a minute," he called out to Sorry as he jumped down from the cab. He wanted to refresh his memory about the layout of the restrooms where Gary's brakes had apparently been tampered with.

Two outside doors opened into a small concrete entrance area where a small separate room holding a telephone was located. The men's and women's restrooms were situated beyond that. The men's room had three urinals and three toilet stalls. Nothing fancy, but reasonably new and clean. A guy would feel quite comfortable and inconspicuous spending a few minutes in one of the cubicles, and would be only vaguely aware of comings and goings inside the building, let alone in the parking lot.

He stepped outside again. There was another, separate rest area on a parallel road just down the slope from the brake check within easy walking distance. Its building was situated on the edge of a large oval of lawn, the far edge of which was dotted with picnic tables and benches. The rest area was clearly designed for the occupants of automobiles and R.V.'s, although there was nothing to stop an automobile from driving into the brake check area. Several people and a dog were wandering around the grassy area, stretching their legs. Hunter rotated each of his arms at the shoulder and stretched his back, then walked toward his truck. A Van-Kam tractor-trailer unit was now parked just beyond The Blue Knight, and a burgundy colored Kenworth pulling a flat-bed trailer, its cargo secure under blue tarpaulins, was just exiting the brake check area. It wouldn't be difficult to tamper with someone's rig, as long as you knew he'd be out of the picture long enough. It would take two. One man to watch, one man to work.

Sorry was standing beside The Blue Knight, his chest thrust outwards in a luxurious stretch while he exhaled a lungful of cigarette smoke. "Nice and cool up here in the mountains. What's that mountain over there, since you seem to know so much." He waved

150

his cigarette towards a smooth upward thrust that looked like it was one solid slab of rock, tens of acres in area.

"The sign back there said Zopkios Ridge."

"This is too far inland to be part of the Coast Range, isn't it?"

Hunter nodded. "Right. It's part of the Cascades."

"Yeah? I thought the Cascades were in Washington."

"Picture this." Hunter drew a rough line with his toe in the dirt shoulder beside the truck. "Over here is the Pacific Ocean. All along the Pacific, from southern California right up to Alaska, this bump is called the Coast Range. It sort of skips a few spots, but that's the general idea. The eastern border of B.C. ..." - he drew another crooked line - "mostly follows what they call the Continental Divide, which is the great big hump of the Rockies. The Rocky Mountain Range goes all the way from north to south, through Montana and Wyoming and Colorado and New Mexico into Mexico. In between, from here down through Washington and Oregon into northern California, is the Cascade Range. That's what these mountains are part of." He gestured at the looming forested slopes on either side of the highway. "Further into California, the Sierra Nevada Range takes over. And there are a whole bunch of smaller mountain ranges here and there, like the Monashee Mountains between Salmon Arm and Revelstoke or the San Gabriel Mountains north of Los Angeles, but that's the big picture. Get it?"

"How do you know all that stuff?"

"Truck stops. If I don't have a book or I don't feel like reading, I sometimes take my road atlas in and study it while I'm having dinner. I wish I had a dollar for every meal I've eaten alone at a truck stop between Edmonton and San Diego. Fun life, eh?"

Sorry dropped his cigarette butt onto the Cascades and crushed it with his heel. "At least you can afford cigarettes, though."

"I don't smoke."

They hoisted themselves up on either side of the blue cab. "Okay, Sorry. I've got an idea that'll keep you in tailor-mades for weeks," said Hunter. The big engine turned over and settled into its husky purr. "Listen to what I've got in mind."

They rolled into Hope just after one o'clock. The restaurant looked pretty busy, so Hunter suggested they go check out the beer parlor first. Sorry greeted Crab, his bartender friend, who returned the greeting with a cool "Hey, man" as Hunter and Sorry took possession of two stools at the bar. Hunter ordered a beer for himself, reasoning that it would make their presence less conspicuous and knowing that Sorry would be eager to take the wheel from here on.

As Crab put Hunter's beer and Sorry's Coke on the counter, he nodded in the direction of a man sitting in a booth near the jukebox. "Remember that dude you asked me about? That's him." Sorry nodded his thanks, exchanged glances with Hunter, and carried his drink over to the table. Hunter swivelled on his stool to watch.

"Hey, pal, don't I know you?" Sorry boomed, sticking out his big mitt. "I'm Sorry. Dan Sorenson, that is. I think we were members of the same country club a few years back, the one near Royal Oak." He leaned on his palms against the table, flexing the muscles under his black cobra tattoo, and studied Wahl's face for an indication that he'd understood the reference to Oakalla, a prison in Burnaby that had been closed down in 1991. "I hear they're buildin' fancy condos overlookin' the lake now. May find a few ghosts haunting their jacuzzi's, eh?"

Wahl must've understood. His eyes grew wary. "I don't remember you," he said, unsmiling.

"I'm hurt." Sorry's laugh bounced across the room as he slid onto the bench. "But I was just a punk then, anyway. I'd just as soon forget me myself!"

Hunter saw Wahl's posture relax, and a hint of amusement played over his face. It was a lined and weary face above a body that seemed used up, almost shrunken. His short hair was a mixture of brown and grey, heavy on the grey. Tanned forearms stuck out of the rolled up sleeves of a faded brown work shirt, and one of them sported a blurry blue tattoo. "If you were just a punk then, what are you now?"

Sorry drew himself up to full height, stuck out his chest and said, "I'm a mother fuckin' trucker now! There's my boss over there." He indicated Hunter. "Hey, Hunter! Come on over here and tell this man what a good trucker I am!"

Hunter sauntered over and sat down. He stuck out his hand. "Hunter Rayne. How do you do. But I'll let Sorry do his own talking, not that I have much choice."

Wahl responded with a limp handshake. "Chuck Wahl. Hi." The attention seemed to be cheering him up.

"Hope you don't mind us moving in on you. We've teamed to Winnipeg and back and we're getting pretty tired of each other's company." Hunter offered an apologetic smile.

"I'm not surprised," Wahl muttered with a glance at Sorry.

"Hey, c'mon! I'm a fun guy. Wait'll you get to know me better," said Sorry, with a mock look of hurt on his face.

"Okay, I'll wait," Wahl replied with a chuckle, which turned into a rattle and a shaking cough. Sorry offered him a cigarette, which he accepted with another cheerful cough. "What're you driving?" He directed his question to Hunter.

"A '91 Freightliner conventional, 350 horses. Do you drive?"

"All my life, pretty much. I'm lookin' for a new rig, makin' do with an '82 Ford for now." He inhaled loudly through his nose and leaned back, his watery grey eyes momentarily unfocussed. Hunter noted the self-conscious effort at muscle control. In spite of the early hour, this wasn't the man's first beer of the afternoon.

"I know what it's like. Expensive buggers, when they get that old. A lot of down time, never sure whether it's worth doing the repairs. This your home base?" Hunter took a disinterested swig of his beer.

"Vancouver," was the reply.

"I'm in Surrey," contributed Sorry. "Can't hardly afford to do more than drive through Vancouver these days, getting so damned expensive."

"You got that right. I actually got a house in Whalley, but I spend a lot of my days off up here," said Wahl. "Who you guys driving for?"

"Watson Transportation. How about you?" Hunter asked.

"Broker out in PoCo, Wayne McCormick. You know him?" When Hunter shook his head, Wahl continued, "Wayne's okay. Used to be a salesman for CP. It's a tough business though. Hard to make a real go of it these days."

"That's a fact. Just ran a pretty good paying load, though. My dispatcher's got me picking up the slack for that outfit that lost a rig on the Coq a few weeks back. You know the one? A guy named Randy Danyluk owned the company. He's the one that died in the crash."

Wahl was nodding with exaggerated glumness. "Did I know him? He was an old buddy of mine. We went way back, Randy and me. Way back." He took a slug of his beer, right from the bottle, and continued nodding. "I hadn't seen much of him the last few years, but I'm gonna miss the old bastard."

"Bad news, man." Sorry shook his head in sympathy. "I know what you mean. I had some good buddies die on me, and it's like you never expect it. It's like, I never got a chance to have a last ride with him, or I never got a chance to tell him about this, or ask him about that. One of the guys, I'd had a fight with. It wasn't nothin', really. I was pissed off at him for somethin' he said about my old lady, you know? But I still ... well, I loved the guy, you know? He was my friend and I fuckin' loved him. And I never got a chance to make up with him. Bad news, man, bad news."

"Had you seen Randy recently, Chuck?" Hunter asked gently.

Wahl nodded, his eyes fixed unblinking on the tip of his cigarette. "Yeah. I saw him the day it happened."

"Yeah?" prodded Sorry.

Wahl raised his eyes to Sorry's. "It was almost like you said, but I was lucky. We'd been friends for a long time, then I got pissed off about something that really wasn't his fault, and I sort of stopped being his friend. But Randy," he sniffed and rubbed his chin, "old Randy never stopped being mine. I'll probably never have a better friend." Wahl blinked rapidly as he took a last pull from the bottle.

Sorry signalled Crab for another round. "I'll buy you a beer, Chuck," he said. "In honor of old friends, old friends who we'll

154

never see again." He rubbed the side of his nose and straightened his lush moustache.

Hunter was mildly surprised to see that Sorry was, indeed, very moved. Then even more surprised to feel a sudden rush of emotion as Ken's image rose in his own mind. He could see Ken raising a glass, smiling broadly, clinking the glass against his own, something they'd done too many times over the years to count. "Yes. Old friends we'll never see again."

They all three sat in silence, in the company of old friends, until Crab broke the spell with the thud of new drinks on the table. "To old friends," they said, and drank again.

"Yes," Wahl said, "I saw Randy the day it happened." He looked from Sorry to Hunter. Their close attention seemed to validate him. He coughed a few times, took another pull from the fresh beer, and continued in the low, sad voice of a melancholy drunk.

"They wouldn't let me drive my truck from the weigh scale in Surrey, 'cause my tires didn't pass their damn standards. Like you said, you don't want to spend money on an old truck unless you have to, especially since I'm thinking about buying a new one, right? So I'm standing there ready to spit nails. How the hell can I get the money to buy new tires if they won't let me drive my damn truck?" He looked belligerently at Sorry, who shrugged and wiggled his moustache.

"So I'm standing there, and who should pull up beside me but Randy. My old friend, Randy. Chuck, he says. Long time no see. What's happening, pal? He says it just like nothing had ever happened between us, except the last time I'd seen him, I told him to go to hell and take his goddamn trucking company with him." Wahl scratched his cheek and sighed. "This company I used to haul for gave him the contract instead. It's a long story. A stupid story. But that had been a very good contract for me. Very, very good, if you know what I mean." He directed a pointed glance at Sorry, half winking at him. "So I says, Damn it, Randy! They've pulled me off the road. I gotta get out of here. And he says, No sweat, Chuck. Hop in and we can talk about it. So he gives me a ride outa there.

"Where you want to go, Chuck? he says. Like an idiot, all I wanted about then was a few beers. And I was supposed to meet somebody ... here." He motioned towards the bar with his chin. "So I said, Take me to Hope, and he says, Sure thing!" Wahl paused to chug his beer, while Sorry managed to catch Crab's eye and signal for another.

"But on the way, we got to talkin'. Talkin' like we were still friends, which I guess we always were, but I was too stupid to realize it. And he says to me, I've always felt real bad about Waicom - that's the name of the company I had the contract to haul for - about them letting you go when they changed their distribution around. You were the one that got them to use Ranverdan in the first place, and it seems to me that you should've got some kind of payback for that, you know? Like a sales commission or something, he says. Maybe I could give you a piece of it, say five percent, on the first year's gross, he says."

Crab replaced the dead soldier with a live one, and Wahl watched him with his eyes wide open, like he couldn't quite believe it. His hand curled around the bottle, his incredulous expression remaining as he resumed his story. "I was amazed, I gotta tell ya, I was totally amazed. Here was this guy, my old friend, who gave me a percentage in the first place when he started helping me out with the Waicom loads, and he's of his own free will offering to give me some kind of commission on the first year after Waicom stiffed me out.

"He dropped me right here that night. I'll be in touch, Chuck, he said. And here, he pulls out his wallet and peels out five hundred bucks. Here, he says. This is an advance, just so you know I mean what I say. It'll help you get your rig back on the road. Five hundred bucks! Just like that. Can you believe it?" He looked, again, from one to the other. "You see what I mean, what a friend that guy was to me?" He covered his eyes with one hand, the other still curled around his beer. "And next thing, I find out he's dead."

Sorry whistled softly. "Wow. That's a friend."

"What a loss, a terrible loss. So you saw him - what? - just a couple of hours before he went off the road? What time did it happen?" Hunter asked.

156

Chuck Wahl frowned. "Let me see. We must've left the weigh scale at about nine o'clock. We stopped for a coffee and doughnut in Chilliwack. He must've dropped me here some time after eleven or so. I hear he went off the road just this side of Merritt, so it wouldn't have been much more than an hour later. Damn!" His fist banged the table. "Maybe if I'd bought him another coffee here it wouldn't have happened."

"You think he fell asleep at the wheel?"

"No, no I don't think so. Not an old pro like Randy. Maybe he lost it because of a deer or moose, or some damn hotshot kid swerved into his lane, or maybe a tire blew. But you know how it is, things happen because a guy's in one particular place at one particular time. Right?"

"Yeah," Sorry commented, nodding sagely. "When your number's up, your number's up. Fate. Like a friend of mine, he decapitated himself running his bike into the back of a beer truck. He just happened to be looking at some chick in the car beside him when the beer truck slammed on its brakes, right? If those chicks hadn't been there at that particular time, if they'd stopped for a piss or something and been one minute later, my friend would still be alive. Or, like you say, if he'd just had one more cup 'a coffee he wouldn't't'a been there."

"So, do you think you'll ever see that commission he promised? Or whatever it was." Hunter put on what he hoped was a commiserative expression.

Wahl shook his head, the glumness even more exaggerated. "Don't expect they'll ever believe me. It was just between me and my friend Randy. And somehow, now that he's gone, the money isn't really important anyway. You know what I mean?"

In the spirit of the moment, they knew what he meant.

"What do you think, Hunter? Is he telling the truth? What I can't figure ... "Sorry took his hands off the wheel and his eyes off the road to gesture his puzzlement. "... is how Chuckie can suddenly be that broke up about a guy he hated for years."

"Drive, Sorenson!" Hunter scowled at him from the passenger seat. "Can't you talk without taking your hands off the wheel?"

Sorry scowled back, then made a show of staring straight ahead with his hands on the wheel at ten and two o'clock.

"Wahl's a maudlin drunk," Hunter continued. "That's why he sounds so broke up about it."

"You don't believe him then?"

"I don't know yet. He's a maudlin drunk and he feels guilty about something. He could start by making up a story like that and then begin to believe it himself because it makes him feel better. But why would he volunteer as much information as he did about that night if he had something to hide?"

"Do you believe that stuff about the five hundred bucks?" Sorry asked, hazarding a glance at Hunter.

"That's another thing. Randy was a good man, but he was also a pretty tough business man. He didn't make that company as successful as it was by giving money away. Chuck must've got his truck back on the road, so I'll believe that he got the money off of Randy that night, but did Randy give it to him?" Hunter made a mental note to ask Garth Pullen about the contents of Randy's wallet.

"You mean, he might have stolen it?"

"Possibly. It might also have been a loan."

"If he did steal it, he could've hit Randy over the head to get it." Sorry got so excited that Hunter could tell he was having trouble keeping his hands on the wheel. "Hey, how about this! He hits Randy over the head and takes the money, here in Hope, say. Randy comes to, and continues on up the Coq. But he's got a concussion, so he blacks out, and drives off the road. Hey, wouldn't that explain everything?!"

Hunter stroked his chin, nodding thoughtfully.

"Or maybe Chuck hits Randy over the head, either for the money, or because he still hates his guts. Then he panics, so he drives Randy's rig up the Coq, finds a suitable spot to send it off the road, and hitchhikes back to town."

158

Hunter shook his head. "Chuck looks like he used to be a tough customer, but I doubt he'd be capable of jumping clear of a moving rig without injuring himself."

"Would it be that hard? How fast do you figure it was going?"

"According to the wrecker who pulled the cab out of the ravine, it was still in second gear. Could've been less than ten miles an hour. But hitchhiking on the Coquihalla in the dead of night?"

"Maybe Chuckie had an accomplice. Maybe the broad with big tits, eh?" Sorry started to giggle. "She could've cushioned his fall." He honked the horn, laughing uproariously at his joke.

Hunter grimaced. "Possibilities," he sighed. "Improbable, but possible."

As Hunter watched the green bowl of the Fraser Valley open up on either side of the Freightliner's navy blue nose, the jolly biker, to his own great amusement, speculated further on the criminal adventures of Chuck Wahl and his buxom moll.

CHAPTER
FIFTEEN

Gord the landlord was puttering in the yard when Hunter turned his
Pontiac into the driveway. Gord hurried over to maneuver the
electric lawnmower out of Hunter's usual parking spot, and with an
electric weedeater in his other hand, he managed to get two electrical
cords wrapped around his ankles in the process. Hunter put the car
into park and went to Gord's rescue. The air smelled of fresh cut
grass, and bits of it clung to the old doctor's bare legs.

"You shouldn't wear thongs to cut the grass," said Hunter.

"I know," said Gord. "I didn't mean to, it just sort of happened."

"Wearing thongs?"

"Cutting the grass."

Hunter laughed.

"Any chance for a game of golf tomorrow?" he asked, once the
car was parked and Gord's weedeater fell silent.

"We just might manage a morning tee-off time at Squamish,"
Gord said, looping an orange extension cord around and around
between the crotch of his thumb and his elbow. "I'll phone and book
a time as soon as I've got this put away. How about a beer in the
back yard? Ten minutes?"

Hunter gave his landlord a cheerful grin and a thumbs up, and
carried his duffle bag into the basement suite. There was a message
from El on his answering machine asking him to meet her for

breakfast Sunday morning. "I've got some interesting dope on Waicom," she said in her message. "Call me first thing tomorrow and we can set up a place to meet."

Hunter groaned and went to the door connecting his suite to the rest of the house. "Gord!" he yelled up the stairs. "Can you book us for around noon instead?"

After an hour or so of indulging in beer and dry roasted peanuts in the back yard, during which he promised to drop in to visit the Youngs' cabin on Shuswap Lake next time he was passing through the area, Hunter settled in at his desk with a mug of microwaved canned soup and the envelope of photocopies Suzanne had put together for him. He pulled a pair of drug-store reading glasses, half-lenses, out of his shirt pocket and perched them on his nose. Suzanne was right about Randy's notes on the computer printouts. On first sight, there was nothing to gain from them except a confirmation that he'd been interested in the Waicom shipments.

The printouts listed the Waicom shipments, in order of date, giving the Ranverdan probill number, the Waicom bill of lading number, a two letter code for the origin and destination cities, specifically the first and last letter of the city in question -- VR for Vancouver, SE for Seattle -- the pieces and weight, and the gross revenue. There were separate printouts for each month. Randy had made large, loose brackets around the shipments from Seattle to Edmonton. There were some sloppy, almost illegible letters in the right margin, something that looked like 'Rybds', followed by a question mark. In addition, there were a couple of scrawled notations at the top of the page. One looked like 'PC Rs', the other like 'TB'. The 'TB' was followed by a dash and '2X'.

Hunter pulled out a foolscap notebook and started playing with the initials. If these followed the same pattern as the city codes, what could they mean? His trucking atlas was in the cab of The Blue Knight, so he called upstairs to his landlord to see if he had one. Gord knocked on his door two minutes later to deliver an old school atlas of the world, evidently left behind in the family bookcase by one of his daughters. Back at his desk, Hunter turned to the P's in the index. The first name that fit the criteria was Pacific, Washington, so he looked it up on the map. It was just east of Tacoma. Unlikely to have anything to do with the two Waicom shipments, but a possibility. He continued on through four pages of cities beginning with P, all over the globe and in small type, trying to pick out cities and towns somewhere enroute from Seattle to Edmonton. Rather than the first and last letters, he had to allow that PC could also be an abbreviation for a two-word name, such as Paden City, but since Paden City was in West Virginia, he moved on. He found his mind wandering repeatedly, distracted by names like Pas-de-Calais in France and Pass Christian, Mississippi. In the end, the only other possibles he came up with were Pincher Creek, Alberta, which was nowhere near Edmonton, and Port Coquitlam, B.C., a suburb of Vancouver.

Maybe it wasn't a place. Maybe it was a person. He checked Pete's last name, which he had forgotten (it was Whitehead), and then skimmed through the list of drivers. Tom Buckingham was a possible for TB, but that was it. He repeated the process of looking up a place name that could be abbreviated as TB in the atlas. Fortunately, there were only two and a half pages. The closest he came was Tonka Bay, Minnesota, although he briefly amused himself by trying to make a case for Tumbarumba, Australia. A search for "Rs" turned up Richmond Highlands and Riverton Heights, both Seattle suburbs, neither of them on the truck route from the Port of Seattle to the border.

By the time he was finished, his eyes burned and it was too late to call his daughters. He took a small block of cheddar from the fridge, along with a paring knife and a carton of Stoned Wheat Thins, and sat down with them on the sofa. He ate chunks of cheese on crackers, washing them down with apple juice, watching a late movie full of senseless violence, and then went to bed.

The next morning he punched in El's number just after seven thirty. He was determined to finish meeting with her early enough to drive the thirty odd miles to Squamish in time for the eleven forty five tee-off time Gord had managed to secure.

"Hello?" Her voice sounded thick and grumpy.

"'Mornin', El! I need my coffee. Where's breakfast?" Hunter asked, sounding as obnoxiously cheerful as he could. He didn't feel at all guilty about waking her up; it seemed a small enough retribution for delaying his golf game.

"Hunter? Just a sec." Then came a slightly muffled, "Damn it, Pete! Get your hairy butt outa my face. Get off the bed." And then louder, "You still there, Hunter? Hold on." He heard rustling and thudding, then a door open. "Go take a leak, you scamp, but keep away from my radishes." The door closed and she was back.

"Mornin', good lookin'! How're things?" She seemed determined to be cheerful right back at him.

"Peterbilt eats radishes?" he asked.

"Nah. He just digs 'em up and carries them around. How about the Knight and Day?"

"The one at Boundary and Lougheed?"

"You got it. Meet you there at eight fifteen." Click.

Hunter smiled. He could picture Peterbilt, a sprightly and mischievous, if not overly intelligent, black Pomeranian, trotting around El's back yard dangling a freshly pulled radish, El bellowing along behind him. Eight fifteen. Good. That gave him just enough time to clean up his golf clubs in preparation for what promised to be a very pleasant afternoon.

The waitress set down a big plate of eggs, bacon, hashbrowns and toast in front of each of them, then refilled their coffee cups. El stirred her coffee thoughtfully. "Do you think Suzanne wants to bail out?"

Hunter swivelled his wrist, his fingers stretched over his plate. "She's pretty scared, but she seems determined to hang on to her dad's company. At least, for now."

El grunted, loading her eggs with pepper, then picked up her fork.

"So, fill me in on Waicom." Hunter scooped up a forkful of scrambled eggs.

"It's like this, according to my good friends at the border." She leaned in over the table and lowered her voice. "Seems that Waicom is already under investigation by Canada Customs. A little matter of undervaluing computer parts on their customs invoices, which they can quite easily do on intercompany transactions, in order to avoid paying Canadian taxes on the stuff they bring in." She nodded knowingly and took a bite out of her toast. "It's no wonder they didn't want to make waves about the smashed trailer when they heard the authorities were involved. They wouldn't want to draw attention to themselves."

Hunter put down his fork and leaned back. "But how ... ? I don't see what that would have to do with Randy." He stroked his chin thoughtfully. "It's not like smuggling or transporting illegal goods, nothing that would implicate the carrier. It's a simple matter of tax evasion. I don't see how that would relate to Randy's behavior, or how it could possibly be a motive for his murder."

El picked up her coffee cup. "It wouldn't. You're right. All it does is explains Waicom's ... uh ... discreet behavior after the accident. Except ... " She pointed at Hunter with her fork. "... remember that shit runs downhill, right?"

"Hmmm. Like, what's sauce for the boss?"

She nodded.

"Well, I'm enlisting Sorry to help out on this. The shipper at Waicom in Seattle hasn't exactly warmed up to me, so I'd like to get Sorry in there to nose around."

"I still don't think that's a good idea. Sorry's about as reliable as a ... a ... as that snake on his arm. And he's got a criminal record. How's he supposed to cross the border?"

"He's an American, El. They can't keep him out."

She shook her head. "I think it's a mistake."

Hunter decided to change the subject. "Anything you can tell me about Randy's drivers?"

El mopped up a mixture of egg yolk and bacon grease on her plate with a corner of toast and popped it into her mouth before she spoke. She didn't know much about the part-timers, but she was confident that both Tom Buckingham and Tiny Kubik had been

164

devoted to Randy. "According to them, his shit didn't stink," was the way she put it. "Same with Murph, the Newfoundlander. You know him. All of 'em are straight, far as I know. Tom and Tiny are both married - responsible family men. Murph isn't married, but he's got a steady girlfriend in Cherry Creek. I think they might be engaged. Of the drivers, he was probably Randy's best friend. Him and Mike Albert, the old guy who's into antiques. He'd be willing to help, I'd bet, if you need any information."

"What about Pete?" Hunter pictured the long faced driver who had been at Waicom the first time he'd been there himself, the driver who was planning to stop over in Kamloops for Randy's funeral.

"Pete Whitehead? Pete's a prick. He's been with Randy a long time, but he's a guy who's only out for himself. Randy used to get pretty frustrated with him. Pete's always whining about his schedules, kept asking Randy to rearrange runs to suit his social calendar, then Randy'd have to scramble to find a replacement or juggle other drivers' schedules. I think the only reason Randy put up with him was because Ronnie had been such good friends with Pete's wife."

"Ronnie?" asked Hunter with a puzzled frown.

"Randy's wife, Veronica. The `Ver' in Ranverdan, except everybody called her Ronnie. Anyway, I wouldn't count on any help from Pete, but you should definitely talk to Mike."

Hunter made a wry face. "I don't know, El. I don't want to come right out and tell any of the drivers I think Randy was murdered." The waitress came by to refill their coffee cups and take away their plates. Hunter waited until she had left. "I wouldn't want to spook them, make them think their own lives are in danger."

El's eyes opened wide. "You think they might be? If they are, they should be told."

"I don't think so."

"Hmmm," said El, scratching the back of her neck. "Suzanne would find it pretty tough if she had a driver or two quit on her, wouldn't she?"

"Besides," said Hunter, "I wouldn't feel comfortable going public with my suspicions, at least not until the RCMP buy into it and make it official. And I can't see any of the drivers willingly cooperating with an unofficial investigation."

"They might, if you talked to them," said El.

"Why would they?"

"They're afraid of you, that's why."

"What?!"

"The other drivers are afraid of you. I've seen it. You intimidate them."

"Why? Because I used to be a cop?"

"Maybe that's part of it, but it's more than that."

"What?"

She frowned and thrust out her jaw, as if she were struggling to come up with the right words. "You're always look so ... somehow ... relaxed. And detached. You remind me of a lion walking around a herd of gazelles on one of those nature shows. You don't look like you're afraid of anything. And then there's your eyes."

"My eyes?"

"Yeah. It's like you don't miss a thing, almost like you can see right through people. See? You're doing it now." She pointed a finger at him. "You half close your eyes and you've got that spooky little smile. You look ... I don't know ... threatening somehow. Like you know something bad about me. If I didn't know you so well, know what a pussy cat you really are ...."

He waved her finger away, a disgusted expression on his face. "Come off it."

El shrugged. "Don't blame me," she said. "I'm just telling it like it is."

Hunter shook his head as he picked up the check. What El was saying wasn't really news to him, though. There'd been times when he'd sensed it himself. He didn't consider himself a violent man, and he felt the best way to win a fight was to avoid it in the first place, but his martial arts training had made him confident of holding his own in a physical confrontation if push came to shove. He guessed it still showed.

166

Some eight hours later, Hunter followed his landlord to an umbrella shaded table on the patio at the Squamish Golf Course. He plunked himself down in the plastic chair with a sigh and studied the score card briefly before tossing it on the table. It landed with a tinny clunk on the white-painted metal surface. "You know, Gord, I've been looking forward to this for weeks, and there were moments on the back nine when I wished I was sitting in a truck." A light breeze rustled the vine maples beside the patio, and he raised his eyes to the rolling grass carpet on the fairway beyond. A slow smile spread across his face. "Just kidding. I loved every second of it!"

The old doctor studied his own score, then tucked the scorecard under the empty ashtray. "For what it's worth," he said, "you beat me. I buy the beer."

"That seven wood is really working for you, isn't it?"

Gord nodded. "I don't know why I bother carting my other woods around with me. Can't get a good hit with my driver to save my life." He turned to the waitress, and they ordered two pints of pale ale. Gord settled back in his chair, looked around at the other patrons on the patio. He caught Hunter watching a foursome of young women decked out in golf togs and sun visors on the adjacent fairway. "So how are your girls?" he asked.

Hunter looked away from the fairway and pulled on his earlobe. "Okay, I guess. They're pretty busy, summer jobs and all. Haven't seen much of them the last few months." His eyes met the landlord's solemn gaze. "I guess they're growing up. It seems the older they get, the less time we spend together." Hunter sighed. "They're always busy. Like I said, I guess it's because they're growing up."

"Good! Children are much more congenial when they become adults. They start to drink beer, learn to golf." Gord's eyes twinkled behind his bifocals. "You might soon find yourself spending more time with them instead of less."

Hunter looked at him sceptically.

"Unless, of course, it's more that you're growing apart. Growing apart generally takes neglect, willful or otherwise, from both sides."

"I don't know if I'd say we're growing apart." He felt a shade of irritation. The subject was already painful to him, and discussing it was like running sandpaper over an open wound. The last thing he wanted was to create more distance between his daughters and himself. He just didn't know how to stop it from happening. "They're young women. They're busy. They've got other things they'd rather do."

"You've been pretty busy, too. I suspect your girls are still too young to shoulder all the responsibility for the state of your relationship." Gord shrugged and smiled apologetically.

Hunter frowned. He suspected Gord wouldn't have risked offending him unless he thought it was important. Maybe he's right, he thought. Maybe he just wasn't trying hard enough. Then he chuckled inwardly. El should see this, he thought. His elderly landlord obviously wasn't afraid of him, x-ray eyes and all.

The beer arrived, and the two men hoisted their mugs.

"Here's to the winner!" Gord toasted. "Who, in my opinion, is anyone who can make it around the course without losing all their balls!"

After he returned from the golf course, with a stop for fish and chips at Troll's in Horseshoe Bay along the way, Hunter threw in a load of laundry, then settled down on the sofa in front of the T.V. He thumbed the remote through a few quick cycles of the channel spectrum, then turned off the sound and stood up. He stood briefly at the sliding glass doors, staring into the twilight muted yard and trying to concentrate on the mystery of Randy's suspicions about Waicom. He knew the next step would be to ask John Semeniuk about his note to Randy, and hoped that it would be possible to get the frightened man to cooperate. Would Semeniuk be willing to talk about it over the phone? His mind wandered, and he headed to the fridge, pausing to examine its meagre contents before closing it again. He walked to his desk, stared for a moment at the photograph of his girls beside the phone, then picked up a Time magazine he'd inherited from the landlord, and leafed through it. He checked on his

168

laundry. Again, he stood at his desk, this time resting his hand on the telephone receiver. He turned away, and paced between the mute T.V. and the washing machine until his laundry had finished the spin cycle.

He started the clothes dryer, fetched a can of Coke from the fridge, and returned to his desk, resolutely picking up the telephone receiver and dialling the number of his ex-wife's home in Burnaby. Christine answered.

"Hi," he said.

"Well, hello! Haven't heard from you for a while. How are you?" His ex-wife sounded genuinely happy to hear from him, and for some reason it pleased him that she was still so quick to recognize his voice.

"Great," he said. "Busy, though. Just got back from a trip to Winnipeg. How about you?"

"Just fine. I've been real busy at work, too. The market's pretty active, so the firm always seems to have more work than it can handle comfortably. They don't want to hire anybody new, though, 'cause they figure it's only a matter of time until things slow down again. That's the way real estate is, I guess. You looking for Jan and Lesley?"

"Well, if they're not too busy ... "

"Hunter, you know they're never too busy to talk to you! Except ...," her voice was sheepish, "they're not home. They went to a movie. Sorry." She paused. "Should I have them call you when they get home?"

"No, that's all right. Uh, maybe tell them I'll try again tomorrow, or maybe Tuesday. It's not important. Just wanted to say hello."

"They'll be sorry they missed you, you know," she said gently.

"Yeah. Sure. Tell them I'm sorry I missed them, too. Good night, Chris."

He let the receiver drop gently into its cradle, then sighed and walked over to the glass doors. He laid his forearm horizontally against the door, the glass smooth and cool through his thin sleeve, and leaned his forehead against it to diminish the reflected glare from

169

the lights in the room behind him. The greens were turning grey and black as the twilight deepened. Stupid, he said to himself. He was planning to visit his old detachment in Burnaby tomorrow morning to see if he could get some background on Chuck Wahl. Maybe if he'd asked the girls to call back, he could have set up lunch, or coffee even. Of course, it was Monday. They'd be working, so they probably wouldn't have time anyway.

Gord had been telling him to try harder. Easy for him to say. Hunter didn't want to make a nuisance of himself. He didn't want his daughters having to make up excuses for not having time to see him. That's just the way life was. Hadn't Suzanne said so? Didn't she say that at that age she didn't have time for her parents? Young women just had better things to do.

El burst through the door from the warehouse and got to her phone just in time to hear a macho curse and a click on the other end. "Jesus!" she muttered. "They know I'm busy on Monday morning. Why can't they let it ring a couple more times?"

She started sorting through the notes on the desktop, making sure that she had all of the pickups covered. There was one she hadn't dispatched yet, a load from North Vancouver to Kamloops, and she held it at arms length, debating how to approach it. None of her regular drivers was going to be free in time to make the pickup, but she was pretty sure that Pete Whitehead was in the area and would most likely be available. Suzanne had asked her not to dispatch Ranverdan trucks directly now that she was back in the office full time, but with Pete being the prima donna that he was, wouldn't Suzanne just have to check with him before she could assign it anyway?

El made a face. No, whether it made sense or not, she had to either talk to Suzanne in order to dispatch Pete, or else find another driver. One way or another, she was going to have to do it soon. She pushed Ranverdan's speed dial number.

"You have reached the office of Ranverdan Transport. There's no one available to take your call at the moment, but if you'll leave your number, we'll get back to you as soon as possible. If it's an emergency, please call El Watson at 526-9393. Please leave your message after the tone." Suzanne had obviously decided on a compromise between forwarding her phone lines to Watson Transportation when she was out of the office, and cutting El out of the picture completely.

"Well, well. This looks like an emergency!" she chortled, and plunked down the receiver. She wondered if Suzanne or Gary had mentioned Gary's brake problem to any of the other drivers. In spite of what Hunter said, it seemed only right that they should know.

El looked up Pete Whitehead's pager number, and made the call.

CHAPTER

SIXTEEN

Hunter turned off the Pontiac's engine and waited for a moment, looking with a mixture of anticipation and trepidation towards the building that housed the Burnaby R.C.M.P. detachment, before he pulled out the key and stepped out of the car. Entering the front doors was like walking into a distorted replay of old memories. In the three years or so since he'd left the force, a lot had changed. The face at the front counter was unfamiliar but not unfriendly, there was a new layout and more computers in the office behind the window. A couple of young constables on their way out brushed past him as he turned away from the counter. He thought he recognized one of them, although no name came to mind, but the young man walked by without meeting Hunter's eyes. He wasn't one of them any more, but he still felt a tug of belonging, a tug of wanting to belong. Corporal Al Kowalski, dressed in civies, ushered him inside his office before clapping him on the shoulder and shaking his hand.

"Great to see you again! How's the trucking business going?"

"It's going," replied Hunter. They swapped the usual pleasantries: the obligatory how's the family exchange, what mutual friends were doing, how age was catching up to them all.

Al had always been tall and lean, but he admitted to wrestling with a spare tire and being warned by his doctor to watch his cholesterol. He slapped his belly, then ran a hand back from his forehead, drawing attention to the receding border of his dark hair.

172

"Looks like being a civilian agrees with you," he said. "You're looking pretty fit, a few more gray hairs maybe." He pointed to his own temples. "But you're not here just to show off your youthful figure, are you?"

Hunter smiled. "No. I'm hoping, Al, that you'll do me a favor. I'm trying to dig up some background information on a trucker we suspect of a little hanky panky. Any chance you could run his name through Ceepik for me?" The Canadian Police Information Computer files was the logical place to start any criminal investigation.

Al winced. "Shit, Hunter. You know I can't do that for a civilian."

"Al," said Hunter, "we've been friends long enough for you to know that no one - and I mean, no one - will even know I have the information, let alone where I got it from. I'm looking for leads, and Ceepik is the logical place to start. Whatever you tell me will go in here," he tapped his forehead, "and never come out."

Al pressed his lips together, eyes closed, and then nodded abruptly. "Okay," he said. "What do you need?"

"The guy's name is Chuck Wahl - W A H L - probably Charles, but I don't know for certain. I know he's done time, but I'd like a few details."

Al typed something into the computer, then scratched his ear, frowning, as he waited for the response. "Rings a bell with me, you know." He scrolled through the screen, then tapped a key that set the printer behind his desk into motion. When the printer had finished, he pulled out the sheets and took a closer look.

"I was on this one," he said.

He gave Hunter a run down on the case. Wahl's conviction for theft took place when he was working as a driver for Transcan Express back in 1981. There had been several Transcan employees under suspicion at the time, but Chuck Wahl was the only one the police could catch red handed. The others, primarily two warehouse workers, had been lucky enough to avoid prosecution. The R.C.M.P. were able to determine that the scheme involved employees in both

Toronto and Vancouver. It appeared that the Toronto group was responsible for misrouting freight, invariably high value consumer electronics items, to the wrong destination.

"A half dozen T.V.'s, for example, being shipped from a distribution warehouse in Toronto would, uh, inadvertently be loaded on a trailer bound for Vancouver instead of, say, for Winnipeg. The suspects, who were part of the warehouse crew unloading the trailer in Vancouver, wouldn't record the cartons as being received, but would quietly load them onto an empty - quote unquote - trailer, which was destined for the storage yard. Later that night, one of the group would retrieve the T.V.'s and deliver them to the group's retail man, who had probably lined up buyers before the shipment had even arrived.

"Meanwhile, Transcan in Winnipeg would have reported the freight short off the trailer and started a trace with Toronto. If the warehouse manager in Vancouver happened to be alerted in time, he might supervise the unloading of the Toronto load to see if the extra cartons had arrived in Vancouver by mistake. When that happened, the cartons were routinely reported as extra and shipped back to Winnipeg. It was highly suspicious that none of the missing cartons ever turned up when the unloading wasn't directly supervised, but, at the time, nobody could prove anything," said Al.

He speculated that Chuck Wahl's main role, as the long haul driver, had been to recruit the accomplices in Toronto and to hand deliver their cut to them when an operation had been successful. The local group seemed to share the most hazardous part of the job, which was retrieving the goods from the "empty" trailer in the wee small hours of the morning and transporting them off the property. The night the R.C.M.P. made the collar, Chuck had the misfortune of doing the dirty work. He very nobly wouldn't implicate his accomplices.

"Hmmph! An honorable man," said Hunter. "What happened to the other guys? I'd have thought we'd have set up a sting."

"After we arrested Wahl, the manager at Transcan strongly recommended to each of the other suspects that they find work elsewhere. We'd suggested to him that he leave the suspects in place

174

and we would look at planting an operative, but his main concern was that the company's theft problem disappear as soon as possible. So he told them that they were about to be supervised so closely, they couldn't scratch their asses without him knowing about it. Appears they both hated that idea, so they moved on."

"Where'd they move to? You ever run across them again?"

Al shook his head. "Can't help you there, Hunter. But, for what it's worth, I can give you their names and particulars."

"Shoot."

"The guy with all the experience was Robert Louis Grant, Caucasian male, six foot one and a hundred and ninety pounds, born 1942. That'd make him sixty two. If he's smart, he's retired to Arizona. The other guy is one Chien Li Mah, Oriental male, five foot nine, about a hundred and forty five pounds, born 1965 in Vancouver. He'd be in his prime now."

"He wouldn't go by the name of Steve, would he?"

"You got it." Al didn't sound surprised. "You know where he is?"

"Assuming it's the same guy, he's now working at the Seattle import distribution warehouse for Waicom Electronics, the company we suspect is involved in our little problem."

"You figure he's using the same M.O.?" Al asked.

"Maybe, but not from a U.S. Free Trade Zone into Canada. Crossing the border has got to make it a lot tougher to pull that scam. If one trailer's short six T.V.'s - computers in this case - and the other has six too many, on every run they'd have four chances of the load being examined and the whistle blown by either U.S. or Canada Customs. With heavy customs fines at stake, the company isn't likely to put up with that for long. Since he's already learned the risks in the business, I don't think he'd be playing those odds." Hunter paused for a moment. "But I don't doubt for a minute that he's involved in something, and that he's got more than one accomplice on this side of the border."

"You'd think this company, Waicom, would've called if they were experiencing any significant pilferage. Let me ask around."

"Hang on a sec, Al. Waicom seems to be a little shy about talking to the law. I heard from a civilian source that Waicom has been engaged in a little hanky panky of their own and customs is on to them. Evidently it involves undervaluing their goods on paper to avoid taxes on imports. You might check that out before you approach anyone at Waicom, make sure you're not butting into an existing investigation."

"Right. Thanks. Say, for a civilian, you sound remarkably like a cop. You getting an itch to come back?"

Hunter shook his head. Sure, there were some things he'd like to change about his life, but being a trucker wasn't one of them. "I'm totally satisfied with being a truck driver."

"Yeah, a nosy truck driver. You want to tell me why you're looking for this information? If there's a crime involved, why not just turn it over to us, or whoever's jurisdiction it falls under?"

"Remember that rig that went off the Coq just south of Merritt? It took a couple of days to find it, and when they did, the driver was dead and the trailer had busted wide open and spilled cartons of computer parts out into the wilderness. You hear about that?"

"Aha! So those computer parts belonged to our friends at Waicom Electronics. The driver was from Kamloops, wasn't he?"

"The driver was a friend of mine, Al." Hunter inhaled and exhaled slowly. "The local officers have reviewed all the available evidence, and there's nothing specific pointing to foul play. I'm working on a hunch. If I get something solid, it goes back to you guys."

"I see," said Al, nodding thoughtfully. "Is there anything else I can do for you while you're here?"

Hunter frowned. Although he had nothing to do with Waicom, Rick Bilodeau was a man with a motive. Hunter decided to take advantage of Al's cooperation and get him to run Bilodeau's name through CPIC, too. He wasn't surprised to find out that Bilodeau had a criminal record. During the past twenty years, he'd been convicted of assault, breaking and entering, and impaired driving on more than one occasion. He'd served eighteen months in Oakalla from 1983 to 1984, which would have put him there at the same time

176

Chuck Wahl was serving out his sentence. Bilodeau's latest assault charge had been laid in Edmonton, Alberta in 1990.

"You know Sam Manji in the Surrey detachment?" asked Al.

"Yes, of course I know Sam. Well. We worked together a couple of times. Why?"

"Might not hurt to get some first hand information on this turkey," said Al, lifting his telephone handset and punching in a number. When Sam came on the line, Al said, "There's an old friend of yours here looking for some information on one Richard Claude Bilodeau. You know the gent?" Al nodded silently at the response. "Well, I'll let you talk directly to the guy who wants the information. Hang on a sec." He winked at Hunter and passed over the handset. "I've got a meeting to go to, but make yourself at home here." Al gestured at his desk. "I'll trust you to show yourself out." Hunter thanked him for his help, and they shook hands before Al went out the door.

Sam sounded delighted to discover who he was talking to, and Hunter went through the same reunion routine as he had with Al before Sam got down to brass tacks. He had had a couple of first hand encounters with Bilodeau in the past six months. At his last arrest, Bilodeau had been ordered to attend substance abuse counselling, had subsequently been enrolled in a residential addictions treatment program but was kicked out in the first week for being disruptive. He currently collected welfare, but spent much more time in the bar than a welfare income would permit. The R.C.M.P. hadn't any hard evidence on whatever he had going on the side, but suspected he was selling drugs, among other things, to supplement his meagre welfare checks. Whatever he was doing, it was bound to be illegal. Hunter asked his friend about Bilodeau's driver's license, whether or not he was licensed to drive a truck with air brakes. If he had been, he'd lost it, said Sam. His most recent conviction was for driving while impaired.

Hunter thanked Sam for his help, and hung up the phone. He sat back in the chair and closed his eyes, mulling over the information he'd just obtained. It might be useful to know if Bilodeau and Wahl had met during the six months they were both at Oakalla. It might also be useful to know how Bilodeau made the extra money that he was pouring down his throat every night at The Goal Post, a bar also frequented by Wahl. It seemed like too much of a coincidence, but it was always possible the two of them were in cahoots. The lack of a driver's license didn't eliminate Bilodeau's possible involvement in Randy's murder. The roads were riddled with unlicensed drivers taking a chance on not getting caught. If a man were prepared to break the law by stealing or repeatedly beating up his girlfriend, he certainly wouldn't shrink from driving without a license. It would be interesting to see what Sorry came up with.

Hunter drummed his fingers on the desk, staring at the phone. Here he was in Burnaby, just a few minutes drive away from where his daughters lived and worked. Hadn't he told his ex-wife that he'd call the girls today? He looked at his watch. They probably weren't home, but he could always leave a message. What would he say? That he was leaving town again tomorrow and wouldn't be home until Saturday? He could just say it was about time he took them out for dinner. They could name the date. He paused with his hand on the phone, then snatched up the receiver and punched in the number. What the hell.

It was Chris's voice on the answering machine, her office voice, managing to sound friendly and professional at the same time. "After the tone, please leave your name, number and a brief message. Jan, Lesley, or I will return your call as soon as possible." The tone sounded. Hunter opened his mouth, then caught his breath. How would he say it? Should he start with "Hi, Chris" or "Hi, Jan and Lesley" or "Hello everybody"? These three women had been the most important human beings in his adult life. He'd lived with them all for more than thirteen years, he'd seen each of them naked and in tears, he'd changed diapers and kissed hurt knees and shared some of the worst and the best moments of his life and theirs, and now he didn't know how to talk to them. The tone sounded again.

Hunter hung up the phone and left the detachment.

178

CHAPTER
SEVENTEEN

The rusty yellow Volvo rattled to a stop in the parking lot at The Goal Post and the driver's door swung open, adding another dent to the side of the multi-colored K-car parked beside it. Sorry slammed the door shut, then bent to examine his reflection in the side mirror. Hunter had given him a hundred bucks for expenses while he sussed out this Bilodeau guy, and he just might have to buy some foxy chick a drink. As part of his cover, of course. It had been a while since he'd been out to a bar with that much cash in his pocket. Hell! It'd been a while since he'd been out to a bar! He preened his moustache, turning his head from side to side, then licked his finger and straightened his eyebrows. He stood back and patted the snarling grey wolf on his teeshirt. Satisfied, he blew himself a kiss. As he walked across the parking lot, he flexed his wrist as if his fingers were curled around the throttle of his Harley. The hooded black cobra slithered along his forearm, sexy as ever. He chuckled out loud. Sexy as ever.

Just as he was reaching for the door handle, the door swung outward and there stood the blonde hag Hunter had brought by to spend the night. Behind her, with a hand on her rump, was a big man, middle aged, wearing jeans and a light colored plaid shirt. A small paunch strained the two buttons above his belt buckle, and a baseball hat sat back on his head exposing a tall, pale forehead.

"Hey, Sorry. Hi!" she said in her smoke and whiskey voice, grinning. "Remember me? Carla. I was at your place last week, with Roy Rogers, remember?"

"Right. Carla," said Sorry. "Roy Rogers. Right." Hunter had told him not to let his target know that he had any connection with Hunter, and this big-mouth blonde could easily blow his cover.

Carla reached behind her and grabbed the guy following her, pulled him up beside her, wrapping both her arms around one of his like she thought he might make a run for it. "Sorry, this is Skip," she said.

Skip didn't look too friendly. "Let's go," he said to Carla, heading on through the door and letting it close behind him.

"Gotta go!" she said to Sorry, then lowered her voice to a whisper. "Guess what Skip does for a living? You know what they say, eh? Lonely truckers make good ..." She flashed her gold tooth roguishly, "... lovers!" She winked and followed old Skip out the door.

Sorry heaved a sigh of relief. He hoped they were leaving for good.

It was just after eight o'clock, a time at the Post when plaid work shirts and steel-toed boots start to give way to clean jeans and cowboy boots. A band was setting up on the raised stage, and a few "test, test"'s burst sibilantly through the speakers. The room welcomed Sorry with the familiar smells of smoke and beer. He leaned against one of the tall tables that ringed the outside perimeter of the room and took stock. At the far side were three or four guys he knew, one of them had worn the patch of the now defunct Black Cobras, like himself. If necessary, he could always approach them and see if they could point out his target, but he'd just as soon not involve anybody who might ask stupid questions. From the description he'd been given, the guy was a string bean over six feet tall, sloppy and ugly, with an overgrown moustache and a broken front tooth. He'd laughed when he heard that, of course, and observed that the description fit most of his friends, except for maybe the string bean part.

"Name your poison, pal!"

180

Sorry put on his best scowl as he looked the waiter up and down. "Where's the chicks with the big tits and the short skirts? I didn't come out to a bar to get served by a friggin' man!"

"You want a drink, or don't ya?" The waiter's expression as he rested the rim of his empty tray against his hip told Sorry he didn't care one way or the other.

"Coke. Straight up!" The waiter rolled his eyes and turned on his heel. "With a lime!" Sorry yelled after him. "And you're not even fuckin' pretty!"

He'd finished five Camels and two Cokes, with ice and no lime, and the band was half way through its first set by the time he saw a guy fitting Hunter's description of Bilodeau. The skinny guy, wearing grubby jeans and a brown shirt that looked too small even for him, was standing beside one of the booths talking to a young, clean looking guy sitting alone behind a glass of beer. Sorry watched String Bean walk out the door, then kept his eye on the kid with the beer. The kid drank the rest of his beer in forced spurts, like a five year old who has to finish drinking his milk before he can go out to play. Then he searched in his front pocket for a coin, slammed it down on the table, and left. Less than five minutes later, String Bean was back. Sorry grinned into his empty glass as he tipped the last piece of ice into his mouth. Lookin' good!

String Bean was much too sociable a guy. He kept stopping to talk at tables, clapping men on the back and putting his arm around women's shoulders, his mug of beer getting lighter the farther he got from the bar. Sorry noticed that most of the women he cozied up to drew their heads away, as if String Bean's breath stank. Two and a half Camels later, during the band's rendition of Achy Breaky Heart, Sorry followed his target into the can. Sorry was still whizzing when String Bean started zipping up.

"I'm celebratin'", Sorry said, grinning at String Bean from behind his cigarette. String Bean turned away.

Sorry spat his cigarette into the urinal. "I said, I'm celebratin'!" he repeated, louder.

"Yeah? So?" String Bean's upper lip curled back to reveal the broken tooth. He paused with his hand on the door handle, the cuff of his brown shirt riding halfway up his forearm.

"I just got a new job, and I wanna get stoned!" The last word exploded from the bottom of Sorry's massive, by comparison, chest. He grinned and zipped. "Say, pal, I saw you out there. I can tell you know a lotta people. Maybe you could introduce me to somebody. Let me buy you a drink!"

String Bean's unruly moustache twitched uncertainly.

And then Sorry lucked out. The door opened, blocking String Bean's exit, and in walked one of the guys Sorry knew wearing leathers and a Harley teeshirt. "Hey, man! How you been?" He punched Sorry's shoulder. "How's your chopper? You got that stuff done you wanted yet?"

Sorry tucked in his wolf shirt and hiked up his jeans, saying "Shit, Max! Fuckin' panhead parts are so fuckin' expensive. I haven't been getting much work the last couple months and couldn't come up with the fuckin' dough." He stuck up his thumb and grinned. "I'm workin' now, though, man. Start tomorrow. So, tonight, I'm gonna party!" He lowered his voice. "Came down to see if I could score some quality weed."

Max nodded discreetly towards String Bean. "Fuckin' A, man. See you around."

Hah! A character reference. He couldn't have planned it better. Five minutes later he was out in the parking lot with String Bean. Sorry flashed some bills, and managed to cajole the skinny man into sharing a joint first. "Quality control for you, man. Taste test for me. You know what I mean?"

String Bean cupped his hands around a lumpy cocoon and lit up, then passed the joint to Sorry.

"You prove you got a good product, then I'm your customer for life, man." Sorry sucked the smoke in through clenched teeth, held his breath and said in a strangled voice, "And I got friends, man. Last supplier we had fuckin' died - fuckin' coronary - and we need a good source." He coughed, hawked, and spit. "Righteous! Good shit, man. Good shit." He clapped String Bean heartily on the shoulder with his big mitt and smiled into his face. "You just made a sale, my man. Lemme buy you that drink."

It was indeed good stuff. Sorry was flooded with a feeling of confidence and well being, and String Bean's hostile attitude towards him seemed to dissolve. The skinny man was becoming less uptight, almost friendly. Sorry ordered a jug of beer for String Bean and another Coke for himself. "You know how it is, man. I drink, I fight. I smoke, I get mellow. Good business for you, eh? Can't take a chance on booze again, or I'll end up back in the slammer. I got me an ol' lady and a couple 'a kids. Can't take the chance any more. My ol' lady would have my balls." Sorry's laugh boomed across the bar. "For breakfast!"

"Bullshit!" The skinny man's grin exposed his broken front tooth. "My guess is you're a mean mother fucker when you get tanked. I don't believe any broad would dare mess with your balls, unless you're married to a fuckin' gorilla."

String Bean practically inhaled the first glass of beer, so Sorry didn't waste too much time getting to the meat of things. "Yeah, man. What's your name anyway? Bilodeau, eh? You a frog? My ol' lady's from Kebec. Nice to meet ya." They shook hands, exchanging moustache shrouded grins. "Like I was sayin', I got a new job starting tomorrow. Drivin' truck. Yeah. Just call me a mean motha' trucker. I'll be drivin' for an outfit called Ranverdan. Randydan." Sorry roared in amusement. "That's me. My name's Dan, right? Randy Dan Transport."

"Ranverdan, eh? No shit? I know that outfit. Guy got killed a few weeks back, old Randydan himself. You hear about that?" String Bean emptied another glass.

"Yeah, I heard. Gotta be pretty stupid to fall asleep on the Coq. You don't mess around with a mother fuckin' highway like that." Sorry nodded grimly. "Gotta keep a few pills in your pocket, keep you outa trouble."

"That's what you heard? You heard he fell asleep?" String Bean looked down his nose at Sorry, his mouth hanging open.

Sorry shrugged. "What else?"

"The guy was a fuckin' prick. Maybe he had it comin'." He lifted his refilled glass and drank. The band was playing Boot Scootin' Boogie.

"No shit? I heard it was an accident. You heard otherwise?" Sorry tried his best to look and sound impressed.

"Maybe." String Bean wiped beer foam off his moustache with a shirt sleeve. "Maybe not."

"Where'd you hear it from? Somebody here?"

String Bean just sniffed and gave a little shrug.

"You're bullshittin' me, man. You never heard dick." Sorry leaned closer. "Listen, Bilodeau. This is my new job we're talking about. If somebody's out there offing drivers, I wanna know about it."

"Cool it, man. Nobody's offing drivers. Maybe I'm just sayin' that somebody had a good reason to want that fucker dead. No more, no less. You understand what I'm sayin'?"

"You ever drive?"

"Me? Nah." String Bean flopped a hand in disgust, then pointed to his head. "I prefer to work with my brain, not break my back workin' for some shit-ass company."

Sorry closed his eyes and took a deep breath. Lucky for String Bean he was mellow tonight instead of mean. "Then what would you know about any fuckin' accident? Sounds to me like you're full of shit." He grunted and squared his shoulders, just in case String Bean had forgotten that Sorry's chest was twice the size of his own.

"I got friends in the business," the skinny man said defensively, starting to squirm.

"Pah!" growled Sorry. This was fun. He shoulda been an actor.

"I got friends," insisted String Bean. "Matter of fact, my old lady -- former old lady -- was sleepin' with that Randydan creep. Like I said, maybe he got what was comin' to him."

"You?" Sorry said incredulously. "You offed the guy?"

"Fuck, no!" Little flecks of beer foam flew from String Bean's moustache. "You think I'd be stupid enough to tell you if I did?" The skinny guy fidgeted with the cuffs of his shirt, looking like he wished he was somewhere else. Anywhere else.

184

"Then who did?"

"Nobody, man. He did it to himself, okay?" String Bean's knuckles whitened around the handle of the beer jug, and his eyes skittered around the edges of the room. "He fell asleep, like you said." His voice was getting loud and squeaky.

Sorry figured the skinny guy was about to become unglued. "Shit. So the guy's dead. As long as it ain't gonna happen to me, let's change the subject." Sorry lowered a bushy eyebrow. "Chill out," he growled. "I'm celebratin', remember? C'mon, lighten up." He clapped String Bean's scrawny shoulder and grinned.

"Yeah. Sure." String Bean emptied the rest of the beer into his glass and buried his nose in it.

"I gotta build a good relationship with my new supplier, right?" Sorry winked. "We're gonna be doin' lots of business, right?"

"Yeah. Right." He craned his skinny neck to look nervously around the room. "That reminds me, I got people to see. Duty calls." He shrugged, making what looked like an attempt at a nonchalant wave. "Thanks for the beer, eh? See you around."

Sorry watched String Bean's hand stop just short of patting Sorry's shoulder. "Yeah, right. Brain duty. See ya." Sorry flashed him a sardonic grin. Under his breath he said, "Fuck off."

He sat there a while, watching String Bean making his rounds and generally enjoying the mellow feeling. He and Mo didn't do pot much any more. They were both getting old, he guessed. Somehow they'd come to prefer comfortable and sober over exciting and stoned. Life was good. He loved Mo. He loved the kids.

He was still sitting there, propped comfortably on his elbows with his back to the table, feeling too mellow to move when he noticed Chuck Wahl heading up to the bar. Old Chuckie looked rumpled and all one color, a drab olive green, and he walked with a limp that reminded Sorry of the gout he'd had in his big toe just after Christmas. The old trucker ordered a beer and stood there watching the bartender pull the bottle out of the cooler and jack off the cap. Sorry looked for String Bean. He saw the skinny man walk right up behind old Chuck. Wahl paid for his beer and stepped back, barely missing String Bean's scruffy size twelves. The two men exchanged a few inaudible words, obviously not friendly ones. String Bean got a pint of beer and attached himself to a group of losers at the pool table. Old Chuckie sat alone and gloomy on the other side of the room. Sorry continued to sit there watching, mellow and contemplative, until he started to feel sleepy. The band was on a break. Time to get up.

It occurred to Sorry that there might be a reason for him to talk to old Chuckie, but he couldn't quite remember what it was. Couldn't hurt to say hello, now, could it? He carried his empty Coke glass over to Wahl's table and relaxed himself into the chair beside the old trucker.

"Hey, man! Remember me?"

"Sure. Hope. On the weekend." Wahl barely touched Sorry's extended paw, then edged his chair away.

Sorry took that as a hint that maybe he was behaving a little too mellow. He straightened up and combed his blond hair back from his forehead with the fingers of both hands. "That's right. We were talkin' about that guy who died, remember?"

Old Chuckie nodded, thrusting out his lower jaw. In regret, or was he annoyed? Sorry couldn't tell, and didn't care.

"Well, guess what? I got a job drivin' for that company, starting tomorrow. Funny thing, eh?" Sorry raised his eyebrows in mock astonishment. "What you might call a real coincidence, eh? A real ko-inky-dink!" He laughed heartily, he wasn't sure for how long. The pot was playing tricks with time.

Wahl made a disgusted face, obviously not amused. He was altogether not very sociable. If old Chuckie was such a tight ass, reflected Sorry, he should fucking stay home to do his drinking.

"So. Anyway." Sorry nodded, pushed his chair back from the table. "Thought you might find that interesting." The old man just took another determined sip of his beer. "Enjoy!" said Sorry. He was glad to get out of there. What a fun bunch of guys!

He smoked half a joint on the way home. It was good stuff, all right. When he pulled into the driveway, CCR's "Who'll Stop the Rain" was playing on the oldies station. Those were the days! Young

186

and tough, they'd raise hell till dawn. He leaned the Volvo's seat back and listened, a warm smile spreading across his face and waves of contentment washing over his whole body.

That's where Mo found him in the morning.

CHAPTER
EIGHTEEN

The phone rang seconds after Suzanne had punched off her alarm and tucked her arm and shoulder back into the warm bedclothes. She raised herself on one elbow and rattled the receiver out of its cradle, almost dropping it. She pressed it to her ear, worrying that she'd cut the line. "Hello?"

"Are you in bed?", breathed a husky male voice. "What are you wearing?" A throaty growl. "Answer me, woman. Are you wearing anything at all?" the voice continued, and began to pant heavily.

Suzanne snuggled down into her pillow, trapping the receiver between her ear and shoulder, hugging herself with both arms. "Silk," she whispered. "Soft, smooth black silk."

"Oooh, foxy lady. Tell me more."

"I'm all alone here in a big cold bed," she said sulkily, "and my manly husband is miles and miles away."

"Your husband must be a fool," said the voice. "Don't you move, you little sex kitten, I'll be right there."

Suzanne giggled. "Great timing, sweetheart. My alarm only just went off."

"I knew that, babe. I wanted to be the first thing on your mind."

Her smile dissolved. She wondered if Gary knew that her father being dead had been the first thing on her mind every morning for the past three weeks. He couldn't know, she decided. "Are you on the road already?" she asked.

"Nope. I just washed up in the restaurant john and I'm about to go for breakfast. Then I'm goin' to Houston, Houston, Houston," he sang.

She laughed. Houston was a tiny town about halfway between Prince George and Prince Rupert in northern B.C. "Well, I hope you're goin' to Terrace, Terrace, Terrace, 'cause that's where you're supposed to be by two o'clock." She wriggled up to a sitting position against the headboard. No black silk. She was wearing an oversized white tee-shirt sprinkled with valentines.

"No problem, babe. You got me a load out of there yet?"

"I think I'll have one in Rupert, but it might not be ready until tomorrow. I'll know by this afternoon. I've called our tap accounts near Terrace, but nothing's moving out of there today."

"Did you check with El to see if she knows of anything?"

Suzanne's jaw stiffened. "I'll find something on my own," she said, unable to keep the anger out of her voice. "You know, that goddamn El dispatched Pete without going through me yesterday. She claimed it was an emergency but that's bullshit!"

"Hey, kitten, settle down. El's a big, tough broad, but her heart's in the right place. Don't be so sensitive about it."

Suzanne frowned. There he was, accusing her of being too sensitive again. Was she overreacting? El would never have dispatched Pete that way when her father was running the operation, why should it be any different now? Was El simply trying to help out, or was she trying to steamroll Suzanne and take control? Either way, it was a clear message that El didn't think Suzanne was capable of staying in control of the company herself.

"Suzanne?"

"I heard you."

They talked about the kids, and Gary promised to call when he reached Terrace.

"I love ya, babe," he said, sounding serious, almost intense. "Don't you forget it."

""I love you, too. Gary?"

"What, babe?"

"Be careful," she said.

Hunter had just tried to call John Semeniuk at work for the fifth time in two days. Each time, the shipper-receiver at Waicom in Edmonton had either been on another line or on a break or in a meeting. Hunter didn't want to leave his number, or even his name. He didn't expect John would return his call, anyway. In fact, he didn't think John would be willing to say much once he did get through. He had decided to connect with him at work first, in order to verify that the number on Randy's note was indeed his, and to ask for permission to call him at home. Hunter didn't want to spook the man. He seemed frightened enough already, maybe too frightened to talk, even from home.

He was packing his duffle bag for his next trip out. El had a trailer for him to deliver to a freight forwarder near Sea-Tac Airport this afternoon, and then he was scheduled to make a pick up in Tukwila bound for Edmonton. He owed El for coming up with the job, because it meant that he'd be able to keep in close touch with Sorry, who was picking up the Waicom load in Seattle and would be following roughly the same schedule to Edmonton. With luck, Hunter might even be able to set up a meeting with John Semeniuk after hours while he was there.

The phone rang and he answered it left handed, a ball of clean underwear and socks occupied his right.

"Hey, man. I need a lift to Annacis." It was Sorry.

"I thought Simone was going to drop you off."

"Goddamn battery died."

"Sorry, ..." Hunter began, then sighed.

"Cheer up, boss. I got some stuff to tell you. I talked to that scuzzbucket at The Post last night, eh? The frog."

"Okay. I'll come get you. See you in about an hour."

An hour later, Hunter was navigating the Pontiac through the winding residential section of River Road, heading for the bridge that spanned the Fraser River between the south side of the delta and

190

Annacis Island. Sorry had just told him about Rick Bilodeau coming face to face with Chuck Wahl in The Goal Post.

"So you think the two of them know each other?"

"Maybe they do, but they aren't buddies. I'd put money on it." Sorry gave a little laugh. "Chuckie's a die-hard booze man, for one thing, and String Bean's an equal opportunity substance abuser, and a shameless dope pusher. Being somewhat of a redneck, I don't think Chuck approves of String Bean. Much like you don't approve of me." He vented a big laugh. "But you at least like me, don't ya? Admit it, Hunter." He prodded Hunter's shoulder. "You can't help yourself, can ya? You like me!"

"Okay, okay. I admit it." Hunter grinned at the big biker. "I like you, you drug addled clown. Even envy you sometimes."

That got a bigger laugh. "Yeah. Sure. What's to envy? C'mon. Out with it. What's to envy?"

Hunter shrugged.

"C'mon, you dirt bag. Now you gotta tell me."

Hunter shrugged again. "You're ... loose."

"Loose?"

"You have fun, you party, you don't let stuff bother you. You can let it all hang out." Hunter looked out the driver side window, then back at Sorry. "I'll bet it doesn't even bother you to go to bed without brushing your teeth."

"Yeah, you're right about the teeth." Sorry bared his gums, showing off a set of front crowns. "Most of them aren't really mine anyway." He nodded, quiet for a moment. "But sometimes having fun and being happy are a zillion miles apart."

"You're not happy?" asked Hunter, surprised.

"I didn't say that." Sorry's laugh boomed again. "I was just trying to be deep. I can have fun AND be happy."

"There. That's it. I envy you for that. And for being - I don't know - I guess for being an `in your face' kind of guy, for not giving a damn about what's the socially acceptable thing to do."

"I can't see you being that way, boss." Sorry shook his head, grinning.

"That's my point."

Sorry's grin faded. "Good," he said. "That makes us even. You envy me for being an outlaw, and I envy you for being respectable. Sort of." Then he muttered, "I can't believe I've spent almost twenty years bein' friends with a fuckin' cop."

Sorry finished filling Hunter in on his conversation with Rick Bilodeau. "I'm not sure whether the scumbag really knows who did it, or if he was just trying to impress me. What do you think?"

"I don't know, but it sounds like he's worth a closer look." Hunter told Sorry what he'd found out about Steve Mah. "From the way the receiver in Edmonton behaved, I'd say that the one to work on at that end is the warehouseman, the mean looking one with the ponytail. I hope to find out more about him today or tomorrow, so I can fill you in before you get there. It'd be nice if we had the time for you to ease yourself into their confidence, but we can't afford it. The longer we wait, the harder it will be to put the pieces together well enough to convince the authorities. Besides, in spite of what Gary says, he could be a target and if he is, the sooner you find out what's going on at Waicom, the better."

"Since when did I become Gary's fuckin' fairy godmother? He's a big boy. I don't want to put my ass on the line for him, tailor-mades or no tailor-mades."

They'd just come to a stop in the left turn lane, and were waiting for the green arrow. Hunter leaned back against the seat and eyed Sorry with alarm. "Whoa! Let's get something straight. I don't want you putting yourself in any kind of danger. All I want from you is to talk to these guys, try to get some information, like you did last night. That reminds me ...." He dug into his pocket. "I guess you smoked your expense money last night. Here's another hundred bucks. Mah likes to talk about little white pills."

Sorry's eyes lit up. He licked his big thumb and counted the bills, then shoved them deep in the front pocket of his jeans.

Hunter pulled away from the light, making a left turn off of the highway onto a curving two lane road. On one side of the road, bumper to bumper and fender to fender, there were acres and acres of imported cars, recently off-loaded from freighters at the Fraser

River docks. On the other, large expanses of land sat empty, waiting for development. It was covered with long matted grass and tangles of young trees. "Remember, just ask questions. Make them sound like stupid questions if you can, so you aren't seen as a threat."

Sorry snorted in amusement. "I'm a natural!"

"You are a natural. I have total faith in you, Dan. You're like some kind of snake charmer. You play your flute or blow in their ears, or whatever it is you do, and these felons all seem to want to tell you how bad they are. I guess they're trying to prove that they're as bad as you are, you think?" They both grinned, and Sorry preened his moustache.

"And whatever you do, don't put yourself at risk. All you have to do is talk to these guys and get them to talk to you. Got that?" When Sorry just laughed, Hunter continued, "Sorry, do you understand what I'm telling you?"

"Yes, boss. I got it, I got it, already. No rough stuff. I'll just try to get over my natural tendency to keep my mouth shut, and I'll try very hard to talk to these guys."

They were passing through an area of light industry, on either side were buildings with small offices attached to large warehouses, with trailers of all sizes and colors backed up to loading doors and parked against chain link fences. They were just blocks from Watson Transportation's yard.

"What time will I have to be on the road?" asked Sorry suddenly.

Hunter shrugged. "I've got to leave right away, but you probably don't have to go until one o'clock or so. Lots of time yet."

"Great. Stop! Stop here. I got a good idea. Let me off here, and nobody has to even know you gave me a lift."

Hunter braked the Pontiac, easing over to the shoulder. He surveyed the signs along the low sprawling building beside the road. "Oh," he said. "I see."

Sorry reached into the back seat for his backpack, hiked it onto his shoulder, and gave Hunter a cheerful wave. Hunter smiled as he watched the big biker stride purposefully towards The Island Kitchen cafe.

Suzanne had fed the kids their lunch of grilled cheese sandwiches and alphabet soup, and now they were playing in the fenced yard behind the house. Even with the windows cranked open and their happy chatter clearly audible, she made a point of looking out the big back window now and then to make sure they were alright. It was while she was watching them, her back to the office door, that Pete Whitehead arrived, clearing his throat and scraping his dry boots on the door mat to let her know he was there. Pete's long face was as morose as ever. The man hardly smiled at the best of times, so it didn't mean much. She greeted him cheerfully, started looking through her out basket for his check.

He stood in front of her desk, eyes on the baseball cap with a Ford logo he was holding in front of him with both hands, like a little boy in front of the school principal. He cleared his throat again before he spoke.

"I ... uh ... heard about the trouble Gary had, with his brakes, I mean. Uh ... a man's got to look out for his own, you know? I ... uh ... I don't wish you any harm, but me and Jason, we've been talking about it for a couple years already, and we've decided the time is right." He cleared his throat again, looked briefly up at her face, then back at the hat. "I guess what I'm trying to say is, me and Jason have decided to buy a truck, go out on our own. We aren't going to drive for Ranverdan anymore."

Suzanne was holding out the envelope containing Pete's check. She let it drop to the desk. "What? Pete? You can't be serious."

He nodded, eyes closed. "I'm sorry, Suzanne. Normally I would've given you a month's notice, but what with Randy's accident and now Gary's brakes ... like I said, a man's got to look out for his own. I made the down payment on a truck this morning. I'd like to stay on, but ... you see what I mean?" He gave a helpless shrug, hit the hat against his thigh.

"Who told you about Gary's brakes? Did Gary?"

Pete shook his head.

"El. It was El Watson, wasn't it?"

194

Pete said nothing, just continued to stare at his hat.

Suzanne swore under her breath. "But, Pete, you were with Dad at the very start, you're a part of this company. Mom and Mrs. Whitehead, they were best friends. Don't all those years count for anything? Please, Pete, give it some more thought. Give it some more time. I'm sure you're not in any danger."

"Are you?" He looked her in the eyes for the first time.

No, she wasn't sure. And she couldn't say it again. "Well, I can't give you any guarantees." It was her turn to look away. "But, listen, Pete. You know Hunter Rayne? He's ex-R.C.M.P. He's looking into it. He'll have some answers soon. Soon we'll all know what happened. We'll know who tampered with Gary's brakes, and what caused Dad's accident."

"That's what guys are saying, that it wasn't any accident. They're saying Randy was murdered, and the police won't do anything about it."

"That's not true, Pete. The police are on top of it, too. Hunter's keeping them informed and they'll be reopening their investigation. They never really closed it, in fact." She knew she was losing the battle. Pete's jaw was set. He was immovable. Suzanne picked up his check, handed it across the desk.

"I'll have final checks for both you and Jason ready on Friday," she said. Her voice displayed her hurt and anger, but she didn't care.

Pete put his hat back on, nodded once, unsmiling, and was gone.

With the big Newfie leading the way, Sorry had no trouble finding the Waicom warehouse in Seattle. The Newfie left his engine running and jumped down from the cab to check in with the shipper, then came trotting back out. He hailed Sorry, pointed to a loading door, then pulled his rig ahead and out of the way so Sorry could back in first.

"Oh, Christ!" Sorry ran a hand across his mouth, leaving behind a grimace of dread. It had been a few years since he'd had to back a forty odd foot trailer up to a loading dock, and now he had to do it with that wise-ass Newfie sitting right there, watching. "Oh, Christ!" He took a deep breath and, face grim with concentration, started slow and easy.

The Newfie clapped him on the back when he caught up with him in the warehouse. "Never mind, buddy! Comes with practice. I seen a lot worse. Don't be sorry about it, now, will ya?" He winked.

Sorry growled. "Go ahead, Murph. Make jokes about my name. I haven't heard a new one since 1978, but I keep hoping." He'd worked up a sweat in the last ten minutes, so the cool of the concrete building was a pleasant change. They had come up to what appeared to be the shipping and receiving counter, but there was no one behind it. The sound of male voices came from behind the warehouse stacks, until they were drowned out by the roar of a forklift motor.

"So I don't have to say I'm sorry, then?" Murph's round face beamed good naturedly.

"Heard that one a million times, at least. Better luck next time." Sorry caught sight of a Chinese guy with curly hair and a goatee walking towards them between the rows of metal shelving loaded with skids of cardboard cartons. He figured that had to be Steve Mah.

"Well, then, what's your favorite joke about your name," Murph continued, "just so's I know what I'm up against."

Sorry stroked his moustache thoughtfully until the Chinese guy was within earshot. "I like it when people tell me that if I do drugs, I'll be Sorry. I figure if I ever have an identity crisis, I'll know exactly what to do." He ended with what was, for him, a restrained laugh. He was trying to create the right impression on Mah. When he'd dug up information for Hunter in the past, it usually just required making small talk with guys he already knew, or else he had his bike and his buddies as props. Character references, like last night at The Post. After what Hunter had said about this Chinese guy and his obsession with little white pills, Sorry hoped joking about drugs would help him get his foot in the door.

196

"Well, I'm always sorry when I drink too much." The Newfie gave him a little nudge and continued, "So I guess we'd best not get drunk together or we'll both be sorry."

Sorry gave the Newfie a weak grin, too preoccupied to enter into the spirit of the conversation. "Yeah. Especially not today. We wouldn't want to fall asleep at the wheel while carrying this good gentleman's very important cargo now, would we?"

Sorry looked at Mah. "We'll get your shit ... er ... shipment delivered on time and in tip top condition."

The Chinese guy's brown eyes were studying him, mildly amused. "I never doubted that for a minute," he said. "You look like a fine, upstanding driver, and it only took you five tries to back your trailer up to the loading door."

Sorry didn't like Mah's smug smile. "I had a bad night," he grumbled. "Didn't get much sleep."

The Chinese guy's slanty eyes narrowed appraisingly. "You're new. You from Kamloops, too?"

Sorry shook his head. "Nope. Born in Yreka, California, raised hell in Surrey, British Columbia, just outside of Vancouver. Drug capital of Canada, from what I'm told." He held out his hand. "Nice to meet you. My name's Dan Sorenson, but as Murph here will tell you, most people say I'm Sorry."

"Steve Mah. You want me to say I'm sorry?" He gave Sorry's hand a firm and friendly shake.

"Hell, no," said Sorry. "I'm Sorry enough for all of us."

Murph and Mah both groaned.

Mah went to talk to the dock workers to get the loading underway, leaving the two drivers standing by the counter. Sorry felt hot breath on his neck, and Murph whispered, "Don't trust that fellow." He continued in a low voice, "If you want to hang onto your new job, then keep your nose clean and your gob shut and don't let that Chinaman get anything on you."

Sorry drew his head back and squinted at the Newfie. "How so?"

"Just a friendly warnin' is all." Murph grinned. "Just wouldn't want you to be sorry, is all." Then he turned his broad back and walked away.

Sorry watched the freight being loaded. The diesel forklift nosed in with a full skid and backed out again empty, like a big stinking bumblebee dumping pollen in its hive. Every now and then, Murph would lean in and say something to the forklift operator, but Sorry couldn't make out the words over the noise of the engine. He looked around for Steve Mah, and eventually saw him stepping lightly off the running board of a second forklift as it slowed down near the shipper's counter. The driver sped up again, and entered Sorry's trailer with a skid of big square cartons. Sorry leaned against the counter. He had already dropped enough hints, and it was time to sit back and wait for the Chinese guy to nibble the bait.

Mah kept messing around with paperwork behind the counter, his unnaturally curly hair all that Sorry could see of his head. Sorry coughed a couple of times. Eventually, Mah looked up at him and said, "Aren't you going to count the pieces we're loading on your trailer? You're going to have to sign for them, you know."

"Aren't you guys counting them?" Sorry asked coolly.

"Yeah. You're going to take our word for it?" There was a ghost of a crafty smile above the Chinaman's goatee.

"Shouldn't I?" said Sorry with a crafty smile of his own.

Mah went back to this paperwork. "Sure, you should. You can trust us. We're your best customers."

Murph's warning came to mind. "Then hell, if I can't trust you, who can I trust?" Sorry said. He grinned broadly but Mah didn't look up. He wished the guy would bring up the pills Hunter had talked about. Here he was with a hundred bucks in his jeans, and looking forward to doing business with the guy. A little deal would help break the ice, kind of establish his credentials. He was sure he'd made the hints obvious enough. So what the fuck was wrong with the damn Chinaman? Sorry glanced over towards Murphy. The final skid was being pushed into position on Murphy's trailer. There wasn't much time left. C'mon, Mah, he thought. Fuckin' say something!

198

"So, you won't fall asleep with our very important cargo on your trailer, now, will you?" said Mah.

Finally! "That would be a veritable tragedy. I'll do my veritable best to stay awake."

"It's not a joking matter." Mah was still fussing with the paperwork, sliding a sheaf of official looking invoices into a big manilla envelope. "I'm sure you're aware that a driver was killed transporting our very important cargo just a few weeks ago." Mah was no longer smiling.

"Yeah. I heard." Sorry hesitated. Mah had brought the subject up himself. How could he get the guy to say more without tipping his hand? And what about the drugs? He decided to give it another shot. "Sounds like he wasn't doing the right drugs."

"I guess ..." Mah drew out the s's in a thoughtful hiss, "... he should've stopped for coffee along the way."

"Yeah," said Sorry, thinking *C'mon, c'mon, what about the uppers?* "He should've stopped for coffee." He looked intently at Mah, waiting for some kind of a signal. A wink, a nod, a little jerk of the head. He saw nothing except a goddamn Mona Lisa smile. What was that word? Inscrutable. Yeah. Inscrutable Oriental. He couldn't read this guy, and the guy wasn't going to talk. His own trailer was now already loaded almost to the back door.

"I never met the guy, but I've heard he was a good driver. The accident shook a few people up." Sorry rubbed his chin. He'd just try to keep the subject alive and see where it led. "So, he went off the road with a load out of here, eh? You lose a lot of stuff?"

Mah shrugged. "Waicom imports computer parts by the thousands. What's one lousy truckload?"

"Only real loss was the driver then, eh?"

Mah hammered his fist several times on the head of a big black stapler, attaching bills of lading to each of the manilla envelopes. "Nope. The driver's somebody else's loss."

Ask stupid questions, Hunter had said. "You didn't like him?"

Mah flashed a suspicious look. "I didn't say that." The words were clipped.

Shit! thought Sorry. He's going to clam up.

Murph walked up to the counter, and Mah handed each of them their paperwork. "Sign here." He slashed a big X on the bill of lading, and Sorry scrawled his name beside it.

Murph peered over at his signature. "Who's Sorry now?" he asked, grinning as he walked away.

"You'll be fuckin' sorry," muttered Sorry through clenched teeth. The Newfie was starting to piss him off. The curly headed Chinaman was pissing him off big time. He ripped the top copy off the bill of lading and thrust it at Mah, who was watching the second copy zig-zag slowly to the dusty concrete floor. "Shit!" said Sorry, kicking at it before he bent to pick it up.

As Sorry straightened up, the copy crumpled in his hand, he saw Mah out of the corner of his eye. The guy was playing with the little diamond stud in his ear, a thoughtful look on his face. Sorry glared at him, then turned on his heel and strode over to his trailer. He checked that the rear doors were secure, then headed towards the warehouse exit.

"Sorenson!" Sorry paused with his hand on the door, slowly turning to face the shipper. The Chinaman was smiling that irritating smile. "Don't forget to stop for coffee."

Damn! Sorry fired up the engine of the big Ranverdan Western Star and sat there fuming while the Newfie pulled his rig out of the way. So, Mah talked about drugs to a clean cut guy like Hunter but wouldn't say a word about the pills to a cool brother like himself. Sorry felt as if he'd thrown in his line, seen the fish play with the bait, and suddenly realized that it was the fish who was reeling him in. So much for being a snake charmer. Hunter was full of shit.

Damn! He sure could've used some good drugs.

CHAPTER _ _ _ _
NINETEEN

He knew it had been too good to be true. The load that Hunter was scheduled to pick up in Tukwila wasn't ready. It's one of those things that truck drivers learn to accept. When possible, they charge for their time, but usually they just grit their teeth, grin, and bear it, rather than risk losing the load, and maybe future loads, to someone else. It's elementary. The law of supply and demand. There are too many truckers fighting over every piece of the cargo pie.

There'd been a production glitch, said the shipper, but they'd be caught up by the end of the night shift. The warehouse manager himself guaranteed to have Hunter's trailer loaded and ready to go by eight a.m. Hunter groaned inwardly, but agreed to come pick up the trailer at seven thirty Wednesday morning. "Thank you, chief," he said to the warehouse manager as he walked away to unhitch The Blue Knight.

Bob-tailing away from the yard in his tractor, Hunter felt light and unencumbered, as if he'd just shed gum boots for running shoes. He briefly considered heading back to Vancouver for the night, but decided that spending another five hours and umpteen gallons of fuel on the road just to be able to sleep at home wasn't going to help the situation, so he set off in the direction of the Flying J truck stop in Federal Way. He called El on his cellular to report the delay.

"Hang on," she said after he'd described his situation. "I've got a message for you."

"Make it quick, El, I'm on my cell," he managed to say before she punched the hold button, as if she couldn't tell from the speaker box sound.

"Okay," she said, coming back on within a few seconds. "Suzanne wants you to call her, but I've got to explain something to you first. She's really pissed at me."

"Why?" He was mired in Seattle's rush hour traffic, inching his way back on to the southbound I-5.

Big sigh. "Pete and Jason quit on her." A short silence. "Suzanne blames me for it."

"Well?"

"All I did was tell him about Gary's brake trouble, but you know how he is, out for himself all the time. He's not prepared to take risks for anybody, not even Randy's kid. It was kind of like the last straw for him anyway, meaning he and Jason had been intending to go out on their own for some time, even had a truck all picked out."

"So Pete's buying his own truck."

"Yeah. He and Jason are going to use the one truck between them, some team driving, singles on short runs. Pete figures he's ready to start cutting down his hours. He's closing in on sixty."

"What kind of work could he have lined up on such short notice? He wouldn't have to leave her in the lurch. He could still haul loads for Ranverdan."

"Uh ... I said I'd broker for him. Suzanne doesn't seem to want to do much business with me any more, so I got some holes to fill." Sounding defensive, she added, "He came to me."

"Jesus, El! What're you trying to do to her? I know, business is business, but have a heart. Besides, I thought you found Pete a pain in the ass to work with."

"Hey! It's not my fault." Her voice got louder. "Like I said, he came to me. I can use another experienced team. What was I supposed to do? Rap his knuckles and send him back to her?" After a pause, her voice dropped a bit. "In this business, them's the breaks. If she can't stand the heat ... the sooner she learns her lessons, the better." When Hunter didn't respond, El added. "Listen,

I like the kid, okay? I feel sorry for her, but ... she wants to run a trucking company, then she'd better learn how. Fast."

Hunter hung up feeling rotten. Poor Suzanne. He was frustrated that he couldn't do more for her, help to ease at least one of the burdens she was now carrying, give her a sense of closure, a sense of justice done. He felt hamstrung trying to investigate Randy's death. As a civilian, he couldn't order forensic tests on Randy's truck, he couldn't assign half a dozen constables to interview possible witnesses, he couldn't even afford to take The Blue Knight off the road long enough to do a decent job of it himself. What's more, he had no authority behind him to help secure the cooperation of those he might want to question, couldn't threaten them with subpoenas or arrests, or hint at favors and plea bargain deals. He was worried that he was pinning an unreasonable amount of hope on the results of Sorry's encounter with Steve Mah.

Hunter checked his watch. Sorry was supposed to call Hunter's cellular to confirm they were both on schedule and could meet for lunch the next day at a restaurant on the Yellowhead highway, north of Kamloops. If Sorry phoned from the border after he cleared through customs as planned, he'd be calling in about two hours. Hunter flipped open the phone again and called Suzanne.

"If Pete knows, they're all going to know," she said after they'd discussed it. "I don't know what to say to them. How can I ask them to put themselves in danger?"

"We don't know that anybody's really at risk," he countered.

"But we don't know that they're not."

"Of course, you're right." Hunter sighed. "So, if everybody already knows, we might as well ask outright for their help, get them to put the word out on the grapevine."

"What do you mean?"

It was something Hunter had thought about already. He had even borrowed the camera El kept in her warehouse to record freight damage, and used it to take half a dozen Polaroid snap shots of a Ranverdan tractor in order to have something to show drivers to jog their memories. The truckers' grapevine could be devilishly efficient at times. He told Suzanne that if they put the word out that they were looking for witnesses who might have seen Randy's truck that night anywhere from Hope, where he was supposed to have dropped off Chuck Wahl, to the site of the accident on the Coquihalla, they might be lucky and turn up some valuable information. "We've got nothing to lose," he reasoned, "now that the cat's already out of the bag. Do you think anyone else might quit?"

"I sure hope not," she said. "I'll do my best not to let them."

Her voice was less discouraged than Hunter had expected, even verging on steely. Randy would be proud, he thought.

"I wanted to ask you," she continued, "Have you been in touch with John Semeniuk yet to see if he's the John who wrote that note?"

"Not yet, but I've tried. The note said don't call at work, which must mean he didn't want someone where he works knowing he was talking to Randy about it, so I'm not even sure that he'll be willing to talk to me over the phone. He wasn't very forthcoming the time I met him."

"He might talk to me. I could just say I came across this note in Dad's desk, and ask him if it was something I should know about."

Hunter paused, debating whether it would put her at risk, and decided it couldn't hurt. "Sure. Give it a try. Don't push him too hard, but see if he's willing to explain the note. I'll try to stop in to see you tomorrow on my way through."

After he hung up, he abandoned his plan to park at the Federal Way truck stop and instead took Exit 149 and looped over to the northbound 405. At least he would feel like he was doing something useful tonight, canvassing drivers to see if they could remember seeing Randy on the Coquihalla, and the truck stops to do that at were north of Seattle, where he'd have a better chance of finding drivers enroute to the border.

When he pulled into the first rest area, a few miles south of Everett, there were two rigs stopped. A tall young man wearing a Seattle Mariners baseball cap and low-heeled cowboy boots was standing beside the restroom reading the glassed in notice board and finishing up a cigarette. Hunter approached him and said, "Howdy."

The man turned and nodded.

"Is that your rig?" Hunter pointed to a royal purple Kenworth hitched to a plain aluminum trailer.

"Sure is." The man flicked ash off the end of his cigarette and grinned. "Or maybe I should say, it belongs to my bank."

Hunter returned the grin and pointed at The Blue Knight. "Ditto." He cleared his throat. "I'm looking for somebody who might have witnessed an accident a few weeks back. You ever been up the Coquihalla Highway northeast of Vancouver?"

"Coquihalla? Is that the one with the toll booth way up in the mountains?"

"Yeah, that's the one. Any chance you might've been there three weeks ago. That'd be Tuesday, May 24th."

The man shook his head. "I normally just run as far as Vancouver. Only time I was on that toll highway was on summer vacation about four years ago." He dropped his cigarette butt and squashed it with his heel. "Can't help ya."

Hunter thanked him, and looked over to see the other rig just pulling out. He hung around for another fifteen minutes and talked to four more drivers, two of whom had never even been to Canada. He decided to try his luck further north.

He drove through a few restaurant parking lots just off the highway in Everett. There were a couple of rigs parked in the vicinity of each, but the drivers weren't in them and he didn't want to go table to table in a restaurant trying to distinguish the drivers of big trucks from the drivers of little trucks. In one parking lot, he pulled up beside a driver who was just stepping out of his cab. The man said that he had driven the Coquihalla many times, and might've been on it three weeks ago. He'd have to check his log.

"What time are we talking about?" he asked.

"Sometime around midnight, I guess." That is, Hunter thought, if Chuck Wahl had been right about Randy leaving Hope around eleven o'clock.

The driver thumbed through the pages of his log book. "Hmmmm. May 24th. Here it is. I've even got the toll receipt here. I went through the toll booth at nine forty five."

Hunter winced in disappointment. Close, but no cigar. It was like having only one winning number out of six on a lottery ticket. What were the chances of ever winning the jackpot?

"Do you remember seeing this rig anywhere that night? Take a look at this." Hunter showed him one of the Polaroids. "Ring any bells for you?"

The driver shook his head. "Are you kidding?! Three weeks ago? You know how many trucks I've set eyes in three weeks?"

"Yes, I know." Hunter sighed. "Believe me, I know."

But he drove away from that encounter with a new idea. Where was Randy's toll receipt from the night he died? That would virtually pinpoint the time he was on the thirty mile stretch of highway between the toll booth and the curve where his rig left the road. If it wasn't still in the cab, it must be in the possession of the R.C.M.P., along with the log book and paperwork for the Waicom shipment, and perhaps Randy's wallet and valuables as well. He made a mental note to check that out, and reproached himself for not tracking it down sooner.

He got back on the I-5 and continued north. When he reached Marysville, famous throughout northwest Washington and southwest British Columbia as the home of mouthwatering pies, he couldn't help thinking of Sorry. If the jolly biker had driven straight through, he could expect a call from him at any moment, but it wouldn't surprise Hunter if Sorry had stopped on this side of the border to eat. He pulled into Donna's Travel Plaza, and was just making small talk in the parking lot with a NW Transport driver who'd never driven the Coquihalla when his cell phone rang. It wasn't Sorry calling from the border, it was Bill Earl calling from Kamloops.

"You'll be pleased to know that I've caught the virus, or whatever it is, that's got you obsessed with this Danyluk accident. I had to make a trip to Merritt on another matter, and managed to convince Garth to spend some time with me going through that trailer before they haul the stuff away. Unofficially, mind you. I'm not convinced enough to want to take this to the brass yet. However ..." He paused briefly. "... I do think you might be interested in taking a look at what we've found."

"Bill, you're a prince! I needed some kind of good news about now."

"Wait a minute, Hunter," Bill growled in a deep voice, "I don't think what we've found qualifies as good news. I'd call it interesting stuff, maybe. No, not even that. More likely, just unexplained shit."

"Okay. Call it whatever you want. What have you got?"

"Garth'll show you if you get time to stop in Merritt. The load must've been pretty loose. Most of the cartons are all crushed and dented and look as if they rattled around and bounced off the walls all the way down. Those are mostly the larger cartons - computer monitors, CPU's, and cartons full of smaller boxes of parts. But there were two skids of smaller, flatter cartons, cartons containing keyboards to be exact, that had been shrink wrapped together. They seem to have been the only skids that weren't loose. The skids are a little out of shape, you know, skewed a bit, but that shrink wrap is pretty skookum stuff and managed at least to hold them all together. As far as we can tell, the shrink wrap around those skids didn't break and didn't unravel. We did a piece count, in fact, we did several piece counts - I don't know how you truckers can stand it - and the number of cartons jives with what's on the customs paperwork."

"Um ... Bill," Hunter ventured, "either I've been retired for too long or you know something I don't know. That doesn't even qualify as unexplained shit, in my book."

"Hold your horses, Hunter, I haven't finished. The unexplained part is that there was a pile of used shrink wrap lying around with no cartons connected to it. It's in a bunch of pieces, but there's not enough of it to have wrapped a complete skid, and it doesn't seem to be off the existing skids, but it was around something because there are places on it that were obviously stretched by the corners of boxes."

"I would like to take a look at that. You don't think it was just wrapped around the top of the skids and came loose?"

"I doubt it. For one thing, the shrink wrap on the top of the skids is intact. I don't see what the point would have been to have another chunk of it wrapped around the top. The other thing is that these pieces were obviously slit with a blade. The original pieces were maybe fifty feet long, now it's in clumps of three layers in lengths of about twelve feet."

"So maybe it was wrapped around something that somebody removed from the trailer."

"That's what I was thinking. Unless there's a chance that garbage like that was left in the trailer from a previous shipment, or that it somehow just got stuck in with the cartons that were loaded in Seattle. You'd know that better than I would. What do you think? Can you hear me?"

"I can hardly hear you. Hold on a sec, chief." Hunter paused while half a dozen loud motorcycles roared into the lot and milled around trying to settle on a place to park. He started off in the direction of the restaurant, figuring it would be quieter inside. Before he reached the door, the engines were stilled, one by one.

"I doubt it, Bill." Hunter picked up where they'd left off. "Waicom runs a pretty clean warehouse, and I don't think customs would take kindly to garbage in trailers crossing the border. My bet would be that the shrink wrap was wound around something that somebody didn't want Randy to find when he got to Edmonton. I've thought all along that whoever killed Randy, it had something to do with what was on his trailer."

"Like what?"

"Your guess is as good as mine. By the way, what's happening with the tractor and trailer?"

"Merritt's ready to release it all. The equipment is a write off, so it'll go to an ICBC lot until the insurance claim is settled, and the contents will be delivered to the bond warehouse in Edmonton, like the paperwork calls for. What happens then is between the owner and customs."

"How about the contents of the cab?" asked Hunter. "You were talking about the customs paperwork. What about the driver's log, the company paperwork? What about any personal effects that Randy might have had inside the cab and sleeper? Or on him? What about his wallet?"

208

"The customs paperwork will stay with the shipment, of course. But the other stuff, that all belongs to the trucking company or the next of kin. You want to pick it up? Get Danyluk's daughter to call me with the O.K. and I'll have Garth release it to you."

"Thanks, Bill. You'll hear from her tomorrow morning. Say, how close are we to making this investigation official?"

"There's that we again, white man. I'm not ready for that, yet. You get me some stand up evidence, Hunter, and I'll take it to the boss. In spite of what your nagging has done to me, the gut instincts of an ex-Mountie don't count for much in court. Sorry, pal."

"Hunh. Could you at least do me a favor, run a few names through the computer?"

"Jeez, Hunter, you're like a goddamn wolf. I show a little weakness and you close in for the kill. What do you need?"

"I'd like to see if you've got anything on any of the deceased's drivers. At present, they're all resident in the Kamloops area." He gave Bill the names of the Ranverdan drivers, including Pete. It was unlikely that any of them had been convicted of a felony or else, like Chuck Wahl, they wouldn't be able to move freely across the border. If any of them had ever been charged, however, it might mean they were worth a closer look.

"A few?! Why don't I run the damn phone book while I'm at it?"

"About that fishing trip, I'll even supply all the grub. Like I said, Bill, you're a prince."

"There are no princes among the Shuswap tribes. You can keep calling me 'chief'."

Hunter entered the restaurant, decided to grab some dinner before he did any more canvassing. He slipped into a seat at the counter and was scanning the menu when he felt a slap against his shoulder blade, and heard a soft thud at his feet. He looked down to find a grimy white baseball cap under the chair. Turning around, he saw Stu Thatcher, a driver who often did work for El. He was a small wiry man with a lined, leathery face and bright blue, twinkling eyes. When he smiled, which was often, his pearl white dentures stood out in startling contrast against his deeply tanned skin. Stu sat in a booth beside the window with a couple of other men. He motioned Hunter to join them.

Hunter took the opportunity to ask for their help in locating witnesses who might have seen Randy on the Coquihalla the night of his death. After they'd discussed Randy's death, he wrote his phone number on the back of one of the Polaroids and handed it to Stu. "We don't know for sure that Randy was murdered, but we're looking for any leads we can get that would help us figure it out. If you ever run across another driver who happened to be on the Coquihalla the night of Randy's accident, maybe you could ask if he saw Randy's rig pulled off the road anywhere along that stretch. Anywhere, say, between Hope and Merritt. I'd sure like to find out if Randy stopped anywhere along there."

"You bet, Hunter. I'd be glad to do anything to help," said Stu. "I sure as hell don't like to think that there's some bastard out there who's responsible for Randy's accident, and he's going to get off scot free. Randy was one of us," he said, looking at the other two men, who nodded in solemn agreement, "and we've got to watch out for each other."

Hunter felt an unexpected warmth in his chest, a shadow of the intense feeling he'd experienced when his graduating troop had paraded in front of their crusty drill sergeant in Regina for the last time. One of us. Truckers were a scattered and diverse fraternity, but a fraternity none the less. He thought of a young man he'd met at a truck stop near Portland. Twenty, maybe twenty one years old. The kid had admired The Blue Knight and said, "I always love it when you guys wave at me - you know, sort of like a salute - that little wave drivers do when they pass each other? It makes me feel like I'm one of you, even though I'm only driving a lousy little five ton sausage truck, delivering cold cuts and wieners to deli's." His face had shone as he looked at the big rigs around him. "But soon I'm gonna be on the road with you. I'm gonna be a real driver. Count on it!" Hunter had often wondered if he'd recognize the kid if he ever saw him again, in the driver's seat of an eighteen wheeler.

Stu copied Hunter's phone number onto pieces of paper torn from his place mat and handed them to the other drivers.

210

"Thanks, Stu," said Hunter. "You'll all make sure the word gets around?"

They all said they would.

Hunter canvassed the truck stop until almost ten o'clock. He talked to at least twenty drivers who wouldn't have remembered Randy's truck even if they had been on the Coquihalla the night of May 24th. He still hadn't heard from Sorry, so he called his voice mail. There was a message in his mail box. Either he hadn't heard the phone ring, or Sorry must have called while he was on the phone to Bill. There was no way that he could reach Sorry now, and he could only hope that Sorry would call back again before he wasted too much time waiting for Hunter in the prearranged spot. For a message from Sorry, the recording was brief.

"Yo, Hunter! I'm at the border, where the fuck are you? I've got nothing to tell you, but I'll let you buy me lunch like we planned. And you were wrong about that Chinese faggot. He didn't want to sell me fuck all. See you in Clearwater."

He'd added, evidently as an afterthought, "That is, if I can make it to Clearwater without falling asleep at the wheel, which is fuckin' unlikely without those little pills you promised me."

CHAPTER
TWENTY

Garth Pullen whistled in admiration when he first saw Hunter's rig, as he and Hunter walked out of the Merritt detachment office. The young constable climbed up to inspect the inside, his eyes bright with enthusiasm. All boys love big trucks, thought Hunter.

"Pretty impressive machine. Funny, I know you're a truck driver, but even though I didn't know you before you retired, I can't help thinking of you as a member. I guess it's because you still talk like one of us." The blond constable looked Hunter up and down. "And you still look like one of us, somehow. You know what I mean?"

Hunter smiled self-consciously, rubbing the back of his neck. "Old habits die hard, I guess. If a guy's been married to the force for over twenty years, what can you expect?" He nodded towards the tractor-trailer. "Okay if I leave this here on the street?"

"You bet. We shouldn't be too long. C'mon. My PC's over there."

When Hunter had called Garth to see if he was free to take another look at the wreck, he'd been guiding The Blue Knight around the slow uphill curve where Randy's rig had left the road. The sun was high in the sky, the wide road was solid and smooth, the patient army of lodgepole pines stood at ease on either slope of the deep ravine. It looked like anything but a deadly curve. Still, he'd felt a small shiver between his shoulder blades.

"They're getting Overland Freight to haul this stuff to Edmonton," said Garth. "Overland has a facility here in Merritt, and they were able to let Bill and I use one of their trailers to unload the damaged cartons into. We had to count the damn things about five times to make sure we'd got it right." The young Mountie opened a padlock on the back of the new trailer parked right beside the wreck and threw open the doors. "Look at this mess! Some of these cartons are so beat up, we had trouble stacking them."

Hunter climbed onto the back of the trailer and Garth handed him a big flashlight. "I see what you mean. So these two here are the only shrink wrapped skids?"

"Yeah. We moved all the loose cartons first, so the shrink wrapped skids were the last things to get loaded. We had to borrow a forklift from a warehouse down the street. Looks like the skidded cartons stayed in better shape than the rest of the stuff."

"Where's that extra shrink wrap Bill was talking about?"

"Right." Garth sprang into motion. "It's still in the old trailer. Stay right there, I'll get it for you." The young constable reappeared a moment later with his hands raised high above his head, holding up several lengths of crumpled shrink wrap. "We straightened this out the best we could, but the damn stuff sticks to itself. It's like Saran Wrap."

Hunter jumped down from the trailer and, with Garth's help, laid the pieces of shrink wrap out along a section of hard packed dirt beside the trailer, avoiding as many oil spots and weeds as they could. The Merritt sun was hot, and the material was soft and almost sticky, but the spots that had been stretched over corners were punctured in places and still quite visible. Hunter climbed back up into the trailer and motioned for Garth to pass the pieces with the most pronounced indentations up to him. The constable climbed up and held one corner firmly against the shrink wrapped skid while Hunter clambered over other cartons to get around to the other side. The stretches fit exactly over the corners of the skid. He unhooked a retractable tape measure from his belt and took the dimensions of the skid, while Garth copied them into his notepad. Then he measured one each of the cartons containing CPUs, monitors, and quantities of smaller parts. When they were finished, Hunter handed the lengths of shrink wrap back down to Garth.

"I'd appreciate a copy of those number before I go. Later on I'll sit down with a calculator and see if this shrink wrap could've fit anything else. Have you got something to keep this stuff in, chief?"

"I always carry a couple of boxes in the trunk. You'll probably need one for the personal effects, too."

"Do you think you could store this stuff in the exhibit room, just in case we turn up enough to open a homicide investigation?"

"No problem, sir." The young constable grinned sheepishly and tossed a loose lock of blond hair off his forehead. "I mean, Sergeant Truck Driver, sir."

Hunter raised an eyebrow. "Knock it off, Constable. I'm a civilian." Then he grinned. "Definitely off the payroll, anyway. Let's take a look in this tractor."

Hunter picked up the acrylic picture frame from off the seat where he'd placed it the first time he'd been to see the cab. He looked at the smiling faces of Suzanne and the little girls, feeling the pang that always comes from handling the orphaned belongings of the suddenly dead. He placed it gently on the console, then climbed into the driver's seat and gathered up all the loose objects he could reach. Inside the console was a vinyl case holding cassette tapes, mostly older country artists like Merle Haggard and Waylon Jennings. Hunter pulled a tape out of the tape player - it was Patsy Cline - and put it into its clear plastic box inside the case. He handed the photograph, a flashlight, a thermos, the tape case, a first aid kit, a small tool kit and sundry trucking paraphernalia down to Garth, who placed them in a cardboard box he'd just assembled.

Hunter maneuvred himself over to the other seat and tried to open the passenger door. It was badly dented and wouldn't budge, so he just reached his hand down between the seat and the door, feeling around for anything that might have fallen into that space during the accident. He came up with a green ballpoint pen inscribed with Ranverdan Transport Inc. and an 800 telephone number.

On the floor of the sleeper he found a zippered black and purple athletic bag containing a shaving kit, four clean shirts, some underwear, and half a dozen pairs of socks. Underneath it was a plastic grocery bag with the sticky remains of two broken orange juice bottles and shards of broken glass. The sides of the bag had stuck together, and parts of it were still wet enough to leave Hunter's fingers infuriatingly tacky. There was also a well-thumbed Robert Ludlum novel, its pages puckered and stiff from having been wet, and a Time magazine dated the third week of May. He found another photograph of Suzanne and the girls, one of a smiling middle-aged woman, and an old wedding photograph. The brass frames of each photograph were intact, but the glass was either cracked or shattered. Hunter picked a small sliver of glass out of his thumb, and noted with disgust that other bits had attached themselves to the sticky places on his fingers. He had to rinse off his hands in the wrecker's garage before continuing.

Straightening the sheets and blanket on the disarrayed bunk, he turned up an empty department store bag, and Hunter assumed that the two child's hats he disengaged from the outer folds of the blanket belonged inside. They were round hats with wide quilted brims, heavy white cotton dotted with small stylized tulips of red, yellow, blue and pink, on curving bright green stalks. He couldn't help wondering how seeing the little hats would affect Suzanne, whether they might become a repeated reminder of her loss, and whether the pain would outweigh the pleasure of this last gift to the little girls from their grandfather. Either way, it was not his call.

When they got back to The Blue Knight, Garth helped Hunter position the sad carton on the passenger seat. He had Hunter come inside the detachment office to sign for an envelope of Randy's personal effects: his wallet, watch, a handful of coins, and a plain gold wedding band. The wallet contained credit cards and two five dollar bills. It was already after two thirty, and Hunter wanted to be in Kamloops by four or soon after, so he didn't wait for a copy of Garth's notes. Garth promised to send it to Bill Earl, along with the entries from Randy's log book and the Coquihalla toll receipt, if he could find it. "We have to hold onto the log book, at least until after the inquest, but I can make copies for you," Garth explained.

"Thanks, chief," said Hunter.

The young constable stood there at the side of the road, holding the evidence carton of shrink wrap against his hip and watching Hunter start up the big engine and maneuver his rig back onto the street. He smiled and saluted as Hunter drove off.

Back on the highway, Hunter punched a number into his cell phone to retrieve messages from his mail box. There was only one.

"I bought my own goddamn lunch. What the fuck happened to you?"

Veri was acting up. She refused to let Suzanne put her running shoes on, and kept pulling off her socks. Suzanne finally gave up and let her wear sandals, even though the ground was still wet from an afternoon thundershower. She shooed the girls out to the minivan and made good time out to the Ranverdan yard, but Hunter's navy blue truck was already parked across the street when she drove up. As she suspected, much of the yard was slick with mud.

"Hi! How are you?" she called from her open window.

"Just tickety boo," Hunter replied with a cheerful smile, climbing down from the cab. "How about you?"

She returned his smile. "Fine, but I'd rather not let the girls out of the van. They'll be mud from head to toe if I let them play outside here. Do you mind if we don't go in the yard?"

"No," he said, shaking his head as he crossed the street towards the van. "There's nothing I needed here, except room to park the trailer for a few minutes." He gestured back to his truck. "I've got that box of ... your Dad's things." His face and voice were both solemn now. He rested his right hand on the door frame.

She nodded silently, not sure if she wanted to see them or not. She kept her eyes on his hand, noticing for the first time how unusual his ring was. It had a greyish milky round stone, within which gleamed a six pointed star.

216

Almost as if he knew she was in no hurry to see what he'd brought, Hunter changed the subject. "Have you heard from Dan Sorenson?" he asked.

Hunter had suggested she hire Dan Sorenson, the driver El had teamed him with for his last trip to Edmonton, and told her to put him on the Waicom Edmonton runs. Suzanne was relieved to be able to work out the Waicom schedules without having to send Gary back there again, and that seemed reason enough for putting a tough character like Sorenson on the run, but Hunter's question reminded her that she hadn't asked for references or even gotten any details about his past experience. After Pete and Jason quit, she was just glad to have another driver all ready to put on the road.

"No," she said. "He hasn't called in yet today. Do you suppose he's unreliable? I don't know much about him."

"I've heard he's okay. Give him some time to learn the ropes. Did you manage to get hold of John Semeniuk?"

"Yes. Just this morning, at work. He couldn't talk. I mean, he didn't want to talk. He was very - I don't know - secretive, almost like he was talking in code. From what I gather, he's going to call me back tonight." She shrugged her shoulders. "He's a strange one - paranoid or something - but I think he's got something to tell me. It was definitely his phone number on the note."

"The R.C.M.P. found something ... uh ... unusual in the trailer: a length of loose shrink wrap that seemed to have been removed from a couple of skids. If he doesn't bring it up, maybe you could ask him if he's ever found loose shrink wrap in the trailers. I'll be in Edmonton, so I can always go to see him if it's necessary. I'll call you tomorrow morning to find out."

"Sure," she said. The kids were getting restless in the back seat. Jolene had ventured a couple of quiet, "Mommy?"s, and Veri had started to whine, straining at the straps on her car seat. Suzanne smiled apologetically at Hunter.

"I'd better get a move on," he said. "But I'm hoping to spend some time on my way back, maybe Saturday morning. Any chance I could take a look at the drivers' logs? And toll receipts. They would help to verify times in the logs." He took his hand from the door frame, and she saw that the star had disappeared from the milky stone.

She nodded. "You won't need the toll receipts. We've got an account, so they fax us weekly statements with all the dates and times on one page."

"Is the back open?" he asked, glancing towards the rear of the van. "I'll just put the box in there, if you like. There are no papers in it, so you don't have to go through it right away. The R.C.M.P. are holding onto all the documents for now."

"Thanks," she said. "That'll be fine."

With the girls coloring on old computer printouts on the floor of the office and the telephones quiet, later that afternoon Suzanne unloaded the cardboard box from the van. She recognized her dad's duffle bag, and decided to put the whole carton in his bedroom closet, out of sight for now. She carried it upstairs. There was a rustling sound as the box shifted in her arms, and she noticed a department store bag. Something on the bottom of the box rattled as she placed it on the floor beside the closet.

She just stood there, looking at it, her hand on the open closet door and her foot ready to slide it deeper inside. Then she reached down and pulled at the corner of the white bag. It rustled again as it finally gave way and broke free from where it was pinned beneath the duffle bag. It was very light, it felt almost empty. She looked inside.

Jolene came thudding up the stairs, her little voice coming closer and closer. "Mommy? Mommy, where are you? Mommy? Can me and Veri have some Kool Aid? Mom?" Jolene fell silent, swinging back and forth, holding on to the door jamb of her grandfather's bedroom. "Mommy? Why are you crying?"

She ran over and wrapped her little arms tight around Suzanne's knees.

"Poor Mommy. Are you all sad about Grampa again?"

When Sorry woke up, his head was fuzzy and when he reached over to touch Simone he banged his elbow on a metal wall instead. He peeled open one eye. He was in the sleeper of a green truck. He ran his tongue around inside his mouth, tasting the acrid residue of several kinds of smoke. Right. He was in Hinton, and had climbed into the sleeper stoned on hash and warm with the camaraderie of his new friends.

They were brothers. Yesterday he'd crossed the Rocky Mountains and run across some brothers discussing their choppers in the parking lot of a hotel in Hinton, Alberta. One thing led to another, and as the evening progressed they were happy to partake of the hash he bought with the money he hadn't spent on little white pills, and he recalled being happy to share it with them. He covered his face with both hands and groaned. His hands were sweaty and grimy and smelled of smoke and grease and piss. So, what else was new?

He poked his head out the door of the sleeper and had to avert his eyes from the brilliance of the sun. He figured he was about three and a half hours away from Edmonton. He should be able to get there by noon, for sure. Squinting at his watch, he swore aloud. It was already after eight thirty. He didn't even have time for a decent breakfast if he was going to get this load delivered on schedule. He plodded half a block to a service station, and asked for the restroom key. The attendant looked like he was going to say something negative until Sorry straightened up and glowered over his tousled moustache, bracing his arms on the counter and rippling his Black Cobra tattoo. The attendant gave him the key. When Sorry came back with the key wearing a clean black Harley teeshirt, looking washed, combed and immeasurably more benign, the attendant even threw in a free coffee and dried up donut for the road.

It wasn't until he was back on the Yellowhead cruising just above the speed limit that he thought about giving Hunter another call. He was a little pissed off at Hunter, although he had to admit that it probably wasn't Hunter's fault they hadn't managed to connect yet. If Hunter was somewhere in the mountains, he probably couldn't even get a signal on his cellular phone. But being pissed off made it easier for him to justify not stopping to make another call. Besides, by the time he parked the stupid truck, found a payphone, collected enough change and pulled the damn number out of his wallet, he'd make himself late for the delivery. He was on schedule and had nothing to report anyway. The only reason for calling was that Hunter might have found out more about that mean looking dude at Waicom's Edmonton warehouse so that Sorry could do his fantastic snake charmer number on him, too. But Sorry figured he had a good instinct for identifying criminal types. He'd just follow his nose.

By the time he reached the Waicom warehouse in Edmonton, he was being bullied and harassed by his stomach. It was just about noon, he was so hungry he could feel the thin edge of a headache, and he was going to have to back the goddamn trailer up to another fuckin' loading dock. He pulled into the yard and left the engine running while he went in for instructions. He felt downright provoked when the shipper, a jowly slob with greasy fingers, bit into a fat sandwich right before he directed Sorry to door number ten. Sorry returned to his truck tormented by the smell of garlic sausage and swiss cheese, but at least it made him mad enough to back right up to the door on his first try. After he turned off his engine, he headed back inside.

The fat guy was whining at a black haired stud with a small ponytail who reminded Sorry of van Damme, cool and lethal. No question that he was the mean guy Hunter mentioned. "Just today, Frank. Sidhu's booked off sick, and I can't get anybody else to start until three. Just this once, can't you put off your lunch, just till the trailer's unloaded?" He looked furtively in Sorry's direction, then continued in a furious whisper, "I can't ask this ... driver to wait around here for you to come back from your lunch break."

The cool stud looked over at Sorry, then back at the fat man. In a smooth, lazy voice, he said, "I'm hungry, John." He smiled like a lizard. "Unload it yourself, John."

Sorry cleared his throat and pulled a crumpled five-dollar bill from his jeans. He waved the bill in their direction. "Say, can either of you gents tell me where I can go around here to get a decent lunch for under five bucks? I'm fuckin' starved!"

John the fat guy just stared slack-jowled at him, but Frank the stud's face eased into a self-possessed smile. "I'll go one better. I'll take you to the best greasy spoon on this side of the city. C'mon, man." He walked towards the door, throwing back over his shoulder, "Don't shit yourself, John. We'll be back by one."

Sorry hitched up his jeans and hurried off behind him.

Frank drove Sorry about a mile in a late model, black Jeep Cherokee. The restaurant featured a brilliantly-colored Chinese smorgasbord -- yellow deep fried prawns, crimson sweet and sour sauce, crisp green broccoli. It wasn't the best he'd ever eaten, but Sorry was half way through his second plateful before he slowed down enough to talk.

"Thanks. I needed that." He patted his stomach. "I partied some in Hinton last night, ended up sleeping in this morning. All I had for breakfast was a fuckin' donut. I'm glad I didn't sleep any later, or I would've missed this." He gestured at his plate with a canary colored prawn impaled on his fork. "If I'd'a had to watch that fat dork take one more bite out of his fuckin' sandwich, I would've ripped it out of his hand and used him as a wheel chock." Sorry grinned, chow mein noodles draped over his chin. "Thanks, pal." The prawn followed the noodles under his moustache.

"De nada," Frank said. "Mind if I smoke while you eat?"

Sorry laughed and waved him to go ahead.

"Hinton, eh? Get ripped last night?"

Sorry nodded as he shovelled fried rice into his face. "Hash," he said. "Damn fine hash."

Frank smiled. "Got any more? Too bad. It's not my drug of choice, but a little good hash now and then helps keep the world in perspective." He fingered what looked like a tiny gold whistle that hung on a fine chain around his neck.

"Yeah, I know what you mean. It's not something I do every day. Can't afford it, for one thing. The old lady always has my paycheck spent before the ink has fuckin' dried." Sorry laughed. He was feeling much better now. "You must do pretty good, nice wheels, nice accessories." He winked towards Frank's gold watch.

"Yeah. That's why I've got to make sure I'm back to the warehouse by one. I can't give fat old John any reason to write me up. I need the job." The stud leaned back and looked at Sorry through slitted eyes.

"Hah!" Sorry rubbed his chin. "No way you pull down more'n rent money working in a fuckin' warehouse. You screwin' a rich old lady, or what?" He mirrored Frank, leaning back and squinting.

"The point is, my friend ..." Frank leaned forward across the table. "... sometimes you have to put up with doing something tedious and menial because it puts you in the right place at the right time. My paycheck is peanuts. Working in that warehouse just gives me easy access to the gravy boat, not to mention it makes a good cover. Know what I mean?"

Sorry's heartbeat picked up, and he knew it wasn't just a reaction to the MSG in the chop suey. He nodded appreciatively. "Yeah. Yeah, I do." He licked some sauce off the ends of his moustache. "I could put up with tedious and menial if the price was right. Hell, I'd fuckin' kiss old sausage face on the mouth if the price was right." He wiped his finger excitedly along his moustache. "Fuck. Would I fuckin' love to be able to give the old lady my paycheck, and then have gravy left over for myself. I could go for that. Fuck, yeah."

Frank smiled. "You look like you might've been on the wrong side of the law a time or two in your life."

"Who? Me?" He laughed. "Moi?" he said in his best Miss Piggy imitation.

"It might be that my partners and I could use another, uh ... associate ... at some time in the near future. You interested?"

Sorry's eyebrows shot up. He was definitely interested.

"That is," continued Frank, "if you're planning to make this Ranverdan outfit a long term thing. For the time being, that's what we need." He stabbed the end of his cigarette into a round tin ashtray, blew smoke across the table. "We need somebody stable and, uh, reasonably respectable, someone who won't draw attention to himself, if you get my drift."

Sorry inhaled Frank's smoke. He was out of tailor-mades again. He was going to have to ask Hunter for a few bucks until payday.

222

That there gravy was looking pretty good. "Like I said, I can handle tedious and menial if the price is right." He paused for a slow, meaningful smile. So what if he had to swear off partying in Hinton. "What do I have to do?"

"Nothing, yet. I've got to consult my partners. We'll talk more next time." He reached in his pocket and pulled out a pack of cigarettes. "Want a smoke, Sorenson?" He held out the package. "Here, take them all. I've got a carton in the Jeep."

Sorry stared him down as he reached for a cigarette. "One's fine, Frank. I can wait." He lit it with a match from a folder of restaurant matches and inhaled deeply. "How do I know that I'm not being set up?" He leaned forward and blew the smoke at Frank. "You got any guarantees?"

"No more than you do, pal. No more than you do."

CHAPTER

TWENTY-ONE

Hunter was standing in the customer's warehouse in Strathcona Industrial Park on the southeast side of Edmonton when he finally heard from Sorry on his cell phone. Sorry said he was finished at Waicom, but had to pick up another load a few miles away and would be tied up for two or three hours yet. Waicom's warehouse was on the northwest side of the city, a couple of miles north of the gigantic West Edmonton Mall and not far off the Yellowhead Trail. Hunter's own outbound load wouldn't be ready until Friday morning, so as soon as this customer signed off his paperwork, he was free for the evening. Hunter told Sorry he'd be waiting for him in the lounge at the hotel near the Yellowhead where he'd met Mel Collins two weeks earlier. It would be easy for Sorry to find and there was room to park their rigs.

When Hunter got there, he circled the parking lot and parked the truck nose out, making The Blue Knight visible from the street. He decided to check in to the hotel so he could get a good sleep and a hot shower before he hit the road again in the morning. His room was on the second floor, plainly furnished but large and bright, with a gold and brown patterned carpet and a south-facing window that looked out over the parking lot. He washed the day's dust and sweat off his face, then sat on the edge of one of the twin beds to use the telephone on the nightstand. He called Ranverdan's 800 number, and

224

the phone rang three times before Suzanne answered. She sounded slightly out of breath.

"Sorry I didn't get a chance to call earlier," he said. "Did you hear from John Semeniuk last night?"

"He called from home, like he said he would. You met him once, didn't you? Is he as strange as he sounds?"

"Strange? He's not a personable sort of man, probably doesn't have many friends. He seemed extremely nervous, very secretive. I'd say you hit the nail on the head yesterday when you called him paranoid." Hunter hoped John Semeniuk's fear wasn't contagious. He didn't want Suzanne any more worried than she already was. "Did he say what that note was all about?"

"Well, he talks really fast and never seems to finish a sentence, so I'm not sure I understood him properly, but it sounds like he's afraid of a guy that works in the warehouse with him. He babbled on about wanting to have the guy fired, but he can't get anything on him. He kept calling the guy `bad news'. When I asked him to explain, he said, `You don't want to know' and then just kept repeating that he was bad news. I got the man's name though. It's Frank Scarfo." She spelled it out. "Will that help?"

"It might," said Hunter. "I saw the two of them together, and there's no question that John's intimidated by him. I'll see what I can find out about him. What about the shrink wrap? Did he elaborate?"

"Again, I don't know if I understood him correctly, but I gather that a few times trailers came in with a bunch of loose shrink wrap in them. He thought something fishy was going on, but didn't know what. He thinks they were smuggling something, but it never made it as far as the warehouse, that it had been removed before the trailer arrived in Edmonton. He was hoping my dad could figure it out, because he really wanted to get something on that Frank guy so he could have him fired."

"Does he seem to connect Frank with your father's death in any way?"

"I asked him straight out. He said he didn't think that was possible, because Frank was at work all day, both before and after the accident."

"That would pretty much rule him out, all right."

"Are you going to try to see John?"

"Based on what you've told me, I don't think there's much point."

There was a short silence on the other end, then Suzanne asked, "Why did you stop hauling the Waicom loads yourself? I don't understand. Wouldn't it have been easier to find out what was going on if you were right there?"

Hunter was prepared for her question. He had decided right from the start that he didn't want anyone other than El knowing that Sorry was doing 'undercover' work at Waicom on his behalf. He didn't want it to be leaked, whether intentionally or inadvertently, to any of the other drivers. "Too many of the drivers know my background, so there's no way I'd be able to gain the confidence of anyone engaged in illegal activity there. My presence would just make them more cautious. You putting a total stranger like Sorenson on the run should set their minds at ease. Meanwhile, I'm going at it from another angle, trying to find witnesses to what happened on the Coquihalla that night."

"If you think they're still doing whatever it is at Waicom, smuggling or whatever, shouldn't we try to do the same thing Dad did? Bring through a load in bond and examine it?"

"For the present, I'm only concerned about your dad's accident and whatever happened to Gary's brakes. The smuggling, if that's what's happening, may be related, but it's not my main concern. Doing something about it would tip our hand, and I don't want to do that unless it becomes necessary. If it does, I'll get one of your drivers to help, one that you trust."

"You suspect one of my drivers is involved?"

"Not necessarily. But they've all had contact with Waicom on a regular basis, and I'm sure you trust one or two of them more than the others."

"Stan. He's an old, old friend of Dad's, and they wouldn't have been such good friends if Dad didn't trust him. I'd have to say I trust

226

him the most. Except for Gary, of course, but I don't want Gary going back in there again, not after that scare."

"I won't let you send Gary back in unless I'm convinced it's safe." Hunter was silent for a moment. If he was right and Randy had been murdered for threatening to expose someone at Waicom, then anyone who got too close to the truth there could be in danger, be it Sorry, Gary, Suzanne, or Hunter himself. He didn't want to put anyone in jeopardy, including Sorry, but at least Sorry had past experience with dangerous criminals and knew enough not to get himself involved in something he couldn't handle. "Like I said, I've put out the word that we're looking for witnesses, so hopefully we'll find some kind of evidence outside of Waicom. Once we do, we'll turn the job over to the police."

He told her he hoped to see her on Saturday, and asked if he'd be able to borrow Randy's Suburban again. "I'd like to take a run out to Shuswap Lake, visit some friends."

"Sure," she said. "See you then."

Hunter tried to reach Bill Earl to see if he'd found anything on the drivers in CPIC, but Bill wasn't available. He left a message that he'd call back.

Downstairs in the lounge, Hunter picked a table near the window and ordered a beer. He couldn't see the parking lot, so he kept glancing over at the door. He hoped Sorry wouldn't be too long. This time, he was the hungry one. He bought a couple of packages of beer nuts at the bar. Popping the nuts into his mouth between slugs of beer, Hunter thought about the Ranverdan drivers and their possible involvement with Waicom. He hated to think that Randy had been betrayed, maybe even murdered, by someone he considered a friend, but it wasn't as remote a possibility as he would have liked to think. In his experience, most murders were committed by spouses or lovers, close relations or friends. Money and alcohol were important catalysts, but what it came down to was a man would murder someone he was close to because of a threat to himself, be it real or imagined. A threat to his freedom, to his family, to his way of life, even a threat to his self respect could cause a man to take a life.

Sometimes even his own.

He refused to let his mind wander down that dark corridor, and forced himself to think about the coming weekend. After putting in a couple of hours on Saturday in the Ranverdan office going over the drivers' logs, he intended to take Gord up on his invitation and spend the night at the Youngs' cabin on Shuswap Lake. By the time Sorry walked through the door, Hunter was on his second beer. The sugar coated nuts had taken the edge off his hunger and he was starting to feel relaxed. Sorry looked a little worse for wear. He held his straw colored hair back away from his forehead and peered into the relative darkness of the lounge. Hunter hailed him.

"Aha! There's the man!" Sorry pulled out a chair, collapsed into it with a heavy sigh. "I've got till Sunday night to drop this load in Vancouver, right? You figure I could maybe crash here for the night?"

"I've got a room here." Hunter didn't really want to share his room with Sorry, but couldn't think of a good enough reason not to. "Forty five bucks," he added.

"Got a couch?"

"Twin beds." Hunter drained the rest of his beer. What the hell, at least Sorry didn't snore. Much. "You buy dinner."

"It's a deal. Can you lend me fifty bucks?"

Sorry brightened up visibly with the prospect of a dinner and a good night's sleep. He ordered a Coke and Hunter asked for another beer. It was one of those days when they went down like water.

"So, tell me about Waicom," Hunter said, leaning forward with his elbows on the table.

Sorry made a face. "You were wrong, man. I ain't no fuckin' snake charmer." He slumped further into his chair. "Your friend Mah did not, shall we say, take to me like he was supposed to. I got almost nothing to tell you."

Hunter nodded slowly, trying to hide his disappointment. "Just start at the beginning, Dan. Tell me everything. You know - you said, he said, then you did, he did. Everything."

Sorry was right. Hunter got almost nothing from the conversation Sorry related to him.

228

Sorry summed it up. "Only thing worth mentioning is that Mah didn't seem to care that the guy was dead. Oh, and I didn't tell you about the Newfie."

"Murphy?"

"Yeah. He whispers at me to watch my back. Says not to trust the Chinaman. The Newfie knows something, I'd put money on it. You got a few bucks for cigarettes? I'm dyin' for a smoke."

"Did you see Murphy talking to anybody at the warehouse?"

"Shit, Hunter. I was trying to stick close to the Chinaman, like I was supposed to. The Newfie was over watching his trailer get loaded, shooting the shit with the guys on the forklifts. Couldn't hear a word from where I was standing." He grabbed the bill Hunter held out to him and waved it at the waiter. "Got any cigarettes, pal?"

The waiter gave him change, pointed out the cigarette machine. Sorry got up and left.

Hunter felt like pacing, but ended up just spinning a beer-stained coaster around and around on its end on the thick acrylic varnish of the wooden table top. He knew he'd been pinning too much hope on what Sorry would find out at Waicom in Seattle. He was still sure that Steve Mah was somehow involved. Mah had escaped prosecution once, and was bound to keep playing the odds until he lost.

But for now it was Murphy's behavior that aroused his interest. Sorry was right. The man knew something about what was going on at Waicom. Murphy's warning to Sorry only confirmed what Hunter had begun to suspect earlier, after the cryptic remark Murphy had made at the Waicom warehouse the night he'd pointed Hunter in the direction of Chuck Wahl. *It should've been me.* Carla Hurley had said that Murphy and Randy had spent some time talking the night before the accident. Even though Murphy was Randy's oldest and closest friend, it was a mistake to assume that he would volunteer information relating to Randy's death. Somehow, Hunter would have to question him further, pressure him to reveal everything he knew about Waicom. Now Murphy was on his way to Winnipeg and wouldn't be back in B.C. until next week. Hunter would have to engineer an opportunity to talk to him as soon as possible.

Sorry came back, a freshly lit cigarette dangling from his lips. "Okay, boss, I'm all yours."

"Good. Now tell me what happened in Edmonton."

Sorry sucked in a lungful of smoke and rolled his eyes at the ceiling as he exhaled. "Tell you what happened in Edmonton," he repeated. "Right. Like, what do you want to know?"

"Same deal, Dan. You said, he said, all that stuff. Who did you talk to? Who talked to you?"

"Right." He sniffed loudly, then closed his eyes and twisted up his face, as if in deep thought. "I walked in there just before twelve noon, and this fat guy tells me to back up to door number ten. I fuckin' did it, too. First try." He snapped his fingers. "John! The fat guy's name was John."

"Then I go back inside, it's twelve o'clock, and the warehouse guy - the mean lookin' stud with the pony tail - he says, I'm goin' for lunch. The fat guy stops eating his sandwich long enough to bitch about it. Seems like he wasn't too comfortable with the idea of waiting around in the warehouse for an hour with a guy like me breathing down his neck. You know, my personal magnetism was maybe a little strong for him, right?" Sorry chuckled. "Nearly shit his pants when the stud tells him he's going for lunch anyway. Frank. Frank's the stud. Unload it yourself, John, he says."

Sorry took a swig of his Coke. "So then I speak up. Where can a guy get a cheap lunch around here? I asked. And this Frank guy, he says, come on with me, I'll take you where I'm going. So we went for lunch, and left the fat guy alone with his stinkin' sandwich." Sorry crushed his cigarette into the ashtray. "And after lunch we go back to the warehouse, they unload the trailer, I phone in to the little girl in Kamloops who tells me where my pick up is ... oh, yeah. She was bitching at me for not phoning in. It's not enough that I deliver the loads on time, I'm supposed to call her every fuckin' day to tell her the truck still runs, or what?"

Hunter's face grew hard. "That's routine," he said. "Go on."

230

"Okay, okay. I'll phone in every day." He pulled out another cigarette and lit it, muttering "She's too fuckin' young to be my mother."

"Keep going."

"That's it," said Sorry, with a shrug, smoke shooting out his nostrils. "I phoned in and the chick sent me off to pick up another load."

"Give your head a shake," said Hunter, his voice hard as flint. "The only reason I got her to give you this job is so that you would get information for me. If you want to keep it, quit behaving like a smartass. What did you and Frank talk about at lunch?"

Sorry bowed his head and thought for a few seconds, then sighed. "Yeah, Hunter, I know, man. I'm being an asshole. So, I did the I said, he said stuff up until we leave for lunch, right? So then this Frank guy drives me to a Chinese restaurant with a smorgasbord. I say, nice car. He's driving this Jeep. He asks did I get ripped last night. I tell him I smoked a little hash with some brothers in Hinton." He looked earnestly into Hunter's eyes. "See, I'm not holding anything back. I toked up last night in Hinton, blew the money you gave me, partied with some brothers I met in a parking lot. That's why I almost didn't make it to Waicom before noon. I got wasted and overslept." He shrugged, his eyes wide. "You know me, Hunter. I'm not like you. I like to party. I've never been straight, and I never will be. You know that, man."

Hunter nodded soberly. He knew that. That's why Sorry could go places Hunter couldn't go, talk to people who wouldn't talk to him. He didn't fully understand why, but he knew that to a lot of people on the other side of the law, he still smelled like a cop. Sorry smelled like anything but. "Go on," he said.

"So he asks me if I've got any more hash, I say no. He hints that he does a lot of coke. I say, how can he afford it. I say, I figure he's banging some old moneybags broad. Some of them go for guys like him - the mean looking types, eh?" He took another swallow of Coke and wiped his mouth with the back of his hand. "So he says, you may be right. Meaning, maybe he's got this rich old lady. I'm busy stuffing my face with beef chop suey and pork fried rice. I wait to see if he's going to say anything more. He talks about the Canucks-Rangers series. Who fuckin' cares? He talks about the fuckin' weather, for Christ sake! I say, yeah, you're right, it is fuckin' hot. I eat more chop suey. We order coffee. I bum a smoke. He looks at his watch, says we gotta go, he doesn't want to be late." Sorry shook his head, shrugging his shoulders. "What more can I tell you?"

Half closing his eyes, Hunter chewed the inside of his cheek. "And back at the warehouse?"

"Yeah, okay. We get back there and the stud climbs on his forklift and starts to unload the trailer. Fine. I go stand around near the fat guy. He stinks of garlic. I say, can I use the phone? He says sure. The handle's greasy and the whole thing fuckin' stinks of garlic. I phone this Suzanne. She gives me the dope on the load I just picked up, and she says you're probably in Edmonton by then and that I should phone you."

"So," Hunter leaned back in his chair, "what do you think?"

Sorry pulled on the end of his nose a couple of times, then ran his index finger underneath his nostrils, snuffling. "What do I think? I think that you think that there's something rotten going on, and I respect that. From past experience, Hunter The Man is usually right. I think that I didn't get the information that you need, and I'm sorry about that. I'm sorry that you're disappointed. I really am. What I think is that these are very cautious dudes, and that nobody should be surprised that they don't tell me their secrets the first time they lay eyes on me." He stuck out his jaw and nodded reflectively. "But I'll get what you need. Count on it. Give me another trip, two maybe three, they'll get slack and sloppy and I'll get you what you need. We go back a long way, man. You know I don't bullshit you when it really counts."

Hunter had to agree. He trusted Sorry about this, although he'd never been sure of him entirely when he was on the force. He always recognized and respected Sorry's allegiance to his brotherhood, as loose as that brotherhood had been at times, and that it was the most important thing in Sorry's life, a part of his very identity. So he never expected Sorry to reveal information about a fellow outlaw biker

232

unless that biker's behavior posed a threat to the brotherhood. If Sorry had belonged to one of the more powerful gangs, Hunter knew he would never have gotten anything from him. As it was, when Sorry was wearing the patch of the Black Cobras, he had put himself at risk giving Hunter information. So, sure, Sorry had sometimes lied to Hunter in the past, or more accurately, omitted to tell the truth. Hunter had expected him to lie. This time, he counted on his own friendship with Sorry being stronger than any rapport the biker might develop with the men at Waicom. Yes, he trusted him.

He already knew he'd had unrealistic expectations for the results of Sorry's first exposure to the crew at Waicom. He figured there'd be no problem with Sorry doing the run a few more times, as long as he kept Suzanne reasonably happy. "Remember, in the end it's not up to me that you stay on the payroll at Ranverdan. The 'chick' is the boss."

"Yeah, okay. I'll be a good boy and phone in like I'm supposed to. Mo's real happy that I'm workin'. I've got to admit, I'd really like to keep this job."

"And let me remind you, Dan, that I don't want you to do anything that's going to put you in jeopardy here. If you can't find anything out by just talking to these guys, don't go any further. If these guys really are responsible for Randy's death, if they're threatened, they may not hesitate to get rough. Don't take any chances. You're a family man now. Got that?"

"Yeah, I got it."

"Great!" Hunter banged on the table with his fist, making Sorry drop his cigarette. It rolled to the edge of the table before Sorry managed to snatch it up.

"I'm starving," said Hunter. "Let's go see if we can rustle up some of that legendary grain-fed Alberta beef."

CHAPTER

TWENTY-TWO

Hunter arrived in Kamloops Saturday morning at around eight o'clock. He parked The Blue Knight just outside the Ranverdan yard, grabbed his duffle bag from the sleeper, and set off on foot for the Rodgers' home. Once he crossed the highway into the residential section, the morning songs of chickadees and robins cascaded down from the trees and bubbled across the green and brown patchwork of lawns and gardens. In spite of the spill of June sunshine across the suburban tableau, it was still early enough to be cool, or at least not uncomfortably hot. He dodged the silvery curtain of an oscillating lawn sprinkler, inhaling deeply the smells of wet earth and grass as he passed.

Suzanne opened the door before he reached it. She was barefoot, and dressed in white shorts and a lavender colored teeshirt. He skin glowed fresh from a shower. Little Jolene peered around her mother's slender legs, giggled at Hunter, and skipped back to where she'd come from, whinnying like a horse. Suzanne invited him in for coffee, and he followed her into the kitchen. Her damp hair, giving off the faint scent of soap, was held in a loose ponytail by a black fabric band.

"Gary's gone out for a run," she said, handing Hunter a mug of fresh coffee. "He's getting restless. I'm not finding enough work for him close to home, so he wants me to put him on the longer hauls again."

"Hasn't El been able to come up with anything for him?" Hunter asked, reaching for the carton of Creamo.

She winced. "I'm trying not to use El, if I can help it."

"Why not? She's got a crusty way about her, but her heart's in the right place."

"That's what Gary says, but I don't think she has my interests at heart." She peered down into her mug for a moment, then raised her eyes to Hunter's. "Pete's gone to work for her, you know."

Frowning, Hunter finished stirring his coffee and looked around for a place to put the spoon. He set it down beside the sink. "Yes, I know. It was his idea, she says."

Suzanne shook her head. "I don't know. It's enough of a struggle trying to keep the business going without her so-called help. I'd like to know how a guy who's bitched for years about just scraping by was all of a sudden able to buy a nearly new Ford tractor. I'll bet she even helped to finance him."

"I can't believe she'd do that," Hunter said, but wasn't as sure about it as he tried to sound.

"You know, the drivers are part of the reason it's seemed so important to keep Ranverdan afloat. They'd always been so loyal to Dad, and to the company, I couldn't turn around and put them out of work." Suzanne stared into her coffee mug again. "Now I'm beginning to wonder if it really matters that much to them."

They both remained standing, sipping at their coffee for a while, then Hunter asked, "Was there anything unusual about your Dad's behavior towards Pete in the past few months?"

Suzanne looked up abruptly, eyebrows raised. "You don't think ...?" She covered her mouth with her hand, thought for a moment. "Dad was always getting pissed off at Pete, but that's nothing new. Pete and him were good friends on one level, like, they'd spent a lot of time together socially because Mom was such good friends with Mrs. Whitehead, but Dad used to get fed up with Pete. He was always turning down runs, or asking Dad to get someone else to switch with him. Dad said that if it hadn't been for Mrs. Whitehead, Pete would've been off the roster years ago." She smiled and shook her head. "Dad was such a mush sometimes. Even after Mom died, he didn't want to do anything that would have upset her."

"What about Stan Murphy?"

"Murph? Why Murph?"

"Just covering all the bases. Anything seem to have changed recently between your father and Murphy?"

"Murph has been Dad's closest friend for years, especially since Mom died. Murph got divorced about the same time, so they kind of supported each other through some rough times. They'd go off fishing together sometimes, have a few beers together when they were both in town, that kind of thing. But lately?" She frowned, searching the kitchen ceiling with her eyes. "Yes, I guess things changed a little about six months ago. Murph got a girlfriend, a woman in Cherry Creek. He and Dad started spending less time together, although sometimes lately Dad would drive out to Cherry Creek and have dinner with Murph and his girlfriend and stay overnight. As far as I know, they still got along fine. Dad never said anything to me about problems between them, and I never heard them argue. It's just that Murph was busy with his girlfriend more often." She sighed. "Maybe that's why Dad got involved with that ... Carla person in Vancouver."

"Have you met Murph's girlfriend?"

"No, but I think Dad liked her a lot. Her name is Kitty. Dad used to call her Miss Kitty of Cherry Creek."

Suzanne turned to place her mug behind her on the counter, and the black band slipped off her gathered hair and fell to the floor. Hunter picked it up and handed it to her, and she held it in her teeth while she shook out her hair and ran her fingers through it. Her movements brought Hunter a sudden, sharp image of his daughter Jan. As she twisted the elasticized band around a new ponytail, Suzanne drew in her breath, then let it out in a sigh. "I'm able to talk about Dad now without feeling like I'm going to fall to pieces." There was pain in her face as she continued, "You'd think I'd be relieved, wouldn't you? But I'm not. I've lost him physically, and

236

now I'm afraid I'm going to lose him here, too." She pointed to her heart.

"He won't let that happen," said Hunter. "Trust me."

The first thing Hunter did after he let himself into the Ranverdan office was call Bill Earl at the detachment office. Bill was off duty so he tried his home.

"You're lucky, pal. Two minutes later and I would've been out of here for the rest of the weekend. I'm taking my kid on an overnight hike."

Bill had Hunter hang on while he went to find his notes. "Okay, we got zip on Albert, Buckingham, Rodgers, and Whitehead. Must be good, law-abiding citizens. Or lucky crooks. But this Kubik, we picked him up for a bar fight one time, and same with Murphy. Neither one was out of the ordinary, the usual drunk and rowdy stuff, a few punches between consenting adults. No charges resulted in either case."

"That's funny," Hunter mused. "Murphy didn't seem at all inclined to get involved in a situation we both witnessed a couple weeks ago. He's what you might call a friendly galoot."

"My brother calls his Rottweiler friendly, too. Maybe the guy learned his lesson. Or maybe he's got to have something at stake. According to my scribble here, the report said they were fighting over a woman. Could be he's the jealous type."

"Were there any other names in that report?"

"Yep. One Robert Charles Williams and one Audrey Eileen Murphy. Wife, no doubt."

"When was that, Bill?"

"October 1991. In a bar at the Stockmen's Hotel."

"I wonder if that was before or after Murphy and his wife split up," said Hunter. "Like you say, maybe he's the jealous type, or maybe he was just going through a rough time."

The report on Tiny Kubik was just as Bill had described it. Two guys, fighting drunk, who slept it off and went home friends the next morning.

"I've got another name for you to run, Bill. Try Frank Scarfo, currently a resident of Edmonton or thereabouts. He's ..."

Bill interrupted. "Okay, pal, I'll do it Monday. Look, my kid's practically standing in my lap here, trying to get me off the phone. Gotta go."

After he'd wished Bill and his son a good weekend and hung up the phone, Hunter sat staring out the office window at the street. He was disappointed, and realized that he'd been looking forward to discussing some of the new developments with Bill - Murphy, for example, and the shrink wrap. It always used to help to brainstorm a case with another detective. It could have been especially useful now that Bill was leaning towards the idea of murder. As soon as he considered the evidence to be strong enough, Bill had said, he would take it to Staff Sergeant Walker.

Hunter wondered how he would feel if the R.C.M.P. decided to take over the investigation, and he was asked to butt out. It could happen. He had every confidence in the force, and didn't doubt the ability of his former colleagues to solve it, but he was developing some strong feelings about this case. As a Mountie, he'd had a few cases that he felt strongly about and was forced to hand over to someone else. The decision was accepted, as it had to be, and he had moved on to other things. This was different. This had become a personal crusade, and he wanted to see it through. Maybe it would be best to keep his distance from Bill until he was ready to hand over the killer, figuratively speaking, of course. In that case, he'd have to solve it on his own, if he could.

He heaved himself out of the chair and went to the cupboard Suzanne had described. The drivers' log sheets were stashed neatly in a series of cardboard file boxes labelled with each driver's name. He carried four file boxes, those labelled R. Danyluk, G. Rodgers, S. Murphy, and P. Whitehead, over to a bare work table that stood against the back wall of the room underneath the picture window. He gazed outside for a moment, admiring the grace of the weeping

238

willow and watching a big bee bumble around the lilacs that bordered the lawn. Then he pulled his reading glasses from his shirt pocket and perched them on the end of his nose.

By law, drivers of vehicles over five tons are required to keep a daily log of their activities, and to make that log available to government authorities on request. Copies of the log must be submitted daily to the carrier the driver works for. The main purpose of these logs is to ensure that drivers do not exceed a prescribed number of hours of driving without taking time off to sleep. Some truckers, often with the help of amphetamines, try to work thirty-six or more hours at a stretch. The DOT doesn't want drivers like that on the road. Sleep deprived drivers see things that aren't there. They fall asleep with their eyes open. Thirty-five tons of freight and speeding machinery out of control on a public highway can do a lot of damage. Some truckers, often with encouragement or even coercion from their employers, will still break the rules, keep two sets of log books, drive too long and ingest too many chemicals, and in doing so jeopardize themselves and others. But they're doing it illegally, if that's of any comfort to their victims.

The information required includes the names of the driver, co-driver (if any), and carrier, as well as the identifying numbers of the tractor and trailer. The driver must record the number of miles driven during each twenty-four hour period, and the origin and destination of the load. The main body of the log consists of a twenty-four hour grid, with each hour divided into quarters. The driver plots his or her activity for the entire twenty-four hour period by indicating for each fifteen minute period which one of the following categories the activity falls into: Off Duty, Sleeper Berth, Driving, or On Duty but not driving. For each change in duty status, he or she is required to write down the vehicle's geographic location at the time of that change. If an activity takes less than fifteen minutes, there's no need to record it in the log.

Hunter was so used to keeping his own log that each grid, looking like a line graph with numerous long plateaus, told him its story in the blink of an eye. The important thing was to match up the dates and locations of the other drivers' logs to Randy's. As he expected, the logs for the last two days of Randy's life were missing. He'd be getting them from Garth in the next couple of days, but in the meantime, he could use Gary's log for the last day instead. Gary's trip to and from Seattle should correspond roughly to Randy's, although Gary had left Seattle before Randy was ready to go. His dry fingers slid on the paper, so Hunter moistened his middle finger on his lower lip and began flipping through the pages to find Stan Murphy's log sheets for May 24th.

Hunter smelled cigarette smoke and turned around with a start to see Gary leaning against the desk, his ankles crossed, one arm across his chest and the other holding a cigarette in front of his face. He smiled at Hunter - it looked forced - and nodded a greeting.

"Good morning! You must walk like a cat." Hunter grinned in an attempt to hide his irritation at being surprised.

"Sorry I missed you at the house earlier. Suzanne sent me over to see if you could use another coffee." Gary pointed at a big thermos bottle on the desk beside him.

Hunter stood up and removed his glasses.

Gary's smile broadened. "You look like an accountant in those things."

"Wait'll you turn forty, chief." Hunter walked over to the desk and picked up the thermos. Beneath it was something he'd overlooked before: a thin sheaf of papers stapled together, with a yellow post-it note stuck to the top. The note read:

Hunter - Here are the toll booth statements for the last few weeks, and a list of the drivers' card numbers. S.

Hunter poured some coffee into the thermos lid and took a cautious sip. It was still scalding hot.

"Still playing sleuth, eh?" Gary motioned towards the file boxes at the back of the room. "What are you nosing around in the log sheets for?"

"Trying to get a fix on where everybody was the night of Randy's accident."

"You know where I was."

240

Hunter glanced behind him at the table, saw that the 'G. Rodgers' on the file box was exposed. "Just for the purpose of comparison. I don't have Randy's sheet, so I'm using yours for that day instead. I'm estimating you weren't more than half an hour ahead of him leaving Seattle. Where'd you stop that night? Here?"

"No," said Gary. "Near Monte Creek. When I run through here late at night, I don't like to wake Suzanne and the girls. It upsets their routine. Besides, it's faster if I get a few hours of shut eye in the sleeper. The sooner I get the load delivered, the sooner I'm home."

"What I really want to find out is where all the other drivers were that night. Any chance you remember? You could save me a lot of time." Hunter picked up his glasses and smiled. "And eyestrain."

Gary raised his shoulders and shook his head.

"Murphy, for example. Any chance you saw him that day? Maybe in Vancouver before you left for Seattle?"

"Murphy?" Gary exhaled, slowly and thoughtfully, his eyes following the smoke towards the ceiling. "Randy switched runs with him. I think he sent him to Portland."

Hunter frowned. "What do you mean, Randy switched runs with him?"

"Just what I said. Murphy was scheduled to do the Waicom pickup, and Randy ended up doing it instead."

"Why?"

"How should I know? Maybe Randy had to be somewhere for a meeting or something, so he decided at the last minute that he couldn't do the Portland run."

"Why didn't you tell me this before?"

"I can't see how it could be important."

"How did Murphy feel about the switch?"

"How should I know?" he repeated. "He probably wasn't too happy, because he liked to spend the night with his little squeeze in Cherry Creek when he did the Waicom run. But if you think he did anything to hurt Randy, forget it. Murph's a fuckin' a teddy bear."

"You're probably right." Hunter forced himself once again not to show his irritation.

"Like I said before, I don't care how you want to spend your time." Gary waved the ashy butt of his cigarette towards the log sheets on the table behind Hunter. "But I'd appreciate it if you'd get over this obsession of yours as soon as possible, so that Suzanne can put this behind her and get on with her life." He turned around, seeking out an ashtray on Suzanne's desk. "And let me get on with mine. You've got her so spooked she still refuses to schedule me for the north-south runs, and it's starting to affect our income."

"Just give it a little more time."

Gary started to say something, then shook his head and walked away.

Hunter watched him go before extracting the papers from under the thermos. He looked at the top sheet. Beside each driver's name was a three digit card number. The subsequent sheets were the toll statements, showing the date, time, direction and card number for each toll transaction. Here at last was some of the key information he'd been looking for.

According to the statements, Gary had been through the northbound toll booth at ten forty three p.m. on May 24th. Randy had been through the northbound toll booth approximately an hour and twenty minutes later, at nine minutes past midnight on May 25th. That was consistent with Chuck Wahl's claim that Randy had left Hope sometime after eleven p.m.

Hunter winced. He had involuntarily visualized Randy at the toll booth. The attendant had probably said, "Have a nice day!" like they always do, and Randy might've said, "I sure will! I hope you do, too!" Within the hour he was broken and dying in a deep ravine. Life sometimes seemed such a fragile thing.

There was no northbound toll transaction recorded for Stan Murphy's card on May 25th at all.

Taking the toll statements with him, he turned back to the file boxes and found Stan Murphy's log sheet for Tuesday, May 24th. According to the log sheet, Murphy had left Vancouver at one a.m. After a half hour breakfast stop, he was in Portland, Oregon making his delivery by seven thirty. He then logged himself off duty until three thirty p.m., which gave him the full eight hours required by

242

DOT regulations, at which time he picked up a load destined for Calgary, Alberta. Hunter surmised it was a case of dropping off a trailer at the customer's dock in the morning for the customer to unload and reload prior to the driver picking it up again in the afternoon. Either that or Murphy had been somewhat lax about logging his On Duty hours in Portland. The log showed him crossing the border back into Canada at nine thirty p.m. He could have legally driven another two and a half hours before stopping, but he showed off duty in Hope at eleven o'clock for a full eight hour layover before getting back on the road. He had logged his arrival time in Calgary at seven a.m. on Thursday, May 26th.

Hunter sighed. If Murphy's log were accurate, he arrived in Hope at roughly the same time as Randy left it, and was still there at the time Randy went off the road some sixty miles away. Hunter double checked the toll statement, but there was definitely no transaction on it to back up the times on Murphy's log.

A log is only as reliable as the driver who records it. A driver might fudge the times in his log for any number of reasons. He might have to drive extra hours to make a tight delivery deadline, or maybe to where he could spend the night nestled against warm, perfumed skin. He might not want to take a chance on his wife seeing he'd passed some time in his old girlfriend's home town, or he might not want his employer or the authorities to know he'd been driving well over the speed limit. Under the circumstances, Hunter figured he couldn't count on a murderer to scrupulously log his presence at the scene of the crime.

What could be the explanation for there being no record of Murphy on the toll statement? Hunter frowned and drummed the eraser of his pencil on the page. One obvious possibility was that Murphy had misplaced his card and had to pay cash. The second most likely possibility was that he'd taken the old highway, the long route through the Fraser Canyon. But why? Perhaps he'd stopped in Cherry Creek, which was just off the old highway, to visit his girlfriend on the way through. Or perhaps he wanted to avoid having a record of his presence on the Coquihalla toll highway that night.

Hunter went back to the cupboard and pulled out the log sheets for the other Ranverdan drivers. Tom Buckingham had been travelling westward across Saskatchewan that night. Tiny Kubik had spent the night in Calgary waiting for a load. Pete Whitehead had returned to Kamloops at four thirty that afternoon with a load from Prince George, then logged himself off duty. That put him within easy driving distance of Randy's accident, so he couldn't be ruled out. Of the part-timers, only Jason Whitehead, Pete's son, had been on the road that night. The tractor number matched that of Pete Whitehead's, which meant that Jason had picked up the truck after Pete had returned from Prince George. His log showed that he left Kamloops at five o'clock and arrived in Vancouver at about ten. In spite of logging off duty for a meal, he was turned around and headed back out of Vancouver by two a.m. with a return load for Kamloops. That put him on the fatal stretch of the Coquihalla several hours before and again several hours after Randy's rig would have left the road. Hunter checked the toll statement, which bore out the times in Jason's log.

Hunter pulled out a handful of Randy's log sheets and flipped through them randomly. A notation caught his eye. He remembered that one of the abbreviations from Randy's scrawled notes on the computer printout had looked like "PC Rs". Just after Randy had left Kamloops on a run, he'd recorded a fifteen minute On Duty stop in his log and labelled it "PC". Right beside it were the words "Fuel Stop". Of course, the "PC" stood for Petro Canada, where he must have stopped for fuel and maybe something to eat. The "Rs" could have been a sloppy "Ks", the city code for Kamloops. Had something connected with Waicom happened at the Petro Canada station in Kamloops?

Hunter racked his brain for the other abbreviations Randy had used. "Rybds" was one. If it was a sloppy K again, what could "Kybds" stand for? He sounded it out. Keyboards. The shrinkwrapped skid. The other abbreviation was "TB", wasn't it? He flipped through the pages again and saw nothing that came close to it, but he thought of a prime possibility. Toll Booth. There was a rest area just north of the toll booth on the Coquihalla. Both the rest area

244

and Petro Canada were places where a truck might be expected to stop for an extended period of time, much like Gary stopped to use the washroom at the brake check just past the Coquihalla Summit. If there was enough time for someone to tamper with a trailer's brakes, perhaps there was enough time for someone to tamper with its load. Had Randy seen it happen? Had he seen who it was?

Hunter took off the reading glasses and rubbed his eyes. He still didn't have all the answers, but this latest discovery made him feel more than ever that he was on the right track. Now, where else could he look for hard evidence that hauling the Waicom shipment to Edmonton that night had somehow led to Randy's death? He'd have to talk to Murphy. And he'd have to wait for Sorry to gain the confidence of Steve Mah. Between the two of them, the answers were there, Hunter was sure of it.

He slid the file boxes back onto their shelf, picked up the keys to the Suburban, and set out for Shuswap Lake.

The Youngs' cabin was almost twenty miles off the main highway. Most of the road was paved, and much of it ran along the shoreline of the lake, snaking in gentle dips and curves beside the water. A few sections were heavily populated, with houses on both sides of the road, and sported rows of power boats bobbing off-shore beside an assortment of home-made and store-bought buoys. Hunter saw a glossy turquoise and white Bowrider lurch away from a weathered wooden dock leaving a long, inverted V of foam on the surface of the lake. A few of the boats he saw skimming across the lake were followed by tubers or skiers, trailing their own shallow wakes or boisterous rooster tails.

Two barefoot and nearly naked brown boys, one almost a head smaller than the other, ran gingerly across the pavement ahead of the Suburban and disappeared down a steep bank towards the beach. What a place for a kid to spend the summer! Outdoor adventure and an escape from city attitude. Maybe a dude ranch wouldn't be such a bad place for a couple of little girls to grow up. In his rearview mirror, Hunter saw a small pickup following too close. He pulled over to the far right and let it pass. Three teenaged girls in the box waved at him cheekily as the little truck pulled ahead. Dumb kids, he thought. They think they'll live forever. Every year, the R.C.M.P. attended too many accidents that proved them wrong.

The population grew sparser as the road continued. He saw a little store called the Eagle Bay General Store and turned into its semi-circular driveway. He purchased a dozen cold cans of beer, choosing Kokanees and Kootenays, and two bottles of California wine with corks. No matter what Gord said about not having to bring anything, he wouldn't feel right showing up empty handed. Gord had told him that by the time he reached the store, he'd be only about five miles away from the cabin. The pavement soon ended, and the last few miles were on a hard packed surface of reddish brown dirt pocked with potholes and strewn with loose gravel. On a few of the hills, the road's surface rippled into a washboard and Hunter had to slow the Suburban right down to keep the beer from bouncing dangerously. The road dipped down towards the water past a row of lakeside cabins. Near the end of the row, Hunter saw the sign nailed to an eight foot tall cedar stump. "Uncle John's Cabin", it said.

This was the place.

CHAPTER
TWENTY-THREE

That night, Hunter and Gord stayed up talking long after the others had gone to bed. They sat out on a huge wooden deck overlooking the lake, nursing their second nightcap of beer and admiring the stars on display in the wide expanse of night sky between the trees behind them and the great shadowy hump of mountain across the lake. The stars were so distinctly bright it seemed unreal. Hunter's arms were tucked in against the coolness of the night, but he was grateful for the breeze that kept the mosquitoes away. He had helped at the barbecue earlier, and found out that there were bloodthirsty droves of them hovering in the woods. He and his landlord talked about the innumerable stars and the wisdom of the ancients and the insignificance of man and the history of time. There were long comfortable breaks in their conversation.

Two of Gord's adult daughters and their significant others had gone to bed in a second smaller cabin about fifty yards from the one with the big wooden deck. Gord's brother, John, had retired early to the main cabin to read. Like everyone else, Hunter had eaten until he was stuffed. Camp food, they called it. Nachos and beer in the afternoon. A cocktail before dinner, accompanied by an appetizer of fat pink prawns doused in garlic butter, with chunks of a crusty baguette. Wine. Salad. Inch thick steaks, barbecued to a perfect medium rare, then strewn with mushrooms simmered in garlic. Baked potatoes with sour cream and chopped green onions. A choice of apple or pecan pie, with ice cream, and fresh brewed coffee for dessert. Right, camp food.

"Your daughter said you've all been coming here for over thirty years." Hunter watched the green light of a boat float slowly through the darkness on the other side of the lake, the lazy buzz of its engine clearly audible at a distance of over three miles.

"Yep. Since nineteen sixty, or thereabouts. Missed a few years, here and there." Gord took a quiet sip from his can of beer. "We lived in half a dozen different houses since then, so this place has been the only thing that's stayed more or less the same. We spent a few years on the prairies, then moved to Toronto for a few, but John lived in Kamloops and kept working away out here in his spare time. This big cabin," - he stuck his thumb over his left shoulder - " used to be the same size as that little one over there. John expanded it himself, bit by bit. Now it's got, what? Five bedrooms, I guess. You should bring your girls up here sometime. A lot of weekends during the summer there's nobody here but John."

Hunter nodded thoughtfully. "Your daughters sure seem to like it. Did they enjoy it as much when they were Jan and Lesley's age? Late teens, early twenties?"

"I think so. We lived in Toronto during those years, so my wife and I didn't come here that often, but I think the girls who were out here did," said Gord. He was silent for a moment. "Look! A shooting star!" He pointed and Hunter caught sight of it just before it disappeared, vanishing so fast and so completely he wondered if it had really existed. "At least there's a flush toilet and a shower here now. There was nothing but outhouses then, and we'd get our water in buckets from the lake, heat it on top of that little propane stove to wash dishes. Do your girls like to water-ski? Can they drive a boat?"

Hunter shrugged, took a swig of beer. It was getting flat and tepid. "I should've done more things like that with them when they were younger. We did a lot of snow skiing in the winter. In the summer, we took them camping a few times. You know, put up a tent in a provincial park or a KOA campground. Go for hikes. Go swimming if there was a lake. The last time was eight or nine years ago. Then Chris went back to work, and we never seemed to get

248

vacations at the same time, and the kids started going places with their friends, and vacations together didn't seem so important to any of us any more. I don't know, Gord." He sighed. "I don't know if they like to waterski, or if they can drive a boat."

The wake of a long-departed boat threw itself against the rocky beach, the sound of the waves receding softly into a watery murmur.

"So you didn't see much of your daughters when they were in their late teens either?" asked Hunter.

"Seemed like one or another was always away at school. Even when they were living at home, we didn't spend a lot of time together talking. Some days it wasn't much more than Hi, Dad and Bye, Dad. Unless they wanted something from my wallet." They both grinned wryly. "And they always came to me for medical advice. Still do. None of them bothered with a family doctor for years. And some school subjects, they gave me credit for knowing more than they did. Not often, mind you.

"But you can't compare the situation with your own, Hunter. My wife and I were still together. That makes a big difference. I always knew a lot of what was going on in the girls' lives - boyfriends and other catastrophes - because my wife gave me a daily recap during the Johnny Carson show." The old doctor sighed quietly, and Hunter assumed he was thinking of his late wife, whom Hunter had never known. "Sometimes grown men don't have much in common with young girls." Gord waved his beer can at the Milky Way. "Things like this, everybody can share, though."

They were silent again, listening to the night.

"No, Hunter, you can't ever expect to be as close to them as their mother is. I never was. They're girls, after all. But there are things you can offer them that their mother can't. The benefit of what you've learned in life from the kind of experiences their mother's never had."

Hunter nodded wordlessly, thinking that offers could be rejected.

"How do they feel about you being a truck driver?"

Hunter looked at Gord with a small frown. "I guess ... I don't know. They've never said."

"Just wondered," said Gord. He stood up and leaned against the railing, draining the dregs of his beer over the side of the deck. "Truck drivers kind of have a bad rap, if you know what I mean. Depending on the social circles they're moving in, some young ladies might not understand why you choose to do it." He shrugged apologetically at Hunter. "If you haven't already, you might want to explain it to them. They probably haven't seen enough of life yet to figure it out for themselves."

Hunter slept fitfully on a foam mattress in the attic. Overindulgence in food and alcohol had made him feel hypertensive and muzzy headed, and the whine of mosquitoes haunted him from outside a screen window just a few feet from his head. Beyond the needling buzz of the mosquitoes, there was a massive silence, broken only occasionally by the slapping of waves against the beach. It had never occurred to him before that his daughters might be ashamed of what he did for a living. They often asked him politely how work was going, but it was never discussed in detail. Having grown up in a family who believed in higher education, truck driving wasn't something he himself had considered a career option at their age. In fact, he would probably have regarded it as one of those jobs a man would only do if he didn't know how to do something better. Gord might be right. But if Jan and Lesley found his occupation embarrassing, what good would an explanation do?

Towards morning, he fell into a deep sleep. The room was bright when he awoke to the sound of a small animal thumping across the roof above his head. A chipmunk scolded stridently, paused for a few seconds, then began scolding again. Hunter rolled over towards the wall and pulled the blanket up around his ears. The chipmunk scolded louder, for longer, and finally Hunter admitted defeat. He pulled on his jeans and made his way downstairs.

Hunter leaned against the wooden railing of the big deck and surveyed the early morning. The cabins faced north out of a slight bay, so the sun was climbing above the slope to his right. The lake was like glass, bearing a crisp reflection of the dappled green north shore mountains and the fragments of stretched cheesecloth cloud that drifted in front of them. An invisible truck rattled along the road

250

on the other side of the lake, the position of its noise lagging behind the dust rising along the distant shoreline. He heard the single note call of a loon he couldn't see. About seventy yards from where Hunter stood, one of Gord's daughters sat in silence at the end of an old floating dock, hands curled around a mug of coffee, a book lying unopened in her lap.

The door behind him opened with a squeak and Hunter's landlord emerged with a faded Hawaiian towel draped over his bare shoulder. In his mid-seventies, he was still well muscled but his skin had started to sag. Hunter hoped he would still be that fit when, and if, he reached Gord's age. "Good morning," Hunter said, almost sorry to break the silence that surrounded them.

Gord bowed, smiling. "Join me for a swim?" he asked, his eyebrows shooting up above the frames of his glasses. The old doctor's hair stuck up in places, making him look like an elderly Dennis the Menace.

"Uh ... ." Hunter searched for a good excuse. He ran his hand over his own hair and realized that he must look much the same.

"It's bracing, I'll give you that, but you won't be sorry once you're in. Clears out the cobwebs."

"Hah," said Hunter. "After last night, I've definitely got my share of those. Okay. I'll be right there."

The old doctor was right. It was cold enough that the first shock took Hunter's breath away, but after half a minute it felt indescribably great. It was like the ultimate cold drink of water for a thirsty man. Quietly treading water, submerged almost to his nostrils, he looked along the surface of the lake. A frog's eye view. Small swarms of insects danced above the water, and a distant houseboat chugged somnolently towards the eastern point of the bay. By the time he climbed out onto the dock, Gord had returned to drop off a mug of fresh coffee, which Hunter accepted gratefully. He felt more than a little self conscious standing dripping wet and half naked beside Gord's daughter, who was still sitting at the end of the dock, so he followed Gord off the dock, and moved a plastic lawn chair to a warm patch of beach beyond the shadows of the tall cottonwoods and cedars surrounding the cabin.

A moment later, footsteps crunched down over the rocky beach from the cabin and Hunter's landlord deposited a second chair beside him, working it back and forth to find a solid footing on the rocks before sitting down. "I always make breakfast when we're up here, but they won't let me do it this morning." Gord sighed heavily. "Father's Day. I'm supposed to relax. I'm retired, for crying out loud! For me, the most stressful thing in life is having nothing to do." He grunted, and held up his coffee mug. "Happy Father's Day, Hunter."

They clinked coffee mugs together and Hunter smiled. "I forgot about Father's Day. I should call my dad. Do you know whether a cellular phone would work here?"

"From what I understand, the signal is pretty weak. Anne's used hers a couple of times, but she usually gets cut off halfway through."

"I'll have to call later from Kamloops, then. Just as well. He and my mother live in Hawaii so they're a couple of hours behind us."

"Your kids might be trying to call you, too. Maybe you should put your phone in your pocket and turn it on. A poor connection is probably better than none at all."

Hunter shrugged. "It's okay. I figure the girls are pretty busy. There'll probably be a message on my answering machine when I get home." Like last year. "You're right though, I should see if they've got time to come up here for a weekend. It'd be nice." He nodded to himself. "Yes. It would be nice."

After breakfast, Gord suggested a cruise up to the Narrows in the powerboat. He explained that the Shuswap is shaped roughly like a big, lopsided H, made up of the main body of the lake and three long narrow arms, the largest of which is Salmon Arm. The place where the four arms of the lake meet, called Cinnemousin Narrows, was roughly ten miles away by water. At a leisurely pace it took them a good forty minutes to reach it. The dirt road stopped a few miles beyond the Youngs' cabins, so the cabins along the shoreline, now accessible only by boat, became sparser and sparser as they approached the middle of the H. Over the roar of the motor, Hunter remarked on the number of houseboats. Gord nodded and hollered back, "Wait'll you see the Narrows!"

They soon came upon a cluster of houseboats - Hunter counted eight - and Gord slowed the boat to an idle. "Those two," he pointed towards two large houseboats festooned with signs, "are floating general stores that are here to service the houseboaters. I've never seen them not busy. They carry everything from tee-shirts, to milk and butter, to rental videos." Two or three houseboats were lined up beside each of the floating stores. They ranged from little beige houseboats just slightly bigger than a truck camper to big new blue and white jobs sporting water slides and gas barbecues. Some of them were towing speedboats. A jet-ski roared up beside them, slowing and settling in the water as it approached the houseboats.

Hunter laughed. "It looks like a great way to escape from the crowds and traffic of the city, doesn't it?"

"The Shuswap isn't exactly a good place for the real wilderness enthusiast." The old doctor swung the boat around slowly. "It would take far too much time for us to drive up one of the other arms, not to mention a lot of gas, but the houseboats thin out up Seymour Arm," he pointed over the back of the boat, "and Anstey Arm up ahead there. With all the little nooks and crannies, they've calculated that there's over six hundred miles of shoreline to spread out along. That much space can swallow a lot of houseboats. For example, they seldom even get close to our part of the shoreline and they sure don't bother us when they're motoring up the other side of the lake. Ready to head back?"

At full throttle, the return trip took only about twenty minutes. One of Gord's daughters was fishing in a little aluminum rowboat about fifty yards from shore. She looked up from her book and waved as they coasted by. Grinning from behind oversized sunglasses, she pointed to something at the front of the boat, and as they got closer Hunter realized it was The Cat. Gord's Siamese roommate was settled comfortably in the sun on top of a lifejacket spread across the front seat. "She doesn't mind being *on* the water,"

Gord explained with a wry smile, "but it's worth your life to try putting her *in* it." Hunter laughed.

He hoped he could get the girls to come up here with him next time.

That morning, Suzanne had crawled back into bed after feeding the kids and getting them settled in front of PBS's Sunday morning children's shows. She had been surprised to find Gary already awake, lying on his back with his hands behind his head, staring at the ceiling. She snuggled up to warm herself against his body, planting a gentle kiss on his stubbled cheek.

"Happy Father's Day," she whispered. "I told the kids you were still sleeping. They've got a handful of Father's Day pictures they're itching to show you."

He mouthed a little kiss in return. "I'm sure they'll be stomping in here like little dinosaurs right after Barney's over," he said with a smile, and resumed his far off stare.

She studied his face. She remembered thinking, the first time they'd met, that he wasn't very good looking. About a year into their relationship, she realized that he'd become the most handsome man in the world to her. Her fingers stroked his skin, from his collar bone across the bulges and dips of his shoulder and biceps, and he trapped them briefly between his forearm and his biceps, squeezing them firmly with a flex of his muscles.

"What're you thinking about?" she asked.

"You sure you really want to know?"

She made a little face. "Now you *have* to tell me. Otherwise I'll be imagining all sorts of horrible things."

"Okay." He licked his lower lip and swallowed, as if he were about to tell a story.

"Once upon a time ...," she prompted, and their eyes met. His sparkled.

"Once upon a time," he began, his voice low and soft, "there was a beautiful young princess who lived in the High Country. No, wait a minute. She *used* to be a princess, but now she's got to be a young

254

queen, because she married her prince charming, who loves her very much, and together they made two little princesses, who were also very beautiful."

He pulled one arm out from underneath his head and hugged her closer against his chest, and his lips brushed her forehead.

"And the prince - no, I guess he'd have to be the king - yes, it's Father's Day, so he's definitely the king. Anyway, the king had a job that took him away from his lovely queen and the beautiful princesses. He had to leave them alone at home every week for many days, sometimes for longer than a week at a time. So one day, the king said to his young queen, How would you like it if we never had to spend another night apart. And the lovely young queen said ... " He stopped. When she didn't say anything, he added, "Well?" and brought the other hand out from behind his head, slipping it beneath the sheet to tickle her.

Between giggles, Suzanne managed to whisper, "He tickled the poor queen mercilessly, until she said, How?"

"And the king said, I know of a place called The Magic Kingdom, where we can all live happily ever after."

"And the queen said, What've you been smoking, King-y?"

"And the king said, Shut up, Queenie! I'm telling the story!" Gary's hand shot out to tickle her again.

"Okay, okay, King. It's your story." She pushed his hand away, giggling softly. "So the queen shut up."

"So the king waved his magic wand, and he and the queen and the two princesses were magically transported to a big, beautiful log cabin. The queen looked down in wonder, for her fancy, stiff and stuffy gown had turned into comfy blue jeans and soft leather boots, and a denim shirt with neat little white leather fringes and pearl buttons. And the king took her by the hand and led her outside, and she saw that the log cabin was on a hill that overlooked a sparkling blue lake. This land is all ours for miles around, said the king, spreading his arms wide. And across from the log cabin, there was a barn, and some stables, with dozens of beautiful horses. And the king took the queen to the stables, and there was a beautiful

Appaloosa mare with big, brown eyes and a soft pink muzzle. And the king said, this one is yours, my Queen. So he helped her into the saddle, and he mounted a big roan stallion, and they galloped off into the sunset and lived happily ever after, forever and ever, amen."

Suzanne poked him in the side. He jumped and made a grab for her hand, missed it, and started to tickle her again. "Wait, wait!" she said, trying to fight him off. "What about the king's job?"

"The king and queen became the proud proprietors of The Magic Kingdom dude ranch, which became very famous and made pots and pots of money, so the king and queen and their little princesses got to meet lots of new people and had fun playing with their horses every day."

"I see," said Suzanne, with an uncertain smile. She wondered what had happened to the queen's father, and whether all the queen's memories disappeared along with her fancy gown and the king's old job. "A magic wand, eh?"

Gary pulled his hand out from under the sheet and waved an imaginary wand above her head. "Whoosh!," he said. "Neat story, huh?"

Suzanne sighed, not daring to look at him. Gary had a right to dream. It was a dream that she had once collaborated with him on, it seemed so long ago. She didn't want to let herself get caught up in it now. Not now, when Ranverdan had fallen like a sudden weight on her shoulders, a weight that she felt herself staggering under, as she tried to cope with the additional burden of her grief. Not now, when things were going badly at Ranverdan and she felt so very vulnerable. Not now. She whispered it under her breath, not wanting to say it aloud.

Yes, Gary had a right to dream.

"Suzy?" He lifted her chin gently and made her look into his eyes. "Sweetheart? Will you go there with me today? Please, Suzy. Come with me, and we can take the girls for a pony ride?"

She closed her eyes, pressed her lips together. Was there any good reason to say no?

"It's all I want for Father's Day, hon. Just for you to come up there, take a look around. Okay?"

256

She sighed deeply.

"Okay, baby?"

She nodded, reluctantly. "Yes, mi'lord," she said, and he hugged her tight.

CHAPTER
TWENTY-FOUR

When Hunter pulled up in front of the Rodgers' house in the Suburban around three o'clock, Suzanne was squatting on the lawn weeding a border of red geraniums that ran the length of the driveway. She looked like a young tomboy, her hair tucked up inside the crown of a fluorescent green baseball cap. As before, he couldn't help but think about how much her father must have loved her. As he got out of the truck, she stood up and stretched her back, her face in an exquisite grimace, and let two oversized, dirt covered gardening gloves drop to the grass at her feet.

"Gardening, laundry, and carrying kids," Hunter said with a smile. "They're almost as hard on the back as driving a truck."

She laughed, wiping her hands on what looked like a man's white dress shirt with the sleeves cut off. It came almost to the hem of her faded yellow shorts. "Yeah. Tell me about it! So, how was the Shuswap?"

"Great! But I spent most of the last twenty four hours eating and drinking." He slapped his stomach. "It should last me for at least a week. You're sure hard at work here. Looks good." He indicated the row of geraniums with a wave of his hand. "Where are the girls?"

"I gave them ten dollars so that they could take their father to the Dairy Queen for ice cream cones. Father's Day, you know?" Her smile faded, and she looked down at her hands, picked at some dirt under one of her fingernails.

Hunter nodded. They were both thinking of her father again.

"Gary took me out to see that ranch," she said. She bent down to pull a weed she'd missed, tossed it into a plastic pail.

He nodded silently again.

"It's very nice." She rubbed her jaw with her wrist instead of her fingers, but still managed to get a little smudge of dirt on her face. Hunter fought the impulse to wipe it away. "I guess you don't know anything more yet ... about Dad?"

"No. I'm working on a couple of leads, but it'll probably be a few days before I get anything new."

"I can't even think about selling the company," she said, sounding almost angry. "How could I? It meant so much to Dad."

Hunter smiled gently. "You know what I think means more to your Dad than anything else?"

She raised her eyes to his, but said nothing.

"I think that your happiness means more to him than anything."

"That doesn't make it any easier," she said in a tiny voice, looking down at her hands again. "I don't even know what would make me happy. In fact, sometimes I can't imagine myself ever being truly happy again."

He reached out and touched her cheek, rubbed gently at the smudge of dirt. "You will be," he said. "I promise you, you will." Then he felt uncomfortable, and looked away.

She rubbed at the same spot, then said, "I guess you need a ride to your truck?"

They climbed into the Suburban, Hunter driving, and headed towards the Ranverdan yard. His mind groped for a suitable opening to a question he needed to ask her, but found none. "Suzanne ... ?" He hesitated.

"Yes?"

He shrugged. "I just wondered ..." He inhaled, exhaled. "I wondered whether you were ever -- I don't know -- maybe ..." He compressed his lips, looked at her and then back at the road. "...

embarrassed that your father was a truck driver -- when you were a teenager."

She looked stunned.

"Oh, damn, I'm sorry. It was a stupid question, especially today. It's not about you, really, it's just ...."

"Ahhh. I see," she said. "It's okay. And yeah, maybe I was - embarrassed, like you say. I usually didn't talk about it, but if anybody asked, I'd tell them my dad was in the transportation industry, or sometimes I'd just say that he had his own company. I don't think I ever came right out and told anybody he was a truck driver. Dumb, huh? At university, a lot of the other girls' fathers were doctors and lawyers and executives in big corporations or whatever, and I didn't want them to look down on me. I was ... ignorant, I guess. Just an ignorant kid."

"Thanks," he said.

"I'm sorry. It doesn't mean ..."

"That's okay." He smiled sadly. "At that age, maybe I would've done the same."

When Hunter got home that night, there was a message from Sam Manji on his answering machine. The message said that something interesting had developed in regard to Rick Bilodeau, and that Hunter should call the Surrey R.C.M.P. detachment Monday morning. Other than half a dozen hang ups, Manji's was the only recorded call.

Hunter was tired. He erased the tape and went to bed.

It was a typical Monday morning at Watson Transportation: phones ringing non-stop, drivers in and out of the door with styrofoam cups of coffee in hand, trucks in and out of the yard, warehouse doors up and down like yo-yos, their metal chains sliding across pulleys with a metallic whirr. El hadn't even realized the Ranverdan tractor-trailer that had been parked in the back lot was gone until she saw it coming back, just before ten o'clock.

"Who the hell is that?" she muttered, catching a glimpse of the blond driver on the far side of the green cab as it passed her window.

The phone rang again. A North Vancouver customer wanted to know when his shipment would be delivered, so she had to raise her city driver on the radio to find out where he was. There'd been a rush-hour accident northbound on the Second Narrows bridge that had traffic jammed up for miles on westbound Highway 1. She reported the driver's ETA back to the customer and looked up just in time to catch sight of the unfamiliar blond driver walking past the front of the building on the way to his car.

"I'll be damned," she said. She squirmed out of her chair and hustled to the door, flung it wide and yelled, "Sorenson! You dip stick! You too good to say hello, or what?" He gave her the finger, several times with both hands, and ambled over. He was wearing a regular shirt, light blue, with buttons and a collar, and his hair came to just below his ears; his moustache was neatly trimmed.

"What the fuck happened to you?" she asked. "You find God in Edmonton, or what?"

Sorry grinned. "Fuck off, Fat Broad," he said. "My kids wanted to take me out for dinner yesterday, and my wife made me get cleaned up so we could go somewhere respectable."

"Yeah? Where'd you go?"

"Denny's."

They both guffawed loudly.

"I see you got the Ranverdan load delivered in good time this morning," El said, nodding towards the back of the lot where the tractor-trailer was parked.

"Damn right. I might even keep that job," he said.

"Any luck with ... you know?"

He shook his head. "Not yet. It'll come."

"Yeah. Let's hope so." Her phone was ringing again. "See you around, eh?"

He waved and turned back towards his car.

"Watson!" she barked into the receiver.

"Good morning, El." It was Hunter.

She told him about Sorry's new look. "If it wasn't for his Harley belt buckle, you wouldn't even suspect he was a biker," she said. "What's his angle, d'you suppose?"

"Good for him," said Hunter. "He's mellowing with age, I guess."

She snorted. "As amusing as he is - and I like the guy, don't forget - I wouldn't trust him any farther than I could throw his bike. He's still part of that one percent, as far as I'm concerned."

"He's got a family now, El. That changes a man."

"Yeah. Charles Manson had a family, too."

Hunter's voice signalled a change of subject. "Listen, El, do you know anything about Murphy's schedule this week? I'd really like a chance to sit down with him - as soon as possible - but I don't want it to look contrived, if you know what I mean."

"I'll probably be talking to Suzanne at some time today - if she's speaking to me - so I'll see what I can do for you. I'll let you know." Another line began to ring. "Hang on a sec."

She put the new caller on hold.

"Hunter? You still there?" And yet another line. "Shit!"

"It's okay, El. I've got to drop by there later this afternoon. I'll talk to you then."

"Well ... " She'd intended to tell him that one or another of his kids had been phoning yesterday, that they'd reached her at home twice to find out where he was, and that they'd sounded worried. But they would have left a message on his answering machine. "Okay," she said, and he hung up.

Besides, she thought as she punched the flashing button on her phone, he probably talked to them last night after he got home.

"Hello, there! How's the highway treating you?"

Hunter had reached his friend, Sam Manji, at the Surrey R.C.M.P. detachment.

"I've got something new for you on that Rick Bilodeau character," said Sam. "We picked him up on Saturday for trying to sell stolen property to a female officer working undercover in a bar.

262

He's trying to unload a CD player, still in the box, with serial numbers that match one stolen in an electronics store break-in about four weeks ago. The wee small hours of May 25th, to be exact. The date ring a bell with you?"

"Yes," said Hunter, nodding to himself. "Randy Danyluk's rig went off the road sometime after midnight on May 25th. So if Bilodeau was involved in that electronics store break-in, I guess I can scratch him off my list of suspects."

"Hang on. There's more to come. At first Bilodeau gave us some song and dance about it being a birthday present from his Mom." Manji snorted. "He should write fiction. The guys pull up his particulars. His birthday's in October. Try again, pal. Next he says, he found it at a bus stop. Sure thing. So the good officers bring him in for further questioning. The only prints we can lift off the box belong to the birthday boy. So we tell him what we're going to arrest him for, and he gives us an alibi."

"An alibi?"

"Right. We verified it to the best of our ability, and it's solid. Bilodeau couldn't have committed the B & E. He and a friend drove to Princeton that night, and stayed there at his friend's brother's house for a couple of days."

"Princeton? You sure?"

"Sure as we can be. His friend and his friend's brother have both backed him up. Their stories jive well enough that we had to drop the charges to possession."

"What time did they arrive? Did you verify that?"

"Bilodeau's friend said they stopped in Hope for pizza at about midnight, and got to Princeton at about two thirty a.m. According to my calculations, travelling time between Hope and Princeton on Highway 3 is just under two hours. You detour via the Coquihalla, then back down from Merritt on 5A, it's not much more than about half an hour longer."

Hunter looked blankly at the photo copies of the Waicom computer printouts, which were still spread out across his desk. If

Bilodeau was in Princeton at two thirty a.m., he was still just as much a suspect as anybody else in Randy's death. Maybe more so.

Because wasn't Bilodeau the only one who had threatened Randy, in public, less than thirty hours before?

Hunter spent what was left of the morning catching up on his mail and doing laundry. He had two pairs of decent blue jeans and after any stretch of time on the road, sometimes going two or three days without a shower, he couldn't forget to wash them or he'd be stuck with dirty jeans for another week or even two.

His thoughts kept returning to Randy's accident and, with a mounting sense of frustration, to the question of what he, a civilian, could do to determine the identity of whoever had engineered it. He hoped that a discussion with the big Newfoundlander would reveal something about Murphy's suspicious behavior: his warning to Sorry at the Waicom warehouse, why there was no record of him passing the Coquihalla toll booth on the morning after Randy's death, and why Carla had described him as being "pissed" at Randy when they left The Goal Post the night before. As far as Hunter could tell, Murphy wasn't a criminal. If he were, he wouldn't have remained a close friend of "straight as an arrow" Randy for as long as he had. He was probably also not a liar, at least, not a good liar. Hunter hoped he would be able to read Murphy well enough to learn what he had to know.

Bilodeau was a different matter. Hunter had already had one run in with the tall, skinny dope pusher, and couldn't expect anything but hostility from a face-to-face encounter. He doubted whether talking to Bilodeau would yield any useful information. That meant his only options were to coax some information from Bilodeau's friend, and possible accomplice, or to find a witness. Sam Manji had given him a description of the car, and the names both of Bilodeau's friend and of the friend's brother in Princeton. The friend owned an old five-ton truck and hired himself out to local cartage companies on their busy days, and did private household moves on the weekends. Hunter had his pager number, but had yet to figure out a good pretext to call.

264

In the early afternoon, Hunter headed out to the Watson Transportation yard to pick up his rig. The Blue Knight needed some attention, including a wash and an oil change. During his last inspection, he'd noticed a broken reflector that would need to be replaced, and his right-side mirror was loose. With all the running around getting things done, and stopping to talk to the guys at the Freightliner parts dealership, it was almost five o'clock by the time he got back to El's office.

For once, she wasn't on the phone. She said Murphy was in Kamloops and couldn't legally be back on the road for a couple of days. She'd found out that he was scheduled to bring a load to Vancouver on Wednesday, and then he'd have to lay over until Thursday morning for a load to San Francisco. If Hunter wanted to pass on a more lucrative air-ride run to Winnipeg this week, she could send him to Eugene, Oregon on Tuesday. He could pick up a load in Portland on his way back north, and be in Vancouver in time to connect with Murphy Wednesday afternoon. "How's that sound?" she said, just as she grabbed a ringing phone.

Hunter agreed. As much as he wanted time to concentrate on solving the mystery of Randy's death, he had to be on the road with The Blue Knight at least enough hours to pay its keep. Early tomorrow morning he'd be back on the road with ten skids of chemicals in drums for an Oregon pulp mill. He'd see Murphy on Wednesday.

"Shit!" said El into the phone. "You let them load it already? How many? What!? *How* many? Jesus H. Christ! Put the shipper on, will ya?" The hand that held her pen drummed raggedly on the desktop. "Hello. Who's this? Bee-oh? Oh ... *Bill.*" She rolled her eyes up at Hunter and silently mouthed, "Chinese."

"Listen, 'Bee-yo'," she said, "we're mainly a truckload operation, but we can make arrangements to do the distribution on your load. Have you got a manifest? Man - i - fest. A list of how many cartons get delivered to each store, you know, with all the addresses on it? Good. We'll need a copy as soon as possible. Can you fax it to me, please? I said ...." She had him repeat back the fax number and made sure he understood that she wanted it done right away, then slammed down the phone and sat back, blowing a big breath into the air above her head. "Shit!"

Hunter raised his eyebrows in question, and she explained. A garment manufacturer in Winnipeg had a load of cartons to be delivered to seventeen different stores in the Vancouver area. According to the driver, the three hundred and seventy-six cartons had been loaded into the trailer loose and in no kind of order at all. That meant the entire forty foot trailer would have to be unloaded, the boxes sorted into seventeen piles on the warehouse floor, and reloaded into smaller trucks for delivery to the separate stores. "I'm gonna have to call in a cartage company. Good thing it'll be a Thursday delivery. Hardly a spare truck for hire in the city on Mondays."

Hunter grinned. "What are you laughing at?!" El roared.

"I know just the guy for you to call," he said, pulling a piece of paper from his shirt pocket. "And I'll help him load his truck."

Half an hour later, Bilodeau's friend phoned in response to the message El left on his pager. He'd never heard of Watson Transportation, but yes, he and his truck were available on Thursday at the rate of thirty-five dollars an hour, and yes, he would be there at eight o'clock sharp. El gave Hunter a thumbs up.

"And you," she said to him as she hung up the phone, "as part-time warehouse help, are entitled to the princely sum of ten dollars an hour."

His informal interviews with Murphy and Bilodeau's friend successfully scheduled, Hunter headed back towards North Vancouver with a sense of accomplishment. Stuck in the afternoon traffic leaving Annacis Island, he pulled out his cellular phone and tried to reach Sorry. No answer. He could try again when he got home. On impulse, he turned off the freeway at the Cariboo Road exit and joined the lines of rush hour commuters returning to their homes in residential areas of North Burnaby. He'd stop in and see if the girls were home. El said that they had tried to call him yesterday, several times. Maybe they'd be free for dinner. He was hungry, and the prospect of eating alone tonight didn't excite him.

He parked on the street across from the townhouse complex, and sat in the car for five minutes after he'd turned off the engine. He felt like he should be bringing something. Flowers, maybe? Not a good idea. There might be no one home. It wasn't yet time for the monthly checks. It used to be so easy to bring little gifts home for the girls. Toys. Chocolate bars or licorice twists. Comic books. Now he didn't know. What kind of music tapes might they want? They probably collected CD's now. Books or magazines? Candy and chocolates were out of the question. They worried about their weight. They were slender and healthy and they worried about their weight! At Easter, he'd brought them each a box of Turtles; they scolded him for it before they'd even said thank you. They might not even want to go for dinner with him, but they had been brought up to be polite and he was sure they wouldn't say so to his face.

Hunter inhaled and exhaled slowly, and heard a meaty thwack as a golfer, hidden behind a wall of leafy young cottonwood branches, connected with a golf ball at Burnaby Mountain's eleventh tee. "Jesus!" he muttered to himself, throwing open the door. "This is getting ridiculous! They're my daughters, for God's sake, not blind dates!" He slammed the car door and strode heroically across the street and up the walk.

Chris didn't return his smile when she opened the door. For a second, her face showed pleasant surprise, but she responded to his cheerful "Hello" with a frown, then a shake of her head and "What the hell is the matter with you, Hunter?"

He opened his mouth, but didn't know what to say. He wasn't sure if she was really angry, or was just pretending. Chris's scowl intensified, but she stood to one side and motioned him into the townhouse. "Come in! Come in!" she said, motioning more vigorously as if she were irritated by his hesitation.

The past few years, he'd been able to perceive Chris more as the mother of his daughters, almost as their older roommate, than as his wife. Moments like this the memory of their former intimacy revived disturbingly, like traces of a faded perfume. She must have just recently arrived home from work, as she was dressed in a tailored white blouse and a tapered blue skirt with a wide waist band that flattered her figure, but she had taken off her shoes and stockings, so that her feet were bare. She held her age well. Hunter felt a tentative sensation in his groin, and was relieved when it passed quickly away. Its ghost lingered, unwelcome, in his mind as he followed her into the living room.

"Sit down," she said. "Can I get you a beer?"

Hunter sat on the couch, straining his ears to hear some evidence that Jan and Lesley were home. He could only hear a faint and fading dripping sound. The sliding glass door onto the sundeck was open, letting the smell of damp earth and vegetation waft in. A big basket of pink and purple fuchsias hung in the shaded corner of the deck, and a green plastic watering can stood just outside the door beside a pair of worn rubber thongs. He could hear no music or movement elsewhere in the apartment. He concluded that he and his ex-wife were alone.

Chris handed him a can of beer, then settled resolutely into a leather recliner opposite him, pushing some stray strands of light brown hair away from her face with an abrupt sweep of her hand. She gave him a wry smile.

"You haven't changed, Hunter, not that I expected you to." She shook her head in mock weariness, and the delinquent strands of hair began to re-emerge. "How can such a nice guy - yes, you are a nice guy and no one can ever make me say otherwise - but how can such a nice guy be such a colossal jerk?"

He lifted his shoulders helplessly, waiting to find out what his crime had been.

"You don't know what I'm talking about, do you?"

He shook his head, a cautious, conciliatory smile playing about this lips. "I'm sorry ... " He faltered into silence. He wished she'd get to the point, but didn't intend to provoke her by saying so.

Chris leaned back in the chair, crossed her arms beneath her breasts. "Remember what I told you the day I asked for a divorce?" She didn't wait for him to reply. "I said that how you feel and what

268

you say don't count for a thing unless you back it up by the way you behave. I knew, on one level, that you loved me and the girls - you certainly told me so - but you didn't act that way. You didn't show us that you cared about us." She sighed, uncrossed her arms, and tucked one bare ankle up under her other thigh.

"I did the best I ... "

"What you showed us," Chris interrupted, " - time after time after time - was that your job was more important to you than we were. I wish I had a dollar for every time you didn't come home when you said you would, every dinner you missed, even birthdays - the kids' birthdays - when you didn't even call and we sat around waiting to hear from you, not knowing whether you were on the way home or not, worried sick that you'd been stabbed by some crazed junkie or mangled in some goddamn car chase." She laughed bitterly. "And then to find out that many of those times you'd been hanging out with your friends in the bar."

Hunter's jaw tensed and he averted his eyes. She was referring to Ken. Long sessions of talking things out used to help them both. Ken would say, "I've got a case of heavy duty burn out today. C'mon, Rayne, let's go put out the fire." One drink would turn into an hour, two hours, before Hunter realized the time had gone by.

Chris must have realized she was hitting below the belt, bringing up Ken, because her voice softened. "I'm sorry. That's water under the bridge, and I don't ... I don't hold it against you any more, not for my sake, anyway. I know that you warned me before we got married that a Mountie's first duty has to be to Queen and country. You did what you had to do. That's who you are."

"But I'm still a colossal jerk," he prompted. "Why?" He realized that he hadn't even taken a sip of his beer. He raised it to his lips and took a swallow. He could feel the cold slide of it down his throat. His throat muscles relaxed, making him aware of how tense he'd become. He kept his eyes on Chris's face.

"Jan and Lesley ... ," her lips compressed and for a second she looked like she was going to cry.

Hunter gritted his teeth. He always hated to see Chris or the girls cry. He'd rather be face to face with a rowdy biker or an armed robber any day. If you hurt somebody like that, you could live with it.

Chris continued. "They love you very much, Hunter. I hope you ... appreciate that fact. They never say a bad word about you. Did you know that?"

Hunter shook his head dumbly.

"Now you've gone from being married to the force to being married to that damn truck, and that damn truck takes you away from them in more ways than one. Almost by definition, your job is being out of town. It's like you've made it harder than ever for them to get close to you, like you're running away from them." She stopped, swallowed, and took a deep breath. "They never come right out and say so, but I can feel what they're thinking. They're wondering what they've done wrong. They're wondering why you don't want to see them anymore."

He frowned, shaking his head and letting his breath burst out in a hiss between his teeth. "Come on, Chris. That's ridiculous."

"Listen to me, Hunter. Being with you is still important to them." She leaned towards him and raised her voice, enunciating each letter as if she were practicing her elocution. "Reach out to them. They still love you. Don't lose that, Hunter. Reach out to them."

Hunter leaned back against the couch, his mouth open in confusion and disbelief. What on earth had brought this on? "But I can't ... I can't believe that. Being with me isn't important to them now. They're always busy, Chris. They're never home. And when I do see them they're always in a hurry to get somewhere else." He shook his head in bewilderment. "You've got it wrong, Chris. Jan and Lesley are grown up. They don't have time for me anymore." He gestured around the suite. "Where are they now? They're busy, right?"

Her eyes narrowed, but she didn't interrupt.

"Isn't that right? And what about tomorrow night?" He tried to sound angry, but when he heard his voice come out, it sounded hurt,

270

almost pleading. "Will they be moping around, waiting for me to call? No. They'll be busy, right? And if I ask them to have dinner with me on Wednesday night, they'll say, Sorry, Dad. We've already got plans. Right?" He swallowed hard. His mouth and throat were dry, and he remembered his beer. He picked it up, looked at it hopelessly, then put it down again.

"Where were you yesterday?" she demanded abruptly, leaning forward and lifting her chin.

"What has that got to do with it, for heaven's sake?"

"It was Father's Day. Where were you?"

His voice dropped. "I was out of town. I was on the road."

"It was Father's Day," she repeated.

"Yes. It was Father's Day. I was in Kamloops." He shrugged. "My father was in Hawaii yesterday. I called him on the telephone." He felt dishonest. He'd enjoyed more than half the day at the Youngs' cabin on Shuswap Lake, out of touch even by cellular phone. He thought about telling her how he'd spent Father's Day last year, waiting for the phone to ring, eating alone at a lunch counter, coming home to a message that seemed to poke fun at him and his lonely day. Then he thought of the hang ups on his answering machine, and of what El had told him, that the girls had called and called, and seemed to be worried about him.

"I'm sorry," he said quietly.

CHAPTER
TWENTY-FIVE

Sorry was choked. This wasn't turning out at all the way he'd expected it to. In Edmonton last week, Frank had made it sound like he was practically going to be in the game this trip, but judging by the way that Chinese asshole in Seattle behaved, he wasn't even on the bench yet. He glanced at a green and white mileage sign. Still about half an hour to Hope, where he planned to console himself with a steak dinner at the Canyon Hotel. His conversation with Mah made him feel like he was on fucking probation, and he didn't dare drive over the posted speed limit. He growled and bared his teeth at a little boy who stared up at him from the back seat of a passing car. Patience had never been one of Sorry's strong points.

He'd played it cool in Seattle, of course. Last week Frank had simply referred to his "partners", and hadn't mentioned any names. It would have been stupid to make the first move in Seattle, so he left it up to Mah. Sorry just made some small talk and acted as dignified and responsible as he knew how. Although he tried not to show it, the slanty-eyed bastard made him sweat, smiling that smug and irritating smile, leaving it until the last possible second to give him any sign at all that he knew they were going to be playing on the same team. By the time Mah finally said something, it took all Sorry had to keep from grabbing the little creep by his fu manchu and pounding that scummy smile off his face.

Sorry had already locked up the back door of the trailer, signed the bill of lading, and tucked the paperwork under his arm, when Mah, stretching and yawning, said, "I could use a little fresh air. I'll walk you out to your truck."

When they got outside, Mah looked him up and down slowly as if he was inspecting a slab of meat, then said, "A friend of mine thinks you might be able to do a little job for us." Sorry clenched his teeth and said nothing, because what he wanted to say wasn't going to win him any points. Mah continued, "I'm not convinced you're dependable. We need a real Rock of Gibraltar type, understand? Somebody who's not going to screw things up by attracting attention, if you know what I mean." He wiggled his eyebrows, like he was expecting an answer.

"You want a fuckin' Boy Scout?" Sorry asked, still being cool.

Mah ignored his comment. "Last week you struck me as being some kind of magnet for the attention of the authorities. You looked like a severe case of attitude." He smiled slowly. "I've got to admit, you look a lot cleaner this week. And you haven't been fishing for uppers. Booze or any kind of dope while you're on the job, just one time, and you're out." Mah's smarmy smile evaporated in the snap of his fingers. His face hardened and his voice froze over. "And we're not afraid to play hardball if somebody fucks us around."

Sorry stared him down. "If the price is right, I'll do whatever it takes. But if the price ain't right, I sure as hell don't intend to risk my butt doing *anybody's* dirty work." As he said this, he drew himself up to his full height, stuck out his chest. "So make me an offer."

Their eyes stayed locked for a full fifteen seconds, then the Chinaman stretched and yawned again, flashing a gold molar, and strolled away.

Still holding himself in, dignified and responsible like, Sorry yelled at the back of Mah's head, "Hey, man! You got the balls to make a decision, or not?"

The Chinaman didn't even turn around, he just called over his shoulder. "Maybe next time, dude."

And that was fucking IT!

273

Sorry straddled the wooden stool at the bar of the Canyon Hotel. He had decided to have a smoke and shoot the shit with his old buddy, Crab, before he went in to order dinner. Crab came back from delivering a jug of beer and leaned both hands on the counter in front of Sorry.

"You're lookin' border-line respectable these days, Sorry. Your old lady holding out on you or something to keep you in line?"

Sorry sniffed. "Just following your lead, Crab, old buddy. Rumor has it, you've been pussy whipped into a fucking pillar of society up here in Hope."

"Then rumor hasn't seen me on my day off," said Crab with a wicked grin. "Say, what'd you do to that Chuck guy last time you were here? He saw you comin' just now and was out the back door like a flash."

"Chuck Wahl? The guy you pointed out to us?"

Crab nodded, and jerked his thumb towards a half full glass of beer going stale on a table by the window.

"What the fuck ...? I wonder what that's all about."

It wasn't until after he'd finished his steak, and was waiting for his pie and coffee, that Sorry noticed Big Tits and her musclebound boyfriend leaving the restaurant. Could it be that they arrived at the hotel at the same time he pulled the Ranverdan rig into the parking lot? If so, that would explain old Chuckie ducking out of the bar like that. If not, what the hell was the old scuzzball avoiding Sorry for?

El had managed to keep Murphy entertained in the office until Hunter pulled in on Wednesday afternoon. The big Newfie was leaning on the front counter, leafing through Truckers News and waiting for El to get off the phone when Hunter walked in and slapped him on the shoulder.

"Hey, Murphy! How was Winnipeg?"

"Flat." He laughed heartily. "How's the world treatin' ya, Hunter?" He made it sound like "warld".

274

"It's a long story, Murph. Got a couple hours? I'll buy you a coffee."

"You make it a beer, buddy, and I'm all ears!"

They decided to meet at The Goal Post in Surrey in an hour. That would give Hunter time to finish up at El's office, and Murphy time to book himself a room at the hotel for the night, since there'd be a load for San Francisco ready for him to pick up in Delta the following morning.

On his way out to Surrey, Hunter used his cellular phone to call his youngest daughter, Lesley. Chris had told him that Wednesday was one of her days off from the job at the mall. She answered on the third ring.

"Dad! Hi!" she squealed. "It's about time! Didn't that lady give you our message on Sunday?"

That lady? "You mean El? Sure she did. She told me you'd called, but I didn't talk to her until Monday. Your Mom told you I came by Monday evening, didn't she?"

"Yeah. But you didn't call first. Remember, I asked you to? How were we supposed to know you were coming?"

"No problem. You were busy, but I knew I'd get hold of you eventually. What are you and Jan up to tonight? Want to go for pizza or something?"

"Jan's going to a play or something with a couple of her friends." She hesitated. "But I'm free, Dad."

"Well, do you want to go for pizza with me later, then, or do you want to wait for a night when Jan can make it?" He wanted to leave her an easy way out, so she wouldn't feel obligated to go if she didn't really want to.

"Um ... well ... would you rather wait until Jan can come too?"

He paused. Was she trying to let him down gently, or was she becoming as insecure about their relationship as he was? He thought of what Chris had said, about how he was running away. "Would I rather wait until Jan can come, too? No, I wouldn't rather wait. I'd like to take you out for pizza, or burgers, or Chinese, or whatever you feel like, tonight. If it's just you and me, that's all the better. We'll have a chance to really talk, right?"

"You're on, Dad! It's a date! How about Greek? What time will you come by?"

He looked at the dashboard clock. This time he would be there when he said he would. She wouldn't have to wonder where he was and when he'd arrive. "I'm on my way to meet a guy out in Surrey right now, and it's already after five o'clock. How about seven thirty? Is that too late?"

Seven thirty was fine with her, as long is it wasn't later. He'd have to leave The Post no later than seven. No matter what.

"I don't blame Pete for lookin' out for himself but, by Jesus, I sure am worried that all these problems are goin' to drive poor little Suzy to bail out of the business. Randy'll be turnin' in his grave, it meant that much to him to be able to pass the company on to her." Murphy tsked out of the corner of his mouth, shaking his big head morosely. "Here's to old Randy! Wherever he is now, may his tires never wear and his load never shift!"

They raised their glasses of beer and drank. They were in a quiet booth against the back wall of the pub, with a jug of Okanagan Springs Pale Ale on the table between them. Hunter was pretty sure Murphy had already had a glass or two before he arrived.

"I know Suzanne wants to hang on to Ranverdan, Murph, but after what happened to Randy, it's no wonder she's badly shaken up. You heard about Gary's brakes?" Hunter watched the big man's eyes carefully.

"Pshaw!" Murphy made a face. "That young buck's always lookin' to blame somebody else for his own mistakes. Now, I don't mean he's a bad boy - he's just trying to make his sorry way from the cradle to the grave like the rest of us - but he doesn't take trucking seriously. Takes no pride in it. Thinks ferryin' forty thousand pounds of freight across the continent is something he can do with one hand tied behind his back, and he's wrong. Real wrong. Thinks he's smarter than us old farts who've been on the road since he was a

276

pup. He makes mistakes. Damn right! More mistakes than he knows." A flush spread from Murphy's already ruddy cheeks up to his hairline and down into his collar. He sighed heavily. "I shouldn't let myself get all worked up about it, but if Suzy decides to pull out, he'll be the one to blame. He never liked trucking. If she decides to sell, it'll be his doing, dollars to donuts!"

"So you don't think Gary's brakes were tampered with?"

"Now, who'd do that? What friggin' good would it do anybody?" Murphy sounded exasperated.

"What about Randy? We all agree, you and me and El, that he was too good a driver to have an accident like that. The doctors say that it wasn't a heart attack, it wasn't a stroke. What was it?"

The big Newfie put down his beer with a thud and leaned forward across the table, peering directly into Hunter's eyes. "I heard that you figure he was murdered," he said in a low voice. "They say you've been looking into things. The drivers - we're counting on you, you know, to find his killer and see justice done."

Hunter smiled sadly and nodded silently as he undid his shirt cuffs, rolling up his sleeves and pushing them up to his elbows. Stu Thatcher's grapevine was at work.

"So you know, then, Murphy, that I'm looking for reports from anyone who might've been on the Coquihalla on either Tuesday, May 24th or Wednesday, May 25th. What about yourself? Think back to what you were doing the day after that little fracas here with Carla's ex, the day you last saw Randy. From then until you heard about Randy's death, can you remember where you were and what you were doing? Try to remember as much of it as you can. Maybe something that didn't seem important to you at the time will turn out to be a crucial lead."

Murphy resettled his bulk on the bench and rubbed his meaty jaw thoughtfully. "I had a rush load on for Portland and I had to make up some time that night, so I was out of here after midnight, about one o'clock, I'd say. I could check my log book when I get home, but I'm pretty sure. It was a quick drop, then I parked it and got some sleep. The customer reloaded the trailer with freight for Calgary and

I was on my way again before you could shake a stick, which suited me just fine. You see, I wanted to be in Cherry Creek that night, to spend some time with my little lady." Murphy's eyes dropped, and he ran the tip of his index finger back and forth through the ring of condensation left by the beer jug on the acrylic coated tabletop. "I had to run over hours, eh? If I'd've stopped when I was supposed to, she'd already've been at work by the time I come through."

"So you were on the Coquihalla that night?"

Murphy leaned back against the bench and shook his head. "No. I warn't. Cherry Creek's west of Kamloops on Highway 1. I took the Fraser Canyon road."

"I wouldn't have thought that was any quicker."

The big man squared his shoulders. "Six o' one, half a dozen of t'other. Shall we say, it's more discreet."

Hunter assumed Murphy meant that a driver who was on the road illegally, who had already driven over the number of hours allowed by law, wouldn't be as likely to run into authorities on the route less travelled by big rigs. Whether Murphy's theory was correct, he had his doubts. "So you weren't on the Coquihalla. That doesn't mean you didn't see or hear something that could be useful in finding out how Randy died." Hunter stopped short. Murphy had raised an arm, covered his eyes with his hand, inhaled deeply. His square fingernails were outlined by black grease stains. When he pulled his hand away, Hunter noticed the effort it cost Murphy to smile.

"I sure miss the old bugger," he said.

"You and Randy were very close." Hunter paused, filling up Murphy's empty glass and topping up his own, which was still two thirds full. He took a few slow sips of beer. "Was there anything in your conversations with Randy in the days or weeks preceding his death that indicated he was worried about something, or someone? Did you talk about anything unusual? Anything illegal? Or perhaps just something Randy suspected wasn't right?"

When Murphy didn't reply, just sat staring at the head of foam subsiding in his glass, Hunter nudged him further. "Anything related to the loads Ranverdan was handling for Waicom, for example. It

278

may not be a coincidence that there was Waicom freight on his trailer when Randy's rig went off the road."

Murphy looked up from his beer, an eager expression on his face. "I knew it! I knew that damn Chinaman was up to no good!"

"You mean Mah? Steve Mah at Waicom?"

"None other! What a crafty bugger that little yellow bastard is!" Murphy said venomously, narrowing his eyes.

"He seemed like an okay guy to me," Hunter lied.

"Oh, ho! Listen up, me bye! Can I tell you a thing or two!"

Hunter frowned quizzically, and topped up Murphy's beer in encouragement. Murphy licked his lips.

"I've known Mah since the days we first started haulin' Waicom's freight from the Seattle docks into the Vancouver warehouse, back when Chuck Wahl was still pulling a combined load to Winnipeg and Edmonton for them once a week." He clicked his tongue against his back teeth. "Never really knew how Chuck could afford to do that, 'cause surely the big carriers with their schedules, needin' eastbound backhaul and all, could do it cheaper and faster than him with his single truck. His old Ford was in better shape then, mind you. But Mah was in charge of the Vancouver warehouse back then, and he pretty much called all the shots at Waicom when it came to choosing carriers. He and Chuck were as thick as thieves." He held up two intertwined fingers as he took a gulp of beer, barely pausing for a breath.

Hunter looked at his watch. Still lots of time.

"Then Waicom got big enough to hire themselves a warehouse manager, and Mah was back to being just a shipper. That must've put Mah's knickers in a knot, by Jesus! He was under the new guy's thumb, and obviously had to cut down on his hanky panky. Pretty soon the new guy gave Chuck the heave ho. Chuck was bitter, let me tell you! But it warn't Randy's fault, anybody could see that.

"Once Chuck was out of the picture, all of a sudden the slippery little Chinaman starts gettin' real friendly with yours truly. You know the sort of thing, eh? Wink, wink. Nudge, nudge. Just between us boys, like. Mah there, he's my best buddy all of a sudden. Murphy, he says, you're a fine figure of a man. I can tell by just lookin' at you that you must have to fight the ladies off with a stick. Me, he says, I'm just a damn shipper stuck here in this warehouse, and I sure would love to hear about the adventures a big guy like you has on the road. Wink, wink. Nudge, nudge. And you know how it is, Hunter, being on the road for days in a row, you got a lot of stories to tell and nobody to tell them to sometimes." He shrugged glumly. "I was married then. Happy as a clam. But that didn't mean I didn't still have a few little darlin's on the road to talk about.

"Of course," Murphy continued, "that's just what Mah was waiting for. So happens he needed some 'favors'. Chuck's not around anymore, so now the Chinaman turns to his good buddy Murph. And he has a little leverage, you might say. What would happen if your good wife found out about the little blonde waitress in Everett? he'd ask, nonchalant like. Then he'd ask me a little favor. Don't count the freight on this load, he'd say, and phone ahead to Scarfo before you deliver it in Edmonton. And I was afraid if I told Randy, Mah would call my dear wife. That scummy ... ." He pursed his lips as though he were about to spit, but thought better of it and swallowed hard, then threw back his head to empty his glass.

"I asked Randy to take me off Waicom. Rather, I asked him to send me someplace else, so's it wouldn't look like my doin'. I guess Mah didn't see any likely replacement at the time, 'cause he phoned me up and 'advised' me to come back. Not only would he not call my wife, he said, he'd also throw in a little grease for my wheels. Maybe my wife would like a new T.V. to watch while I was on the road? Would you believe it?" He paused, wide-eyed. "Stupid Stanley fell for it. Hooo, bye! Then my goose was really cooked. Randy would've had my balls if he'd found out."

Hunter checked his watch again. Murph was opening up like a dam, but he only had twenty minutes to take advantage of it. "How long did that go on?" he prompted.

"Hah! I was Mah's donkey for almost a year. I wish I could say that I finally had the balls to end it, but I can't take the credit. My little wife run off on me, so I didn't give a damn. It wasn't until then

I told the little prick to shove it up his ass." He grunted. The beer jug was empty. Murphy hoisted it up and waved it at the waiter.

"No more for me, Murph," Hunter said, and immediately regretted it. Murphy looked annoyed. He must have assumed that Hunter would be his drinking buddy for the evening. "I'll have one more glass," Hunter countered quickly, taking a ten dollar bill out of his shirt pocket and slapping it on the table. "Go on, Murph. Please."

Murphy made a show of watching the waiter fill a new jug and bring it to the table. The waiter refilled both their glasses, and Murphy raised his to Hunter's in a toast. "To Randy," he proposed, "a man you could trust with your life." His eyes glittered with melancholy.

"To Randy," Hunter repeated. He had to somehow resuscitate Murphy's good will towards him. After a respectable pause, he said, "So you walked out on Mah? That took a lot of guts, no matter what you say."

Murphy responded with a preoccupied nod.

"Did Mah do anything? Did he tell Randy?"

"Use your brains, bye." Murphy shot him a look of disgust. "You think Mah would shoot himself in the foot just to get back at me? Of course not!"

"Did he recruit someone else?"

"The bugger was transferred to Seattle not long after that, when the brass at Waicom decided they needed their own warehouse down there. He was King Shit again, once he landed in Seattle. Maybe his boss was suspicious, I don't know. He might've moved him across the border to cramp his style. Goin' through customs, you've got to watch your p's and q's. You can't just short loads willy nilly, or ship half a dozen cartons to the wrong place every month." Murphy took a big sloppy slug of beer, wiping his mouth on his sleeve. "Who knows what the slimy bugger got up to after he moved." He shrugged loosely. "But his kind never go straight. You can take that to the bank." He shut up, scowling into his beer.

Hunter debated whether to ask the same question again and decided to go at it from a different direction. "Did Randy suspect something?"

The big driver stared at him dumbly, and Hunter was about to repeat the question when Murphy finally spoke. "Randy was a prince among men. He trusted me." The Newfie leaned across the table and waved his finger in Hunter's face for emphasis. "Randy trusted me. He always gave me the benefit of the doubt." He pulled back, his big shoulders sagged and his whole body seemed to shrink towards the floor. His voice faded almost to a whisper. "Now, shouldn't I have trusted him? How could I ever have suspected that man of doing something behind my back?" Murphy abruptly revived and straightened, raising his glass to Hunter's again, insistently this time. "Here's to an honorable man. Randy was a prince among men."

Hunter's next question to Murphy, about whether Randy had made a last minute switch with him the night before the accident, met with a hostile, "What if he did?" followed by a sullen silence. The dam had shut, and Hunter had no time left to try to pry it open again.

It was after seven o'clock by the time Hunter pulled out of the parking lot of the Riverside Inn. He edged the Pontiac a few miles an hour over his usual cautious speed on the way to Burnaby. Replaying parts of Murphy's conversation in his mind, he visualized the big man's moments of discomfort. *The drivers - we're counting on you, you know, to find his killer and see justice done.* He seemed sincere, but Hunter was convinced that he wasn't telling everything he knew. His warning to Sorry about Mah had been explained, but whether or not he had again been recruited by Mah was left unsaid. Would Murphy have been so open about his previous involvement if he were still doing something illegal? Would he have said anything about it at all if he himself were somehow involved in Randy's death? *Shouldn't I have trusted him?* he'd said. Trusted him in what way? He obviously had serious regrets about something, but was it related to Waicom? Was it related to Randy's death?

Hunter felt like he'd blown a good opportunity. Too bad he couldn't go back and start his conversation with Murphy all over again.

CHAPTER
TWENTY-SIX

Lesley directed Hunter to a little restaurant called the Neighbourhood Hideaway just a few minutes away. They were shown to a table for two in a raised section of the restaurant divided from the main floor by a wooden railing. It was relatively dark, and their table was screened by plants. *This is what they mean by intimate*, thought Hunter. While Lesley arranged her jacket and purse, a big denim bag, on the back of her chair, he rolled down his shirt sleeves and buttoned his cuffs.

The waitress came and lit the candle that sat inside a globe of nubbled amber glass on the table. Lesley asked for an appetizer of tzatziki and pita bread. "I'm absolutely starving," she said, catching the swatches of her hair that hung down in front of each shoulder and flipping them behind her neck. Hunter marvelled at how unlined her skin was, and how fragile her chin and nostrils looked, lit from below by the candle's steady flame. *She still looks brand new*, he thought, glancing from her smoothly sculpted fingers to his own knobby fingers and corded hands.

The waitress brought the appetizer almost immediately, along with two glasses of water and two Cokes. For their meals, Lesley ordered souvlakia and Hunter ordered prawns. Lesley dunked torn pieces of pita in the garlicky dip, chatting away furiously about her job and her friends and her sister and her mother. She talked about little things, like what happened today and yesterday, things that she had found funny, and things that had exasperated her. Hunter leaned on his elbows and stared at his youngest daughter with a broad, irrepressible grin. It made him happy just to sit and watch her and listen to her talk. God! He missed them! He'd forgotten just how much.

She suddenly stopped, a chunk of pita bread in each hand. "Jeez, Dad! I've been doing all the talking, haven't I? Feel free to tell me to shut up, you know?"

He shook his head, his grin still fixed in place. "I like listening to you, Lesley." He motioned her to go ahead, keep talking.

"No, Dad. You talk for a while." Tiny frown lines appeared above the bridge of her nose. "How's your job?" she asked.

"It's fine. My truck's running well. The weather's been good. I've been getting some good trips, mostly short." He gestured with open hands that he had nothing much to say. "I'd rather listen to you. What are your plans for school in the fall?"

She thought for a moment, her frown deepening. "How about if I ask you some questions first?" she said.

He shrugged agreeably.

"Why did you resign from the R.C.M.P.?"

Hunter caught his breath, then slowly and deliberately picked up his Coke and took a sip. She'd gone right for the jugular. A jumble of reasons ran through his mind: feeling burned out by years of trying to be strong and unflinching because that's what a Mountie's supposed to be, feeling heartsick at the sight of yet another senseless death, yet another hostile juvenile, and ... seeing his friend, Ken, like seeing a reflection of himself, dead with a bullet in his head. Had Ken's death been the beginning, or had it been the final straw? Either way, he couldn't talk to Lesley about it.

He felt assaulted by the blur of confused emotions and images that still haunted him and that he didn't want to remember, tried hard not to remember. He thought about what Chris had said, about her and Jan and Lesley forever worrying that he was lying dead somewhere when he was late coming home. Surely they'd talked about how his job was such a big part of the reason for the separation. The girls must have known or sensed the toll being a cop took on a man's personal life.

"Well ..." he said slowly. He suddenly remembered what Suzanne said, that she'd always told her college friends that her father was 'in transportation', and it occurred to him that Lesley's real question might be, Why is my father just a lousy truck driver? He took a deep breath.

"I needed a break, I guess. Police work is pretty intense, pretty demanding sometimes." He dropped his eyes from her face (why did she look so cute and funny when she was trying to look serious?) to the burning candle. "Police see so much of the negative side of human life - highway accidents, murders, crime, domestic violence. It was like ... thinking about the ugly things I saw at work sometimes took up so much of my ... time that I didn't pay enough attention to ... to other things in my own life that should have mattered more."

She said nothing. He glanced back at her face. She expected more.

"Even though I didn't quit until a couple of years after your mother and I split up, there were still a lot of things to do with the divorce that I hadn't ... dealt with, sort of, ... uh, emotional type things, and I guess finding a less demanding job seemed like a good idea at the time." He hated the idea of his daughter thinking about him having 'emotional things' to deal with. He was not a nineties kind of guy, and he didn't want to be. This was becoming an uncomfortable topic for dinner conversation.

"I have to tell you, though, that driving a tractor-trailer unit isn't the mindless job some people think it is. Drivers aren't all like the cowboys they show in the movies, you know." He grinned at her, and she wrinkled her nose at him, obviously confused. Confused, or sceptical.

"If you could do it again, would you still join the R.C.M.P.?" she asked, leaning forward, closer to the candle.

"That's a hard question to answer, Les. The R.C.M.P. is all I ever knew, really. I think I had my sights set on being a Mountie before I was even ten years old. It was hard for me to imagine being anything else, right up until I quit. And by then I couldn't face taking a job at a desk, or behind a counter, or even just being in one place all the time. There's a lot of good people in the trucking business. Restless, maybe, but good." He grinned at her again and this time she managed a quick, preoccupied smile under her frown.

"So you liked being in the R.C.M.P. more than you didn't like it, right?"

Cripes! She had fastened onto that topic like a bulldog. He didn't know what she was fishing for, and wondered if she wanted to make him confess that he'd still rather be a Mountie than a truck driver. He couldn't. It wasn't true. He toyed briefly with the idea of telling her about his investigation into Randy's accident, and was relieved when the waitress appeared with their meals before he'd had a chance to reply.

"Smells terrific," he said. A robust odor of garlic and seafood wafted up from his plate. "I had some great garlic prawns up at my landlord's cabin on Shuswap Lake." As they both dug in, he told her what a great place it was, about how bright the stars were and the way the sound carried across the water. Reach out to them, Chris had said. At least try, he told himself. It won't be the end of the world if they say no.

"My landlord invited me to bring you and Jan up there for a weekend this summer. What do you think?" he asked, and was relieved when Lesley, her mouth full of souvlaki, nodded vigorously.

By the time they left the restaurant, they'd worked out that the second weekend in July would probably be the best weekend for all of them, providing Jan hadn't just made other plans, and he'd even suggested that he take them for a ride in his truck one day soon.

"That would be nice, Dad, but I don't think you're allowed to drive big trucks up our street," she said. "Except maybe for moving vans, I guess."

Lesley was quiet on the short drive back to the townhouse. He walked her to the door. Just before she went in, she burst out "Dad, in case you haven't noticed, I'm not a little kid any more. Maybe some day you'll start to talk to me -- I mean, really talk to me -- like

I'm an adult." Stunned, he stood there with his mouth open for almost thirty seconds after she closed the door.

He was still trying to figure out what he should have done differently when he arrived home. There was a message on his answering machine.

"I'm trying to reach a guy named Hunter. My name is Cal Burmeister. I'm a driver with Norco Transport out of Calgary. I hear you're ... uh ... I just want to tell you I saw Randy Danyluk on the night of May 24th. I'm calling from a restaurant in Gilroy, California and ... um ... I don't have a cell phone so you can't call me back."

El covered the mouthpiece of the phone with her hand and laughed out loud when Hunter walked through the door. "Slouch a little more. Your spine's too straight," she said.

He was wearing his oldest jeans, a pair he kept for painting and yard work, and the only black tee shirt he owned, one with the bulldog crest of Mack Trucks on the front. The shirt was inky dark and new, but badly wrinkled from lying at the bottom of his underwear drawer. A reasonably well-worn jeans jacket and scuffed steel-toed boots completed his uniform. He rubbed his hand self-consciously over the stubble on his chin. "How's my hair?" he asked.

El squinted at the top of his head and motioned him to turn around. "It's okay. Looks real. What'd you do to it?"

"I wet it down, put in some hair goop, and combed it with my fingers." He ruffled the top of it with his hand. "I didn't shower."

El flapped her hand at him. "It'll probably do you good. Most days, you look too damn clean. Anyway, you'll have plenty of time to shower and change before your load for Calgary's ready to pick up this afternoon. I sure as hell don't want you out there fraternizing with Watson's customers looking like a middle aged punk." Although she practically spat out the last word, she couldn't keep the corners of her mouth from turning up.

Hunter tried to call his sense of humor into play, but he felt wretchedly embarrassed. He didn't remember feeling this uncomfortable doing undercover work on the force, but that was a

288

long time ago. He was younger then, and going undercover added excitement to the game, a game that he and Ken were always confident of winning. Not for the first time since he'd left the house that morning, he wished he hadn't made such a drastic change in his appearance. But recent experience had reminded him that his every day persona still looked and acted too much like a cop. If Bilodeau's friend was anything like Bilodeau himself, he'd either clam up or be openly antagonistic in response to questions coming from any man with an aura of law enforcement around him, no matter how casual he might try to make his conversation sound. As foolish as he felt arriving at El's office in this get up, it would be even more foolish to pretend he could be as effective in obtaining information without it. It had barely worked with Stan Murphy, let alone someone like Steve Mah.

At eight o'clock when Bilodeau's friend drove up in his battered five ton, Hunter was helping El's warehouseman, Wally, unload and sort out the cartons of garments from the trailer. Wally had opened all of the loading doors to encourage a cross breeze through the warehouse. It was hot work, and the climbing sun wasn't helping. Dust and the heavy smell of motor oil from the forklift mingled with their sweat. Through the open door, Wally signalled the driver to back his truck up to the loading dock, and a minute later El walked into the warehouse with Bilodeau's friend in tow. He was a wiry guy of average height with brown hair, the kinky ends of which poked out from beneath a black baseball cap. He wore a clean white teeshirt and boot-cut Levis that were a little too big for him.

"Unfortunately, Rob," she was saying to him, "the freight's not quite ready to load. I've gotta send Wally here out to the border to help one of my guys reload his trailer. Goddamn customs pulls his load apart and won't lift a finger to put it back together." It was a lie. El was sending Wally to McDonald's to eat breakfast and read the paper. "At thirty five bucks an hour, I'm sure you won't object to helping Dean here finish unloading."

Hunter rolled his eyes discreetly. El had insisted on referring to him as Dean James, and had even typed it onto a warehouse time sheet. "Well," she'd said in defense of her inspiration, "the hair and all. Right? You look like James Dean in Giant, except twenty odd years older. Dunked in crude oil, nobody could tell you apart." Hunter had never been too impressed with James Dean, but it wasn't worth arguing about.

They worked in near silence for almost forty minutes, Hunter pushing stacks of cartons to the back of the trailer and tossing them one by one to Rob, who carried each one from pile to pile looking at the labels until he found its proper place on the warehouse floor. Each of the seventeen piles was destined for a different store. The limited warehouse floor space was so crowded there was barely room to walk between the piles, and as Hunter helped sort the last few cartons, the two men repeatedly got in each other's way. Hunter wiped the sweat out of his eyes with his forearm, then checked his watch. "Time for a break," he said. "Wan' a Coke?"

Rob followed him to the lunch room. Hunter tossed him a cold Coke from the fridge and opened one for himself. "Too hot for coffee. I'm sweatin' like a pig! I'm not used to this manual labor shit." He emptied half the Coke and burped. El would love to see this performance, he thought. She once told him he talked like a school teacher, and claimed she had never heard him utter a four letter word.

Hunter told Rob that he used to play in a touring country band, but decided he was too old to hang out in smoky clubs night after night. "Small town bars! Christ! Got so that I could never tell which goddamn town I was in, every bar and every crowd looked just the same. 'Play me and Bobby McGee'," he simpered, and took a hearty slug of Coke.

Rob laughed. "I been there. I grew up in a small town. Princeton. I can't understand how people can stay there, man. Like, the big city scares 'em, or something. Small towns make me claustrophobic. I scrammed outa there as soon as I was old enough to get a job." He sounded younger than he looked.

"Never been back since, huh?"

"Yeah. Sometimes." Rob lit a cigarette. "Wouldn't live there again, though."

290

"I passed through there myself, just a few weeks ago." He paused to rub the back of his neck. Didn't James Dean used to do that?

"I was back there about then, too. Visiting my sister and her husband."

"Yeah? Just for fun?"

Rob shrugged. "I took a couple days off, needed a change of scene." He drew on his cigarette and exhaled slowly. He clearly wasn't planning to elaborate.

Hunter tried another tack. "That friggin' Hope-Princeton highway gives me the creeps. Especially at night." He pretended to shudder.

Rob's eyes lit up. "Do you remember when that happened? The Hope-Princeton slide, I mean? January 9th, 1965. I'll never forget," he said, shaking his head. "I was still in Princeton - just a kid - so it was really a big deal. Whole side of the fuckin' mountain came down on the highway. Two bodies were never found." He tipped the last of his Coke down his throat. "Mother Nature can be a pretty awesome broad, eh?"

"You ever take that truck of yours into the interior?" Hunter scratched his chin nonchalantly.

"Yeah," he said. "I'm not licensed for it, but I've done it a few times. Personal moving jobs. Stuff like that."

"Recently? You can get that beater up to the Coquihalla summit? I can barely get my car up those long hills."

"Nah, not up the Coq. I've only ever taken it to Kelowna, which seems to be a pretty popular place to move to these days, so I always take the Hope-Princeton. It's bad enough."

"A guy'd have to be pretty patient to drive one of them big rigs up the Coq, eh? Can't go very fast uphill, don't dare go fast downhill, I guess. Ever done it?" Hunter watched Rob's eyes closely.

"Nope." He seemed to be thinking, so Hunter let the silence hang there undisturbed. "It's probably pretty boring, all right."

"I heard one of them rigs went off the highway a few weeks ago. Didn't even find it for two days. Poor bastard. Imagine if the guy was alive and all busted up and just lyin' there waiting for somebody to come along."

Rob shrugged. "I never heard. I don't read the papers much." He stubbed out his cigarette. "Guess I should get that truck loaded. Thirty five bucks an hour, eh?" He grinned at Hunter, hitching up his pants and wiggling his eyebrows. "She ain't payin' me to stand around shootin' the shit."

They loaded everything they could destined for the north side of the river into the box of Rob's truck. While they worked, Hunter expressed his interest in buying a truck of his own, and asked Rob if it was a good business.

"I'm barely scraping by," the driver admitted. "Something's always breakin' down, the price of gas is stupid, and there's always some dickhead who pays you with a rubber check. I always tell them up front that I only work for cash, but when you've already spent the time and gas to move stuff for a guy, and he doesn't have the money on him, you take whatever you can get. The good thing, though, is you don't have to punch a fuckin' time clock and you're your own boss, eh? That's worth a lot to some guys, like me."

After he finished the north side deliveries, he would be coming back to load up the south side deliveries so he could end the day in Surrey, and finish delivering anything that was left over the following morning. When Rob had finished getting the paperwork from El for what they had already loaded, Hunter walked him to his truck..

"Listen, Rob," he said. "I'd like to maybe buy you a beer sometime, hear more about the local delivery business. Where do you hang out?"

"You know The Goal Post at the Riverside Inn, just south of the Patullo Bridge?"

"Yeah, I've been there. Say, would you happen to know a guy, hangs out there, named Rick Bilodeau? A friend of mine said to look him up if I ever went there."

"Yeah, I know him, sort of."

"Friend of yours?"

"Hardly." Rob shrugged and made a face. "I've done some business with him, you might say."

292

Hunter grinned. "You might say, that's why my friend gave me his name." Hunter looked at the ground, debating whether to pursue this any further. He was pretty much convinced that Rob had nothing to do with Randy's accident. He didn't seem like the type of guy to be in league with Bilodeau, but given his financial struggles, he might well have been persuaded to provide the dealer with a ride to Princeton and an introduction to a few dope users there in exchange for gas money and a percentage of the profits.

"Sure," said Rob. "Give me a call some time."

As Rob climbed into his truck, Hunter noticed a Ranverdan rig pulling into the yard. Rob didn't give it a second glance.

This time, Sorry arrived at the Waicom warehouse in Edmonton well before noon. He hadn't run into any of his brother bikers in Hinton, and he figured it was just as well. He wanted to make a good impression on Frank, to finally clinch his membership on the team. Mah had made it clear that they didn't want him attracting any undue attention when he was carrying the goods, whatever those goods might be.

The fat guy wasn't chewing on sausage this time, but he reeked of garlic and his hands looked greasy. Frank came tearing down the center aisle of the warehouse on an electric forklift and jumped off before it had fully stopped. He wore black jeans and a black teeshirt that looked like it had been sprayed on. Sorry discreetly sucked in his gut.

The fat guy muttered something into his chest and shook his jowls.

"What's that?" asked Sorry, leaning forward and cocking an ear.

"Speak up, John," said Frank, sauntering over to the counter. "We couldn't hear you."

The fat guy glared at Frank, eyes livid with hate. "I wasn't talking to you," he muttered.

"What?"

"I wasn't talking to you," he repeated. Then louder, "I never said anything," jowls trembling.

Frank pulled out a swiss army knife, pulled it open. He backed the fat guy into a corner, smiling his lizard smile, and held the knife up between their faces. "Good man, John. I like you better when you don't say anything, remember?"

The fat guy's mouth hung open. You could almost see him sweat. Frank slowly and deliberately moved the tip of the blade closer to the fat guy's nose, slowly, slowly, let almost an inch of it disappear into the porky nostril, sharp side up. He held it there for fifteen seconds while the fat guy held his breath, eyes screaming silently behind thick lenses as his glasses slid down his sweat-slick nose, then he pulled it away and wiped the blade on the front of the fat guy's shirt. "All clear," Frank announced, then turned to Sorry with a grin. "Booger check," he explained, tucking the knife back in his jeans and walking away.

"He'll look after you," the fat guy blurted out in Sorry's direction, then waddled, with haste, over to a door that read "Employees Only".

Fatso probably had to go change his underwear, thought Sorry as he strolled over and met up with Frank at the back of the open trailer. Hands on his narrow hips, Frank was surveying the load. For the first time, it occurred to Sorry that he could have been transporting something for these guys without even knowing it.

"Looking for something special?" he asked with a tight smile.

Frank turned slowly and met his stare with hooded eyes. "Oh, John would like that," he said in a low voice. "It'd give him a big fat hard-on to be able to tip off the high mucky mucks in the inner office, and get them to catch me redhanded right here in the warehouse." He turned his attention back to the freight. "No," he said with a sigh, "my interest in this load is purely professional." He pulled out some cardboard dunnage from between the skids. "I hope you don't have to be anywhere in a hurry today, man. I'd like to buy you lunch."

"No problem," Sorry replied. "I just won't call in until later. The boss can't send me anywhere until I tell her I'm clear, right?"

294

Frank said to meet him at noon in the parking lot of the Chinese smorgasbord. "Drive around the block and park your truck on the south side of the street that runs behind the restaurant. It's usually clear during the day. Got that?"

Yes! thought Sorry, nodding solemnly but doing a little goalpost dance inside his mind. Now we're getting somewhere.

After his trailer was unloaded at Waicom, Sorry drove directly to the Chinese restaurant and parked in the street behind it, like Frank had told him to. He was twenty minutes early. He locked up the cab and strolled back up the street to a gas station with a convenience store attached, where he bought a fresh pack of Exports. There was a telephone booth in the corner of the gas station's yard, right next to the cement sidewalk. Sorry lit a cigarette and leaned against the frame of the booth, occasionally glancing inside at the phone. Someone had painted the initials D.G. inside a crooked heart on the stainless steel shelf beneath the phone in what looked like nail polish. Bright fuckin' red.

Sorry hadn't talked to Hunter since before he'd left Vancouver, but this wasn't a good time to call. He'd wait to hear what Frank had to say, wait to see just how far he could get with this game. Hunter wouldn't approve of what he was doing. Sorry knew that. He tried to tell himself that he didn't care what Hunter would think, but something nagged at him whenever he thought about it. So, don't think about it, he told himself, throwing his cigarette butt into the street. Hell, Hunter knew better than anybody that Sorry had never been a play-by-the-rules kind of guy. When the time comes, I'll tell him, he decided, and not before. He thumped the aluminum frame of the phone booth lightly with his fist before walking away.

At two minutes after twelve, Sorry watched Frank's Cherokee turn into the restaurant parking lot and nose into one of the empty spaces. Frank then backed the jeep into a space between the building and its dumpster, the kind of place a guy might want to park if he were more concerned about avoiding damage to his paint job than about the smell of the kitchen's trash. He got out of the jeep, and

Sorry saw that Frank had put on a loose fitting shirt of a light, charcoal colored fabric over his teeshirt. It looked like fuckin' silk.

Signalling Sorry to follow him, Frank walked around behind the dumpster, where he opened a gate in the eight foot high fence of weathered wood that surrounded the parking lot. Sorry followed him through. Directly in front of them was the familiar green cab of the Ranverdan tractor. Frank slapped the passenger door with his hand, his sleeve billowing like a parachute and his watchband making a little click against the panel.

"Next week," he said, "we'll do a little transaction right here, same time, same place. I'll explain it all when we get inside."

Yahoo! thought Sorry, and offered Frank one of his tailor-made cigarettes.

CHAPTER
TWENTY-SEVEN

Suzanne knew she should be doing something else. She knew she should be phoning around - to current customers, past customers, manufacturers in the industrial directories, or even just companies listed in the Yellow Pages - trying to find more business, trying to find even just one load for Gary, for today. But she couldn't. She couldn't seem to find the drive, or the courage, or the heart - whatever it was that it took to make a business grow. Instead, she stood at the back window, watching the river and thinking about death.

It was hard to accept that there was nothing left of her mother and father, that when their physical bodies had died, their personalities and their accumulated knowledge and their lifetime of memories had ceased to exist, completely and irrevocably. She intuitively believed that something of them yet survived. A spirit. A soul. Some form of consciousness. She wondered if they knew what she was thinking. "Show me a sign," she whispered. "Please, show me a sign."

The river continued to make its way towards the Pacific Ocean, its surface textured with swirling pock marks of current and wrinkles of light. A light breeze ruffled the big willow, a fountain of gold and green in the bright sunlight, and a crow landed on the clothes-line post, then flapped its way to the neighbour's fence and hopped along the top rail until it was out of her sight. Suzanne sighed. It would be easier, perhaps, if she believed that there was no chance her mom and dad existed any more in any way, that their beings had disappeared like last winter's snow. Bad analogy, she decided. Last winter's snow had seeped into the ground and become part of the river, evaporated into the air, rained onto the fields, become part of millions of living cells, remained part of an endless cycle. Perhaps, then, their beings had been extinguished like a candle flame. Gone. Vanished. Never to return. If she believed that, she wouldn't have to worry about whether or not what she was doing needed their approval, or might cause them pain.

She heard a car door slam and seconds later the front door opened, loosing two giggling whirlwinds into the room. The two little girls chased each other around the sofa and made their noisy, roundabout way to Suzanne, where they started to chase each other around her legs. "Whoa, there!" she said. "Settle down, you little monkeys!" To Gary, she said, "My goodness, they're wound up. What have you been doing?"

Gary grinned. "We went to the big kids school and they got to play on the big swings and the jungle jim. Didn't you, you little goofballs?"

"Mom. Daddy says we can go ride the ponies again," said Joli, getting serious. "When, Daddy? Tomorrow?" she said, looking up at her father.

"Not tomorrow. I said we'd have to ask Mom, remember?"

"Can we, Mom? Can we? Please, can we?"

Veri's contribution was a wide-eyed, "Po-o-oh-nies!" She looked up at Suzanne with a goofy grin, hopping up and down.

"Maybe."

"Goodi-i-i-e!"

"Only maybe," cautioned Suzanne. "Now go upstairs and wash your hands, get ready for lunch." It took a little more discussion, but eventually the girls stampeded out of the office. Suzanne turned to Gary.

"That's not fair," she said.

298

Gary snorted. "You know what's not fair? It's not fair that I haven't had a load since Monday, that's what's not fair. You find something?"

Suzanne turned back to the window. "Not yet."

"Did you call El?"

"I told you ... "

"Fuck what you told me! You can't keep this business going if you don't have work for your drivers. You hire on some guy you don't even know to replace Pete, because you don't want me doing the Waicom, and even though you're still short one truck and two drivers, you can't find enough loads to keep me working. What gives? What the hell gives?"

Suzanne shrugged, looking back over her shoulder at him. "I think some of the customers have stopped calling us. I know Dad used to call people to ask for loads, but I ... I'm not sure who I should talk to, what I should say ... " Her voice trailed off and she turned back to the river.

"What are you going to do? Just let the customers drop away one by one until there's nobody left and the company's not worth shit? I know your dad used to talk to El, a couple of times a day at least, to see if she had anything she couldn't handle and vice versa. That might be a good place to start." She heard him pick up the phone and punch in a number. "Hello, El? Suzanne wants to talk to you," he said. "Hang on."

"Here," he called, his hand over the mouthpiece, "El's on the line. You talk to her."

Suzanne hesitated.

"I said, talk to her!"

She walked over, her face like stone, and grabbed the receiver from his hand. "Hello," she said. A Reba McIntyre song was playing in her ear. She was on hold. "Go feed the kids," she told Gary, her face still expressionless, and turned her back to him.

Outside, the gold of the willow faded as a cloud obscured the sun.

Hunter called and left a message for Cal Burmeister with the linehaul dispatcher at Norco Transport. It said, "Hunter Rayne would like to talk to you about the night of May 24th. Please call him collect on his cellular phone" and the number.

The dispatcher, who had a voice like coarse sandpaper, said he didn't expect to hear from Cal again until the end of the day, or maybe even the following morning. "He picked up a load of produce this morning in the Coachella Valley, and he's on his way back to Calgary. So long as there's no problems, he won't call in more'n once a day." Hunter thanked him and hung up.

By four o'clock on Thursday he was on the way to Calgary himself, carrying a clean, palletized load. The several hundred cartons he picked up in Vancouver were of various sizes, shapes and weights, and contained cans, jars, bottles and bags of non-perishable grocery items imported from the Orient. The load had an easy delivery deadline of Friday afternoon, so he considered investing some time in trying to make contact with Murphy's girlfriend, Kitty, in Cherry Creek. However, after the rather sour note their last meeting had ended on, he didn't want to set it up through Murphy, and he wasn't quite sure how to find her.

He thought about it as he cruised up the smooth stretch of highway just past Abbotsford, heading east towards Mount Cheam and her sisters, whose rugged green-black humps were humbled by the white pyramid of their regal American brother, Mt. Baker, some thirty miles to the south. He used his cellular to call Suzanne, and she found Miss Kitty's number after flipping through the pages of her father's address book. Her full name was Katherine Dunn.

At Hope, Hunter steered onto the Coquihalla. He felt no need to be "discreet", and it was an easier drive than the older two-lane Fraser Canyon route, with fewer twists and turns, and plenty of passing lanes so there was less chance of getting stuck behind a dawdling motor home. He intended to drive through the canyon some time soon, though, by car. It was a more interesting route, and allowed some great views of the Fraser River's tortuous rapids.

300

He hadn't used the Canyon highway since the Coquihalla opened in 1986, and was curious to see what changes the little towns along it had made since then in an effort to attract tourists. It was hard to believe that during the gold rush of 1858, little Yale was the biggest town west of Chicago and north of San Francisco. And tiny Spuzzum was once the site of a Cariboo Wagon Road toll station. Maybe the girls would enjoy taking the trip. They could ride across the Hell's Gate rapids on the air tram, and have lunch at the Salmon House near Boston Bar. It was one of those things he'd always meant to do, next time through.

But a man could suddenly run out of next times. Some time soon, he told himself again with a sad smile.

He stopped at Merritt for a Dairy Queen hamburger and a large Coke. He sat outside on a stone bench at a stone table, enjoying the feel of the warm dry air on his skin after a few hours in air conditioned isolation. It was late afternoon, and although its rays had lost some of their sting, the sun was still hours away from the western horizon. The sleeves of his blue cotton shirt were rolled up to above his elbows, and he'd undone an extra button at the neck. The breeze carried no coolness, just the smell of french fries and the sound of children's voices from the table next to him. He wiped his hands one more time on his jeans before he took the cellular phone out of his pocket and called the number Suzanne had given him.

The voice that answered was clear and friendly. Hunter introduced himself, then said, "Did Stan Murphy tell you about me?" The woman couldn't recall.

"I'm a friend of Randy Danyluk's. Randy's daughter has asked me to do some investigating, talk to people he knew in order to address some unanswered questions about her father's death. I understand that you and Stan saw a lot of Randy, socially, and I was wondering if I might drop by to discuss ... the situation." Although he'd tried to sound casual, he could tell that his "on official police business" voice had broken through.

"Are you with the police?"

"No, Miss Dunn, not anymore. This is strictly unofficial. I'm a friend of Stan's, and had meant to get him to introduce me to you. I do apologize for calling you out of the blue like this."

She told him she'd be home for the evening, gave him directions to the house, and said he was welcome to drop by for a visit. "I liked Randy very much. He used to talk about his daughter and his little granddaughters so much that I almost feel like I know them. This must be very hard on Suzanne, and I'd be happy to help." Somewhat doubtfully, she added, "If I can."

Hunter began to look forward to meeting her. She sounded like a real lady, this Miss Kitty of Cherry Creek.

Hunter looked back over his shoulder at The Blue Knight. It was parked on the side of the asphalt road, and he'd left its parking lights on as a precaution. Although the sun had not yet set, the shadows were deepening. He'd have a bit of a hike from the main road, she'd told him, on a narrow unpaved driveway to reach her house. Turning around a forty eight foot trailer in her yard would definitely be a problem. He enjoyed the walk, inhaling deeply the dry smells of sage, pine and warm earth. Bees buzzed in patches of white clover and around the nodding lavender heads of mountain daisies beside the road.

He spotted the neat little house, not much more than a cabin, about a hundred and fifty yards ahead of him through a stand of scrubby whitebark pines. Its wooden siding was painted a soft, pleasing yellow, and the door and window frames were white. Sitting at right angles to the house, a small garage with an attached lean-to shed sported the same cheerful paint. Half barrels of flowering plants were placed at the corners of the house, and he saw that the sandy ground around each of them was dark with spilled water.

A little black Scottie came tearing around the far corner of the house, his unbroken barking sounding like the ignition of a stubborn old car. The dog came to an abrupt halt, standing its ground about ten feet away from Hunter, engine still turning over and over without catching. Around the same corner came a woman wearing long

302

shorts and a scoop necked sleeveless blouse, and carrying a big aluminum watering can.

"JoJo! Settle down. That's enough out of you."

The Scottie looked inquiringly at his mistress, then turned back towards Hunter. He barked again, but his stub of a tail began to wag tentatively. Hunter bent down and held out a hand for the dog to sniff. Formalities over, the Scottie's tail began to wag so furiously that its rear end began to seesaw. Hunter scratched the dog's ears as he watched the woman approach.

"Hunter, I presume," she said, putting down the watering can and extending her hand.

They strolled to the south side of the house and Hunter admired Kitty's two raised beds of vegetable seedlings and her little fiberglass greenhouse while she finished watering her plants and explained how she'd had rich topsoil trucked in when she first built the beds. "It gave me quite an advantage over my neighbours," she said with a smile, "until they followed my example and built their own raised beds. You never walk on them, you see, so the soil doesn't get packed down and the roots can grow deeper. That means you can set plants closer together in the row. Easier on the back, too."

The watering done, she invited him to sit on her screened back porch while she went inside the house to get some iced tea. The porch faced the setting sun, and looked out over a collection of gentle brown hills dusted with various greens. The greens sharpened in the yellow light of the slanting sun, but dulled almost to grey wherever the early shadows lay. It was a peaceful place.

They traded polite remarks for several minutes before Hunter felt comfortable about asking questions. "I understand that Randy used to visit you and Stan here now and then, and that you sometimes spoke with Randy on the telephone. Did he ever say anything to you that indicated he was worried about someone or something related to his business?" Hunter had planned his opening carefully in order not to let on that he was checking up on Murphy.

Kitty Dunn placed her glass on the arm of her adirondack chair and seemed to be considering it thoughtfully. Hunter studied her out of the corner of his eye. She looked to be in her mid-fifties, and had the boxy matronly figure that many women that age seem to get without being noticeably overweight. Her face was pleasantly full and smooth, sagging just a little on either side of her chin and at her throat. Her hair was a pale blond, cut short like a man's just above her neck, but a mass of feminine curls from her forehead to the level of her ears. She was squinting from the sun.

"Randy never confided in me," she said. "I wish he had." Her eyes searched Hunter's face, perhaps for some sign of sympathy or for some promise of confidentiality. Whatever she was looking for, she must have found it, for she sighed resignedly, dropped her eyes to the hands clasped in her lap, and began to speak.

"I'd known Stan Murphy for several months before he invited his boss over to dinner. By then, Stan and I were engaged in a stable sort of relationship. You see, at my age, a woman stops expecting love, and learns to be content with a convenient and comfortable ... arrangement. It suited me that Stan was on the road more often than not. I had a man to cook for now and then, which is an activity that gives me great pleasure, and a strong pair of shoulders to do some of the heavy work around the place. As for him, he appreciated a warm cuddle and a hot meal whenever he was in town. He says he loves me, and maybe he really thinks he does." Her voice trailed off on the last sentence, and she lifted her eyes to the brown hills.

"Yes, it suited me well. Over the years, I'd gotten used to being alone, and I like having my own home without the clutter of a full-time husband. Set in my ways, I guess," she said with a smile. "And then Stan introduced me to Randy." Her smile faded, and she gazed silently at something beyond the hills for what seemed like a long time.

"You know ... I can't believe I'm telling you this. I've never spoken of it to anyone. Ever." She looked him in the eyes.

He nodded, a faint smile on his lips.

"Randy and I ... we ... I believe it was something special, something truly precious. Randy and I communicated it - our feelings - by looks, never by words, really. I believe that we truly loved each other." She smiled sadly. "You probably think I'm crazy."

304

He shook his head.

"It's true. No, neither of us ever came out and said so, not to each other or to anyone else. Sometimes you don't have to talk about it. You just know." She closed her eyes and swallowed.

Tipping his glass slowly so the ice wouldn't rattle, Hunter sipped quietly at the iced tea. It tasted strongly of lemon.

"Neither of us would have said anything to Stan," she continued, "nor ever done anything at all about it as long as he was still around. Hurting Stan would have, I don't know, cheapened it somehow. I used to pray that Stan would find another woman and break it off with me. I imagined that Randy was waiting for the same thing. We were both very patient." She smiled again, her sad gentle smile. "Looking back, perhaps unwisely so. Suddenly ... and tragically .... we ran out of time. Before we'd even had a chance to spend a single evening alone."

"I'm sorry," Hunter said. It was easy to imagine Randy Danyluk and Kitty Dunn living out their golden years in warm kindredship, puttering around the little homestead and sharing a thousand sunsets on this very porch in deep and modest joy. They were both silent for a moment, and Hunter felt the familiar heavy weight of hopeless regret deep in his chest.

"Do you think that Stan ever guessed?" Hunter asked gently.

Kitty nodded mutely.

The hills on the horizon glowed like bubbles of molten metal beneath a sky ranging from gold to rose to blue when he bid her goodnight and left her sitting on the porch. From beneath Kitty's chair, the mournful eyes of the Scottie watched him ease the screen door shut. Murphy hadn't told her about Randy's death until after the funeral, she said.

She would have been there to say goodbye, if only she had known.

Hunter planned on driving as far as Revelstoke before he stopped for the required eight hours off duty. After seven hours in the bunk, he could go for a walk to stretch his legs, have a good breakfast, and be on the road again shortly after nine, which would put him into the customer's yard in Calgary well before two in the afternoon. He drove through the lowering dusk from Cherry Creek to Kamloops, tinkering in his mind with the nuts and bolts of his conversation with Kitty.

Murphy was a jealous man, especially when he'd been drinking. It was seldom a problem, because they spent most of their time together at her home. "If I liked going out, I'd live in the city," she'd said matter-of-factly. He never mentioned Kitty's platonic relationship with Randy, but more and more frequently, after Randy had left from one of his visits, Murphy would be in a foul mood.

She couldn't remember if Murphy had spent the night of May 24th with her or not. "Good heavens! I can barely remember what I do from one day to the next," she'd exclaimed. She did confirm that around that date, one time he'd arrived almost in the middle of the night and was still in bed when she left for work early the following morning. "We barely exchanged half a dozen words. I have no idea whether he came up the Coquihalla or up the Canyon, and we certainly didn't discuss anything he'd seen or done on the way. I was half asleep when he arrived, for goodness sake."

She balked completely at any implication that Murphy could have been responsible for Randy's death. "You can't seriously think that Stan needs some kind of alibi." Hunter said that he agreed with her, the idea was completely absurd, it was just the habit of covering all the bases that came from his years as a Mountie.

In spite of her brief sense of outrage, she remained pleasant and cooperative throughout Hunter's visit, and he carried the sensation of being wrapped in the warm mantle of her goodwill when he left. He smiled as he passed the turnoff to Randy's house in Kamloops. So that self-contained, generous lady was Randy's Miss Kitty of Cherry Creek.

From Kamloops to Revelstoke, he was trapped inside the dark cab. The more he tried to ignore them, the more his darkest thoughts muscled their way into the confined space around him. His meeting with Kitty had aroused a relentless, oppressive meditation on the

306

theme of opportunities not grasped that slipped away and would never come again. "Some time soon." The phrase played over and over in his mind like a broken record, an endless taunting chant. Randy and Kitty, denying themselves the sweet fulfilment of their love, waiting patiently for the time to be right. Ken. Hunter should have seen it coming, he should have been there to help, or did Ken himself even know he was that close to the edge? Suzanne and Randy. What was left forever unsaid between a father and daughter, forever undone? He and his girls, Lesley and Jan.

There is never enough of tomorrows left, he thought.

Never enough time.

Hunter was awakened the next morning in the sleeper by the cellular phone ringing beside his ear. He jerked up to a sitting position and gave his head a few groggy shakes while he wriggled his arm out of the tangled top sheet, then grabbed the phone and flipped it open. "I have a collect call for Hunter Rayne from Cal Burmeister in Nephi, Utah. Will you accept the charges?"

"Yes," he said. "Yes, I sure will." Hunter swung his bare legs down off the bunk, stretching his legs out and rotating his feet one at a time as he listened.

Cal Burmeister had what Hunter called a Canadian prairie accent. He not only dropped most of the "g"s the occurred at the end of words, but his "t"s came out sounding like something between a "th" and a "d". Hunter suspected that the accent developed through generations of living in close proximity to the French-speaking Métis. Cal told Hunter that he had been travelling north on the Coquihalla the night of May 24th, and had seen a rig broken down on the side of the road somewhere north of the toll booth. He thought it wasn't far from the junction of the Coquihalla and 97C, the highway that went over the mountains to Kelowna. "What's the name of that town there? Merritt, i'n't it?" The rig was parked on the shoulder, and the driver had set up three emergency reflective triangles at intervals from the rear of the trailer.

"When I got close, I seen it was a Ranverdan rig, eh? So I slowed right down and hailed him on the CB, eh? Is that you, Randy? That's what you get for drivin' an old clunker like that, I said. Me and Randy, we'd have coffee sometimes when we run into each other somewheres. I'd always give him a hard time about his trucks, eh? I'm a Kenworth man myself. Don't matter that his truck was three years newer than mine, it wasn't a Kenworth, eh? You drive a Kenworth?"

"I drive a '91 Freightliner."

Cal Burmeister chuckled. "Say, no offense, eh? Nothin' personal or anything."

"So did he answer you back? Was it Randy?" Hunter did his best to stretch his arm and shoulder muscles without moving the phone from his ear.

"Yeah, he comes back at me all right. Says, no problems, Cal. Help's already on the way, or somethin' like that."

"Did you stop and talk to him?"

"Nope. Wasn't a good place to stop, unless it was an emergency. Dark, eh? And on an uphill curve."

"Did you see him? Did he wave or anything?" With his shoulder hiked up to hold the phone, Hunter grabbed his jeans from the floor and worked his way into them.

"Nope. Like I said, it was dark, he didn't have no light on in the cab, and I couldn't do more'n just sneak a quick look as I went by."

"Could it have been someone other than Randy that you talked to?"

There was a short pause. "Well, I never thought about it. But he called me Cal, I'm sure of it. Well, I think he did. He's the only guy drives a Ranverdan rig that would know my name, eh? From my moniker? Mind you, he had his radio playing pretty loud, I remember that. Damn song stuck in my mind, like it does every time I hear it. You know that song about bein' stuck on the L.A. freeway? Guy's afraid he's gonna die there? I always hear that song in my head when I'm drivin' through the basin there, eh? Smog city, eh?" Cal Burmeister chuckled again. "Just like, every time I'm headin' north on this damn highway, I start hearin' that Ian Tyson song about goin'

308

to Montana, eh? You know? About he's leavin' Ol' Paint in Cheyenne? No matter I'm five hundred miles east of Cheyenne, I just like the song, eh?"

Cal wasn't able to pinpoint the time, because he'd turned in his toll booth receipt to the Norco office. "Must've been sometime after midnight, I'd guess. Between midnight and one o'clock."

Hunter asked him if he could check his toll receipt when he got back to Calgary. "Sure thing," he said. "You know, since I heard about Randy gettin' killed like that, I keep thinkin' that maybe if I'da stopped there, he'd still be okay. There's talk that maybe it wasn't any accident, and that just gives me the willies, you know what I mean? You hear about that kinda thing in the States, eh?, so you take precautions. But in Canada now? Cripes! That's real bad news! Must've been somebody comin' along behind me there, eh?, maybe just after I talked to him. Sees him stopped and decides to take advantage. Can't help but think that if it was my truck broke down, it could've been me. I hope you find out who did it, before the bastard does it to somebody else."

Hunter thanked him and promised to look him up and buy him a beer next time he was in Calgary. "Hell! I prob'ly spend less time in Calgary than I do anywhere else on this damn continent. But our paths'll cross somewheres, sometime, eh?" Cal was chuckling again as he hung up.

CHAPTER
TWENTY-EIGHT

Hunter's delivery in Calgary was routine. He checked in with El, to see if she'd been able to line up a return load for him. So far, no luck. He didn't want to hang around waiting for something to turn up, but running back empty would hurt. Running empty miles didn't cost that much less than full miles, and the dollar a mile he'd made on the run east wasn't going to cover his expenses for the trip home. He asked her to keep trying, but if he hadn't heard from her by six a.m. on Saturday, he'd be starting back empty.

His next call was to Bill Earl.

"Hah!" said Bill after Hunter had made it past the detachment switchboard. "I'd begun to think we'd be playing telephone tag for the rest of our lives. I ran that guy Scarfo, like you asked. Even made a few long distance phone calls. He's bad news, man."

"How bad?" asked Hunter.

"Attempted murder, for starters. But the victim refused to identify him and there wasn't enough else to prosecute with. Also, suspected murder. Ontario. The OPP say they know he did it, but they had to let him walk for lack of evidence. The body, to be exact. Don't mess with him, Hunter."

"Don't worry," he said. "I'll make sure we don't get too close."

"We? Who else you got in on this?"

"I just meant I wouldn't let anybody at Ranverdan get too friendly with him. The guy works for Ranverdan's biggest customer, remember?" Hunter wasn't about to divulge anything about his confidential informant, even to Bill. He felt a spasm of guilt for sending Sorry to nose around in a potentially dangerous environment, but reminded himself that he'd already warned Sorry to keep his distance. "What else?" he asked.

"Frank Scarfo grew up in The Family, if you know what I mean. Crime is a way of life for him, although he hasn't been convicted of anything since he was a juvenile. Fraud, theft, assault, murder, or whatever, he's a good all around suspect from the looks of things. Got anything we can use?"

"Not yet," said Hunter. "If I get anything solid, you'll be the first to know."

Just in case there was no backhaul load to cover the cost of his trip home, Hunter decided to spend another night in his sleeper and save the price of a hotel room. He found a place to park the truck near the western outskirts of Calgary and locked up the cab. His cell phone a heavy bulge in his shirt pocket and the Tom Clancy novel tucked under his arm, he set out to find a quiet restaurant where he could nurse a couple of beers and read his book before dinner. He knew he should be doing something physically active, but couldn't summon up enough imagination to figure out what. With any luck, he'd be home in time for a round of golf on Sunday anyway.

Sorry's call came through before Hunter had found a restaurant. After they had set up a rendezvous for dinner Saturday in Kamloops, Hunter asked, "How'd it go this time, Sorry? Find out anything?"

"As good as can be expected. Uh ... look, boss, I'm using the customer's phone and he's standing here waiting to make a call. I'll talk to you tomorrow, okay?" Hunter had no choice but to agree.

Hunter's decision not to get some kind of physical exercise came back to haunt him that night. He'd sat as long as he could in the restaurant, even ordering pie and coffee, then an after dinner beer that he didn't really want, in order to retain possession of a comfortable table in a family restaurant. In the brightly lit booth, he managed to concentrate well enough on his book, but back in the sleeper, his attention continually wandered from the page. Knowing he had to be ready to hit the road before six o'clock, he turned out the light at about ten and lay in the dark. The meal still lay heavy on his stomach, and he couldn't keep his eyes closed. He tossed and turned for almost two hours, his mind buzzing with scraps of recent conversations and a vicious circle of unanswered questions.

If Randy had broken down and was waiting for assistance that night, who was he expecting when he told Cal Burmeister that 'help's on the way'? Had he summoned help from another driver by CB or cellular phone? If so, who? And why? Unless he needed a part, Randy was as capable as any driver of doing emergency repairs on his vehicle. And if he had broken down, why didn't the mechanics find anything wrong with his Western Star tractor, except for damage attributed to the crash? Had they missed something? If he hadn't broken down, why would Randy have stopped his rig on that uphill curve? Randy seemed to have been a soft touch where the weaker sex was concerned. Could he have stopped for a woman in distress? A decoy?

Murphy had been jealous of Randy's unspoken bond with Kitty. Had he been jealous enough to want to hurt his best friend? Or if Hunter's gut instincts about Waicom's involvement in Randy's accident were correct, someone connected with Waicom did the dirty work. Could Mah still have some kind of leverage on Murphy? R.C.M.P. files had revealed a past link between Mah and Chuck Wahl, but what about Bilodeau? Was Hunter being too quick to write him off as a suspect, based simply on the fact that Bilodeau's friend, Rob, didn't seem like the criminal type? If it was someone involved with or hired by the suspects at Waicom, how would they have known Randy was going to stop where he did? And there were still some wild cards, like Pete and his son Jason. Where did they come up with the money to buy a new truck?

Or was Cal Burmeister right? A crime of opportunity. A passing car, a couple of crack heads or heroin addicts mugging a lone trucker

312

they found stranded on a highway for the contents of his wallet. If so, why did they leave a ten dollar bill and his credit cards?

Hunter tried to tell himself that Sorry would soon be able to shed some light on the setup at Waicom, perhaps even tomorrow. But something was starting to eat away at his confidence in Sorry. Was Hunter putting too much stake in what he hoped Sorry could find out? By concentrating on Waicom, was he being blinded to other possibilities? He felt like his thoughts were endlessly turning back on themselves, like a snake eating its tail. Let it go. Don't try to force it. Sleep, and let the subconscious take over for a while.

Think of something relaxing, he told himself. Think of lying in sunshine, imagine a weightless sensation of warmth, imagine the sound of waves lapping on the shore. His mind moved on to the thought of visiting his parents in Hawaii, and that perhaps he would invite the girls to join him. Jan and Lesley. His thoughts again slipped out of his control and he saw Lesley's angry adorable face, heard her say, "Maybe some day you'll start to talk to me like I'm an adult! I mean, really talk to me, Dad!" and he wondered what he was doing wrong. Again. He had tried to reach out to her, but his reach had somehow fallen short. What should he do? He groaned in frustration, then got out of his bunk, pulled on his jeans and sneakers, and stepped out into the cool dark air. Finally, after an hour of walking past hushed warehouses and shadowy vacant lots along the midnight streets, he went back to bed and slept.

When Hunter pulled up at the Pizza Hut in Kamloops, Sorry was stalking up and down in front of the restaurant, one hand hooked onto a front belt loop, the other ferrying what was left of a cigarette to and from his mouth. Before Hunter had time to get out of the Suburban, Sorry was pulling on the handle of the passenger door and signalling for Hunter to unlock it. "I get enough fucking pizza at home. Let's go to a steak house, eh?" he said as he jumped into the passenger seat. "Besides," he added with his usual booming laugh, "you're buyin'!"

Hunter winced inwardly as he thought of his empty trailer, but had to admit that a steak house was probably a better place to talk. The Pizza Hut was often crowded with boisterous teenagers, and families with noisy young children. Within ten minutes, they found a place that met with Sorry's approval, and settled into a corner booth in the smoking section. Sorry lit a fresh cigarette as soon as they sat down, and his eyes swept the restaurant's interior, back and forth, back and forth. His body jiggled slightly, and Hunter realized that he was bouncing one knee up and down rapidly underneath the table.

"OD'd on coffee?" asked Hunter.

Sorry grinned. "Pepsi. Been mainlining Pepsi. Shows, eh?" He laughed. "Besides, I'm fuckin' starved. Let's get some kind of starter." He pulled a menu out from behind the salt and pepper stand. "Hey, they got wings. How about wings?" He beckoned over a middle aged waitress wearing a shirt and tie and a little brass name tag. "Hey, Eva darlin'," said Sorry, "How about bringing us an order of hot wings and a side of fries for starters? And light a fire under the cook, eh?" he called out as she walked towards the kitchen.

Sorry babbled on about the day's drive until the appetizers showed up, then limited his conversation to slurps and grunts until there was nothing left but a plate of bones and a wicker basket full of greasy paper and ketchup smears. Hunter asked him what had happened at Waicom.

"We're gettin' close, boss. I haven't got the story yet, and I know the chink in Seattle still doesn't like me, but I'm getting along okay with this Frank dude in Edmonton. We had lunch again."

Hunter waited for more details. Sorry needed prodding again. It wasn't just laziness, which was something he expected from Sorry. Sorry seemed to be testing him, trying to see how little he could get away with saying about what had gone on at Waicom.

He told Hunter that Mah made a snide comment about his haircut, indicating that it was a big improvement but he still had a long way to go. "Said I looked like a bad case of attitude. I don't know whether I'll ever get anything out of him. It's like, there's no rapport between us, if you know what I mean."

Hunter knew what he meant. He had the same problem with Mah.

"But this Frank guy, we're almost buds now, boss."

Eva brought the steaks, chunks of Kamloops beef, thick as baseballs and dripping with juice, and they both started in on their meals. Hunter was impatient to hear more, but knew that Sorry would be more amenable when his stomach was full. While they ate, conversation was minimal. Sorry finished first, pushed his plate to the edge of the table, and pulled a cigarette from his shirt pocket. Cigarette in one hand, disposable lighter in the other, he looked at Hunter expectantly.

"Go ahead." Hunter pushed his plate away and leaned his forearms on the table. "Tell me more. What happened in Seattle?"

"Fuck all, like I told you."

"Did you see anything out of the ordinary in the warehouse?"

Sorry thrust out his jaw thoughtfully, then shook his head.

"Okay, so tell me about Edmonton. You said you and Frank went for lunch again. Whose idea? His?"

"Yeah, that's what I've been trying to get across. The guy likes me. We went for lunch again, at that little Chinese smorgasbord."

"In his jeep again?"

"Nope. We met there. Trailer was empty by then, so I had to pull out of the Waicom yard."

"You took your rig?"

"Yeah, but wait. We gotta back up a bit. This time I got there earlier, about ten thirty. First Frank does a number on John, the shipper. Sticks a little blade up his snout, just for respect, you know? Doesn't hurt the guy, just scares the shit out of him. Probably did it for my benefit, to show me he's got things under control. Then Frank comes and looks in my trailer and lets out this big fuckin' sigh. I say, lookin' for something special in there, Frank?, half joking like, giving him an opening, sort of. And he says, wouldn't old garlic breath there just love it if I was?, or something like that. Seems like he might be letting his guard down with me a little, don't you think? The way he said it, the sigh and all, I figure he's under pressure."

"Could be. Could be their operation's been on hold since Randy's death and they're starting to feel the pinch." Hunter rubbed his jaw. "Did he say anything else while you were in the warehouse?"

Sorry took a slow drag on his cigarette, blew the smoke out towards the ceiling. "Just that I should meet him for lunch at this Chinese place again. Hard to talk, anyway, with work to be done and the fat guy hanging around."

Hunter asked for the restaurant conversation, word for word, and Sorry groaned. It was Hunter's turn to groan once Sorry had started in.

"First off, I asked him why the hell he's living in Edmonton. No, wait. We start with the weather. The fuckin' Edmonton weather. Then I ask him why the hell he lives there. He just says, opportunities. Then he says, when the time comes, he wants to live in Miami. He wants to be some place with a lot of action, and good weather. Not thirty below in the winter and a furnace in the summer. Then I asked him if he'd ever spent much time in Vancouver, and he said ... " And so it went on.

Sorry's word by word replay of the conversation included a discussion of Vancouver's new NBA team, The Grizzlies, plus a mild disagreement about the future of the Canadian Football League. They also discussed Sorry's Harley and whether he'd be better off buying a brand new bike instead of dumping more money into custom parts for his chopper. "A new bike's got no soul, I told him. No personality. My hog's like my best friend, man. No way I'm gonna walk away from my best friend."

I asked for it, Hunter told himself. Word for word. He didn't want to interrupt, but fervently hoped that the recitation would soon swing around to something involving Waicom and Ranverdan.

"So then, he says he's gotta get back to work, but to plan on lunch again next trip. I wanna talk to you, he says. About what? I ask. He doesn't say. He just smiles like a rattlesnake and says, I gotta go." Sorry's eyebrows lifted. "I said to myself, shit! I need to get something more for my pal, Hunter, but I don't want to push, eh? Don't want Frank to get paranoid and clam up completely, not when things are going so good between us, you know?"

316

Sorry opened his hands out on the table. "So I still don't have anything real good for you. The only thing I can say is that we're gettin' closer, and if I hang in there a few more weeks, I'll have something for you. I can feel it."

Hunter was leaning back, arms crossed on his chest, eyes steady on Sorry's face.

"Not great but pretty good, don't you think, boss?" Sorry's eyes wandered around the room as he took another cigarette from the pack, held it loosely between two fingers and bounced the filter end on the table. "The guy likes me. We're simpatico. It's just a matter of time, right? Right?"

"Hold on. I just want to think about it for a minute. You say you met him at the restaurant this time. You managed to park there?"

"Not right there. I didn't have far to walk. So what?" Sorry lit the cigarette and tossed the lighter back onto the table.

Hunter shrugged. "It's not much, but like you say, it's just a matter of time. Thanks, Dan. I appreciate it."

Hunter drove Sorry back to where the Ranverdan rig was parked about a block away from the Pizza Hut. They got out of the truck and talked a while longer, leaning against the Suburban's front fender. It was still only seven thirty, and Sorry planned to make it home before midnight. "I wake up three or four times a night," he said, "and reach for Mo. I fuckin' miss her and the kids like crazy." Sorry laughed sheepishly. "I guess I wasn't born to be wild after all."

Hunter passed him five twenties. "Dan, listen to me. Don't - even for a second - think that I don't appreciate what you're doing. And remember what I said at the start. You don't ever, ever, put yourself in any kind of jeopardy for this. This isn't a game. These men play hardball, your buddy Frank included. You've got a wife, you've got kids, they need you. Don't even think of doing anything to get in deep with these guys. You understand?"

Sorry nodded, frowning. "Hunter ... ." He suddenly looked away, inhaling deeply as he tucked the bills into the pocket of his jeans.

"Yes. What?"

"Hunter ... ." Sorry extended his hand. "Thanks. I know I act like an asshole sometimes, but that's just the way I am. I really ... appreciate that you always take the stupid things I do and say with a shitload of salt. You're a true friend." He nodded, his moustache twitching. "Thanks."

Hunter smiled, just a little, and watched him walk away.

Sometimes what Sorry didn't say told Hunter more than what Sorry said.

It was at least an hour until sunset, but in the shade of the hills the heat of the day had passed. Suzanne was out in the front yard watering her geraniums with a green garden hose. As Hunter approached, she released the nozzle's handle and the spray abruptly stopped. "Hi. Gary told me you'd arrived. He just left for the pub. So, how goes it?" she asked.

"Just tickety boo," said Hunter with a smile. "And you?"

She shrugged and made a face. "Not so good. Business has fallen off and Gary's pretty unhappy, with things the way they are. I have some tough decisions to make, I guess." She pressed her lips together and sighed, then brightened. "Like a beer?"

"You betcham."

They settled on the patio. The sun still gilded the tops of the sand hills on the other side of the river. A gentle wind rustled the trees at the edge of the yard and carried with it the sounds of a backlot ball game from somewhere in the neighbourhood, mostly yelling but occasionally the faint pop of leather on leather or the crack of leather on wood. The smell of damp earth and leaves came from Suzanne's freshly watered patio pots, where snowy alyssum and electric blue lobelia spilled down the sides.

Suzanne was twisting the gold wedding band round and round on her slender finger. "Anything new?" she asked.

Hunter frowned. "Yes." He debated how much to tell her. There were definitely things he didn't want her to know, at least not yet. "Nothing conclusive." He leaned forward, elbows on his knees.

318

"Suzanne? I don't know how to say this." He sighed. "You are probably hoping for a cut and dried answer, a revelation that will make some sense out of your father's death. I have to warn you that the answer, if and when it comes, might not bring you any relief, any real sense of resolution."

She looked puzzled.

"I'm sorry. I guess I'm just trying to apologize for not having something better to tell you." He paused, then tried again. "You see, there may not be any justice for you, Suzanne." He searched for a better way to say what he wanted to get across. "I sincerely wish I could make this come out happily ever after for you, but I can't."

"I'm not expecting happily ever after. Nothing will bring him back, will it? I just want to feel that I've done my best for Dad." She smiled wanly. "Especially if I end up letting him down in other ways. What have you found out?"

"I talked to a witness yesterday who said he saw your father's rig the night of the accident. It was stopped not far from where it went off the road, parked on the shoulder with emergency reflectors set up. The man knew your father, and he hailed him on the CB. He said it looked like your father's truck had a mechanical breakdown of some kind, and he was waiting for assistance from somebody. The man offered to get help, but your father said help was already on the way. One possibility is that he called a service station or towing company on his cellular, or a passing CBer might have volunteered to send somebody."

Her eyes widened. "That means we could check with the local service stations, see if they had a call? Oh ... but, if someone had come to work on his truck, or even just talked to him, wouldn't they have already come forward when they heard about the accident?"

"Quite possibly. Merritt's a small enough community. Unless they were worried about being held responsible, of course."

"But there was no indication of mechanical problems ... " Her voice trailed off, and she frowned.

"Right. Another possibility is that there was no breakdown. Maybe the truck was stopped there for other reasons."

319

"Like what?"

Hunter shrugged. "I wish I could tell you."

"But, if Dad said that help was on the way ...?"

"He might have said that just to keep the other driver from getting involved, either for his sake or the driver's." He paused. "Or someone else's."

"Like who?"

Again Hunter shrugged. "It wouldn't be unlike your dad to play Good Samaritan, stop to help someone in distress on the highway."

Suzanne's eyes widened. "A woman?"

"Possibly."

"That could happen," she said softly. "Dad would've just stepped out of his truck and offered to help. It never would've occurred to him to be afraid, would it?"

"No. Your dad gave everybody the benefit of the doubt."

"And then somebody - her husband, maybe - showed up and became violent?"

"Or her accomplice."

"Oh. I see." She tried to smile. "What you're saying is that maybe Dad was the victim of some random attack? A robbery?"

"That's quite possible."

"But what did they steal? Why didn't they steal the load?"

"Your dad's wallet was almost empty. I can't believe he'd go on the road with no more than ten dollars in cash." He purposely didn't mention the five hundred dollars that Chuck Wahl claimed to have received from Randy that night. "Not only that, we think something was taken from the trailer, that some of the cartons from one of the skids are missing, but we can't be sure, because everything listed on the invoices seems to be there. But think of it. If the perpetrators were from out of town, which is highly probable, what were they going to do with a trailer full of computer parts? How would they find a place to hide, and then fence, that kind and quantity of merchandise? And the truck itself? A highway mugging is a crime of opportunity. The victim's vulnerable. They just want to grab his money and run."

"That will make them hard to find, won't it?"

"There's no way to link the killer to the victim without a witness. Unless they strike again and get caught somewhere nearby using the same M.O., there might be no way to link the killer to the crime. In fact, the chances are pretty slim they'll ever be identified. They could be in a different state or province every day. They could be in California or Illinois or Florida by now."

"That's why you warned me not to get my hopes up."

Hunter smiled weakly, but said nothing.

"So the answer is that there'll never be a solution, we'll never know who did it?"

"That's possible, I'm afraid."

They were both silent for a while, sipping on their beer and gazing at the sunset, which had turned stretches of high cloud into pink cotton candy.

"What now?" she asked. "Are you finished?"

He shook his head. "We've found one witness who saw the truck there, there's always the chance we'll hear from someone else who drove past half an hour later and saw a second vehicle. I won't drop it, not unless you want me to." He knew she wouldn't call it off. Even if she did, Hunter knew he couldn't stop pursuing Randy's killer now, in spite of how continuing with the investigation would probably not bring Suzanne the peace he wished for her.

"So, at least nobody's out to get me." She laughed, harshly. "Except maybe El. And if that's the case, I don't have to worry that somebody's out to kill Gary, too. What do you think? Can I send him back on the road again? Back to Waicom?"

Hunter nodded. "You say he's been pretty unhappy without the work. It would probably be a good idea."

"I guess I'd better. Until Dad's estate has gone through probate and I can sell the company, which could be months away, we'll have to keep the revenues up as much as possible, to get a good price." She stared down at her hands, watched her fingers twist the wedding band, round and round. "We've decided to buy that ranch."

Hunter felt his stomach drop. It surprised him. He hadn't realized how much he was hoping Suzanne would stick it out, make

Randy's company work. "Are you sure that's what you want?" he asked, his voice low.

She shook her head. "No. It's not what I want." She closed her eyes, pinching her mouth closed as if to keep from speaking out. "What I really want is to keep Dad's company going, to see Ranverdan prosper. I want my parents to look down on me, from wherever they are, and be proud. And for them to know how much I value them and the things they accomplished in their lives." She sighed. "But it's looking more and more like I can't keep the company profitable. We're losing more business every week, and I can't seem to figure out how to bring it back.

"If it was just me, it wouldn't matter. I wouldn't give up so easy. It's ... well ... Gary's never really been happy as a truck driver. He moved up here to Kamloops and started working for Dad for my sake. But marriage is ... a compromise, you know? The ranch ... a ranch ... is something Gary's always wanted. I can't have everything my way, can I?" She didn't seem to expect an answer. "Jolene and Veronica, they need their father. I don't want him to start drifting away from us because he's unhappy. And he will be, if I run the company into the ground and lose everything. This may be our only chance to sell at a decent profit. It would be different if I felt confident I could keep the company going, make it work, but there's so much about the business I don't know yet."

They watched the silver green patterns of fluttering birch leaves play against the sky. A dog barked somewhere close by.

"Have you talked to El Watson?"

Suzanne snorted bitterly. "El can hardly wait to see me quit," she said. "At first, I thought she was on my side, but she's not. She hates me for some reason. She wants me to go under."

Hunter stared thoughtfully at his beer can, maneuvering it this way and that, trying to peer down the hole in its top. It was nearly empty. "El's jealous," he said. "It's not that she hates you, she's jealous of you."

Suzanne stared at him incredulously. "What?"

"Look at you. You're young. Pretty. You've got a handsome young husband and two beautiful little daughters. Then a father who

322

worshipped you leaves you a healthy, well run trucking company, free and clear. Whereas El ..." He smiled a half smile. "El had to fight her way, tooth and claw, in a man's world to get where she is. She wants it to be just as tough for you as it was for her. Just think of how, if you achieved immediate success, without any pain or struggle, your success would cheapen her own. I don't think she wants you to fail, she just wants you to have to work at it." He smiled apologetically. "To tell you the truth, I think her feelings were hurt when you seemed to be in such a hurry to reject her help so quickly after your dad's death."

Suzanne seemed struck dumb.

"Have you asked her for help?"

"Um ... I asked her if she had any loads for us. She just gave me one. Just one."

"Don't ask her for handouts, ask her for help. Ask her for advice. Tell her you're coming to town and want to buy her dinner and pick her brains, then hire yourself a baby sitter for a day and do it."

"Do you really think she'll help me?"

"El will help you," said Hunter. "There's no doubt in my mind."

He wished he could help her, too.

CHAPTER
TWENTY-NINE

Hunter was dreaming about the Lions Gate Bridge. He was driving across the suspension bridge, high above the water, in the direction of Stanley Park. As he watched, a small plane flew beneath the span, heading out towards the Straight of Georgia, while an ocean liner that looked like the Love Boat, with repeated blasts of its deep, echoing horn, steamed in the opposite direction, into Vancouver harbor. The whole bridge began to undulate beneath him like the back of a giant snake, and he suddenly found himself on foot in a crowd of people, walking calmly along a narrow sidewalk that was partly submerged in sea water. He looked up, and the bridge deck was far, far above them, while the waves broke over the sidewalk and soaked their pantlegs and shoes. A bell was ringing from the lighthouse at Prospect Point.

Hunter jerked awake and grabbed for the phone. It was Monday morning, and Cal Burmeister was back in Calgary looking at his Coquihalla toll receipt from May 25th. "Twelve oh two," he said. "That's when I went through."

Hunter thanked him, and his fuzzy head cleared enough for him to ask, "Did you stop at all between the toll booth and Merritt?"

"Nope."

"Have you thought of anything else since I talked to you last? Anything Randy might've said on the CB, or anything else you might have seen?" The day must be overcast. The yellow curtains of his bedroom weren't glowing like they did when the sun was bright.

Cal thought not. "If only I knew something was gonna happen," he said. "I never thought twice about it at the time. I just thought to myself, Oh, Randy's broke down. Bad luck. And joked to myself that he shoulda bought a Kenworth. I never knew it was important, eh? ... or I would've paid more attention, if you know what I mean. Hell, I would've stopped in a heartbeat."

Hunter knew what he meant. "You couldn't have known, Cal." Hunter knew, too, the curse of *if only*. "Nobody could've known."

After he hung up, Hunter stayed in bed, lying flat on his back and staring up at the ceiling. Cal had told him what he expected to hear, but he had hoped for something else. Something more. Something different. Something unexpected and apocalyptic. Life isn't fair. He'd realized that during his first year on the force. He liked to think that, forewarned, he had set his jaw and seized life by the horns, that he was prepared for the ride. He guessed that Randy and Ken had felt the same. But why is it, his heart cried out, that innocent and fragile beings, like Randy's daughter, Suzanne, and Ken's wife, Helen, ended up with more than their share of life's unfairness. He tried not to think of the two innocent and fragile beings that he had fathered into the same arbitrary life.

He was still staring grimly at the ceiling when the telephone rang the second time that morning. He swung his feet to the floor and reached for the receiver.

"What the fuck is going on!? The bitch canned me! She fuckin' canned me! What do you know about this, Hunter? What the fuck are you trying to prove?"

Hunter grinned and gave Suzanne a silent thumbs up. "Whoa! Settle down, chief. Take a couple of deep breaths and count to ten."

"Hunter! I'm fuckin' telling you ..."

"Shut up! If you can't talk like a rational human being, call me back when you can."

Hunter heard some growling and muttering, but gradually the heavy breathing subsided.

"Okay. Explain it, Hunter. And it better be good."

"All right, Sorry, think back. It wasn't supposed to be a permanent job. I asked you if you'd be interested in making a few bucks driving for Suzanne and getting some information for me about this Waicom outfit, you remember?" Hunter's voice was low and measured.

"Do you think I'm fuckin' stupid? Of course, I remember! Now you think back. That's exactly what I've been doing, man! Right? We talked about it on Saturday, and I said I'd have everything you need in a few weeks, remember?"

"Yes, I remember. But it was never up to you to decide how much information I needed. All the same ... ." Hunter yawned discreetly and ran his hand over his sleep warped hair. "... I guess I owe you an apology. I should've warned you, but I gave it a lot of thought and decided to let it play out like the real thing. Did she give you a reason?"

"Some bullshit story about me running illegally. Over hours. Jesus! The log looks legit. Everybody does it, and the only time anybody says anything about it is when some poor fuck gets caught."

Hunter sighed. "No, not everybody does it. And I would've reminded you about it on Saturday if I didn't want Suzanne to have a good excuse to let you go. The thing is, I can't let you do the run on Tuesday and I can't risk them planning on you being back to do the run next week. If they're under as much pressure as I think, they've got to make a move as soon as possible. I've got to get them to do the same thing they'd planned to do the night Randy was killed. You're out of it now. Understand?"

He heard a low growl, then stubborn silence.

"Listen to me. You did good. You gave me enough. You did your job."

He heard Sorry's breath ricochet thunderously off the mouthpiece.

"Sorry?"

"How can I help you solve the goddamn case if you fuckin' go and pull me out before I get all the facts? Another week, two at the max, I can deliver the fuckin' goods right into your hands. No fuss, no muss. Hard evidence. Give me a chance, Hunter."

"I can't, Sorry. The smuggling is incidental, remember? I'm looking for a murderer. You being a Ranverdan driver is no longer part of the plan."

Sorry sighed again. "Shit! I went and told Mo she could buy a bunch of new clothes for the kids. She'll cut my balls off." He paused, and in a softened voice said, "No, she won't. That's the damn trouble. She'll just get all quiet and make me feel like a piece of shit.

"Jesus, Hunter! I thought I'd be workin' steady for a few weeks. Why'd you go and spoil the whole thing?"

"Just hang on tight for a couple of hours. I'm going to need you tomorrow. Easy job. Easy money. Besides, you could be driving for Ranverdan part-time again before the week is out."

"The little bitch just fuckin' fired me, you asshole!"

"And I'm glad. In fact, I'm really, really glad that she did such a good job of it. It's probably the first time in her life she's ever had to fire a man, and I can't think of a better way to boost her confidence than successfully firing a mean old grizzly bear like you."

"You asshole!"

"Give it a rest, Dan. It probably did you good. Listen, don't do anything stupid. Just hang around the house for a while. I've got a few important calls to make. It'll probably be a couple of hours, and then I'll call you back."

Not for the first time, Hunter asked himself why he put up with Sorry's unbridled roaring. "He's like a big, noisy, clumsy, slobbering bear cub," he muttered as he stepped under the shower. "I just can't help liking the big clown."

El called just before noon. Hunter's jeans were already flopping around in the clothes dryer, and he was sitting on the back lawn with his landlord debating whether or not it was time for the first beer of the day. "It's almost four o'clock in Halifax," was the deciding argument. "And four thirty in Newfoundland," added Gord as he headed upstairs to get the beer, and Hunter went inside to answer the phone.

"Okay," El said. "You're all set for tomorrow. I've found you three quarters of a load of low-end T.V.'s and stuff for Calgary. It'll be ready for pick up in Richmond by three o'clock. It doesn't pay great, but it doesn't have to be there until Friday, in case you get hung up. I'll see what I can find you for backhaul outa there. I hope we're luckier than last week."

"Yes, me too," he said. Another week like the last one and he'd fall behind with his checks to the girls. "Did you talk to Suzanne?"

"Gary and Murph are driving down together. Gary'll pick up the other rig here before the two of them head down to Seattle."

"She have anything else to say?"

"Yeah, she's made Gary promise to call her every couple of hours, and he's going to park it in Kamloops for the night on his way through. Says she's not taking any chances. Shit! Hang on a sec."

Hunter was on hold again. He watched the landlord's cat stand just outside the sliding glass back door of his suite, delicately sniffing at the air inside.

"So, where was I?" El was back on the line.

"Suzanne wants Gary to lay over in Kamloops instead of stopping to sleep on the road."

"Right. For his first time back anyway. She's still a little nervous. And she also says she's gonna be in Vancouver in the next week or two and wants to spend some time with me here at the office."

"Good," he said. The cat set its brown paws daintily onto the sill and rubbed its jaw on the frame of the open door. "She really admires you, El, but you scare her, so go easy on her. She thinks she might learn a lot by watching you work."

"Moi?" said El, with her tommy gun laugh.

"She might as well learn from the best."

El cleared her throat. "It wasn't her idea, was it, Hunter?"

Hunter smiled as he heard another line start to buzz in the background.

"Gotta go," said El, and was gone.

328

The cat refused to get out of his way, so Hunter stepped over its bobbing head and reached out his hand to take the beer Gord offered him. "Cheers," he said. "Here's to innocence."

The old doctor shrugged agreeably. "I lost mine long ago, but I'll drink to anything."

"What good is innocence," Hunter muttered, "if all it does is keeps you from seeing the gun just before the bullet hits you smack between the eyes?"

"This is Black Rabbit calling the rig pulled over on the shoulder. Do you need any assistance? I can send somebody back for you from Merritt. Do you read me? Over."

"I read you, Black Rabbit. Thanks for the offer, but no help required." Hunter turned down the volume on his CB radio. He had debated turning it off completely, or ignoring any hails that he might receive from passing truckers, but he didn't want some Good Samaritan pulling over to investigate if he didn't respond. He'd keep his responses, he figured, much like the one Cal Burmeister heard the night of Randy's accident. The digital signal gauge on his cell phone remained strong, and the green light pulsed steadily. He looked at his watch.

It was ten o'clock, still twilight but the sun had long since sunk behind the blunt mountains. Once Sorry's call came, he guessed it would be at least another hour before the vehicle he was waiting for arrived. Or else he would have to carry on up the highway past Kamloops. It might turn out to be a long night.

His windows were open, but the high winds that commonly scoured this stretch of mountain highway were subdued in anticipation of darkness. The breeze bore a faint scent of pine. He listened to the sporadic swish of passing cars, and the intermittent brisk stuttering of grasshoppers, and the trills of crickets warming up for their nightly performance. Hunter's right hand played scales on the rim of the steering wheel. His narrowed eyes were trained on his side rearview mirror, following the progress of approaching headlights. He wasn't looking for anything specific, yet.

Betrayal. It had to be one of the most gut wrenching blows life could deal you. Someone who claims to love you, someone you trust and believe in and open your heart to, becoming the author of your worst nightmare, your deepest pain.

Dad would've just stepped out of his truck and offered to help. It never would've occurred to him to be afraid, would it?

No. Your dad gave everybody the benefit of the doubt.

He jumped when the phone finally rang.

"Hunter? Bingo. I just followed him into the rest area. He parked the rig on the outside rim of the truck side, and I stayed on the car side. It's pretty dark, but I saw the back doors of the trailer swing open. Want me to get closer?"

"No. Stay where you are. Whatever you do, keep out of sight."

"Do you want me to call you again when he pulls out?"

A pair of headlights in the mirror blossomed into a low-bed chip truck, its white, ridged trailer distinguishable even in the near darkness. "Only if it takes longer than ten minutes. Otherwise, just call when he passes the sign for Coldwater Road. That's Exit 256. Okay?"

"Gotcha."

Hunter flipped the phone shut, and watched the sky deepen from indigo to black.

A set of truck headlights approached at a steady speed. Alongside The Blue Knight, the truck abruptly lost speed. Its red brake lights brightened, and the CB started to hiss. "Hunter! Is that you? It's Murph. You need some help? Over."

"Thanks, Murph. I'm fine. Must've been something I ate. Carry on."

"Roger dodger."

Hunter picked up his cell phone again and punched in the number of the Merritt R.C.M.P.

Sorry's next call came at four minutes to eleven. "I'm a quarter mile behind him and I just passed the eight hundred meter warning sign for Coldwater Road."

"Thanks. I'm parked exactly fifteen miles away. Keep on him and call me again if he doesn't stop here."

"You got it."

"Hold it!"

"What, Hunter?"

"If he does stop, keep out of sight."

"Damn it, Hunter! You never let me do any of the fun stuff."

Seventeen minutes later, Hunter once again saw the headlights of a rig in his side mirror. He spoke into his CB mike. "This is TBK, calling any good sams in the vicinity. I've got some kind of electrical problem. I need another pair of hands to hold a flashlight. Any offers?"

He caught himself grinding his teeth waiting for the reply. "TBK, this is Hasty Pudding." Damn! It was a stranger. "I see you up ahead, but I'm on the downhill side of the road and this don't look like a good place to stop. Good luck."

"Thanks, Hasty Pudding. This is TBK. I need a pair of hands for a couple minutes. Any good sams coming up over the hill? Over."

The CB spit and popped again. "That you, Hunter? This is Margaritaville, coming at you from behind. I'll try to pull over just ahead of you and give you a hand."

"Hey! Gary. Am I glad to see you. TBK out."

Hunter saw the lights in the mirror slow and the rig's turn signal start to blink. The Ranverdan vehicle eased onto the shoulder in front of him and came to a stop a full truck length ahead. As Hunter opened the door to step down from the cab, a car slowed alongside, then increased its speed and continued on up the hill. Hunter wiped his palms on his jeans.

Gary was already out of his cab and had walked back as far as the end of his trailer before Hunter reached him. Marker lights from the rigs threw an anemic orange wash over the two men. "Thanks, Gary.

I really appreciate you stopping." Hunter was acutely aware of Gary's youth and size. He had fifteen years and twenty pounds on Hunter, easy.

"Hey! No problem. You'd do the same for me."

"And, uh - sorry - I should've said. I not only need a pair of hands, I also need a flashlight. I've pretty much drained mine's battery trying to do this repair job with one hand. You got one?" Hunter shrugged apologetically.

"Sure." Gary's voice seemed to have gone flat.

Hunter fell into step behind Gary. Gary looked over his shoulder once, stopped irresolutely, then turned and continued on. Hunter couldn't see his face. The moon had not yet risen, and here there was only a pale reflected light from the silver skin of the trailer. A couple of cars sped by on the other side of the highway, followed by a slower truck, a tractor pulling two pup trailers. The noise momentarily obscured the crunch of their footsteps on the gravel strewn shoulder.

Gary climbed into his cab, and Hunter rested his foot on the lowest step, holding onto the open door. "You afraid you're gonna lose me?" Gary asked. In the light of the cab, Hunter saw him crack a smile.

Hunter smiled back. "I need the exercise," he said. He leaned back to watch a pair of headlights approaching from the rear. A car whooshed past without slowing and the whine of its tires receded up the hill. Gary found his flashlight and started to back down out of the cab. He shut the door, and it was dark again. Dark and quiet.

Where the hell were they? Aloud, Hunter said, "Here, you go first, Gary. You're the one with the flashlight."

Gary clicked on the light. Hunter shut his eyes as the beam leapt at his face. "No. Age before beauty," Gary said. "You go first." The cone of light travelled first to Hunter's feet, then lengthened along the ground behind him.

Hunter started walking backwards, running his right hand lightly along the dusty aluminum wall of the trailer. "Deja vu, Gary?"

The beam of the flashlight swung back up to Hunter's face, and he narrowed his eyes to slits, squinting into the light from behind his lashes. "What?!" Gary's voice snapped from behind the vortex of the light. They both stopped dead. The light barely wavered. Hunter brought his right hand down to shield his eyes.

"I said, deja vu? Haven't you been here before?"

"I don't know what you're talking about." Hunter could hear Gary's breath now. "You're behaving weird. You're starting to make me nervous, pal."

"Take the light out of my eyes, Gary."

"I want to know what the fuck you're talking about. Tell me!"

Hunter tried to smile, but his upper lip was already raised and curled by the squint. "Take the light out of my eyes, Gary."

"Fucking tell me! I said. What the fuck are you getting at?" The light dropped for a split second, then returned to Hunter's face again. "Forget the fuckin' light. Tell me!"

Hunter thought he heard the faint crunch of tires on the gravel shoulder back of The Blue Knight. He hoped that's what he heard. But Gary would have seen lights, and Gary didn't react. Gary took a step forward.

"Deja vu. That means you've been here before. You have, haven't you, Gary?" Hunter stood his ground, straining to hear noises in the dark behind him but not daring to turn his head. "In fact, weren't you stopped here, oh, about five weeks ago? Make that exactly five weeks ago."

Gary's breathing grew rougher, heavier. "You haven't got a damn thing on me, Hunter. Not a damn thing."

"I don't have to have anything on you, Gary. I'll leave that up to the R.C.M.P." He thought he heard footsteps on the other side of the trailer. Was he hoping too hard? "There's a witness. A witness who saw a Ranverdan rig parked near here at about twelve thirty."

"So? That was Randy's rig, obviously."

"The witness went through the toll booth almost ten minutes ahead of Randy. He said that whoever was stopped here was listening to a Jerry Jeff Walker song. Randy didn't have a J.J. Walker tape in his truck ... but you did." Hunter paused, listening. He heard nothing but the whine of approaching traffic and the trilling of crickets and Gary's ragged breathing. "Randy stopped for you just like you stopped for me, didn't he? But I can't believe you planned to kill him, Gary."

The sound of Gary's breathing stopped abruptly. Several seconds passed. "Kill him? Why would I kill Randy?"

A car and a truck sped by, going uphill, just feet from where they stood. Hunter let the silence that followed settle around them. He became aware of the booming of his own heart inside his chest, the rush of blood beneath his eardrums.

"What are you talking about? Why would I kill my own father-in-law?"

"He switched trailers with you at the last minute in Seattle, didn't he? At Waicom that night, Randy made sure the Edmonton trailer was fully loaded, then he made you unhitch your tractor and hitch it up to the Winnipeg trailer, didn't he?"

"Who told you that? Mah wouldn't ... That's a lie!"

"Easy enough to check, Gary. The R.C.M.P. have Randy's log book. Besides, the trailer numbers will all be on file at the border."

"Jesus!" Gary kicked at the gravel beneath his feet and took a step closer.

"Don't make them think you're guiltier than you are. Make it easy on yourself. Tell them what happened. Give them Waicom. Tell them you didn't plan to kill him."

Again, silence. Gary cleared his throat, then spat on the road. The beam of the flashlight wavered briefly before it returned to Hunter's face.

"What ... what would that mean, if I didn't plan to kill ... anybody. If I explained it was an accident. Like, in terms of what would happen to me, what would it mean?"

"It could very well mean attending Jolie's high school graduation. Or maybe teaching Veri how to drive." Hunter's palms were slippery with sweat, but he didn't want to move his arms from a ready position to wipe them dry. He let the silence close in again, gave Gary time to think it through.

"What if I gave myself up? What if I went and told the cops just how it happened? I really didn't mean to ... I ... didn't think. I just panicked. I ... it was Waicom. Mah said to fix it, or I was a dead

334

man. I figured those guys'd kill me if I screwed up." Gary started gesturing with the flashlight, throwing the circle of light on the gravel, on the trailer, on the road. "I told Randy my headlights kept cutting out. I thought maybe if I could get him tinkering with my truck, I'd be able to get his keys and sneak into the back of his trailer and get the stuff without him knowing. But the goddamn trailer was sealed! I knew he'd be on to me right away if I broke the goddamn seal."

Gary breathed heavily, wetly, and he swore again.

"I'd decided to break it anyway, and then I heard Randy coming up behind me, so I ducked behind the trailer. I didn't have time to think. He saw me, and I hit him." He gestured with the flashlight. "Jesus! I fuckin' hit my father-in-law. I knew that was it. Suddenly it wasn't just that Scarfo might cut my throat, but I knew that after I'd hit him, Randy would fire me. Not only would he fire me, he'd turn me in to the police for... for ...." He waved the light at the trailer. "It was good money. I was puttin' away damn good money so I could get out of this fuckin' business. But if Randy found out, he'd ... Suzanne wouldn't understand. I'd lose my wife, I'd lose my kids, and ... I just panicked." The light condensed to an intense circle beside Gary's boot heel.

"Jesus! I'm fucked. I'm totally fucked. Tell me, Hunter, what do I do now?"

"My guess is, if you turn yourself in and agree to testify against Mah and Scarfo and whoever else is involved, you'll get away with a lot less time than if you try to run. It's not just me who knows about it now. I guess you already figured that out."

"Yeah. Shit! Look, I'm not a fuckin' degenerate. I hate what I did. Life has been hell for me since it happened, since even before you started nosing around. My brakes. I tried to throw you off, but you figured it out, didn't you?" A snort, almost a sob. "Maybe I should've run away, but I couldn't leave Suzanne and the kids. They'd probably be better off if I had."

"It'll be hard on Suzanne. No getting around that, either way. And confusing for the kids. But Suzanne's a strong woman. And she's a good woman. She won't turn your kids against you." In spite of himself, Hunter felt himself relaxing his guard. He wiped his palms on his jeans.

The headlights of an approaching truck swept towards them. Gary turned and leaned up against the trailer's burnished wall, his face buried in his folded arms. In the light, Hunter saw Gary's shoulder heave once, and the light was gone.

"Okay," Gary said. "Okay. Will you come with me, Hunter?"

"That won't be necessary, Mr. Rodgers." The voice came from near the front wheel of Gary's tractor. "Constable Garth Pullen, Merritt R.C.M.P." A flashlight flicked on behind the officer and its beam splashed across Gary and Hunter like luminescent skim milk. "I'd be happy to escort you to the Merritt R.C.M.P. detachment office. Hunter and his friend, here, can make arrangements to take your truck, but first, I have a warrant to search your vehicle."

"No," said Gary resolutely. He pulled open the door to his cab, and Hunter saw Garth Pullen tense up and his hand dart to his holster.

Hunter held up a cautioning hand, and the officer hesitated, hand still poised over his gun.

Seconds later, Gary backed down out of the truck, hauling a large plastic bag out behind him. He handed it to Garth, and went back into the cab's sleeper for another one.

"I'm voluntarily surrendering this stuff, okay? It's CD's. Computer CD's. Pirated stuff. The warehouse supervisor at Waicom in Seattle, his buddies in the Orient copy the real thing and smuggle the copies over in Waicom containers, packed in Waicom boxes. Keyboard boxes usually. The warehouse is a free trade zone, so U.S. customs never looks at the stuff. Mah stacks a bunch of these boxes on top of the other keyboards, and shrink wraps them together. Customs at the border never check the count. Sometimes the dogs sniff for drugs, but they never bother counting a shrink wrapped skid of computer keyboards. Keyboards are the cheapest part of the load, so nobody pays any attention."

Gary put both hands to his head and closed his eyes. "Fuck! I can't believe this is happening!" He turned around and slammed the

336

side of the trailer with an upraised fist. The aluminum wowed and reverberated dully.

He took a couple of deep breaths and continued in a defeated voice. "Somewhere along the road, at night, I stop and cut off the shrink wrap on the top of the skid. I empty the packages of CD's into these bags. The keyboard boxes I stomp on, and then dispose of them in a few more garbage bags in dumpsters along the road. I meet Frank Scarfo for lunch and pass the CD's on to him. Nobody else in the Waicom warehouse in Edmonton ever sees them. He pays me cash. I've been doing this since last April. What else do you need to know?"

In the white glow of the flashlight, Gary Rodgers looked pale and very, very tired.

Hunter called El from Calgary on Thursday morning. "Have you talked to Suzanne?" he asked.

"She'll be fine, Hunter. She's a trooper, just like her father was. She'll be fine." El said that Suzanne had appreciated having Kitty come by to help her with the kids on Wednesday. "That was a good idea you had. Sounds like it did them both good. Kitty took the kids to the park while Suzanne had a nap. She said she hadn't gotten any sleep at all that night after Gary arrived."

Hunter nodded mutely into the receiver. In his eyes, Gary had taken at least a step towards redeeming himself by insisting on being the one to tell Suzanne about what he'd done. Garth Pullen had taken him to Kamloops to break the news to her, then delivered him to Bill Earl at the Kamloops R.C.M.P. detachment.

"Yes, I'm sure she'll be fine," Hunter said. "She's decided to keep Ranverdan?"

"I don't know," said El. "If she does, she's got my help for as long as she needs it. Her phones have been forwarded to my office again."

"Did Sorry call in?"

"Yep. Things are all set for his arrival at Waicom, but it seems he got hung up in Hinton, so he's running a bit late. Said something about spending some time with his brothers there. Did you know he had relatives in Alberta?"

Hunter smiled. "Sorry has brothers all over the place," he told her. "Like the Teamsters do." Gary had helped set up a sting. The Edmonton R.C.M.P. were going to be there when Sorry met Frank Scarfo for lunch. Sorry had said he was looking forward to being in on the action for a change.

After El hung up on him, Hunter called Bill Earl. "How's it look, chief?"

"It's in the hands of the lawyers now, Hunter. Your young friend's cooperating fully so far, I can tell you that. He says he doesn't know anything about this Murphy guy being involved as well. If he was being blackmailed into it again, like you suspect, our only chance of pinning it on him is if the other two roll over."

"His biggest crime was not revealing their dirty scams years ago." Then all of this would never have happened. *If only* ...

"Say," continued Bill, "you going to be around next weekend? It's about time we went fishing, don't you think?"

"I'll have to take a raincheck on that, Bill. I'm spending next weekend with my girls. We're going to a friend's cabin on the Shuswap. The girls want to do some swimming and waterskiing, soak up some sun. Maybe I'll even get them to come with me to that golf course I've always admired from the highway."

"Next time you're passing through, then."

"Next time, for sure," said Hunter.

The day after Gary's confession, Suzanne moved herself and the two girls into her father's house, leaving everything of Gary's behind in what had been their home, and putting the house up for sale. She stood now, in darkness, at her father's bedroom window, looking out at the night sky. She couldn't sleep. There were moments when she thought she'd go crazy. If her world had been turned upside down by her father's death, now it was being turned inside out, twisted and

338

mangled and torn apart. How could you go from loving a man to hating him in the blink of an eye? You couldn't. At least, she couldn't. How could you continue to love a man who had hurt and betrayed you on such a scale, someone who had lied to you and witnessed your pain and kept on lying?

Her eyes wandered from star to star to star, tiny pin pricks in the wall of blackness. The sound of a truck gearing down came from the highway half a mile away.

Funny, she thought. Her living husband had been wrenched from her life more brutally than her dead father. Severed completely, as if by the blow of an axe. With her mom and dad, she could call up treasured memories, and remembering would bring her comfort. But could she ever allow herself fond memories of the man who murdered her father and destroyed her happiness? She didn't think she could forgive him. Ever. But what about Jo and Veri? Gary was their father. He would always be their father, and she couldn't take their father away from them. It would not be simple, sorting out her emotions over the next few months.

Take it one day at a time, Suzy Q.

It was almost as if her father's voice were inside her head. Yes. Take it one day at a time. Tomorrow she would switch the phones back to the Ranverdan office and get to work. Now was not the time to make decisions for her future. She would just take it one day at a time.

Wind rustled the willow branches, and a warm breath of air came through the window screen carrying the scent of her mother's lilac bushes. The long strands of willow bobbed and swayed, colorless in the soft light of half a moon.

CHAPTER
THIRTY

So far, it had been a great day. The girls had made bacon and eggs and pancakes for breakfast, and the three of them sat in the little cabin for an hour over coffee afterwards, watching a million silver shards of light dancing across the surface of the lake. Even though the girls did most of the talking, much of it between themselves, Hunter didn't mind. He got the impression that they were showing off for him, and that they welcomed this chance to be together as much as he did. His face ached from smiling.

He sat on an upended cinderblock near the base of the dock, picking flat rocks off the beach and skipping them across the water. The sun sneaked through a gap in the trees behind him, and he felt its warm hand on his back. He could hear laughter and muffled thumps coming from the cabin, where Jan and Lesley were getting themselves ready to go swimming. The cabin door slammed, and he looked over his shoulder to see Lesley running down the beach. Without stopping, she dropped a towel and a book at his feet, and ran out onto the dock. She stopped at the edge, kicked off her thongs, and turned back to look at Jan, who was walking down from the cabin with the dignity appropriate to an older sister.

"Beat ya!" Lesley cried, and cannonballed into the lake. She came up screaming. "Eeeow! It's like ice!" Kicking her legs and rotating her arms, she brought the water around her to a furious boil.

Hunter picked up the book she'd dropped and turned it over. It was a heavy, grey textbook titled "Canadian Criminal Justice". He held it towards Jan, who had come up beside him to deposit her own towel and a Cosmopolitan magazine. She was gathering her honey-streaked hair into a ponytail. "What's Lesley reading this for?" he asked.

She shrugged and said, "She's nuts!" as she began walking down towards the dock. "She's already bought half the textbooks she's going to need in September."

"She's studying criminal justice?"

"She didn't tell you?" Jan called back over her shoulder as she walked out onto the dock. "At S.F.U. She's taking Criminology. She says it'll help her get into the R.C.M.P." She raised herself lightly on her toes and vaulted neatly into the water.

Hunter stared at the sleek, wet heads of the two human beings he loved more than anyone else in the world, but who he didn't really know at all. "I'll be damned," he said softly. He was so surprised he couldn't think straight. He found himself blinking furiously, so he closed his eyes, took a deep breath and swallowed hard. "She can't ... She's too ... Damn!" Too what? Too female? Too weak? Don't be stupid, he told himself. He thumped the textbook with his fist. "Damn!"

His mouth twitched a few times, then his frown broke into a bewildered smile.

"My little Lesley," he said. "Well, I'll be damned."

THE END

ACKNOWLEDGEMENTS

Slow Curve on the Coquihalla has been through several incarnations since the first manuscript was completed in 1995. At the time, as a beginning writer, I received a great deal of support and encouragement from the community of writers on the Compuserve forums, as well as participants on the DorothyL listserv. I've lost touch with them in the intervening years, but I particularly appreciated my cyber-friendship with fellow mystery writers Sharon Zukowski, Walter Satterthwait and Kate Grilley

I also owe Ed Griffin and the Surrey International Writers' Conference a big thank you for giving me the opportunity to learn from such accomplished fiction authors as Diana Gabaldon, Jack Whyte and more recently, mystery authors Anne Perry and John Lescroart. Attending SIWC panels, as well as those hosted by Bouchercon and Sisters in Crime, helped me not only to improve my writing skills, but to better understand the industry. Thanks also to mystery author Elizabeth George, who helped me take my writing to a new level at a 1998 workshop hosted by The Book Passage in Corte Madera, California.

Feedback and encouragement (in spite of rejection!) from several literary agents who read my manuscripts, especially Michael Congdon, kept me going, but the biggest boost to my confidence came - and still comes - from the readers who have enjoyed my novels, and say they can hardly wait for the next one. Thank you to Judi Hayward, Yvonne Hillsden, Denise Beaton, Barbara Macartney, Marie O'Neill, Vivian Harder, 'Nash Black', Margaret the 'Literary Chanteuse', and others who early on read and commented on my books.

The wonderful covers on my novels are thanks to the team of Chris Hunter and the exceptionally creative Steve Johnsen.

ABOUT THE AUTHOR

R.E. Donald is the author of the Hunter Rayne highway mystery series. Ruth worked in the transportation industry in various capacities from 1972 until 2001, and draws on her own experiences, as well as those of her late husband, Jim Donald, in creating the characters and situations in her novels.

Ruth attended the University of British Columbia in Vancouver, B.C., where she studied languages (Russian, French and German) and creative writing to obtain a Bachelor of Arts degree. She currently lives on a small farm in Langley, B.C. She and her partner, a French Canadian cowboy named Gilbert Roy, enjoy their Canadian Horses (Le Cheval Canadien) and other animals.

Also by R.E. Donald in the Hunter Rayne highway mystery series:
Ice on the Grapevine
Coming as a digital edition in the fall of 2012:
Sea to Sky

Visit **proudhorsepublishing.com** or **redonald.com**
for information on new releases.

www.ingramcontent.com/pod-product-compliance
Lightning Source LLC
Chambersburg PA
CBHW051231260626
47162CB00002B/370